THE GUARDIAN'S CURSE

CURSED BLOOD: BOOK ONE

J.D. MONROE

Editing by Three Points Author Services

Cover Design by Yocla Designs

Formatting by J.D. Monroe

I

The curvy brunette smelled of sweet cocktails and a heavy perfume that didn't blend well with the sweat of dancing all night in an under-ventilated nightclub. Black stilettos conspired with too many Cosmopolitans to keep her off balance as she stumbled across the darkened parking lot on wobbly fawn legs. Her pulse thrummed beneath her skin, singing that wickedly sweet siren song.

Alistair Thorne ran his tongue across his teeth, savoring the sweet ache as his needle-sharp fangs descended. Beneath the shadows of the alleyway, he might as well have been on another planet from drunk, vulnerable Stacey, who'd been popping in and out of the Alley Cat bar all night to talk to a string of girlfriends. Based on her progressively less coherent conversations, she was partying to forget a regrettable sexual escapade with a Grade-A douchebag.

Her words, of course.

Now she wandered across the parking lot, with stray receipts fluttering out of her oversized purse.

A good predator was patient, waiting to strike when his prey was most vulnerable. He waited for her to stray from the safety of the pack, out in the open with nowhere to hide.

At the end of the alley, a wiry human was pressed to the graffiti-covered brick, like a lion hiding beneath the tall grasses of the savanna. No. More like a vulture. A scavenger who was too cowardly for a real hunt.

Stinking of sweat and stale beer, he shifted nervously on his feet. The tail of his black shirt was tucked into his paint-stained jeans, barely concealing the gun in his waistband. A stained ballcap covered his greasy short hair and cast his face in shadow. Harder to identify, of course. He could have been any one in a lineup of the usual dirtbags. The thumping of his heart was a noisy drumbeat to Alistair's sensitive hearing.

Gravel scuffed under Stacey's shoe as she walked past the alley. In the hazy floodlights, her shadow danced across the narrow alleyway. Another choking wave of her too-sweet perfume drifted toward him. Now her back was to both of them, to Alistair and the man who'd been watching sweet Stacey for the last two hours.

Her backless dress revealed the faint outlines of her summer tan. And with her wavy hair piled in a messy bun atop her head, her slender neck was exposed. The wiry man inched forward, his right hand creeping back to his gun.

Before he could emerge from the alley, Alistair pounced. Brick blurred around him. With the smell of blood in the air and fury igniting his nerves, he cleared the length of muddy ground in half a second. The burst of energy awakened the primal killer in him.

Dark-gloved hands yanked the skinny man back into the shadows. As they folded into the darkness, the man jerked in surprise. Alistair clapped one hand over his prey's mouth before he could cry out and alert Stacey. Muffled screams vibrated against Alistair's firm grasp.

Keeping the man's mouth covered, he leaned in close. His lips brushed the human's ear and caught the taste of dirt and salt. He preferred a much cleaner meal, but this would have to do.

"Watch her go," Alistair whispered. "You've been watching her all night, haven't you?"

"Mmm," the man protested, wriggling in vain against his steel grip.

Alistair tightened his hold. There was a clipped whimper. Was that a crack? Maybe a rib or two. Possibly his sternum. Oops.

"Don't lie," Alistair said. Across the parking lot, Stacey had finally located her keys and was climbing into her car. She sang some pop song, a little off-key and made of more *da da da* than words. "She came alone, drank a few too many cocktails. And you were watching her. Were you going to rob her? Rape her?"

The man let out another sound of protest. He'd seen the scumbag patting his crotch, tongue darting over his lip in anticipation. Even now, he could smell the change in his body chemistry, the distinct smell of a man who wanted to fuck.

The engine of the white Jeep stuttered, then fell silent. In Stacey's car, there was a whining sound of despair, then a muffled *god dammit.* Alistair was no mechanic, but thirty seconds on Google yielded enough knowledge to disconnect a few wires so Stacey didn't go swerving down the interstate and kill herself or some other innocent bystander.

Go inside, he thought.

After another failed attempt to start the car, Stacey headed for the bar again. Her stylish black stilettos had been abandoned in favor of ratty white sneakers. Wise choice. As she strolled past, she was on the phone again. "Joanie? Yeah, I know it's super late, but I need a huge favor. Do you think you could pick me up?"

After seeing her return to the relative safety of the dive bar, Alistair hauled his struggling prey back to the fenced-in Dumpster. The smell was nearly overpowering to his sensitive nose, but it was hidden and dark. All the better to finish what he started, and efficient cleanup to boot.

The man strained against Alistair's grasp, but he was weak as a baby compared to nearly three centuries of supernatural strength. Fully cloaked in shadow, Alistair yanked the man's head to the side. The blue line of a fat vein was tantalizing, just beneath the tiniest layer of skin. The smell of that fresh, hot blood overpowered his revulsion at the stench of unwashed human.

"And now, a treat," he growled. The man whimpered, then let out a muffled squeal as Alistair bit. There was the faintest hint of resistance as needle-sharp teeth pierced through skin and sinew.

Blood rushed over his tongue, warm and rich and full of life. His senses ignited. The metallic bite mixed with a boozy burn, sliding down his throat. The roaring hunger in him, almost a living creature in itself, purred with delight as he drank deep.

The would-be rapist gave another weak twitch, then relaxed against Alistair. If it was his choice, he wouldn't have made it so pleasant. The man didn't deserve the euphoria tingling through him from Alistair's fangs. He deserved to be consumed in terror as his life was drained away, realizing he would never again hunt innocent prey.

A hand fisted into his collar and swung him around violently. Before he even saw his attacker, Alistair released one hand, tightening it into a blade to drive up into his opponent's belly. He whirled to see a familiar silhouette standing next to the rusted brown Dumpster, the faint silver of moonlight playing off his perfectly coiffed chestnut hair.

Surprise and anger twisted through him at the sight of his old friend. Drunk on fresh, hot blood, he hadn't even heard Paris coming. Idiot. He'd be hearing about it for decades.

"Eating on the run is so déclassé," Paris said wryly. God, he could be so smug and infuriating. "What happened to sitting to savor a meal?"

He bared his teeth, knowing how monstrous his blood-caked smile was. "I'm the paragon of etiquette normally."

"You used to be," he said, folding his arms over his chest. He leaned, as if to prop himself stylishly against the Dumpster, then thought better of it. His nose wrinkled. "What the fuck are you doing out here? I told you I was picking you up for tonight. I drove all the way to Midnight Springs and your house was empty."

"I was craving a midnight snack," Alistair said, turning his head. The man's pulse was slowing, but he had another few minutes of feeding left in him if they were careful. "If you hadn't interrupted me, I might have shared."

In a blur, Paris shoved him and wedged one strong arm between him and his prey. Alistair resisted, but Paris flipped his arm up to elbow him in the chin. His teeth clacked together and drove his fangs into his lower lip. As he was snarling in pain, Paris shoved him away. The wiry human crumpled to the ground at their feet.

Alistair snarled, but his friend glared back, his eyes flashing red for a moment. "Don't snarl at me, you son of a bitch." Despite the harsh words, his tone was almost playful. Paris nudged the man with one foot. Blood still trickled down his neck, but it was a steady, slow rush, not arterial spurting. He didn't bite carefully to spare the man's life, but rather to make sure he got to drink his fill before it spilled onto the ground and went to waste. "What'd this one do?"

"He was following a drunk girl to her car," he said. "You figure out the rest."

Paris sighed and bared his fangs. Opening two deep punctures on the fleshy part of his hand, he hauled the man up by the throat and pressed his hand to his cracked lips. The man's head jerked to one side, bloodshot brown eyes going wide. His lips were smeared with crimson. He coughed, and then tried to pull away. A metallic *clang* rang out as Paris slammed him against the Dumpster and leaned in. His power was palpable as he enthralled the hapless human. "You're going to leave here and think about your life choices. If you ever think about touching a woman who hasn't enthusiastically asked for the miserable little worm in your pants, then my friend and I will find you. I'll rip off your cock, and he'll tear your throat out. Understand?"

Thanks to the vampire blood making its way to his brain, the little shitstain was staring up at Paris with a look that was somewhere between abject terror and pure adoration.

Paris snarled, a guttural sound that resounded from his chest. "Understand?"

"Yes," he whimpered. When Paris released him, he took off running. His feet skidded out from under him, and he scrambled along on all fours before he finally got up and ran again.

Paris turned slowly to glare at him. "You. Car. Now."

Two minutes later, Alistair was sinking into the cushioned seat of Paris's black SUV, parked illegally across the street from the Alley Cat. Alistair winced at his reflection in the tinted glass. Just the hint of twisted gray across his cheekbone was enough to make him feel ill. He turned away and faced his angry friend instead.

"Allie, we've talked about this," Paris said mildly. His fury had dissipated into something even worse.

Pity.

"Don't call me Allie," he replied.

"When you stand me up and make me late so you can eat a human behind a dive bar, I'll call you whatever I please," Paris replied. "Jason, we can go. We're already late."

"Wait," Alistair said. "Until she leaves."

Paris sighed, but said, "Wait."

While they waited in uncomfortable silence, Paris fussed

over his blood-stained hand. The oozing punctures would heal in the next hour. His eyes, usually a lovely bright blue, were still dark scarlet from the use of his power.

Eventually, the drunk girl emerged from the front doors of the bar, where a car waited. Alistair rolled down the window a few inches to hear more clearly. A sleepy-sounding woman's voice rose above the clamor of the bar. "No, Stace, it's fine. I was up. I'd rather you called me than end up in a ditch," she said. "Get in. Jesus, did you drink all the tequila?"

The girl climbed into the car, and it pulled away, fading into the anonymity of the night. Sweet, foolish girl, who would never know what might have happened to her if not for one miserable, bored vampire.

Paris raised an eyebrow. "Happy now?"

"Thrilled," Alistair said drily.

"Jason," Paris called without breaking eye contact. "Infinity."

"Just take me home," Alistair said. "I've no desire for you to parade my failings in front of the others."

"If you'll just come along and quit complaining, I won't tell them about it," Paris replied.

The glow of the city blurred beyond the dark windows. Atlanta seemed like the kind of place he would have loved, at least before everything went to shit. Now it was just another city, no different from the rest. A world where he was unwelcome, a monstrosity to be hidden away.

Paris sighed. "What were you thinking, Allie?"

"I saved a woman from a disgusting fate," Alistair said. "Are you faulting me?"

"Fine. It was lovely of you to defend her honor. You're a saint," Paris said. He propped his foot on his knee, displaying his black designer sneakers. Paris had always been a vain little peacock, though his beauty certainly deserved some bit of vanity. "But we both know you were on the hunt, and this was convenient."

"Do we both know that?"

"Allie—"

"Don't."

"Alistair," Paris said, gritting his teeth. His frustration emerged as his native French made his name *Ahl-ee-stair,* with that lovely curled *r* at the end. As if he'd realized it, he pursed his lips, and resumed in his precise North American speech. "You are going to attract the wrong kind of attention, and we cannot afford that right now."

"He only survived because you interrupted me. You left a witness, not me," Alistair said. "Do you lecture Nikko when he goes out on his vigilante hunts?"

"Nikko blends in much better than you do and hides his own bodies," Paris said. "The carjacker in Midtown was you, wasn't it? The one who swore a demon beat him bloody in front of a MARTA station?"

"Did you ask Nikko the same thing?" Paris sighed. Alistair folded his arms over his broad chest. "Did you see the papers? Midnight Springs was named the safest place on the East Coast."

"Maybe for humans. If you keep leaving witnesses, it's going to become the most dangerous place for vampires," Paris said. "You're practically writing invitations for hunters to come looking. It may already be happening."

"What?"

"A shitty dive downtown got hit. At least half a dozen vampires dead," Paris said.

"Ours?"

He shook his head. "We don't think so. Julian and Nikko are there tonight to figure out who they were."

Alistair shrugged. "Not Auberon, not my problem."

"If there are hunters in town, they're not going to stop and ask you who you are," Paris said. "Those fuckers are creating problems for all of us."

The vampires of the Casteron Court had come to Atlanta just over a year ago, bringing their usual blend of mayhem, violence, and disregard for subtlety. More than a few times, Paris had come to Alistair's house to gripe about the bastards over expensive Scotch. Alistair could muster a hint of sympathy, but it only reminded him of how far he was from the society he had once loved. The problems of his court, the Blade of Auberon, were no longer his.

"I adore vampire politics," Alistair said. "Please, tell me more."

His friend glared at him. "Don't be a petulant little shit. I'm telling you this because things are a mess. We enjoy our relative peace because we are quiet. And when bored idiots go out hunting behind dive bars, that makes noise. We do not need any further attention on us right now. What if someone thought you were a threat?"

"I am a threat."

"You know what I mean. If a hunter came upon you, they would not hesitate to relieve you of your head."

"Would that be so bad?" Alistair asked quietly.

A firm grasp closed on his wrist. The familiar touch sent a shiver down his spine. Reluctantly, he met Paris's eyes, now their normal light blue. "If you talk like that, you and I are going to do more than argue."

It was easy for Paris, who was as beautiful and charming as he had ever been. He had his own suffering to bear, but it did not stop him from walking amongst humans, nor their own kind. Others did not recoil from him, nor force themselves to look upon him while failing to hide their disgust. He could move through the world with no one the wiser to his curse.

"I changed my mind. Take me home, please," Alistair said.

Paris raised an eyebrow. "Zephyrine Lenoir is in town. I told her you were coming to see her."

"You lied to her."

"Alas. I would hate to be the one who disappointed Zephyrine," Paris replied, giving him a coy smile.

"One drink," Alistair said. "And then you take me home."

2

Working in the posh, secure office suite of Infinity, Shoshanna York felt like a gazelle sniffing around a lion's den. Burnished gold decor gleamed against dark wood and black paneling, making the whole place feel decadent and intimate. Through the soundproofed walls, she could feel the faintest thump of the music from downstairs, where the vampires of Atlanta gathered for debauchery and blood on tap. Six vampires lingered nearby, including the Elder of the court, his three advisors, and two of his most formidable bodyguards.

At least she had pepper spray on her keychain, which was conveniently tucked into her purse in the next room. She was a tasty little appetizer in a half-priced cocktail dress from the clearance rack. The only thing keeping the vampires from snacking on her was courtesy, not fear. It made things even worse to know they could hear her heart thumping. She just hoped the temptation wasn't too much.

Chill, Sho, she thought. It wasn't like this was her first time around vampires.

If her best friend Ruby knew what she was up to, she'd shit a brick. As it was, Shoshanna had told her she was only working at the club during the day, when the vampires were asleep. To be fair, that was mostly true, up until the last few nights when she'd had to come and start tying all of her wards together. The final steps required the presence of the Elder, only the most powerful vampire in the city.

No big deal.

Her heart kicked against her ribs as she scrawled the final details onto the chalk array. Several hours of painstaking work had yielded the intricate geometric design on the concrete subfloor of the club's inner sanctum.

When she looked up from her work, she found Eduardo staring at her. The Elder's golden-brown skin gleamed in the low light, which reflected off his eerie red eyes. He raised an eyebrow, and she swallowed the lump of fear climbing up her throat. "Mister Alazan?" she said.

His lips curved into a faint smile. "Call me Eduardo," he said. "My friends do."

Her eyes widened. "Yes, sir. Eduardo." She wasn't sure she wanted to be friends with someone with his reputation, but it was better than the other option. "I'm ready for your blood."

At the mention of blood, a pale, dark-haired man in the corner shot a dark look her way. His posture shifted, and she could see the protective intent in his coiled pose.

"Of course," Eduardo said. He handed his glass to one of his subordinates and approached. "Tell me what to do."

"That probably doesn't happen often, does it?" she said.

His smile faltered, and anxiety swelled like a bubble in her chest. Why the hell would she think it was okay to crack a joke with the most powerful vampire in Atlanta? *Please don't kill me.*

Then he chuckled. "No, it does not, Miss York."

She let out a shuddering breath. "I need your hand. Non-dominant is better."

"I'll heal fast," he said, extending his right hand to her. She took a small silver knife from her bag of supplies. There was a rustle of fabric as one of the bodyguards, Dominic, moved toward her. He had supervised her for the last few days, though he'd said no more than two dozen words the entire time. Eduardo glanced up. "*Calmati,*" he said quietly. "Miss York means us no harm."

"No, sir," she said. She wanted to walk out of here with her five-figure paycheck and her head still connected to her shoulders. She gestured to the inscription. "I'll cut your hand and place blood here. Then here, here, and here," she said, gesturing to different points. At strategic intersections were small piles of powdered herbs, precious metals, and even a small ruby imbued with stormwater. An open circle was placed at the center, with shavings of elder wood in a neat pile. "This will anchor all of the club's protections to you and those who are connected to you through the Covenant. As you asked."

"Wonderful," he said.

"I'm sorry if I hurt you," she said.

Dominic snorted in derision.

Eduardo scowled over his shoulder. "I appreciate your courtesy, Miss York. Perhaps my subordinates could learn from your example." Dominic scowled at her.

She gripped Eduardo's wrist lightly. His skin was cool to the touch, the rich gold-brown slightly lighter than her own. The cold prickle of vampiric energy swept over her. After glancing at her notes, she recited the first incantation. "Spirits above, hear my will, may my intentions be bound in crimson spill," she intoned. With a quick flick of her wrist, she sliced the silver blade across Eduardo's palm. He flinched, but made no sound. Blood streamed over his brown skin and pattered onto the chalk lines below.

The vampires surrounding her faded into the shadows as she focused on her Weaving. She closed her eyes for a moment and allowed her arcane sight to take over. Magic swirled around her like tiny currents in the air. Wispy gray tendrils and pale blue motes floated around her, while rich, dark red enveloped Eduardo. Little pinpricks of light like tiny flames reflected from the blood on his palm. As it struck the chalk lines, the array ignited. A tingling sensation zipped up her spine as her magic took effect.

Without missing a beat, she pressed one hand to Eduardo's cheek, then moved his hand to each of the nodes that required his blood. "As I have spoken, so may it be."

The vampire Elder gasped and went rigid as the array was completed. Tendrils of bright blue radiated into the corners of the dim office, through the walls, extending over the entire nightclub like a spider's web. Eduardo's eyes darkened to a rich crimson, fixed on hers as his fangs descended.

She swallowed back her fear, hoping he was reacting to the power, not the smell of her jugular. "Do you feel it?"

He nodded, rubbing his fingers together as if he would find threads tangled there. "That's quite potent." His eyes faded to a reddish-brown, though she could still see the razor-sharp points of his teeth as he spoke.

"It should fade after a few days," she said. "It's kind of like putting on jeans right out of the dryer."

His head tilted in confusion. Right. Vampires with an eight-figure net worth probably didn't relate to the perils of drying their skinny jeans on hot. She took a clean cloth from her bag and gently wrapped his bleeding hand.

"And this will do what for us?" the pale man asked. His sneering expression told her what he thought of her work.

"This is the foundation of all the protective spells I've been building," she said. She walked to the tinted glass windows overlooking the nightclub. Low music played, while clusters of vampires and other patrons gathered. Below them, she could see a young woman with an older, silver-haired man. Her hand slid up his thigh as she suckled at his neck. The expression on his face said he didn't mind a bit. "See the woman in the green dress at the end of the bar? She's not one of yours."

Like a halo, sparkling light wreathed the pretty blonde's head. "A light show," the man said. "We paid you ten thousand dollars for a light show?"

"Hugo," Eduardo said sharply. "Forgive my Scythe. His zeal for duty sometimes exceeds his social graces. Continue, Miss York."

She gulped. "You'll be able to immediately identify any

vampire that is not connected to Mister Alazan through the Covenant. Furthermore, humans will not be able to enter without permission of an Auberon vampire. That should keep hunters out."

Hugo's expression eased ever so slightly. "What about dhampir?"

She eyed him warily. "Still working on that," Shoshanna said. "It's complex."

"Perhaps we'll find someone with more skill," Hugo said.

"Perhaps you will," she said evenly. "But not someone who can work on your timetable. I may not be the best, but I'm the best you've got right here and now." His eyes narrowed at her. She raised her eyebrows back at him. "I'm designing another layer of protections to essentially fireproof the club. I could probably protect the glass, but you'd be better off just putting safety glass there."

"That will do for a start," Eduardo said, giving his advisor a nod. They spoke in rapid Spanish, and she could just make out *hablamos*. Whatever secrets they had, she didn't want to know.

Well, she did. The nosy part of her that couldn't resist celebrity gossip and behind-the-scenes drama definitely wanted to know what was going on in the vampire underworld that had prompted a quick and somewhat desperate search for a *tisserand*. They'd told her time was an issue, but money was not.

But the practical part of her that valued her safety and the normalcy of her life wanted nothing to do with it. Whatever tangled webs the Blade of Auberon was weaving, they could do it on their own.

The platinum-haired woman she'd met several nights ago nodded to her. "Miss York, I've already arranged for the wire transfer," she said. Violette Baudelaire served as the Gilded Hand to Eduardo, handling all of his finances. Of all the vampires in the room, she was the one Shoshanna liked the most. The Gilded Hand delivered the cash, and she was both generous and prompt, qualities Shoshanna found most appealing in an employer.

"Thank you," she said. She quickly packed her things, taking care to seal the containers of precious reagents. Though the vampires were paying her close to ten thousand dollars for her work, she had spent almost two grand on expensive ingredients, which had yielded several calls from her credit card company about suspected fraud. Next time, she'd bump up her quote. Still, she was coming out on top with seven thousand dollars for a week's hard work.

"I'd like to make my offer once more," Eduardo said. "We can discuss your fee to stay on retainer."

Her throat clenched. Wasn't that a serpent's offer? *Just one sweet bite.* "I appreciate the offer, but I can't."

"Can't or won't?" Eduardo said, his gaze sharpening.

"Does it matter?"

His lips curved slightly. "Thank you for your time, Miss York." He glanced at Dominic. "Dominic will escort you downstairs. Please enjoy drinks on us, if that doesn't offend your sense of neutrality in vampire matters."

She nodded to him. "Thank you for your business."

Hefting her bag over her shoulder, she spared one last glance at the vampires in the room. At the door, a woman waited with a glass pitcher full of thick red blood. Shoshanna averted her gaze and followed Dominic to the lounge outside the office. He veered to the right as they descended to make room.

Coming up the spiraling staircase from the ground floor was a familiar man, one she'd missed this evening amidst the crowd of somber, serious men. The well-dressed vampire with bright blue eyes crested the stairs, talking over his shoulder to a man in a hooded coat. His eyes lit up with recognition.

"Dom," Paris greeted. "You're looking as dour and unpleasant as ever. That color brings really brings out your sullen attitude." Blood speckled his otherwise pristine white collar. She gulped at the thought of how it had gotten there.

Dominic let out another snort of derision. "Paris."

"Shoshanna!" Paris said with a burst of cheer. The handsome vampire stepped in, kissing her cheeks lightly. Along with Dominic, Paris had overseen her work on the club the last few nights. Unlike his comrade, Paris talked constantly, about everything from his favorite wines to his blood type preference to which Hollywood celebrities would make the best vampires. He was distracting but oddly comforting.

The hooded man brushed past her without sparing a glance. As he passed, she glimpsed a hint of eerie red light from beneath his hood, as if a low flame smoldered there. A bolt of fear twisted through her as she watched him go.

"Ali..." Paris sighed as the dark-clad man faded into the shadows down the hallway. "I'd introduce you, but my friend has the manners of a stone statue." He tilted his head and grinned. "May I say that you look positively delicious tonight."

"You may," she said with a smile. Even knowing that he surely had ulterior motives, getting a compliment from a stone-cold hottie like Paris was a nice ego boost.

"Are you staying? Have a drink with me."

"I really need to go home," Shoshanna said. "Maybe another time."

"I'm over two hundred years old," Paris said. "I know a rejection when I hear one, Mademoiselle York. You wound me."

She smirked at him. "Good night, Paris."

He recovered from his heartbreak quickly. After giving her a jaunty nod, he hurried past, calling "Allie! *Attends-moi!*"

Dominic gave her an expectant look and gestured toward the stairs. She followed him, her steps silent on the thick crimson carpet. Though the upper floor was quiet, the lower floor was more typical of a nightclub. The music was loud enough to surround her in a heady atmosphere, but not deafening.

As she stepped onto the smooth hardwood of the club's ground floor, she felt hungry eyes on her like a summer swarm of gnats crawling on her skin.

Instead of leading her to the doors, Dominic headed toward the bar. She had taken only two steps into the dim club when a handsome man with salt and pepper hair stepped up to her and took her hand. His thumb pressed to the tangle of veins on the underside of her wrist, sending a shiver down her spine. "May I offer you company?"

She shook her head and pulled her hand away. "No thank you."

His head tilted, and he glanced up at Dominic. "I apologize. Is she yours?"

"I am no one's," she said sharply. The older man's eyes narrowed.

"Excuse us," Dominic said. He pressed one hand to Shoshanna's back and led her to the bar. "Sit."

"I don't want to stay for drinks," she said.

"I'm not getting you a drink," he replied. He stepped behind the bar, where there were carved glass shelves laden with liquor bottles and glass bottles of red. She'd been here enough to know the blood bottles were just for display, since they kept the red stuff on ice and heated it to their patrons' liking once they ordered.

Her eyes drifted past the bar, to a raised corner table where two handsome men fed on a human woman in a red dress. One stiletto had slipped off, forgotten beneath the table. One man had his teeth buried in her throat, his hand cupping her breast. The other fed from her wrist, and his free hand was under her dress. Her head was thrown back, lips parted with a hazy smile on her face. They weren't just feeding; they were consuming her. Devouring her.

Heat flared between Shoshanna's legs, her body clamping down on the emptiness. The Lady in Red was clearly enjoying herself. Considering the dry spell she was on, maybe she should have taken Paris up on his offer to stay for a drink, even if she was on tap. There was something about his self-deprecating bluster that made her suspect he was an absolute monster in bed.

But the monster was precisely the problem. Sure, it would

start with a nice little bite and a hand on her thigh, but where would it stop? She could appreciate their fine suits and unnaturally gorgeous faces, but she knew better than to trust the creatures beneath those beautiful masks.

And if someone could pass the message along to the heartbeat between her thighs, she could move on with her business instead of imagining dark, decadent wonders.

"See something you like?" Dominic asked. Her cheeks flushed as she snapped her gaze back to him. He grabbed her hand and secured a cool metal bracelet around her wrist.

"What the..." She examined the bracelet, a thin silver band that tangled into a stylized rose. Five red stones like drops of blood adorned its petals.

"This is a vampire club," he said. "Humans here are assumed to be food. That indicates that you're claimed as one of ours."

"I'm not—"

He rolled his eyes. "I've no time for your defiance, Shoshanna. Keep it on your wrist or handle the hungry vampires yourself."

Regardless of how pretty it was, this was a collar for a pet. She wanted to tell him exactly where he could shove his stupid rose, thorns and all. Instead, she crossed her arms. "Can I go home now?"

"I'll walk you out," he said.

As they walked out of the club, a young blonde woman stepped into her path, red eyes sweeping over her appreciatively. Then her gaze caught on Shoshanna's wrist. Her expression changed, and she gave Dominic a little nod before continuing on her hunt.

One point for the fancy bling, then.

"Shoshanna?"

A familiar voice caught her attention, and she turned over her shoulder to see a man in a black button-down hurrying toward her. Lean build, narrow waist, dark brown hair...she tilted her head. Lose the well-fitted shirt and substitute a ragged Blink-182 t-shirt. Subtract a little bit of the muscle on his shoulders and make his features a little more ruddy... "Elliott?"

"Yeah," he said. "Holy shit, you look amazing!"

He stepped in, grasping her shoulders gently as he hugged her. She stiffened in his grasp. The last time she'd seen Elliott was back at her ten-year high school reunion. He'd been human then, but the man hugging her was definitely a vampire. His cold energy enveloped her. "Thanks," she said. "Wow, it's uh...wow."

Her stomach tied in a knot. Their history was complicated, to put it lightly.

A halo surrounded Elliott's head, marking him as an outsider. "This is crazy. Are you two together? Hey, I'm Elliott," he said, sticking out his hand.

Dominic glanced down at his hand but didn't take it. "Dominic."

Elliott let out a nervous laugh. "Right. God, I can't believe it's you. What are the odds? Hey, can I buy you a drink? I'd love to catch up."

She would rather chew her foot off and cauterize the

gushing stump with battery acid. Her tongue was rooted in place, and she looked helplessly at Dominic. His nostrils flared. "Miss York has important matters to attend to," he said. He offered his arm, and Shoshanna took it. "Come on, love."

Her heart thrummed as led her out. There was a weird comfort in knowing that he was probably the scariest thing in a five mile radius. And with his impeccably groomed goatee and tailored suit, he was in another universe compared to Elliott.

Once they were outside the club, she let out a sigh. "Love?"

"Did I misunderstand? You looked as if you wanted nothing to do with him."

"No, you got it right," she said. "Thanks for that." It surprised her that he was that perceptive, honestly.

Elliott had been her first boyfriend, though things had gotten ugly when they broke up in their first semester of college. Despite filling her high school notebooks with *Mrs. Shoshanna McAvoy* inside hearts, distance had made the heart grow not fonder but increasingly aware of how big the world was. When she broke it off with him over Christmas break, she apparently shattered his heart and the fantasy of marrying his high school sweetheart.

On Valentine's Day, he'd driven two hours to show up at her college dorm in one of those gestures that was romantic in movies and stalker-creepy in real life. When she refused to go out with him, he'd bombarded her with increasingly vicious letters and emails accusing her of leading him on, until her father finally intervened and informed Elliott that they'd be looking for his body for years if he didn't leave his daughter alone.

Though he'd apologized profusely a few years later, she didn't exactly have fond memories of Elliott McAvoy. If he thought that she belonged to Dominic, that was probably for the best. Especially since Emmanuel York was no longer here to put stalker ex-boyfriends in their place.

Even once they were out of the club, Dominic held her hand tightly as they walked around the corner to the guest parking lot. It was embarrassing to walk up to her beater of a car with Dominic in tow. The ancient Buick was as well-maintained as it could be for a fifteen-year-old car, but it was humiliating to know that Dominic's suit probably cost three times what her car was worth.

He waited at the curb as she tossed her belongings into the back. When she turned the key, the dashboard lights flickered. No rumbling engine, just an ominous clicking. "No, no, no," she murmured. "Shit." She tried again, getting another death click.

"Battery's dead," Dominic said.

"Yeah, I figured that out," she said sharply.

His eyebrows lifted. "Sit here."

He was gone in a blur. A minute later, a gleaming BMW pulled up next to her. As if it wasn't bad enough for him to see the Blue Monster in its death throes, here they were looking like the Transformers edition of the Town Mouse and the Country Mouse.

"Pop the hood," he said. He laid his jacket over the driver's seat and rolled up his shirt sleeves. While she opened her hood, he hooked jumper cables to his own battery.

"You know cars?"

"I've been driving since they were invented," he replied,

attaching clamps to her battery terminals. He frowned, then started his car. "Go ahead."

She turned the key and let out a heavy sigh of relief as the car rumbled to life.

He peered closely at the battery. "Your terminals are corroded," Dominic said. "You need a new battery."

"Great," she said.

His lip curled. "Honestly, you need a new car."

"We don't all have money coming from our four-hundred-year-old bosses," she replied. "How much does he pay you to stand around and glare?"

"You're the one who keeps refusing an easy paycheck," he retorted. "Blame your pride, Shoshanna."

Easy paycheck? That paycheck came with an obligation to a vampire king and all of his bloody politics. "Can I go now?" she asked.

"Let it run for a few minutes," Dominic said, folding his arms over his chest. It was impossible to ignore the boulder shoulders under those sleeves. God, she needed to get laid, because every hot vampire with an ounce of fashion sense had her heart racing. "Who was that man at the door?"

"Jealous?" she teased.

Not even a hint of a smile. "I want to know why a vampire from another court was so familiar with you," he said.

"I knew him in high school," she said carefully. "I haven't seen him in a while."

"He seemed familiar."

"We dated for a few years," she said. "There's nothing. Not anymore."

Dominic frowned. "If he contacts you, I want to know about it."

"It's not your business."

"If it becomes Auberon business, then it is."

"And if that happens, you'll be the first to know," she said. He glared down at her, and she glared back.

Finally, he shook his head slightly, as if to say *suit yourself*. After carefully removing the jumper cables, he coiled them up and closed her hood. "Get a new battery, Shoshanna."

He waited for her to get into her car and shut the door. His crimson eyes followed her as she backed out of the parking spot. She didn't release her breath until she was around the block from Infinity and cruising toward her apartment across town.

Freaking vampires. She glanced at the clock and groaned. It was already three in the morning, and she had to be up for an early shift at Average Joe's. Maybe she was doing it all wrong and should have taken up Eduardo on his offer.

The woman in the red dress was probably having a much better night than she was. Two hot vampires devouring her whole and paying her for the privilege. There were much worse ways to make a buck. The Lady in Red was way smarter than she was, that was for damn sure.

"Blame your pride," she mocked.

Freaking vampires.

3

The scent of the human woman lingered in Alistair's nose, even as he stood in the luxurious upper lounge overlooking the club. He watched through tinted glass as she followed Dominic through the crowd. A dozen heads turned her way, hungry scarlet eyes sizing her up.

He could hardly blame them. Wrapped in a glittering black dress, her narrow waist and curvy hips were magnetic. Short black curls framed the face of an angel with full cheeks and kissable red lips.

"Has Dominic finally found a girl?" Alistair asked as Paris approached him. He accepted the warm glass placed in his hand, still watching the beautiful woman from above.

Paris scoffed. "Hardly. She put all the protective wards on this place. I would have introduced you if you hadn't walked off like a brooding cliche."

"Ah, yes," Alistair said. "I'm certain that every human

woman is dying to meet the hideous monster of the Auberon court. It's what fairy tales are made of, truly."

Paris rolled his eyes. There was a quiet knock on the door, and he called, "Come in."

A woman with short, dark hair bustled through the door. Her petite frame and pixie cut gave her an elfin beauty that was untouched by time. "Alistair!" she exclaimed. The woman bustled past Paris and launched herself at Alistair. He stiffened as her strong arms encircled him, squeezing him tight. When she looked up at him, she flinched for a split second before recovering her bright smile.

"Zephyrine," he said politely, extricating himself. "You look stunning as always. The hair suits you."

"Everything suits her," Paris said.

"Go find us a snack," Zephyrine said. Paris sighed and left the lounge. Rolling her eyes at the door, she muttered, "Sycophant."

"He means well," Alistair said. "And he's not wrong."

"Flatterer," she murmured. She clasped his gloved hand and drew him to the long leather couch, giving him no choice but to follow. He went to pour her a drink from the warming carafe on the low table, but she waved it off. "Alistair Thorne, how long has it been? Ten years? How have you been? Tell me everything."

He hesitated. Ten years of living alone, hiding from the world. Ten years to stew in his mistakes and to know that all he suffered was his own doing. "To be honest, I've done very little. Tell me of yourself."

"Oh, not much," she said. "I've spent the last few years in

Japan. You know I've always loved to learn languages, and what better way to learn? And the shopping, Alistair, my God," she babbled. If there was one thing Zephyrine Lenoir always enjoyed discussing, it was herself. And she was quite an interesting woman, to be fair. Even so, he would have rather avoided her, if only so he didn't have to see that flinch and the quick fake smile. It was easier decades ago, but the Internet and smartphones had made it much harder to avoid her zealous need to stay connected.

As she detailed the colorful Akihabara shopping district, there was a shuffle of feet at the door. He heard a sharp breath just before the door swung open. A human male, dressed in an expensive but poorly tailored suit, stood in the open doorway. He shifted nervously. "Miss Lenore?"

"Lenoir," she said, emphasizing the French pronunciation. "Are you here for me?" He nodded. Zephyrine crooked her finger, scooting over to make room between them. Alistair watched hungrily as she stroked his brow. Her eyes were already brightening to a rich red, the venom on her fangs filling the air with a potent sweetness. "Is this your first time?"

"No, ma'am," he said, averting his eyes from her intense stare.

"What is your name?"

"Thomas," he said. "Ma'am."

"Thomas," she purred, gazing at Alistair as she unbuttoned the top of his shirt. "You're wonderfully polite. A lost quality these days." Her graceful fingers traced his throat, then his collarbone. Thomas's pupils dilated as the first hints of arousal took him, even before her lips touched his skin. One small hand slid over the older man's belly as she slowly bit into his throat. He gasped, back arching as he let out a quiet sigh. Pain creased his face, but it quickly faded into pleasure. His eyes were glazed as Zephyrine drank from him.

The scent of blood awakened the hunger in him, but he gritted his teeth. He'd at least gotten a snack from the dirty scumbag in the alley before Paris so rudely interrupted him. This Thomas seemed like a nice enough fellow, and the blue pocket square signified he was vetted as a *veravin*. That meant he wanted to be bitten, and he underwent regular health screenings to ensure his safety and prevent unfortunate accidents. Poor Thomas didn't need to have Alistair's true face seared into his memory. He'd probably never leave his house again, let alone return to the vampire club.

"Allie, won't you taste?" Zephyrine asked. "He's very well-nourished." Her tongue darted over her lip. "You must take your vitamins, Thomas."

"I do," he said dreamily. "Extra vitamin B every day."

"I've eaten," Alistair replied. "You enjoy."

With a shrug, she returned to feeding on Thomas. She drank a while longer, then gently nicked her thumb with one sharp fang. Dabbing the dark blood over Thomas's pierced neck, she kissed his cheek lightly and continued to stroke his hair absently. "I think I found a lead on the witch. I could kill her for you."

His stomach plunged through the floor. "Stay far away, Zephyrine. It isn't worth it."

"I wish I could fix this for you," she said with a sigh.

There was a knock at the door, and this time, a cluster of vampires bustled in. Nikko was at the front, talking animatedly on his phone, with Dominic close behind. Paris followed, with a woman in a tight red dress clinging to his arm. And at the rear, much to his surprise, was Julian. His eyebrows lifted at the sight of Alistair. He carried a bottle of whiskey in one hand, balancing a stack of glasses in the other.

"Zephyrine," Julian greeted warmly.

"Hello, handsome," she purred. "Bite to eat?"

"I'm satisfied, but thank you," he said. "Eduardo's finished with his business if you'd like to see him now. He's in his office with Valentin."

She beamed. "I'll return later."

"Can't wait," Dominic said quietly.

"Silence your tongue or I'll tear it out for you, Cattaneo," Zephyrine said, as sweetly as she had spoken to Thomas. She beckoned to the human man. "Come, sweet Thomas. Let's find you something to replenish those lovely red blood cells of yours, shall we?"

Dominic just glared after the woman as she left the room. He'd never understood if Dominic disliked Zephyrine because of her inability to tolerate silence, or if there was something deeper and more personal between them.

It was difficult to be there among his brothers, tied together by the ravages of the Midnight War. They all bore scars, and each of them endured a curse that was uniquely painful. But the others were as beautiful as they had ever been. Women and men alike would watch them pass, not understanding why their bodies were suddenly aflame with desire. They could move comfortably through this world's shadows.

Not Alistair. Awkward and out-of-place as a gargoyle in a boudoir, he perched at the edge of the couch, pressing himself tight into the corner. He wanted nothing more than to retreat to the solitude of his home, where he could play the piano and read in peace.

Paris plopped onto the couch and patted his muscular thigh, giving a wicked grin to the girl in red. She sank onto his lap, doing her best to kiss his neck. He ignored her, though one hand stroked her thigh gently while he spoke. "Got a hunter in town," he said in French. "Likely a team, two or three. They wrecked a nest downtown."

"Any of ours?" Dominic asked.

Julian shook his head. "Some of the remains were burned, but we found personal effects. It seems that most of them were connected to the Casteron."

"That's good, then," Alistair said.

Nikko's pale eyes narrowed as he tucked his phone away. "Not if they were killed by hunters."

The door bumped open again, and a pretty redhead in a glittering white dress entered. Her red curls were piled in a bun atop her head. "You bastards started without me," she complained.

"*En Français*, Safira," Paris said, tilting his head toward his human companion. "I brought a snack. Come and eat with me."

"You know I love a redhead," Safira said, flashing a fanged grin at them. "Good evening, boys." As she crossed the room, she sidled to Alistair and kissed the top of his head. He cringed as her touch pressed the hood against the bony protrusions on his skull. "Good to see you, love."

"Be on time and it won't be an issue," Julian said.

She shot a glare at him. "I apologize. I was explaining to a couple of idiots from Casteron that they can't send their thralls to rob a blood bank in broad daylight. I swear to God, these morons don't deserve their immortality."

"Explaining?" Alistair said. "With your words?"

As she settled onto the other couch with Paris, she examined her nails. "Yes, go with that. With my words."

"Careful, Safira," Julian said. "The last thing we need is conflict with them."

"That's exactly the thing we need," she retorted. "Playing nice is playing weak. That's why they're still here a year after stepping into our territory."

"I agree," Dominic said.

"Eduardo does not," Julian said sharply. "The rest of your opinions are irrelevant."

There was a little giggle that broke through the tension, and Paris looked up from his snack with an expression of guilt. He pressed his finger to the human's red lips. "I thought we came to drink." He tilted his head. "And since Alistair won't leave the house again for another decade, shall we enjoy it?"

"Don't be a tool," Nikko said. "Perhaps he'd join us more often if you weren't such a dick."

The look of mock offense on Paris's face lifted his spirits ever so slightly. Alistair cleared his throat and said, "Paris has been a dick for two centuries. This is hardly news."

Paris laughed. The girl in his lap whimpered and pawed at the lapels of his coat in search of his attention. "Patience, kitten," he said in English. His blue eyes lifted to Safira. Paris cupped the woman's jaw and eased her head to the side. He kissed the exposed flesh, following the sinuous curve to her shoulder. The human let out a soft moan as Paris bit slowly into her, a single drop of blood trickling over her collarbone. His other arm encircled her waist, holding her close to him. Safira joined him, one hand cupping her breast as she bit into the woman's wrist.

Just watching them brought back flashes of better times, when they had fed and fucked to their heart's content.

He looked away and caught Julian's eye. At that, Julian rose and took the seat Zephyrine had vacated. He poured a glass of whiskey and handed it over. "It's good to see you, my friend," he said quietly. "I apologize that I've not made the time to see you recently."

Alistair took the glass and drained half of it. "You're a busy man."

"Always," he said. "Still, a vampire has nothing but time. Have you been well?"

"As well as can be," Alistair said.

"And Lucia?"

"The same," Alistair said quietly. As they all were and ever would be.

While Paris and Safira enjoyed their snack, Nikko and Dominic spoke quietly, both of them wearing intense expressions that said they were talking business rather than enjoying themselves.

He missed this, and at the same time, he wanted to be as far away as he could get. Seeing his circle gathered here only reminded him of how much they had lost. And no amount of forced smiles and half-hearted jokes would lift their curses.

Nothing had changed in over a century, and it never would.

4

After three days of long shifts at the coffee shop and late nights at the vampire club, Shoshanna York was headed home for a hot date with her couch. If she was really feeling frisky, she might consider a foursome with a Korean sheet mask and a slice of dark chocolate raspberry cheesecake from work.

The wire transfer from Violette had cleared that morning, so she had treated herself to takeout sushi that was normally well out of her budget. Then, she'd immediately paid down her credit card and preemptively paid next month's bills, like a responsible little witch. Okay, maybe one Amazon order of non-essential kitchen gadgets and cat toys.

One large order.

The savory smell of steamed dumplings drifted from the paper bag in the passenger's seat. Her stomach growled as she fought the urge to tear into her dinner in stop-and-go traffic.

She silently willed the traffic light to change. Fifteen more minutes and she could ditch the bra and have an eel roll feeding frenzy.

Despite the appeal of a quiet, relaxing night, she couldn't help feeling guilty in advance. Tonight would be the perfect time to work on her long-neglected *grand travail,* the project that would complete her intermediate training as a *tisserand*. It was gathering dust these days, since she rarely had the time to devote to magical studies. She'd completed her last intensive training over a year ago, and most of her classmates had already submitted their work for approval. Then again, most of her classmates came from rich families with long traditions of magic, and were baffled by the concept of minimum wage and subsidized health insurance.

When she returned from her final class in the French countryside last summer, she was motivated to tackle the massive project. Once it was done, she'd ascend to adept training, where her room and board would be covered. No expensive rent payments, no disappointed mothers. She'd even done the non-magical mundane woo by declaring her intent to the universe. But even for a disciplined and organized witch, the best-laid plans didn't last when fate stepped in.

First she'd had a tooth that broke and revealed a cavity. Thankfully she'd gotten away with a filling and not a root canal that would have cost five times as much. Then her cat had gotten a kidney infection that set her back even further. The nest egg she'd saved before the trip quickly evaporated.

Instead of cutting back, she'd ended up taking more hours at the coffee shop to try to recoup her losses. And so, when one of her mentors from the Grand Guild called to tell her that the Auberon vampires were looking for someone with her exact skillset, she couldn't turn it down. Now when she had time off, she was just too damned tired for intense magical study. Best intentions ended with her books discarded on the floor while she snored on the couch.

The Blue Monster's brakes squealed as she pulled into the parking lot of her apartment complex. The car had miraculously started that morning, and she'd thanked her lucky stars all the way to the auto parts store where she reluctantly bought a new battery that put a hefty dent in her cash surplus.

The water-stained stucco betrayed the age of the complex. It was a decent place, but she hated running faster and faster on this financial treadmill to go absolutely nowhere.

One of these days, she was going to make it. Her younger brother Elijah had just bought his first house, which her mother mentioned every time they spoke.

As if she could forget.

Unlike Shoshanna and her arcane pursuits, Elijah had gone into the far more respectable field of medicine. He'd also finished an advanced program last summer and completed his certification as a nurse anesthetist. Six-figure salary, no debt. Though he'd inherited none of their father's magical talent, Elijah had far surpassed his sister in every other way.

Maybe she'd have been better off without it, too. Right now, the York magical talent wasn't doing her much good, considering she'd refused a cushy job offer from Eduardo. Judging by what he'd paid her to build the wards, he would be more than generous with a retainer.

But that meant she was theirs. Her father had served the Casteron vampires until he died. Dad had been sparse on the details, but she suspected he wasn't just making nice little protection sigils. In the York home, no one inquired about Dad's job, especially when he went to Mass in the middle of the day or when you found a blood-stained shirt in the garbage.

Even if it meant breaking her back to earn a living, her freedom was worth something. But it was hard to reconcile working for ten bucks an hour slinging overpriced coffee when a couple of vampires were willing to pay her four figures a week to be on call.

Shoshanna grabbed the takeout bag and got out of the car, breathing in the balmy night air. "Sushi in my tummy. Yummy yummy yummy," she sang quietly, adding to her repertoire of stupid songs typically reserved for her cat's entertainment. Her song dried up in her throat as she climbed the stairs.

Dressed in jeans and a gray t-shirt, a man stood just outside her apartment. His back was to her, revealing only a slender frame and short, dark hair. His posture was relaxed, thumbs hooked in his pockets. There was nothing inherently threatening about his appearance, but an unexpected visitor at eight at night was automatically suspicious.

When her foot scuffed against the concrete, his head whipped around. The bright halogen bulbs cast his features in sharp relief. "Elliott?" she murmured.

The handsome vampire turned toward her, his face lighting with recognition. "Shoshanna!"

The growling hunger in her belly turned to gnawing fear.

She forced a smile, hoping he couldn't hear her heart playing a bongo solo in her chest. "What are you doing here?"

His smile broadened, but it was the toothy white grin of a hungry predator. "I thought we could catch up since you left so quickly the other night."

She was ten feet from safety. Frozen in place, her mind sheared in two; part of her wanted to walk confidently past him, broadcasting that she was unafraid. And the other part of her wanted to run. A chilling thought prickled over her. Elliott was no longer the skinny college kid who was scared off by a protective father. Undead Elliott could snap her neck like a twig if he didn't like how she looked at him.

Setting her jaw, she took another step closer. "Showing up at my place is not okay," she said, her voice shaking. Her eyes swept over the still parking lot of her quiet, cozy complex. Just this once, she wished she was in a boisterous college neighborhood with plenty of witnesses with phones at the ready.

He gave her an incredulous look. "What? I thought you'd be happy to see me."

"I'm not happy to see anyone unannounced at my house in the middle of the night. It's not personal." It was very personal. To hell with him. She was going to walk away and call...who was she going to call? Atlanta Police, who would never get here in time? It wasn't like she had a vampire slayer on call. "You need to leave."

Cold air rushed around her, and he was suddenly in her space. Icy fingers dug into her bicep. His genial tone faded into a sharp-edged command. "Shoshanna, don't be rude." His eyes darkened to red. "Let's just chat."

"Let go of me," she demanded, twisting against his strong grip. But he twisted the keys from her hand and dragged her to the door. A scream bubbled on her lips, and then she saw the scene play out in her head.

Her elderly neighbor, Miss Joan, would stick her head out the door like she did every time someone got food delivered or had a nighttime guest or got a package from UPS. And Elliott would twist her head off like he was popping a bottle of old-lady flavored champagne.

"Just talk to me for a few minutes, and then I'll leave," Elliott said, still gripping her arm. "I promise."

He unlocked her door and pushed her inside. She stumbled in and frantically surveyed the cluttered space. She was a witch, not a warrior. The closest thing to weapons she had was a drawer full of mismatched cooking knives.

Elliott stepped over the threshold and wrinkled his nose. "Your house is warded, too?"

"Of course it is," she said. But her sigils weren't designed to keep vampires out. They were meant to give a mean case of the heebie-jeebies to would-be burglars and rapists, making them avoid the complex. But such elementary spells wouldn't do much more than make Undead Elliott's neck itch. Her top priority after investing in wooden stakes would be upping her security game.

Elliott slammed the door and secured the security latch. His eyes wept around her apartment. "Cute place, though I'd have expected something a little fancier for the pet witch of the Auberon."

"I'm not—" She froze. *He doesn't know.* "My place is just

fine." She folded her arms over her chest. "Speaking of the Auberon, they won't appreciate you putting your hands on me."

His lips pursed. "I know you're not their witch," he said. "The last time Cristiano reached out to you, you told him that you weren't taking any contracts for vampires. Casteron or Auberon. Has that changed?"

"How do you know about Cristiano?" she said. Cristiano Moretti ruled over the Casteron vampires here in Atlanta. She'd heard the name from her father when she was younger, and it was always tinged in dread. It was a personal goal to never cross his path if she could help it.

Elliott's hand drifted to his throat. "One of Cristiano's Vessels turned me," he said. "Imagine my surprise when I discovered our connection, Sho. The Casteron protected you until you up and left town. We're practically family."

"I didn't ask for their protection," she said.

"You would think that kind of loyalty would prompt a bit of gratitude." He pushed her big armchair in front of the door and plopped onto it. Her throat clenched around a lump of ice.

This was the nightmare she'd feared for years in college, when he kept showing up, kept calling, kept writing. That she'd come home one day and find him there with a knife, finally snapped and ready to punish her. It was bad enough when he was a college kid just growing into his frame. Now he had fangs and a grudge.

Her calculations changed rapidly. Beyond the locked glass door behind her, the balcony overlooked a stone courtyard. If she jumped, she might break her leg, but that was better than Elliott getting his hands on her.

Mrow?

A black blur ran out of her bedroom, then froze in the middle of the open living room. Magneto's baleful yellow eyes stared up at Elliott. "Hey there, kitty," he said, beckoning with one finger.

Magneto's tail flicked rapidly as he let out a low growl. Good boy.

"Come here, Maggie," she said, her voice shaking. Despite his usual contrary personality, the little black cat came running. She cradled him to her chest. "Look, you need to leave. I'm not interested in working for the Casteron. And you being a creep isn't helping your case."

His eyes narrowed. "All I'm asking is for a meeting. Cristiano is willing to pay you way more than the Auberon. Name your price."

"I said no," she said sharply. "Now leave."

He sighed and dusted off his knees as he stood. "I was really hoping that you would be more reasonable. I told them that you were friendly but you've obviously changed. Now I have to tell them that you're uncooperative."

Her eyes drifted to the bottle of cheap Moscato on the counter. It was supposed to be her treat with her sushi. Elliott was about to get himself a generous helping.

Please don't burn the place down, she prayed as she made her plan. Her arm tightened around Magneto, and he let out a little chirp of displeasure. His tail whipped against her arm, but she kept him tucked tight like a quarterback on a touchdown run.

With a deep breath, Shoshanna thrust one hand out and made a rapid twisting gesture. Fiery red tendrils of magic twined around her fingers. *"Mettrez à feu,"* she exclaimed in French.

Like an arrow shot from a bow, a thin stream of flame materialized from her palm. It zoomed toward Elliott. The backlash of power licked through her, like she'd gulped down burning gasoline. He let out a terrible roar of pain, but she didn't look back. She grabbed the bottle of wine and sprinted for the hall.

His hand fisted into her shirt and yanked her back. She screamed and smashed the bottle against the counter, then swiped at Elliott with the jagged glass. He bellowed in pain and released her. Without looking back, she bolted into the bathroom and slammed the door.

As soon as she was in the bathroom, Magneto wriggled out of her arms in a flurry of claws, leaving a thin scratch down her arm. From behind the toilet, he glared at her with his ears laid back.

The door shook in its frame. Bracing her left hand on the door, she used her right hand to trace another symbol, Weaving the tiny strands of magic into a simple sigil. *"N'entrez pas,"* she said. A glowing sigil ignited against the wood. Another wave of backlash hit her, clamping like a vise around her belly. She couldn't do much more before she was tapped out.

Elliott pounded on the door, then went quiet. The silence was shattered by the terrible wrenching sound of shearing metal and splintering wood. He tore the door clean off its hinges, but her sigil still hung in the doorway. Blood trickled down his slashed cheek and onto the burnt crater in his shoulder. Fangs out, eyes red, his expression was pure murder.

She just stared at him as she swiped through her phone contacts. Just under a long text message chain with her best friend Ruby was a curt text from Dominic, with just the letter *D*.

One ring. Nothing. Two.

Fuck.

He was probably fangs deep in some *veravin* draining her dry, and—

"This is Dominic."

She nearly wept with relief. "Hi Dominic. It's Shoshanna York," she said, hoping she sounded calmer than she felt. Elliott's head tilted. "I have an uninvited guest from the Casteron Court in my apartment. He doesn't believe that I'm under your protection."

In the silence that followed, she aged ten years. *Back me up. Please.* "Put me on speaker."

"Shoshanna, really?" Elliott complained. "All these dramatics are unnecessary."

"I know you can hear me," Dominic said, his deep voice issuing from her phone. "If you're still there when I arrive, I will let you crawl away with a message for your Baron. However, I assure you that you will wish I had simply killed you instead." His voice was eerily calm. "Shoshanna?"

"Yeah?"

"If he tries to bite you or make you drink from him, put your thumbs in his eye sockets and don't stop until they rupture," he said, as calmly as he'd told her that she needed to replace her battery in her car. Elliott took a tentative step back, then disappeared. "Someone's coming."

She clutched the phone tightly as Dominic hung up. It was silent for a few seconds, then came a telltale rattle of cellophane from the kitchen.

"Oh God," she murmured. Another rattle, then the tiny chirp of a fat cat who was accustomed to chowing down on treats when his human got home. A black ball of fur shot past her. She bounded for the door, then hesitated before crossing the sigil.

Elliott stood at the end of the hall with the cat tucked under his arm, one hand buried in his scruff. The cat's tail whipped back and forth violently. "This is so juvenile," he said. "Come out and talk."

"Just put him down," she said. "You're not doing much to win me over by threatening my cat."

"Who's threatening? I don't want this cute little guy to run out the door. Something bad could happen to him," he said. He stroked Magneto's head, and the little traitor stilled, eyes closing halfway. His panther ancestors would be ashamed to see him. "The way the Casteron see it, you owe them loyalty. They protected your family. They still protect Elijah and Sherry."

The mention of her brother's name sent a chill down her spine. "My family was only ever in danger because of the Casteron."

He shrugged. "Who's to say? You owe them a meeting at

the very least." His eyes narrowed. "You owe me that. We used to have something, Sho. Please."

There was something oddly fervent in his voice. "You stalked me," she protested.

"I loved you," he said incredulously. "I just want you to be part of something like I am now. You could be living in a penthouse in Midtown instead of working in that crappy coffeeshop."

Her blood went cold. "What do you know about the coffeeshop?"

"I know a little black dress suits you far more than that red apron," he said.

Her skin crawled. He was watching her, and had been for God only knew how long. And the crazy thing was that he sounded earnest. Her voice trembled as she said, "Please let my cat go. I might be willing to hear you out."

His mouth pulled into a crooked smile. "I can hear your heartbeat, Shoshanna," he said. "I know you're lying."

There was a firm knock at the front door, then it flew inward. A barefoot woman in a slinky black dress entered, a pair of red-soled high heels hooked in one hand. Her red hair was windblown in waves around her face. She gave Elliott a once-over and wrinkled her nose. "You must be the uninvited guest."

His smile twisted into a snarl. "We were just talking."

"Your conversation is over," she said. The woman darted forward and grabbed Elliott's face in one well-manicured hand. He backed into the counter, feet crunching over shattered glass. The cat wiggled out of his grasp and bolted to her bedroom.

The red-haired woman glanced over her shoulder. "Hey there. You okay?"

Shoshanna nodded, her mouth going dry. "Yeah."

The vampire woman smiled brightly, then turned back to Elliott. Her scarlet-painted nails dug into his face, and his knees buckled. "Listen up, you little shit," she said. "This witch is under the protection of the Blade of Auberon. You're new in my city, so this is your one and only warning. If you even think of touching her again, you will have the entire Shroud up your ass. And in case you're wondering, I do not mean in the fun way. Do you understand?"

"I was just talk—" He let out a terrible, muffled cry of agony. His face was suddenly misshapen in her grasp, like a jack o'lantern left too long on the stoop.

"I didn't ask for an explanation, boy. Do you understand?" the woman said again. Blood trickled down her pale forearm. "Take the message to your Baron. Write it down if you can't speak clearly."

Elliott wrenched away from her. Blood streamed from his nose. His jaw hung crooked and loose. "You're going to regret that." His words were slurred.

"I sleep fine in a pile of regrets," the woman said. She snarled. "Get out before I change my mind and rip your nuts off for a midnight snack."

In a blur, Elliott was gone, leaving them alone in the apartment. Shoshanna let out a sob of relief and ran for the bedroom. "Mags? Maggie?"

She found his glowing eyes under the bed, his go-to spot when he got busted for digging in her flowerpots. He dodged and retreated behind a plastic tote full of winter clothes. The feel of his tail slipping through her fingers prompted a sudden wave of tears.

The vampire woman appeared in her door. She casually caught the trickle of blood on her arm and licked her fingers clean. Freaking vampires. "Hey, are you okay?"

"Yeah," she said in a breathless rush, still slumped on the floor. "No. I mean, yeah."

The woman's feet were dirty and streaked with blood. Shoshanna followed her shapely legs up to see her cocktail dress and heavy jewelry. Despite her strange appearance, she was smiling. "We haven't met. I'm Safira."

"Are you okay? Your feet," Shoshanna said.

Safira lifted one filthy foot, then cursed. "*Scheisse,* I left a mess on your floor."

"Good lord. Forget about my floor," Shoshanna said. "Do you need first aid?"

"Honey, I'm a vampire. I'll heal fine in a few hours," she said. "I was headed out when Dom called me." When she pointed her toes, she had the dramatic, graceful curve of a ballerina's foot. "I kicked off my shoes and ran. No one's fast in stilettos. Plus, those were limited edition, and I would have actually murdered that little prick if I'd broken one of them because of him."

Her throat clenched. "You don't even know me."

Safira shrugged. "Dom said it was important. That's enough for me. Plus, I hate guys who don't respect boundaries." She busied herself with the front door, which was swinging loose on its hinges. "I think I ruined your door, although I have to admit that I didn't even try to open it. It's a bad habit. You have no idea how satisfying it is to kick in a door."

Despite herself, Shoshanna laughed. "I think I have bigger problems right now."

The redhead jumped, then stared down at her cleavage. "My tits are buzzing. Just a sec." She fished into the snug dress and took her phone out. "Yeah, she's okay. Obviously, Dom. Hey, bring me a snack. Please? Dammit," she swore. "Do you have blood here?"

"Sorry. How about coffee?"

She expected Safira to scoff, but she nodded. "Caffeine is a close second to hemoglobin," she said. "Black and strong, please."

Ten minutes later, Shoshanna had prepared a respectable espresso for the vampire woman and wrapped a warm, wet towel around her bloodied feet. While Safira sipped her coffee, Shoshanna swept up the shattered glass and propped a chair against the broken front door. As long as she kept busy, she wouldn't panic. She was about to make her third attempt at extricating the cat from under the bed when Dominic shoved the door open. Paris was on his tail, eyes sweeping around the apartment.

Both men were poised to kill, with eyes glowing furious red. She could see the point of a wooden stake at Paris's palm, barely concealed in his sleeve. Things changed quickly, because she'd never have thought she'd be so pleased to see two angry vampires barging into her place.

“I told you we had it under control,” Safira said mildly. She shot Shoshanna a look. “Men. They don’t listen.”

Dominic brushed past her and gave Shoshanna a once-over, red eyes skimming from head to toe. “Did he hurt you?”

She shook her head. “Just threatened me.”

“Tell me what happened,” he said.

“Did either of you bring snacks?” Safira asked. “I’m starving.”

Paris rolled his eyes. “Priorities, Saf. Jesus.” Then he gave her another slow, scraping look and smirked. “You look great, by the way. That neckline is delightful.” Safira beamed at him. Then he sniffed at the air. “Is there coffee?”

“What. Happened?” Dominic repeated. Shoshanna gave him the quick version of the story, up to the moment when Safira arrived. Dominic wrinkled his nose. “Did you burn him?”

“A fire spell,” Shoshanna said. “I didn’t know what else to do.”

“You don’t keep stakes?” Paris asked. He had already made himself at home and poured a cup of coffee for himself. Watching him sip from the bright pink coffee cup, she was keenly aware of her kitschy décor and how it probably looked to a couple of centuries-old vampires from Europe.

“No,” she snapped. “Vampires stalking me home wasn’t a problem until I started working for you two.” Then she tilted her head. “Did you tell him where I lived?”

Dominic scowled. “You are dangerously easy to find.”

“I am not,” she said.

Safira winced and nodded. “I literally just typed your name into Google and came up with your address to get here.”

Dominic sighed. "Pack whatever you need for a few days. We'll take you to a safehouse."

"Wait, what?" she spluttered.

"He knows where you live and he clearly wants you," Paris said. "We can't stay here to protect you round the clock."

"Can I bring my cat?"

Dominic closed his eyes as if he was in pain. "If you must."

Paris smirked. "Bring your witchy things. I have an idea."

AN HOUR LATER, Shoshanna had packed a suitcase with enough clothes for a week, a bin full of spell supplies, and another suitcase filled with Magneto's bed, treats, and toys. Dominic's expression was incredulous as he watched her zip the huge bags. "That's all for the cat?"

"They're creatures of habit," she said, her cheeks heating. She spritzed catnip spray in his carrier and coaxed the cat from under the bed. After some nips and swipes, she got him into the carrier and was rewarded with a baleful glare.

"A witch with a black cat," Paris mused. "You are a delightful cliche, Shoshanna." He grabbed one of her bags while she tucked Magneto's carrier under her arm. After doing her best to secure the broken door, she followed the two vampires down to the parking lot.

It was dark and quiet, with night finally settling over the city. A couple of her neighbors stood outside, chatting quietly as they smoked. She surveyed the concrete expanse, wary of Elliott lurking in the shadows.

A black SUV was parked directly behind her car, one door open and interior lights still on. She suppressed a smile. It was nice to have such intense backup. Paris loaded her bags into the back, then opened the back door. She hesitated with one foot into the car. "Where are we going?"

"A safe place," Dominic said. "Get in."

She settled into the back seat with the cat in her lap. The vehicle was impeccably clean, with the luxurious smell of leather. "I need to know more than that."

"Do you?" he said. "You called us for help. We're helping."

"Safira helped," Shoshanna said. "You're basically kidnapping me."

"Get out of the car if you don't want our help," Dominic said, turning to glare at her. "I have no patience for this."

"Dom, I'm pretty sure you have no patience for anything," she said. His eyes widened, and he leaned toward her. His broad frame filled the space between the seats. She was painfully aware of how close he was, with the smell of good cologne and the faint bite of vampire venom. His eyes still gleamed with that deep red sheen that said he was in predator mode, ready to bite anything that struck him as tasty or annoying.

"My name is Dominic. And while you may choose not to show your gratitude, you will show respect," he said quietly. "Unless you prefer to deal with the Casteron yourself."

Her heart kicked against her ribs as she stole a look back at her apartment. Thanks to Elliott, the Casteron would know where she lived, and most likely where she worked. What was to stop Elliott from coming back tomorrow night with an All-Star team of bloodsuckers who wouldn't ask nicely?

"Okay," she said meekly. "Thank you."

He stared at her for another few seconds, as if he was debating whether to tear her throat out just for kicks. Then one brow arched slightly, and he turned around to start the car.

In the middle of the night, Atlanta traffic was slightly less terrifying than normal. They zipped along the tangle of interstates, through tunnels of hazy orange-yellow light. As Dominic drove, he spoke quietly to Paris in German. At one point, the discussion got heated, and Paris snapped at him. Dominic glanced back at Shoshanna, then shrugged.

Nervous energy fluttered in her chest. What exactly were they planning, and why did they have to hide it? It took a tremendous amount of willpower to not blurt out *speak English!* but she didn't want another scolding from Dominic, who had a way of making her feel like a slimy little worm.

She thumbed through her phone. Who else was she supposed to call? Ruby was a green witch with connections to every practitioner in the city, but she had no hand in vampire politics. With his ties to both vampires and witches, her father might have been able to give her advice, but unless she could raise the dead, that ship had long sailed.

It was well after midnight when they pulled off the highway and into a ritzy suburb. A wooden sign read *Midnight Springs* in ornate calligraphy. Her stomach plunged as she watched the buildings blur by. Even the chain restaurants and stores were built from monotonous stacked stone, uniform in their cookie-cutter fanciness. Of course this unnaturally clean and bright pocket of suburbia was home to bloodsucking monsters.

They drove past the edge of town and turned down a private drive. Mounted in a high brick wall, a wrought iron gate blocked the drive. Rising over the wall, she could make out the peaked roof of a big house against the silhouette of Georgia pines. Dominic pressed a button on a remote clipped to the visor, and the gate silently swung open. "You'd better tell him," Dominic said to Paris. "He'll take it the best from you."

"Tell who what?" Shoshanna asked.

Dominic parked in front of the huge house, a gorgeous two story with a Victorian facade. It had clearly been updated over the years, but there was a sense of age to it, like it had been here long before the rest of the town. There was a cool, tingling energy around the place, and a thrumming undercurrent of natural energy that she often missed living in the city.

Paris gritted his teeth and headed for the house. The red door closed behind him, and Dominic turned to glance at her. "This house belongs to one of ours," Dominic said. "You'll stay here until we make other arrangements."

Her jaw dropped. "I'm sorry, what? You want me to shack up with a strange vampire? Absolutely not."

Dominic folded his arms and stared down at her. "Don't be melodramatic. You'll never even cross each other's paths. There are far worse fates."

Tears stung at her eyes. "We're not all superpowered, you dick. A vampire just stalked me home and broke into my house. Then another terrifying vampire crushed his face in her bare hands. Now you want me to have a sleepover with a complete stranger who is equally as terrifying as the rest of you. Forgive me for being scared."

His stern expression softened slightly. It might have been the tiniest shred of compassion, or maybe just indigestion. "You have nothing to fear here. Alistair is one of our brothers," he said. "No one would know to come here, and if they did, Alistair would quickly make them regret coming within a mile of this place. He will not lay a hand on you. I swear it."

She pursed her lips. This was why she didn't want anything to do with vampire politics. "After this, I'm done with the Blade of Auberon. Let Eduardo know."

He shook his head sadly. "I don't think you are," he said. "If you want the benefits of our protection, then you owe us something in return."

"Great," she said. "So you guys pull me into your crap, and now I'm the one who has to pay—"

"That isn't—"

The red door flew open, and Paris practically ran out onto the big porch. Despite his forced smile, he looked uneasy. "Welcome to your home away from home, Shoshanna."

5

It had been at least a decade since Alistair and Paris had gotten into a proper tussle, with claws and fangs and the occasional gouged eye. Their scuffle in the alley behind the bar barely counted. With Paris's unwelcome visit and even more unwelcome announcement, Alistair realized it was well past time to put his friend in his place. Perhaps a stake in his belly would drive the point home.

"Did you just say that you brought a human to stay here?" Alistair said, glaring over the edge of his manuscript. He'd been having a perfectly lovely evening alone with a Tchaikovsky piano concerto and a tall glass of A-negative.

"I can say it in German if that's easier for you," Paris said, sidling up to him. As if to be as obnoxious as possible, he repeated himself in German. The low light gleamed off his bronze hair as he leaned on the piano seductively.

His former lover's charm scraped rather than soothed, and

Alistair stalked around the piano to put distance between them. Being within arm's reach was dangerous for Paris. "Why?"

"She needs somewhere to stay," Paris said, as if that explained anything.

"We live in one of the biggest cities in America," Alistair said. "There are other options that do not involve a human under my roof." He did not need someone here to gawk at him, to interfere with his solitary existence.

Paris scowled. "I need you to keep her safe."

The *her* caught his ear. "Who?"

"The witch who worked on Infinity's protections," Paris said.

"A witch? Are you—"

"Eduardo values her," Paris interrupted. "And I owe her. I would trust no one else with this."

"You know that's bullshit. You're asking me because I'm stuck here, not because I am uniquely capable."

A clear voice rang out in the night. "Forgive me for being scared!"

The sweet feminine voice was edged in steel, but he heard the keening edge of fear beneath it. He darted for the front window and peered through the one-way glass. A young woman glared up at Dominic with fire in her eyes.

The sight of her caused a seismic shift inside him, the sort of deep movement that reshaped entire worlds and defined eras. He had glimpsed her pretty face in the club a few nights earlier and quickly forgot her, but now it rushed back to him. There had been a sparkle in her eye then, a flicker of mischievous joy when Paris greeted her. That sparkle was gone now, replaced by defiance and fear.

And though Paris had not mentioned the injury, he saw the distinct imprint of fingers on her arm. Someone had dared to put their hands on her. He knew nothing about her, not even a single syllable of her name, but he was overcome with fury at someone marring such a beautiful creature.

"Allie, it's just for a few days," Paris said. "I just need—"

"I'll do it," he interrupted, still gazing at her intently.

"You to help me handle this, and...wait, what?"

"I'll do it," he said absently, watching as she turned away from Dominic. The moonlight reflected in her eyes, which welled up with tears. A fierce battle played out on her face. After one big sniffle, a look of angry determination furrowed her brow.

"After this, I'm done with the Blade of Auberon," she declared to Dominic. The dour vampire scowled at her, but Alistair had already turned back to Paris.

"I don't want her to see me," he said softly. "Not someone like that."

"I understand," Paris said, his usual sarcastic bluster gone. "I'll handle it."

He nodded, then rushed up the stairs quickly. Paris stepped outside and interrupted the argument. "Shoshanna, welcome to your home away from home!"

Shoshanna.

Even her name was a song, every bit as exquisite as she was. Paris's voice echoed in the quiet house. "This house belongs to one of our comrades, Alistair Thorne."

From the shadows at the top of the stairs, Alistair stared down at the open living room where his piano stood. Quiet steps shuffled over the hardwood as the witch walked into the living room. Her eyes shone as she surveyed the house. "Is he home?"

"He's here. You should know that Master Thorne has an unusual affliction." Alistair gripped the banister tightly. "He is unusually sensitive to light. Therefore, he tends to remain in darkness for his safety." It was uncanny how easily Paris lied.

"Oh," she said, craning her neck as if she was hunting for him. Though there was no way she could see him from below, he backed further into the shadows.

"You can make yourself at home," Paris said.

"This house is incredible," Shoshanna marveled. Then there was the crystalline sound of middle C from his piano, shimmering into silence. "Gorgeous piano, too."

"Do you play?"

"I took lessons for most of my life," she said. "I don't get to play often anymore. No piano."

"Well, I'm certain that Master Thorne wouldn't mind if you played."

He listened closely as Paris gave her the grand tour of the house, pointing out the bathrooms, the kitchen, and the library in turn. Thankfully, his old friend steered clear of his bedroom, simply telling her to leave the basement level alone so she didn't introduce light into his quarters. Clever vampire.

"Is there anything I can do?" she said as they circled back around the bottom floor. "Like with the house? I can cook if that would be helpful."

Paris chuckled. “We don’t eat. But I do have work for you. I want you to design wards like what you put up at Infinity. Maybe more. I’ll write you a list.”

“I can do that,” she said eagerly. Her voice was more serious when she asked, “What are you going to do about Elliott?”

“I don’t know yet,” he said. “Fifty years ago I would have hunted him down and torn his head off and called it a night. Things are more complicated now. But I give you my word—as does Alistair—that you will be safe here.”

“Thank you for all of this,” she said.

“Don’t thank me too soon,” he said. “Dominic was right. This won’t come without strings. But for now, just get some rest. Try not to leave. Order out if you need anything.”

There was the faint sound of a kiss, sending a flare of envy through Alistair. Paris had failed to mention that he was seducing the pretty human witch.

Of course he was. She was mildly interesting and had a heartbeat, so of course Paris was seducing her. And he was Paris, so of course the witch would want him in return.

There was a clatter as someone carried bags into one of the long-empty bedrooms. He noted with a hint of gratitude that Paris had guided her to the room farthest from the door to the basement. Though his old friend could be a real shit when he wanted, he had his moments of consideration.

He listened for the sound of shoes on the porch, and then there was a clear voice, speaking in his native tongue. Paris didn’t speak German nearly as well as English, but he was fluent enough. With their sensitive hearing, he could hear him through the glass. “This could start something ugly, Alistair.

You must keep her safe. This witch could be critical in surviving another war."

"I understand," he said quietly.

The engine of the SUV roared to life, then faded as his brothers left him alone with the woman. Shoshanna's soft scent of vanilla and sage wafted through the house, startling in its strangeness.

It was strangely thrilling to have a guest, and a beautiful woman at that. Once upon a time, he would have been confident and bold in her presence. He'd charmed many beautiful women from the piano bench, meeting their eyes across a crowded room. One such meeting had led to his transformation into a vampire, and another had resulted in his curse.

But those days were long gone. Shoshanna would not look at him and hear a silent invitation to bed. She would only see a monster. And though he had no illusions about what he was, he could not bear to see the disgust on her face.

He heard her tiptoeing around the kitchen, speaking quietly. "You better behave, Maggie," she said. "Or the big bad vampire might eat you."

"What?" he whispered to himself. Moving silently, he crept down the stairs, keeping to the shadows. If she noticed him, she didn't say a word. Now that he was closer, he could smell the faint animal scent of a cat, and heard the gentle purr.

"Blood, blood, and more blood," she said, pulling the refrigerator open. "Not surprising. Groceries tomorrow."

A few minutes later, she retreated to the guest room. The door closed, but he could hear her chatting quietly to the cat. She was stern as she told the feline he better not get her kicked out of the nice vampire's mansion by pooping on something expensive. The water ran for a while, and finally, it was quiet. He waited a few minutes longer before creeping downstairs.

He intended to go to his library for a book, but instead, he found himself drawn toward the guest room. Her intoxicating scent drew him to the closed door. If he stilled, he could hear the steady, quiet thump of her heartbeat, along with a subtle thrum of a purring cat.

The witch's curse had taken his looks and his dignity, consigning him to the shadows. He had been isolated from his kind and their dramatics for nearly a century. And he had long felt like the cold, undead creature that folklore held him to be. The world was unaware of him, and little would change if he faded from existence. The closest he came to feeling connected, to having some tiny impact on the world beyond his door, was on his late night hunts.

Somewhere, sweet, foolish Stacey was a little safer than she had been. There were dozens of Staceys in the city, and there was a very good reason that Midnight Springs had been rated the safest place in the Southeast to live. Perhaps he could no longer enjoy the warmth of making love to a beautiful woman. But he knew the visceral satisfaction of tearing apart a would-be rapist or abuser, ensuring they wouldn't hurt anyone again. That was something.

And now there was Shoshanna, who surely mattered to someone.

He could not do much, but he could ensure her safety. Standing there, listening to her breathe so soft and slow, he silently vowed, *You will be safe here.*

With that, he silently crept to his library. In addition to the usual book of Shakespearean sonnets, he took down a copy of *The Cherry Orchard*. His Russian was rusty, and he'd been doing his best to brush up for the last few months. After pouring a glass of Scotch, he retreated to the cozy alcove overlooking the barren gardens.

Moonlight poured through the open window, casting a silvery pall on the stone statue keeping silent vigil. Though it was a fool's wish, he always hoped that he would arrive one night to find Lucia smiling, or better yet, to find her gone. Instead, he found the ever-present somber expression on her face, her graceful hand reaching for the cursed lover who could not save her from her fate.

"Good evening, Lucia," he greeted. After setting down his books, he took a soft cloth from the nearby shelf and gently dusted her from head to toe. He took care with her face, using a light touch as if she could still feel the fabric scraping over her eyes and lips. When he was done, he brushed a kiss over her cold stone fingers. "We have a guest for a while. I may have to abstain from playing in the evenings, so long as she sleeps at night. I trust you'll understand, and when she leaves, I'll make it up to you." He opened the book of sonnets. "Now, where were we? Ah, one hundred twelve. A continuation of the prior, as you well know. He cleared his throat, though the foul witch's curse had left his voice permanently rough. "Your love and pity doth th'impression fill which vulgar scandal hath stamped upon my brow..."

When he finished the sonnet, he glanced up at Lucia, unmoving and silent.

"One more, you say?" He spared a smile, thankful that her dull stone eyes did not reflect the monstrous twist of his mouth. "Number eight, then. Music to hear, why hear'st thou music so sadly?" When he completed the sonnet, he closed the book quietly. "It's too bad you don't speak German. You would enjoy Rilke, but the translations are simply not the same. Maybe I can read you both and explain."

Her silence was an admonishment. The witch's malice was not just skin deep, though in Alistair's curse, it certainly lay upon the surface like filth encrusting a stagnant swamp. Eternally mournful Lucia reminded him of the dangers of falling in love. It was not enough that she punished Alistair and his brothers. Anyone close to them was subject to her wrath. Lucia was a reminder that they could still lose so much more.

He sat in the quiet to read the Chekhov play. Despite his attempts to focus on the Cyrillic letters, he was distracted by Shoshanna's breathing. Her scent still lingered in the air, though he wasn't sure if it was reality or his own fixation on the strangeness of having someone here. A maid visited once a week, but she was gone long before he woke, leaving only the fading scent of cleaning products.

Now there was a heartbeat here. Movement in the air as another soul existed dangerously close. It was fresh and constant, not a fading memory that he could ignore.

With a sigh, he rose to bid Lucia farewell. Closing the curtains, he gently touched her cheek. "Good night, Lucia. May your dreams be as lovely as you are."

He retreated to his bedroom to read. The richly appointed room was cast in low light by a single lamp on the nightstand. Though she was out of sight, even his bedroom felt different with Shoshanna here. He closed the door, effectively blocking out the sound of her presence, and settled in to read.

Like many vampires of the Auberon Court, he was fluent in multiple languages. His Russian was rusty from lack of use, so he spent the next few hours reading Chekhov aloud, twisting his tongue around the unfamiliar consonants.

His phone chirped an alarm to remind him that sunrise was rapidly approaching. He preferred the old ways in many things, but he could not deny the utility of the smart phone. An enterprising younger vampire had developed several apps for the modern vampire, including one that tracked local sunrise and sunset times and issued alerts.

Books and movies about his kind were steeped in superstitions and folklore, though they occasionally stumbled upon a nugget of truth. Exposure to sunlight was not instantly lethal, but it would weaken him and cause horrific burns within minutes. Even when not exposed to the scorching rays, vampires were far weaker during the day.

He peeled off layers of dark clothing, leaving just loose pants. There were no mirrors in his bedroom, but he couldn't avoid glimpses of his wrecked body; the dark, mottled gray skin on his hands turned his stomach. After brushing his teeth in the dark, he slid into his bed and pulled the heavy curtains tight around him. Pure pitch darkness engulfed him in its pleasant embrace.

The twisted bone protrusions on his brow made it difficult to lie down comfortably, but he'd learned to deal with it. The heavy, deep sleep of day would come soon enough, and he could forget the cold loneliness of this life for a while longer.

As he lay down, an odd, unfamiliar thought danced through his mind. This was not just another night in this large, echoing house. Though she was as far from him as she could be without sleeping outside, he somehow felt Shoshanna's energy nearby. It was a faint vibration just at the edge of his hearing.

What would it be like to touch her soft skin? A human witch would be warm, practically vibrating with energy. And there was her hair, in those dark, round curls. He could just imagine twining one perfect spiral around his finger as her perfume engulfed him.

And if he dared, to brush his lips across hers. The thought of her breath on him, that little hint of life...

He shook his head, squeezing his eyes to push the image away. The thought of these hands on that beautiful face was an atrocity. She deserved more.

And yet, hope lingered. He hoped it would leave before it became a flame he could not extinguish.

6

An undeniable magnetism drew her down the long, dark hallway. Flickering candles in sconces cast dancing shadows that beckoned her to the stairs at the end of the hall. The pull grew stronger as she descended into hazy darkness.

Something awaited her. Something wanted her.

A filmy nightgown billowed behind her as she crept through the open doorway to the vampire's chambers. Dark oil paintings overlooked the massive canopy bed wreathed in heavy black curtains. Silver moonlight poured in through an open window, casting the strange man in silvery light.

Her breath caught in her throat at the sight of him. Dark, slightly curly hair framed a strong-featured face with a broad jaw and high cheekbones. Blue-green eyes gleamed from the shadows of the canopy. With the moonlight playing off his bare chest, she could imagine him posing for a sculptor, preserving his perfection in pale white stone.

"M...Mister Thorne?" she asked hesitantly.

In a blur, he was on his feet, staring down at her. She was a quivering mouse in front of the hungry lion. "Miss York," he said. His voice was the rumble of distant thunder in a summer storm, the smell of wood smoke in the fall. "Have you brought my dinner as I requested?"

She stared down at her empty hands. Her skin was lined with silvery tendrils, as if a spider's web enveloped her. With sinking reluctance, she murmured, "I forgot it. I'll get it." She didn't want to leave, but wasn't that the expectation?

When she stepped back, he grabbed her wrist and pulled her closer. "My hunger will not wait," he said. Her heart thrilled with anticipation as he grasped her waist and lifted her onto his bed. Graceful fingers untied the nightgown and revealed her body to the moonlight. His icy gaze raked over her. "What a delight," he said with a toothy smile. "Where shall I begin?"

Anywhere you like, she thought. A dim thought whispered somewhere. She shouldn't allow this. She should say no. But she couldn't. Didn't want to.

Cool hands encircled her wrists, pinning her hands to the soft bed. "Exquisite," he murmured as he loomed over her. His lips were shockingly warm as he marked her skin with his kiss, making his way from her lips to the hollow of her throat.

Sharp teeth grazed her tender skin, but he didn't bite. His gentle kisses followed the curving path of her collarbone down to her breast. She gasped as his tongue flicked at her, teasing her nipple into a hard bud.

"You taste delightful," he murmured. His teeth scraped slightly over the sensitive flesh and sent a shiver down her spine. When he raised his head, she saw that his eyes had gone deep red. "I hunger, Miss York."

In that hungry gaze, she was helpless prey, something to be conquered and consumed. She didn't care, so long as he kept touching her. "Then drink your fill, Mister Thorne."

Sharp fangs descended, glinting in the moonlight. A drop of venom dripped from one tooth and splashed onto her skin. He scooped her into his lap, and with no fanfare, he sank his teeth into her throat.

The pain was quick and sharp. Electric cold spread from his teeth as one hand tangled into her hair, keeping her throat exposed. His other hand settled between her thighs. The icy tingle of his bite shot down her spine, colliding with the fiery burn of his fingers below. Like hurricane winds, they spiraled around her. She was the eye of the storm, at the center of something terrifying and amazing. Amidst the roaring winds, she heard the waterfall of piano keys. The world trembled around them.

The phone buzzed against the nightstand, screaming an obnoxious alarm. Shoshanna gasped and opened her eyes to find a notable lack of sexy vampires in her bed. There was a throbbing ache between her legs. She slid one hand down, and the lightest touch of her fingers sent a shiver twisting through her. Wet warmth soaked through her panties.

Holy shit.

A furry tail snapped against her cheek, and she looked up to see Magneto sitting on the pillow next to her. His silent glare was thoroughly judgmental, as if he knew she'd just been having a sex dream about her new employer.

"Who I haven't even seen," she muttered. Magneto's eyes narrowed. "What are you looking at? You don't even have balls anymore. You cannot possibly relate."

She sure as hell wasn't going to chase the Big O with the damned cat watching her. With a growl of frustration, she rolled out of bed, still clinging to the hazy bliss of her dream. There was a sting at her neck, and she leaned close to the mirror to inspect her skin. It was unmarked, but she could still feel his phantom kiss.

"Good lord," she muttered. She hadn't had a dream like that...maybe ever. A steady pulse throbbed between her legs. She stole a glance at the shower. It was tempting to take care of the mounting frustration, but what if he heard her? What if he knew somehow?

After covering her hair with a shower cap, she trudged into the shower. The warm water cascading down her back reignited the memory of his touch on her skin. Her fingers drifted downward, finding that warm, ready place. Closing her eyes, she tried to hold on to the fragments of the dream, of those lips on her breast, and strangely, his teeth in her throat.

Bracing one arm against the wall of the shower, she stroked and circled, imagining the handsome vampire's hands instead of her own. His blue gaze stared down at her, filled with hunger and lust.

I hunger, Miss York.

Pressure gathered into a desperate ball of flame between her thighs. Energy pulsed from her, and there was that one perfect, frozen moment of pleasure as her body tightened. She breathed hard, leaning against the granite wall of the shower. Not the most satisfying, but it was better than walking around all day thinking about him.

After scrubbing herself from head to toe, she emerged to find Magneto sitting on the bathroom counter. His yellow eyes followed her, as if to say *I know what you just did.*

"Don't judge me," she muttered. "If you'd seen him, you wouldn't blame me one bit."

But she hadn't seen Alistair, not really. And yet, she knew beyond a shadow of a doubt that it was him. Still, she did not need to spend her days having sex dreams about the vampire. He was protecting her from Elliott by being a bigger, badder monster, and she would be a fool to forget that.

After getting dressed, she pondered her suitcase. Completely unpacking felt too much like accepting this strange situation. Instead, she placed one set of clothes in a drawer and left the rest in her suitcase. After feeding Magneto his morning feast of pungent fish chunks, she settled back in bed with her phone.

Late last night, she'd texted her boss Jolene with a story about a stomach bug that would keep her home for a few days. Hopefully, Elliott would be dealt with by the end of the week, and she wouldn't have to maintain her lie too long. She hesitated to text Ruby, her best friend and fellow witch. Everything with Ruby was a family affair, so Ruby's mother, grandmother, and aunties would all know Shoshanna's business by lunchtime. Still, if their positions were reversed, she'd be furious if she only found out after the fact that Ruby had been in trouble.

Hey, give me a call when you have time. Got a weird situation and wanted to let you know.

Ruby was never away from her phone for more than a few minutes. Shoshanna managed to finger-comb her hair and apply mascara to one eye by the time her phone started ringing. She hit the speakerphone and kept working on her other eye.

"Sho! Are you okay?" Ruby asked.

"I'm okay," she said hesitantly.

There was boisterous laughter in the background, and Ruby let out a furious tirade in Cantonese. "Like a bunch of little kids," she complained. A door slammed in the background, and the noise faded.

Ruby worked at her family's upscale health food store, Jade Breeze. In addition to expensive organic juices and local produce, the Wangs also sold protective herbs and tea blends that were quickly becoming famous. Ruby had put the store on the map with her "Dusklight Blend" sleeping tea, which she'd only named such because Auntie K said she couldn't call it *Better than Ambien.* The last time Ruby put a batch up for sale, the customers were lined up at four in the morning to get their orders.

"How's business?" Shoshanna asked.

"Aunt Eileen is working on a hangover tea and trying to pay college kids to try it, but I keep telling her that her sales pitch sounds like she's the villain in a horror movie," she complained. "We're working on her marketing skills. What's up?"

"Well, for starters, I spent the night in Midnight Springs," she said.

"Damn, girl. Did you get laid?"

Almost. "Not exactly. It's a vampire's house."

"What?!" Ruby spluttered. "If you banged a vampire without telling me, this friendship is off."

She laughed. "No banging. Do you remember me telling you about the stalker boyfriend from college?" She told Ruby the story of Elliott showing up at her place, up to getting dropped off here at the mysterious Alistair's house.

"Oh my God! Are you okay? What about the kitty?"

"Yeah, we're both fine," she said. "But I think I'm going to be here a few days while they figure things out."

Ruby was quiet for a while. "Do you want to come stay with us instead? This seems like a lateral move from the frying pan into the fire, babe."

She nodded to herself. "You're not wrong. If it looks like it'll be more than a day or two, that sounds better."

"I'll tell Miles to clear his gaming crap out of the guest room," she said. "He'll be excited to have you, although you'll have to put up with hearing about Twitch streamers."

"Thanks," she said with a laugh. She wasn't sure Ruby's cousin was a big improvement over a reclusive vampire. "I'll keep you posted."

"Send me pictures of the house!" Ruby ordered. "And obviously of Hottie McFangs."

"I'll try," she said, shivering again at the thought of that gorgeous face. "Talk to you later."

Shoshanna spent the next few hours roaming the house. She convinced herself that she was looking for cleaning products to make herself useful, but she took her time looking into every nook and cranny of the breathtaking home. The interior was done in dark colors, with rich ruby red walls and oil paintings framed in decadent gold. The centerpiece of the open living room was a polished grand piano, surrounded by leather couches.

The house was oddly dark, with all the windows covered by heavy blackout curtains. Even when she peeked out the front windows, there was the grayish-brown tint of tinted glass.

She ventured across the house and lingered at Alistair's door. There was no sound, and she was suddenly tempted to descend the stairs and see him sleeping. He probably looked like a male Sleeping Beauty, with those beautiful lips and long lashes.

With a shiver, she stepped away before she made a stupid mistake. Instead, she returned to her snooping upstairs. In addition to several more well-furnished bedrooms and a study, he had an actual library lined with overflowing bookshelves.

Across from the library was a bay window overlooking a barren patch of dirt where there might have once been a garden. But stranger than the empty garden was the eerie, life-like statue of a woman who faced the window.

A strange energy surrounded the statue. Shoshanna circled it slowly before gently touching its cheek. Bitter cold prickled down her spine, and she gasped. Her arcane sight overwhelmed her, revealing a tangle of dark, blue-black energy running through the statue like veins. Most recently, she'd seen that same bruise-colored energy entangled around Paris and Dominic. It wasn't vampiric energy, which had a rich crimson hue.

This was a curse, a powerful act of spell-weaving imbued with malice and cruelty. She hadn't brought it up to Paris, but she'd gone back to her textbooks to confirm what she was seeing after the first day that they met. The same distinctive energy ran through the stone statue. There was no mistaking it; even touching it made her feel uneasy.

Why would Alistair Thorne have a cursed statue in his home? A centuries-old vampire might find all manner of things fascinating, but this was the only thing that she'd noticed with such obvious magical power. Shoshanna gazed at it. The face was remarkable. It was eerily lifelike, as if someone had been frozen in time. But that was absurd. Such powerful magic was practically nonexistent in modern times.

She shook her head and walked away from the statue, though the mournful look lingered in her mind. If the vampire showed himself, she'd work up the nerve to ask him about it.

Shoshanna finally located a closet filled with cleaning supplies and linens tucked in the closet of an immaculate guest bathroom. It only seemed right to do something around the house if she was staying. Even if he didn't ask for it, the lemon fresh smell of cleaning products would shout *I'm making an effort to not be a complete leech.*

After scrubbing the kitchen, she sat down with her phone to order some groceries. There was no TV in the house, so she watched a true crime documentary on her laptop while she waited for her delivery. Once it arrived, she sauteed chicken thighs in a savory sauce, then added a rainbow assortment of vegetables. After she'd eaten and cleaned up, she paced the living room.

It was strange to be in the big house all alone, without the pressure of going to work tomorrow. She felt like she was on a vacation into a parallel universe. With nothing else to do, she went to her room for the notebook where she'd kept her notes on her *grand travail.* She'd been working on a large, multi-layered array that could be installed in homes or even hospitals to aid in healing work. When Dad was sick and getting sicker by the day, she'd searched every book she could find to no avail. Her work would be too late to save Dad, but maybe it could help someone else.

Staring at the notebook felt like trying to remember a song from middle school. She flipped through her neatly organized notes to refresh her memory. Halfway through the notebook, her phone buzzed. It was swiftly followed by a knock on the door. Her heart thumped, and she was immediately tense at the thought of Elliott standing outside.

She grabbed her phone and found a text.

Paris: *It's me at the door. I'm coming in*

By the time she rounded the corner, Paris was already walking through the door with a bag slung over his shoulder. "Something smells good," he said. When he leaned down to kiss her cheeks, his lips were cool on her skin.

"Do you want some? There's a lot of leftovers."

"I don't eat," he reminded her. "But if you want to warm up something for me to drink, I wouldn't say no."

She hesitated. "You mean blood."

"No, I mean chocolate ice cream," he drawled. "Yes, *ma sorcière,* blood. There's a double boiler around here somewhere. Around one hundred degrees, if you please."

She planted her hands on her hips. "Can I get you a glass of whiskey? Perhaps a massage?"

"If you're offering..." he said with a grin. He perched on a stool at the kitchen island and took a tablet from his bag. She rifled through the cabinets. "The one next to the microwave."

She found the double boiler in the cabinet as directed. "Can I just microwave it?"

"Shoshanna." His look of disgust was all the answer she needed.

"Sorry," she said, setting the double-decker pot in the sink to fill the bottom layer. "I'm not educated in the fine art of blood preparation."

"Go ahead and make two. Alistair will be up soon," he said. "Have you seen him at all?"

She shook her head. "I tried to be quiet so he could sleep."

Paris laughed. "You could tap dance outside his door and he'd still sleep. If you'll forgive the expression, we sleep like the dead."

"You're awake," she said.

"I'm an early riser," he replied.

She wrinkled her nose and took two of the blood bags from the refrigerator. They were marked only with labels indicating their type, which was odd. Usually medical supplies would have barcodes and addresses and all sorts of markings. "Where are these from?"

"We have our own blood bank," Paris said absently. "He'll probably get a delivery this week."

She braced herself for the coppery smell and dumped the bags into the upper part of the double boiler, then hunted down a wooden spoon. *Cranberry sauce,* she told herself as she stirred the viscous fluid. In the depths of the pan, it could have passed for a dark sauce. People sauce. Yuck.

She tamped down her disgust. If the worst thing they asked her to do was heat up a glass of blood, she was getting off easy.

"Violette and Hugo prepared a contract for you," Paris said. He pushed the tablet toward her. "We want this house warded. What you did at Infinity at the bare minimum, and more if you can. If you can turn the basement into a panic room, that would be ideal."

"Why not just use physical security measures?" she asked. "You know...locks, alarm systems."

"We will eventually, but those things take a while to build. Furthermore, short of installing steel vault doors, our kind can tear through anything we build," he said. "Hence the magical request."

She skimmed the list of requests. "Magical tasers for vampire hunters," she said with a laugh. "Really?"

"I didn't know how to describe it," he said defensively. "Can you do something that targets hunters?"

"Not specifically." He sighed. "But I can target humans. If you don't expect many other humans to come here, that would work."

"Fair enough," he said. "What about you?"

"I can tie my blood to it so I'm recognized as a safe person. I can do the same if you have other humans you want to have access. Easy enough."

"And the containment?"

She kept reading. "Seal in a vampire. Like a prisoner?"

"Like someone who needed to be protected," Paris said. His gaze skimmed away from hers.

"I can do that, but it'll be expensive if you want to be strong enough to hold them for a while. The materials are going to cost you," she said.

He raised an eyebrow. "I cannot overstate to you how little of a problem that will be. Go stir." While she stirred the blood, he continued talking. "How long do you think this much work will take?"

"At least a few weeks," she said. Some of the ingredients would have to be steeped or prepared, and there was the issue of her own energy levels. This wasn't like writing a term paper the night before it was due.

He nodded. "We'll pay for all your materials, plus a rate of fifteen hundred dollars a week. I know that's much less than what we paid for Infinity, but considering we're providing protection and shelter, it's a fair offer."

"No argument here," she said, glancing over her shoulder. "But I don't see myself staying here for a few weeks. I've got a friend who will let me stay with her."

He gave her an appreciative smile. "This matter is complicated, Shoshanna. The easiest way for us to protect you is to keep you here."

"And I don't want to stay here for two weeks," she said.

His smile never faltered, but it transformed from a pleasant expression into a dangerous one. The shift in his eyes was like a cloud passing over the sun. "Let me be very clear," he said. "If you decide to leave, that ends our commitment. And if you end up with a pissed off vampire trying to drag you away again, Auberon will not jump to your aid."

"You'd let them hurt me?"

"If you refused the safest option you have, then I'd be sad to lose you, but I wouldn't jump in," he said. His casual tone was chilling.

She leaned on her elbows and stared at him. "I think you're full of it. You couldn't let something bad happen to me."

"You don't have a clue what I'm capable of." He sniffed. "It's going to burn. Go stir."

She tore her gaze away and hurried to stir the blood. Then she hunted through the drawers for a thermometer. An arm snaked past her. Paris stuck one finger into the pot and tasted. "That's warm enough," he said, pulling down a crystal glass from the cabinet. Her hands shook as she filled his glass, then a second for Alistair. "Take that one to his door. I'll wait."

Her heart pounded as she carried the warm glass to the bottom of the stairs. His door was dark wood, with a thick foam seal around it. She knelt and put the glass on the floor, then knocked lightly. "Alistair? Uh, Mister Thorne?" Her cheeks flushed as she remembered those words spilling over her lips.

Yes, Miss York?

A wave of heat rolled through her. "There's some blood here if you're hungry. Okay, uh...good evening."

She hurried back and found Paris back at the counter. He sniffed again. "Are you all right?" His eyes drifted down, as if he was looking at her...

Oh. God. Could he smell...no. Absolutely not. She would not even begin to entertain the thought that he could detect the situation in her panties because that was a whole new universe of privacy violations she couldn't even venture into.

"Fine," she blurted. Down the hall, she heard the click of a lock, then the creak of the door. She wanted to bolt down the hall to see him, but she managed to stay put.

Paris pushed an envelope toward her. Inside, she found a thin stack of one hundred dollar bills and a black credit card with her name on it. Beneath her name was *Alazan Holdings, Inc.* "Cash if you need it. Order what you need on the card. I don't want you leaving the house, but if there's an emergency, here," he said, dropping a set of keys. "There's a car in the garage for you."

"This is so much," she murmured. "What are the strings, Paris?"

He nodded. "Right now, the strings are that you do the work described in the contract. Protect this house. That's it."

"Why is this house so important?"

"I thought you wanted no part of vampire politics," Paris mocked.

"Fine," she said. He flashed that obnoxious, cocky grin. Then he took a small black case from the bag and slid it across the counter to her. She opened it and froze. There was a gun inside, with a row of what looked like wooden bullets. "Uh..."

"I have no reason to think that dickhead will find you here,"

Paris said. “But I have protected my court for over two hundred years, and I’ve never regretted being too careful. Those won’t kill us, but they’ll pack a punch and give you time to get somewhere safe. Do you know how to use it?”

“Point it at the bad guy and pull,” she said quietly.

“That’s about it,” he said. “It’s already loaded, but let me show you.” He took a few minutes to open the revolving barrel, eject the large wooden bullets, and then reload them. Her fingers fumbled as she imitated him, but eventually, she did it to his satisfaction. “Good girl. Can you shoot fire like you did at your apartment?”

She shook her head. “That’s an emergency thing only. It’s exhausting,” she said. “Doing a couple of fast spells like that is like running a marathon in an hour. It’s not reliable enough that I’d depend on it.”

“I see. Then stick to the firearms.” He glanced at his watch. “I’ve got to run.”

“Did you find Elliott?” she asked. Her voice trembled. “Are you going to kill him?”

He hesitated. “That’s complicated, Shoshanna. We can’t just kill another vampire because he came into your house.”

“But he wants to…” she trailed off. “So how does this end?”

“That’s up to you,” he said. “If he tries to hurt you, we’ll intervene. But you can’t expect Eduardo to have a diplomatic incident with the Casteron for a witch who insists she isn’t loyal to him.”

“That’s pretty shitty of you guys,” she said.

“That’s pretty entitled of *you*,” he retorted. “We’re navigating it. You’ll have to be patient.” A cool wave of energy rolled off him, and it reminded her of the sense she'd gotten from the statue.

"Paris, are you cursed?" she blurted.

His pale eyes widened. "That's quite personal, *chérie.*"

"I was just wondering," she said.

He slid the tablet toward her. "The amount we're paying you every week is more than enough to quell your curiosity. Sign, please."

She lifted her eyes to him and scanned the contract. She was hoping for a nice parchment with gothic script on it, but instead it was a simple text document in PDF form. It was written in surprisingly plain language for a bunch of centuries-old bloodsuckers. She signed with her finger, then typed in her email address before sliding it back to Paris.

"Violette will transfer your payment on Fridays," he said. "I expect you to start work on this place tomorrow. Fair enough?"

"Got it," she said.

He finished off the glass of blood, then set it on the counter. "Thanks for the snack. *Bonne nuit, mon petit sorcière.*"

He left her with more questions than answers, and more than a little frustration. They'd taken Elliott seriously enough to bring her here, but they seemed perfectly content to squirrel her away indefinitely like a princess in a tower. And why wouldn't they? Immortal vampires probably had no sense of urgency.

And really, who was she to complain? They wanted to pay her good money to sit in this beautiful house, work on her spells, and occasionally pour a glass of blood for a reclusive vampire. A girl could do worse.

She cleaned the kitchen and put away the dishes, leaving it as spotless as she'd found it that morning. Then she retreated to her bedroom to get ready for bed. Magneto was sprawled across her pillow, and he simply raised his head to look at her as she entered. "Hey bud," she greeted. "Did you have a busy day of sleeping?"

A big yawn revealed a mouthful of tiny panther teeth. She chuckled and retired to the bathroom to wash up. After a long, luxurious shower, she smoothed on a minty-scented moisturizer from Ruby's shop. It was nice to contemplate the morning without having to get up early to brew overpriced coffee.

She carefully wrapped her hair to protect her curls, then changed into her loose pajama pants. When she returned to the bedroom, Magneto had vacated the plush pillow. She plopped down and tucked her feet under the covers.

"Mags," she called. "Come to bed if you want bedtime scratches before I sleep." She clicked her tongue to get his attention, then reached over to turn off the lamp.

The room was quiet without the steady sound of his noisy purr. Way too quiet.

"Mags?"

She sat up and peered around the room. The glint of the doorknob caught her eye, revealing the door that was open just enough to let out one little, sneaky cat.

"Shit," she hissed, leaping out of bed. She never closed her doors at home, because he would yell at the sight of a closed door.

Shoshanna grabbed her phone for light, then hurried down

the hall. Across the house, a melancholy tune drifted from the piano like a whisper on the wind. Her chest tightened.

"Maggie," she murmured, barely raising her voice for fear of catching Alistair's attention. Knowing him, he was in the kitchen poking his face into anything that smelled interesting.

She emerged into the open expanse of the living room and froze. A candelabra with a single lit candle sat in the corner of the room, casting a hazy yellow glow. It took a few moments for her eyes to adjust well enough to see him.

A dark figure sat at the piano bench, its head concealed in a hood. The fingers dancing over the keys were covered in black fabric, and a robe of some sort hung down his back and pooled on the floor.

And to her absolute horror, there was a nine-pound black cat sitting next to the cloaked man. His tail hung over the edge of the bench, completely relaxed and still.

Oh God. As she crept closer, she could see Magneto, the ruiner of her life, nuzzling his head against the man's elbow. "Magneto," she whispered. "Come here."

Of course, he ignored her.

The piano playing stopped, though the man didn't turn. Silence hung between them as the final chord died out.

"Uh, Mister—Master Thorne," she blurted.

"Alistair," he said. What a voice. It ran down her spine like warm water. There was a rough edge to it, but it didn't entirely mask the rich depth, a bass sound like a bow drawn across a cello string. There was a faint British tinge to his accent. It wasn't quite the voice she'd heard in her dream, but it was all the better for being real.

Her legs threatened to turn to Jello. "Alistair, I'm so sorry about the cat. I hope he didn't bother you. I'll keep him in my room. If it's a problem, I can—"

"It's fine," he said gruffly. His gloved hand rested on Magneto's back, and the little cat stared up at him. "We have an understanding, don't we? You are not the master of this house, are you?"

Magneto let out a tiny, chirping sound.

Alistair rubbed between his ears, and Magneto head-butted his arm in a signature sign of affection. "I thought not."

Then he turned. In the low light, she could only see the dark fabric covering him. Was he so sensitive to light that even the candle would hurt him? His head lifted, and she realized the hood hung low over his face, casting him in shadow. All she could see was the glowing red of his eyes.

Ice cold trickled down her spine, followed quickly by the hot flush of embarrassment. Here was her grand meeting with a respected vampire of the most powerful court in America, and she was dressed for bed without a stitch of makeup, wearing the obnoxiously cute llama pajamas that Ruby got her for Christmas.

Alistair was quiet. Probably wondering why in the hell his friends had bothered protecting a complete moron with llama pajamas. "You must be Shoshanna."

"That's me," she said. *In all my childish flannel glory.* "I hope I didn't wake you during the day."

"No," he said. "If you're planning a schedule, I'll take my dinner at ten beginning tomorrow night."

She stood up straight, already feeling like she'd disappointed him. "Would you like something now?"

"No," he said. "The snack you brought was sufficient. For the future, I prefer a bit hotter."

"Sure," she breathed. "I can do that."

He sniffed the air. "Have you been cleaning my house?"

Her heart thumped. "Yes. Is that all right?"

"Of course. However, you will not go into my chambers." It was polite, but very clearly an order.

"I understand," she said. Her heart pounded. And worse, she knew he could hear it.

As if he felt sorry for her, he nudged the cat. "Go to your mistress. And remember the rules."

Magneto leaped down from the bench and barreled for her, winding around her legs before she scooped him up. His rapid purr vibrated against her chest as she squeezed him like a stuffed animal. She wanted to turn and run. Those deep, red eyes burned within the shadow like coals behind glass. She'd never seen a vampire with eyes that intense.

Closing her eyes, she used her arcane sight to inspect Alistair. Deep blue entangled him like a net, with a gnarled knot around his heart. Just like Paris and Dominic. That had to be why he avoided the light. How had they all ended up cursed?

"Was there something else, Shoshanna?" His voice broke through her concentration.

"You play the piano so beautifully," she blurted.

"I know." He chuckled to himself. "Playing for over two hundred years yields a certain amount of proficiency."

"I play too," she said. "I mean, not like that, but..."

He turned. "Good night, Shoshanna."

The abrupt dismissal left her reeling, cheeks hot. With the cat cradled close to her chest, she hurried back to her room. As she made her hasty retreat, the piano playing began again behind her.

Well, that hadn't been what she expected. With embarrassment turning her guts to a twisting knot of snakes, she closed the door and deposited Magneto on the bed. "Really?"

He stared up at her, yellow eyes wide and innocent.

"Don't play cute," she said. "You're lucky he didn't eat you."

But honestly, it seemed like Alistair had liked the cat better than he liked her.

Not that it mattered. He didn't need to like her. He was just here to scare away Elliott and the other Casteron vampires. And she was here to put some witchy security on his house. It was business.

Nothing more.

7

Sweet vanilla hung in the air long after the witch left him alone in the dark. Her scent was light and pleasant, with a faint hint of something richer that he couldn't quite place. And she was a work of art with the candlelight illuminating her rich brown skin. Even in the low light, he could see the light dusting of freckles over her full cheeks and the tiny corona of amber against the deep brown of her eyes.

Shoshanna was utterly exquisite.

A familiar, though long-distant, heat stirred in his belly. Despite the loose nightclothes she wore, with their inexplicable cartoon figures drawn on the fabric, he remembered her sumptuous curves from when he'd seen her from afar at Infinity. Strangely, he was even more intrigued by her now.

Despite its vivid perfection, his dream hadn't done her justice. During the deep sleep of the day, he'd been drawn to her, climbing the stairs in the darkness to find her lying on the bed in a sheer nightgown. She'd invited him in, first kissing him, then baring her neck with an invitation. Her skin had warmed to his touch, her whole body thrilling to him. The rest of it was lost to a red haze of lust and sated hunger.

When her quiet knock left a goblet of blood at his door, her scent hung in the air. He could almost imagine that he broke his fast in her embrace.

He sat at the piano alone, tracing the keys idly in silence as he listened for the sounds of her returning to bed. Water ran, a strange sound in the house where he had lived alone for so long. Then a heavy sigh, affectionate whispers to the cat, then slow breathing as she drifted off to sleep.

There was a faint purr as the lucky little feline settled, and then it was quiet. With his sharp hearing, there was no true silence; there was always the noise of distant birds, the whirring hum of electronics, and a thousand tiny voices in a quiet symphony.

Alistair shook off the heavy hood. It was hot and uncomfortable, but with a beautiful woman in the house, he had no choice. He carefully closed the lid on the piano, and peeled off the black gloves as he silently crossed the lower level of the house.

He poured himself a glass of Scotch from a cabinet in his study, then went to the library to collect his reading for the evening. With the blue leatherbound tome tucked under his arm, he headed to Lucia's alcove. As always, he dusted her, kissed her fingers, then sat down to read to her. But as he read, he was distracted with thoughts of Shoshanna.

After Armina cursed him, he had resigned himself to a life

of solitude. And that had seemed simple enough when he lived alone, determined to not subject anyone else to his curse. When Paris and the others were not here, he could almost imagine that he was the lone inhabitant of the universe. He could go months without seeing anyone, and in fleeting moments of deep concentration, he forgot about his curse.

But Shoshanna was not an abstraction, a theoretical wisp of a person floating through his head where it was safe. She was a flickering flame, casting a warm glow and heat into the space that had been empty and cold. He could not ignore the sound of her breathing, nor the smell of her in the air. And though it had been only a day since she arrived, something had awakened in him.

It was only an ember, nearly unrecognizable after so many years. It was desire, tinged in the faintest flicker of hope. It was as dangerous as sunlight and a sharp blade.

Lucia was proof of that. Desire was a curse, and love was unthinkable.

The presence of the lovely woman in the house felt like a rock in his shoe. He paced the bottom floor, unsure of what to do. His usual piano practice would disturb Shoshanna. Perhaps a late night hunt would burn off some of his nervous energy. Midnight Springs was usually quiet, but there was no end to the supply of would-be dirtbags in the city.

And what would he do if someone attacked Shoshanna while he was out? He'd given Paris his word to protect her.

With a little growl of frustration, he retreated to the basement. His lavish bedroom took up a small portion of the large underground area. Another large room was a spacious training room, with dummies, targets, and a rack of weapons. While it had been many years since he fought with the Shroud, he had plenty of time to practice and keep himself in shape. He took out a set of short knives, occupying his mind with throwing them at targets across the room. One by one, he buried blades to the hilt in the wooden targets.

When he had satisfied himself with his aim, he went through a long string of shadow combat exercises, imagining himself destroying a number of targets. There was the faceless threat to Shoshanna. The witch, Armina. Sometimes, Paris. Sometimes, himself.

Finally, he had worked himself to exhaustion, and hurried upstairs for another snack of blood. He didn't bother to warm it, though it tasted like bad wine and cigarette ash when it was cold. Heat stirred in his chest as he crept toward Shoshanna's room. He froze at the end of the hallway, afraid to step any further. Her quiet breathing was a gentle whisper, interspersed with the little snores of a well-loved pet.

He spared the tiniest smile, then shook it off. He was lurking about like some lovesick beau. He retired to the basement and sealed the door. Several wall sconces lit the basement hallway. Though the house was thoroughly modern, with all the wonderful conveniences of the twenty-first century, he favored decor that was reminiscent of when he was still human. Electric candles flickered in the ornate gilded sconces, lighting the path to his bedroom.

After showering, he dared to look in the single small mirror hidden beneath a curtain in his bathroom. It took willpower, and no small amount of self-hatred, to stare into his own, molten-red eyes. With disgust stirring in his belly, he lightly touched his lower lip, watching the monstrous gray fingers touch his darkened lip.

Who could love this?

He lunged to cover the mirror again, his chest tightening. After donning a pair of loose pants, he settled into bed and pulled the curtains tight. With the dark to protect him, he could almost forget how things were. He could imagine that he was still the vain young artist who took his reflection for granted.

What a fool he was.

1827 - Vienna

A DIZZYING ARRAY of silks and glittering necklines swirled through the salon in a kaleidoscope of riches and exuberant energy. Heady aromas of brandy and tobacco smoke hung in the air, filling the room with an intoxicating haze. And there at the center of the whirlwind was Alistair Thorne, fingers dancing gracefully over the ivory keys to the delight of his patron, Franziska Bauer. A talent like no other, she claimed, showing him off at every opportunity like a prized jewel.

He had met the charismatic and mysterious Franziska at one of an endless string of parties in Vienna. His days were spent studying piano, dabbling in composition with dreams of his name being uttered in the same breath as Schubert and Beethoven. The wealthy socialites of the city were constantly on the search for young talent to show off in their private salons, in hopes that they might find the hidden gem of the city. And the next best thing to being a rising star was to be the patron who had made them.

During one such party, the guests dined on decadent chocolates and fine cheeses. All but one, a woman in a richly embroidered blue gown that looked like she had wrapped the night sky around herself. Though her clothes were in fashion, her porcelain pale skin and otherworldly beauty made her glow like the North Star among the crowd. Furthermore, she was unaccompanied. He had heard rumors of the wealthy widow, with wild tales of her ill-fated husbands, claims of a harem of lovers, and even tales that she was a witch who feasted upon virgins to keep her unnatural beauty from fading.

The much-discussed Fraulein Bauer sauntered toward him, resting one hand upon the piano while he played. Her dark-lined eyes fell upon him, and his fingers slipped, striking a D-flat in the middle of the B-flat major passage. Her crimson lips curved into a smirk. He forced his attention back to the keys, but he could still see her at the edge of his vision. Soon, he could smell the sweet perfume on her skin.

When he finally finished, there was a smattering of applause before the guests returned to their meal.

"What lovely playing," she said quietly.

"Thank you, my lady," he replied. He rose and adjusted the tails of his jacket before bowing deeply to her.

She extended her hand to him with the imperious air of a queen. He grasped it and brushed a kiss over the back of her hand. Electricity tingled down his spine as he looked up at her. "Alistair Thorne."

"I know," she said. "Franziska Bauer."

"I know," he replied.

Her smile split wide to show dazzling white teeth. "Smart lad," she said. "Alistair Thorne, if you would let me, I will change your life."

Despite the oddity of it, there was something mesmerizing about her. Her confidence and allure overwhelmed him. "Fraulein Bauer, I would surely let you have whatever you wish."

"Careful what you promise, sweet boy."

And that had been the start of it. That night he had gone home alone, but the echo of her remained with him for days. He dreamed of her at night, and thought of her when he was awake. Each hour of practice found him daydreaming of her. The thought of her watching him, enchanted by his playing, turned even the most mundane and tedious of exercises into an act of worship at her feet.

It did not take long for Franziska to find him again and deliver an invitation to the first of many private salons in her lavish home. After the second engagement for her guests, he found himself alone with her, and that was the first of many passionate dalliances with his alluring patron.

This went on for nearly a year, until one midwinter party when he was the featured entertainment. The endless medley of dance tunes were insultingly simple compared to the masterworks he prepared during his studies at the university. But the elite revelers wanted to dance, not have their ears challenged by the new compositions. And with what Franziska paid him to entertain at her parties, he would not complain about the musical selections.

At the end of a galliard, his eyes searched the room for Franziska, who sat upon a settee surrounded by admirers. With rich chestnut hair in curls piled high upon her head and a scarlet neckline that plunged far deeper than was socially acceptable, she looked like the sort of woman a priest would warn good boys to avoid.

He was no good boy, and he had enjoyed the decadence of Franziska's generosity for many months. And if history repeated itself, he would end the evening in her arms. As if she sensed him thinking increasingly amorous thoughts, her eyes drifted toward him. Her full red lips curved into a smile, baring her gleaming white teeth. Her eyebrows lifted in a tiny motion, and he smirked at her. Her head tilted downward as if to say *well?*

His stomach rumbled with hunger as he continued to play. It was odd, but Franziska's late night salons never featured the lavish spreads of food he had enjoyed at other homes. Liquor and dark, pungent red wine flowed freely, but no food would be served this evening.

The night passed in a blur, and when the last of her guests had gone, the front door was barely closed before she pounced upon him. Sweet perfume overwhelmed his senses as her teeth grazed his neck. Graceful fingers turned his face up, and she claimed his mouth in a hungry kiss. A hint of pain lanced through his lip as she nipped him, holding his chin firmly.

"Alistair, dearest," she murmured.

His heart pounded as blood pooled in his groin. He barely understood her, as he was already rapidly working through a plan to get her out of the silken cage that encased her lovely body. "Hmm..." His hands roamed over her waist, searching for the fiddly ties. Damn these fashions that made it so difficult to get her naked.

She laughed, a rich echoing sound. "Eager boy."

"Always," he said.

"That word." She grasped his wrists and pulled them away. With a little growl, he tried to reach for her again, but she held him firm. How odd. Her strength was at odds with her slender frame and delicate bones. Her head tilted, and there was a glint of red in her eyes. Just a trick of the light. "Would you be at my side forever?"

He gave up fighting for his hands, and pressed his lips to the soft ivory skin of her breast, letting his teeth graze her. If she would just hike up her damned skirts, he would do whatever she wished for as long as she wished. "You know I would."

Her hand suddenly tangled in his hair, yanking his head back. He gasped in surprise as she straddled him, hips undulating slowly against him. He'd always appreciated Franziska's voracious appetites, particularly when she was hungry for him, but there was something unusually aggressive about her tonight. It only made him want her more. The ache in his groin was maddening. He pried at the tight laces crossing her back.

"Forever?" she whispered, stealing a kiss. Her deft fingers unlaced his trousers, freeing him. In a rustle of skirts, she shifted in his lap. Then there was the blissful, decadent heat as she welcomed him into her, deeper and deeper until they were one. There was nothing hesitant about Franziska. He was certain that she had never been timid a moment in her life.

"I am yours," he said.

"Indeed," she purred. Her body embraced him, and he could only grip her hips tightly as she took control of him. A quiet moan slipped from her lips as she let her head loll back. Tension and pleasure wound together in a knot in his belly, and he was lost in the sheer sensation; the heat of her body, the smooth skin of her breast at his lips, the sweet perfume, the rustle of silk beneath his hands.

Who needed the pleasure of wine or the stupor of opium with a woman like Franziska Bauer?

He groaned and gripped her shoulder tight as he finished within the searing warmth of her body. She yanked his head back again and kissed his throat. "Good boy," she said. "I hunger for you. Just this once."

The strangeness of her words jutted through the soft haze, like a sharp rock in his shoe. *Just this once?*

Through heavy lidded eyes, he gazed up at her. The scarlet in her eyes deepened to a bright, bloody red. This was no trick of the light. A discordant sound rang out as he startled, leaning back against the piano keys. Her white teeth lengthened, until her canines were needle sharp and glinting in the light. He had heard rumors of demonic creatures, of beautiful succubi who prowled the chambers of lonely young men, but this was no drunken fantasy. Primal fear cut through his warm haze.

Sharp teeth pierced the side of his throat, sending a lancing pain down his spine. An impassioned moan ripped from her as her teeth closed on him, and he felt her tighten around him, her climax in sharp contrast to the pain. He tried to push her away, but she locked her legs around him in a mockery of the way they so often made love amidst her lavish bed. With a desperate cry, he grabbed a handful of her curls, trying to wrest her away, but her free hand grasped his wrist and twisted, snapping the bones.

He saw white as pain radiated up his arm. Despite the desperate situation, all he could think was *how will I play?*

His heart pounded, and the world began to sway around him. The noises that came from Franziska were animalistic, primal and terrifying. They were not the breathy moans, or even the impassioned cries of their midnight romps. This was the sound of a beast devouring its prey.

His limbs felt far away, and the pain soon receded into a heady bliss, the hazy glow as he lay next to his sated paramour, with the burn of good brandy in his belly. When the world was small and cozy, all calm and warm and soft. His head lolled back. Black pressed around his vision, which faded quickly.

"*Scheisse,*" she cursed.

The world spun around him, and he was suddenly resting against her, his head pressed back into her bosom.

Suddenly something warm dripped on his cheek, and then there was blood on his lips. He gagged at the taste, but Franziska held him tightly, forcing the spill of crimson down his throat. He was too weak to fight back, caged against her body with her wrist pressed to his mouth.

"Oh, my sweet boy, you have no idea the things we will see together," she whispered. He groaned and struggled, but it was like fighting a stone statue. She kissed the top of his head. "You will be young and beautiful and never know the pain of faded beauty. This world will lay before us like a feast."

Something seared his belly from within, as if his stomach burst into flame. Fire crawled through his veins. He let out a bellow of sheer anguish, blood bubbling over his lips. She released him and let him tumble to the floor.

He pressed his hand to his bloody throat and brought red-stained fingers up to his eyes. "What are you? What have you done?"

"I have granted you communion, *mon coeur,*" she purred. Her eyes glowed like a fire behind amber glass. She licked his blood from her lip slowly. "When this is over, you will forgive me, and soon, you will thank me."

8

A full day's work had yielded several basic arrays on the house in Midnight Springs. Shoshanna had spent most of the morning and early afternoon designing the base array, sort of like a magic generator for the house. The smaller spells on individual rooms would tie into the base array, drawing power from the environment and continually renewing.

After sketching out plans for Paris's requests, she made a preliminary list of materials. The estimated price tag made her wince as she composed an email to Violette Baudelaire for approval. She read the email approximately forty times before sending it, then immediately unsent it, tweaked it one last time, and finally sent it.

With the base array drawn, she sat down with several of her textbooks and wrestled with how to block out vampire hunters. As she was contemplating how to detect murderous intent with a spell, her phone alerted her that it was nine thirty.

She scrambled to pick up her things, then got out the pot to warm Alistair's dinner. As she was heating the bag of blood, she got a call from Ruby. "Hey," she said. "What's up?"

"Uh, so I don't want to alarm you, but some guy called here asking about a *tisserand*. He acted like he didn't know the name, like 'oh, uh, Shawna, Sheila, Shayna...Shoshanna?' So freaking obvious. I asked who was calling, and he said his name was Andrew," Ruby said. "But that's the guy, isn't it?"

"Probably so," she said numbly. Andrew was Elliott's middle name. "You didn't tell him anything, did you?"

"Of course not," Ruby said. "I mean, I'm all about hooking you up with work, but not under these circumstances. I told him I didn't know anyone by that name."

"How do you think he found you?"

"Same way everyone does," Ruby said. "He didn't ask for me by name, so I don't think it was about me being your friend so much as my family knowing everyone."

That much was true. The Wang family were known for being the most skilled green witches in the city. And if they couldn't do a task, someone in their vast network of connections could. Shoshanna had benefitted from that connection more than a few times.

"Okay, I just want you to be careful," she said.

"Obviously," Ruby said. "How's the vampire life?"

"I'm heating up blood on the stove," Shoshanna said. "It's thrilling."

They chatted for a few minutes before hanging up. She'd

finally located a thermometer, and she slowly heated the blood to one hundred and ten degrees, hoping it would please him. She contemplated the plain glass and wished she had some black paper umbrellas for garnish.

Her heart thumped as she walked down the hall to deliver his breakfast. She knocked and waited. Stairs creaked. A gloved hand slid out to grab the glass, and she cleared her throat. "Mister Thorne?"

"Alistair."

"Right," she murmured. "Do you want me to report how things are going?"

"No. That is Paris's concern."

Her mouth went dry. "Um...do you need me to do anything around the house?"

"Not at the moment."

His gloved hand withdrew beyond the doorway, and for some reason, she was desperate to hold on to this tiny connection. "Alistair!"

"Yes?"

"Would you mind if I play your piano?"

He was quiet for a while. "Go ahead. There's music in the bench. Please cover the keys when you're finished."

"Thank you," she said hastily. "Um...just yell if you need something."

The door closed, and she let out a heavy sigh.

With her heart still thrumming, she retreated to the living room. The piano bench creaked open, revealing a messy sheaf of sheet music. There were several books of etudes mixed with dozens of pieces of sheet music. Dense notation spilled over the pages in a deluge of ink; far too complex for her rusty skills. The pages were marked with pencil, just like her own books from childhood. Some of the music looked old and handwritten, as if he'd bought first editions. She finally found a familiar piece, the *Carnival of the Animals* by Camille Saint-Saens.

The thought of Alistair listening to her made her nervous, but this place was a dream come true. It was like being in the salon of some wealthy prince, with one of the most gorgeous grand pianos she'd ever seen. It was practically a sin not to play it. She hesitated, then placed her fingers to the keys, rolling them across the first chord. The vibrations resonated through her, the clear sound shimmering in the air.

Her chest swelled as she took a deep breath and began to play. She'd spent years learning to play with her father, and then with a tutor when Emmanuel no longer had time for frivolities like time with his daughter. She caught herself humming the melody quietly as she played the familiar tune.

A throat cleared behind her. She jumped in surprise and spun around to see a dark silhouette behind her. "Alistair? Did you need something?"

He was cloaked in black from head to toe. Like yesterday, a hood hung low over his face. Even his hands were covered in sleek black gloves, leaving no skin exposed. A pleasant, woody smell wafted from him.

"Nothing," he said gruffly. "Would you take instruction on your technique?"

Her stomach churned. "Oh...sure. I know I'm not very good, just—"

"You're quite good, actually," he interrupted. "But your

technique is keeping you from playing as well as you could. Face the piano, please. You're sitting too close." There was a quiet *thump* as he set his glass on a nearby table.

She raised her eyebrows, then faced the keys. Excitement bubbled through her. He crept behind her, so close she felt fabric against her shoulder. Suddenly, she jolted as he pulled the piano bench back. Her shoulders pressed into his chest, and the edge of his hood whispered over her bare skin. God, he smelled good.

"Straighten your wrists," he said. This close, she could feel the deep vibrations of his voice, rich and dark. He gently touched her right hand and straightened her wrist before placing it over the keys. "Always straight wrists. When you sit too close, you must bend to play. Proper placement is as important as playing the right keys."

"Got it," she said. She glanced back at him. It was disconcerting to talk to that void, with only the glowing red of his eyes peeking from the darkness. "Miss Jean told me the same thing, but I forgot, apparently."

His gloved hand lightly touched her upper arm, sending a shiver down her spine. "Now you can use your arms to play," he said. "Your fingers should not do all of the work. Again."

She drew a deep breath, then started at the top. With him looming over her, it was hard to focus. When she fumbled a tricky passage, she yanked her hands away and shook her head. "Sorry."

"I make you uneasy," he said. "I'll leave you to it."

"No," she blurted. "I don't mind."

"Keep practicing," he said, fading into the shadows. She

was strangely disappointed to watch him go. The echo of his touch still prickled across her skin.

Though it was disappointing be alone again, she found herself smiling. Perhaps he was willing to risk the light to be around her.

No, she told herself. She needed to keep all eighty-eight keys of this piano between them at all times. Between the rich voice, the masterful musicianship, and the clean scent that made her stupid, she was playing with fire. There were plenty of beautiful things in the world that could kill careless witches.

Maybe they could be friends. She was friends with Paris at a respectful distance.

"Playing with fire," she muttered to herself.

THE NEXT DAY, Shoshanna began her workday with good news from the vampire court. She had received authorization from Violette to order the expensive supplies. The vampire woman's response was short and simple:

I trust your judgment. Ensure that you obtain the lowest prices. Order whatever is necessary.

-V

It was thrilling to spend someone else's money, to the tune of nearly ten thousand dollars just for the preliminary ingredients. She was tempted to add a few things for herself, but she didn't want to end up on the bad side of a vampire accountant.

With her supplies ordered, she began sketching the smaller sigils for individual rooms. Some would be long term protections like the ones at Infinity, and others were temporary wards with more pronounced effects. Those were the *smash glass in case of emergency* of Weaving, but they could be handy. She placed a sunlight sigil at the front door, painting it onto the hardwood floor with a dyed ink to conceal it against the brown plank.

As she worked, she checked the time obsessively as she anticipated Alistair waking. She knew her job here didn't require his attention. But damn if she wasn't intrigued after his impromptu lesson last night. And she was fully aware of being a walking cliche; seeking attention from the distant vampire who was an eerie echo of her emotionally distant dad. If a therapist was in her modest budget, they'd have had a field day with it.

Nine thirty took its time arriving, and she exploded into action when the first tinkling alarm sounded. She was filled with nervous anticipation as she prepared his meal, then delivered it with a quiet knock. Again, the door opened just enough to reveal one gloved hand. "Alistair?" she asked quietly.

"Yes?"

"Can I show you part of the spell work I did today?"

"I told you that I don't need updates," he said.

"But you need to know in case the house is attacked," she said. "Your reaction will be faster than mine." Manipulation 101; appeal to the big manly vampire's superpowers.

He was silent. "Fine." When he emerged, he was cloaked in black again.

His steps were nearly silent behind her. He followed her to the front door, where she knelt next to the sigil. With a flick of her hand, she cast a tiny veil of light that glowed within the neatly drawn lines of her sigil. Precise geometric shapes were connected by circles and arcs. The neat work filled her with pride.

"If anyone you don't like tries come in, this will hold them off for a few minutes," she said.

"Just a few minutes?" There was a note of disdain in his voice, and it made her feel both irritated and embarrassed. It wasn't like *he* could build a protective ward from scratch.

"It's temporary," she said hotly. "This will basically put up a wall made of sunlight. Humans can't pass through and vampires won't want to unless they like getting deep-fried. It's self-powering, so it won't last long. Once I get the central array done, I can do better. But I thought you might want something to keep us safe until then."

"I see," he said.

Nothing else? No *good job, Shoshanna? Thanks for making sure no one decapitates me while I sleep?*

She scowled at the floor, taking a moment to compose herself before she let her mouth get her in trouble. "If you need to activate it, you'll need to touch it and say *allumez*. It's French."

"*Oui, je sais,*" he said. "*Merci.*"

"Oh," she said with a sheepish smile. "Then you're all set. I know you told me not to go into your chambers, but I need to get in sometime this week to place a sigil on your door."

"I'd rather you didn't," he said.

Her temper flared. It wasn't like she was going to creep on him. "Paris put it in the contract."

"This house does not belong to Paris," he said coldly.

She drew a deep breath through her nose. "I can wait if you want to talk to him about it. It won't take long, and I can do it at night so you're not there to be disturbed."

"We shall see."

She rose and took a deep breath to settle her nerves. Arguing with him was an inauspicious start to her mission. "I was also wondering if you'd listen to me play again and tell me if my wrists are better tonight." She braced herself for another resounding *no*.

His silence stretched for hours. "I can spare a few minutes."

While she perched on the piano bench, he settled onto one of the big leather couches, long legs crossed neatly. All she could see were those fiery eyes from the shadows, intent on her.

Her heart thumped as she rested her fingers on the smooth ivory keys. The music unwound itself beneath her touch. She briefly wondered if he was looking, but the steady spill of black ink over the page kept her attention. It wouldn't win an award, but her rendition of *The Swan* was respectable, with only a few missed notes. When she finished, she let the final chord ring before stealing a glance over her shoulder.

No Alistair.

When she looked back to the music, he was at her left side, one gloved hand on the keys. She yelped in surprise.

Freaking vampires.

"Can I touch you?"

God yes, she thought. The little voice that told her to be careful was fading into the lovely white static of his attention.

"Your fingers are collapsed," he said. His fingers curved over hers, forcing her left hand to cup as if she was grasping a ball. "That's better." He repeated it on her other hand, and a shiver rolled up her arm. Then he gripped her upper arms lightly and shook her, just enough to jolt her. "Relax. You play with tension. Are you anxious?"

"Am I anxious with a two hundred year old vampire watching me play? Yes."

"You asked me to watch," he said sharply.

Her cheeks heated. "No, I was just being...sorry. Sarcasm is a bad habit of mine."

"I know it well. Paris is a connoisseur." He gently pressed on her shoulders. "Release the tension here." Her body ignited with a thrill of excitement at his touch. His hand drifted to her throat, then lightly touched her jaw. "Even here. When your body is tense, you lose your strength and fluidity. Play the first line again, but take a deep breath and exhale as you play. Let your tension and anxiety flow out on your breath."

The anxiety was going to linger as long as this vampire was nearby, but she didn't hate the feeling. It was a bubbling sort of energy that walked a razor's edge between fear and delight. With a deep breath, she began to play again. His voice rumbled at her back. "Fingers." She obliged by curving her fingers more, and he was quiet as she played the first page again.

When she went to turn the page, he placed a hand over hers. "That was lovely, but you're tense again."

"I spend most of my life tense. Especially these days," she said with a nervous laugh. She slid the page aside and hesitantly set out the Liszt *Fantasie* on the stand. "Alistair? I found some of these pieces for four hands in your music. Would you play with me?"

He took a step back, and the distance felt like miles. "I'm afraid not. I have things to attend to."

"Oh," she said, cheeks heating. "Okay. Maybe another time."

His noncommittal *hmm* left no doubt what he thought of her pending offer. "Good night, Miss York."

"Goodnight, Alistair."

Her shoulders slumped as she watched him go, his shadow fading into the halls. She wanted to slink away in defeat. Why did she want him to like her so much? Dominic clearly didn't like her, and she didn't give a damn. Paris *did* like her, or at least did a good job of acting as if he did. And neither of them crossed her mind more than once a day. But Alistair was living in her head just like she was living in his guest room.

She stuck her chin out and returned to the piano, playing through the top part of the *Fantasie,* as if to say, "See what you're missing?"

But her attempts to bait him with music were fruitless. It was probably for the best. Left to entertain herself, she spent time working through some of the difficult passages slowly, remembering Miss Jean's admonition not to practice fast before she was ready.

Playing the piano reminded her of a time when life was simpler. Some of her earliest memories were sitting next to her father, who patiently taught her to plink out familiar tunes with her impossibly tiny hands. As she grew, her reward for a good lesson was to play from old hymnals while he sang in his rich baritone. Eventually, she'd moved on to lessons with a local music professor, who'd tried to convince her to audition for a conservatory for college. But by then, her heart was set on pursuing her magical craft.

Still, there was something incomparably soothing about music. It didn't depend on unseen forces or the unpredictable moods of brooding vampires. Placing her fingers in the right place at the right time would produce something beautiful. If only everything was so easy.

After another half hour of practice, she covered the keys, but left the music on the stand as a message. She returned to her bedroom and let out a heavy sigh. What was she doing? "Just stop," she muttered to herself. Desperation wasn't a good look.

It was just so hard to shake the dream. It was just a stupid sex dream, the sort that came after a year of being single and celibate. It didn't mean a damn thing except that her hormones were on overdrive. Vampire pheromones made everyone horny. Her desire was no more trustworthy than a late-night ice cream craving.

After a shower, she went through her nightly routine and put on her pajamas. When she climbed into bed, Magneto emerged from under the bed to snuggle against her. Right on cue, he curled into her side like a furry little spoon. She scratched under his chin while he wrapped his paws around her wrist and purred like a little motor. "At least you like me."

9

"At least you like me."

Her whispered words stunned him as sure as a slap to the face. He wished he could tell her how he'd fought to hold back his *yes* when she asked for his company. But the thought of seeing his hideous visage reflected in those huge, warm eyes...it was too much.

And despite the risks, he'd played a dangerous game just to have a taste of her. She was open and effusive, with the warmth of sunlight and the sweet scent of summer blooms. She did not take and consume, as so many of his kind did. Touching her gently to guide her hands, he'd been drowning in the natural perfume of her skin, the sheer warmth of her being.

He growled in frustration and paced the living room. The music on the stand was tempting, but he feared waking Shoshanna. Except that he *did* wish to wake her and demand her attention. Before he could make a regrettable decision, he poured himself a glass of whiskey and headed to the alcove to read to Lucia.

The book of French poetry remained closed in his lap as he stared up at her cold gray eyes. “What am I doing, Lucia? I should stay away from her. I have been alone this long, and there is no reason I cannot stay in my chambers for the next few weeks.”

He sighed.

“But I cannot remember the last time I spoke to someone like this, without the weight of the past,” he said. “The dance, the uncertainty, the friction of conversation...I missed it. But I know it will not end well. So why bother?”

Staring at the cold stone statue, he had all the reason he needed not to bother. Even if Shoshanna could somehow tolerate what she saw, he could not risk Armina’s fury. Kova had made that mistake, flaunting his beloved at every chance. And then the witch took the most precious thing of all from him.

Even with that grim spectre hanging over him, he knew that his resolve would not withstand another opportunity. It was as if she had cast a spell on him. No matter how determined he was to stay away, he only wanted to be closer.

He gritted his teeth and drained the Scotch before reading to Lucia. He read to her for an hour, translating carefully from French to her native Czech to the best of his ability. If Paris was here, he’d likely correct Alistair left and right, but this would have to do for Lucia.

After his reading, he bade her good night and headed to his studio to work off his frustrations with a punching bag. The sunrise alarm found him exhausted and sweaty, but as soon as he stopped flinging fists and stepped under the water to shower, he was thinking of Shoshanna again. His dream returned to him as he gripped himself tight, wishing that it was her body clamped tight around him as he chased a wave of pleasure.

This would not end well.

For the next two nights, Alistair carefully avoided Shoshanna, other than to accept her nightly delivery of blood. Each night, she went to bed a little later, as if she was slowly becoming nocturnal. It kept him penned in his room even longer, listening to her rattle around upstairs.

On the fifth day after her arrival, Alistair emerged from his chambers to retrieve the blood she'd left. It was warmed to perfection. He was about to close the door when he heard an unfamiliar female voice speaking in rapid French from upstairs.

At the stroke of midnight, the carriage will turn back into a pumpkin.

His curiosity piqued, he crept out of his room and climbed the stairs. Shoshanna was in an open sitting room just down the hall. The other voice came from her laptop, sitting on a plush armchair.

He lingered in the doorway and watched her work. Several large sketch pads were strewn across the floor. Rulers and compasses were scattered over the rug, along with half a dozen pencils and charcoals. Both pads were covered in intricate geometric drawings with colorful notations. And Shoshanna was carefully measuring distances to create a new design on a single sheet of paper.

Her face was furrowed in determination, as if she was angry at the drawing for not already finishing itself. A smudge of charcoal on her cheek gave her a delightful charm. Chalk dusted her golden brown forearms. Her presence filled the room, and it made him content simply to bask in this place, like standing in a kitchen where fresh bread baked.

Meanwhile, the laptop continued playing the story of Cinderella in French.

He finally broke his silence. "*Bon soir, Mademoiselle York.*"

She startled and turned. A faint smile played over her full lips. "*Bon soir, Monsieur Thorne. Tu as bien dormi?*"

He smiled. "I slept quite well," he continued in French. "Thank you for asking."

"I didn't know you spoke French," she said. "Are you originally from France?"

"Austria, actually," he said. "But I spent a great deal of time in France after I was turned. What is your excuse?"

She gestured broadly to the supplies all around her. "I'm a *tisserand.* We love our French. I listen to children's books sometimes to keep it fresh when I'm here in the States." Her smile faded, and she switched to English. "Do you need something?" Along with her speech, her entire demeanor changed. As if he had blotted out her light, her face was shadowed with tension and uncertainty.

He shook his head. "I heard your story and wanted to see what you were doing."

"Is it too loud?"

"Not at all," he said. "What are you working on?"

"I'm waiting on my ingredients to get here," she said. "In the meantime, I'm drawing up some test arrays for your central piece. I'm working with some very powerful ingredients, so I've got to make sure my channels are all correct and balanced. Too small and they'll overload. Too big and they won't keep enough power flowing, and..." She trailed off into a laugh. That was a delightful sound. "I'm boring you."

"That would be impossible, Miss York," he said seriously. Her cheeks flushed, and he heard the thump of her heart. "This all looks very involved. Not what I expected from a witch. I expected more herbs and lizard parts."

"In some ways, a *tisserand* is more engineer than witch," she said. She yawned and rubbed her eyes. "I've been staring at this for hours. I should take a break or go to bed." He watched her gathering her pencils, neatly arranging them into a small box.

Walk away, Alistair. Return to your room. Let her go to bed.

Many years ago, wiser friends had told him to leave a witch alone, and he ignored them. He knew best, after all. That encounter had left him cursed to be the monster he was now.

He had grown no wiser since then, it seemed. While she stacked her sketch pads, he inched forward. "Would you still like to play the piano with me?" As his question hung in the air, he felt like a gawky teenager again, standing in front of the lovely Clara Hurst and asking her to dance.

Her lips parted in a broad smile. "I would like that very much. Can I wash my hands first?"

Dangerous hope raged through him like wildfire in a drought-stricken forest. "Join me at the piano."

He darted for the piano, suddenly mired in worry. What was he doing? He needed to disappear. And before he could, her footsteps whispered across the floor. The scent of soap greeted him, and he realized he was too late.

"Top or bottom?" she asked him.

Lust smoldered through him as his dream echoed once more. He smirked beneath his hood. "I am pleased either way."

Her eyes widened, and then her lips pursed into a faint smirk. An invitation to dance, and an acceptance. "Then I'll be on top."

"Lovely," he said. Wait. Was she...no. There was no way.

Her pupils dilated slightly, and her smile widened. The realization that he awakened her desire filled him with pride that he hadn't felt in decades. He sat to her left on the bench, close enough that their arms brushed.

He leaned into her slightly. "From the top, shall we?"

"Sure," she said. "I'll follow you."

He tilted his head, then began to play, immediately enrapt with the rich vibrations of the piano beneath his fingers. Music had always been the language of his soul, but since becoming a vampire and developing super-powered senses, it had only become more intense. The sound was almost too loud, but it drowned out everything else, lifting him to a place beyond his ravaged body.

He nearly jumped in surprise when Shoshanna joined him a few measures into the piece, playing the melodic line. She'd taken his advice to heart, keeping her fingers curved. Her posture still needed work, but he didn't have the heart to correct her and ruin the moment.

A sour note rang out. "Dammit," she swore.

"Keep going," he said quietly. "No need to weep for one lost note."

She muttered and scanned the page before rejoining him. He started to push the tempo, bringing the volume into a gradual crescendo. She followed him easily, matching his tempo and volume.

A good follower, a lovely quality in a fellow musician and a lover.

As they finished a tumultuous section, he murmured, "Shhh. Now a secret."

Her eyebrows lifted in surprise as she played quieter, with a light touch. As the notes spun and swirled around each other, her quiet breaths marked each phrase as if she was singing. There was a heart-stopping moment when her left hand pressed close to his right, their fingers dancing dangerously close together.

With his hands upon the piano and a lovely woman at his side, he could almost forget the curse. This was the happiest he had been in years.

Finally, they finished the first movement, and he glanced at her. "That was lovely playing."

"Nowhere near as good as you," she said shyly.

"Well, I do have two hundred years more experience."

She laughed again. "There is that."

He reached for his glass of blood and took a sip. Her nose

wrinkled a little, but she didn't comment. "I hope that you have felt safe in my home."

She nodded. "It's been very nice."

"Paris only told me a little about your situation," he said. "Someone attacked you?"

"Sort of," she said. "He wants me to go work for the Casteron vampires, and he was willing to drag me out of there to do it."

"Who was this person?"

"His name is Elliott McAvoy. We..." Her shoulders slumped. "We dated in high school and he didn't take it well when I broke up with him in college. But I haven't seen him in ages. Last time I saw him, he was human, but that's changed, clearly."

The thought of someone daring to terrorize this lovely witch made his blood boil. "And have they found him?"

"I don't know," she said. "Paris says it's complicated, and I just have to be patient. That's easy for him to say when he's not stuck somewhere. No offense to you, but I miss my neighborhood and my job."

And there was the gentle reminder that she did not belong here. The light she had shone into his home was temporary.

"Is being a *tisserand* not your job?" he asked.

She shook her head. "I work at a coffee shop. I just do this on the side."

"And why do you not work for the Auberon already? Surely Eduardo's payment is more generous than this coffee shop," he said mildly.

She shrugged. "I'm not sure I want to be beholden to the court."

"But you welcomed our protection," he said. "Wouldn't you prefer to be cared for?"

She scowled, and he realized he'd overstepped. "I only need your protection because I did a job for the Auberon. I don't need vampires to pay my way."

"Why are you angry at the thought of someone paying for your skills?" he said. "You're obviously quite talented. Do you not value your work?"

His compliment did nothing to soothe her. "Of course I do. It's just...it's complicated."

"Complicated," he mused. The warmth in her eyes had turned into angry heat. He nudged her with his elbow, hoping to contain the flame before it burned the tenuous connection between them. "Shall we play again?"

"I want to ask you a question first," she said. His mouth dried. "Are you cursed? Is that why you can't be in the light?"

"That's right," he said carefully. That was Paris's cover story.

"How did you get cursed? Is it related to the statue in the alcove?"

He felt as if she'd punched him in the gut. "What do you know about the statue?"

"It's obviously cursed," she said. "I can sense it. And you have the same thing, along with Paris and Dominic. What did you guys get into?"

He hesitated. "It's related, but it's a long story. As you said, it's complicated."

"I'm here for a long time," she said.

"We made enemies of a powerful Night Weaver," he said. Her eyes widened again. "And she cursed all of us."

"That's terrible," she said. "What's wrong with Paris and Dominic? Obviously the light doesn't bother them."

He shook his head. "Their afflictions are their own, and not my place to tell."

"But..." she sighed. Then she gave him a determined look. "Is the statue a woman? Or a statue?"

"Do you want the truth?"

"I think your evasion answered my question."

He nodded grimly. "Lucia drew the ire of the witch. She was innocent, and her only mistake was loving one of us. The witch made her pay for it."

Shoshanna's face fell. "That's horrible." Then she averted her gaze, picking at one nail. "What would you say if I wanted to try to break the curse?"

"I would say that much more experienced witches have tried, and the Night Weaver is much more clever than we gave her credit for," he said.

"Maybe I am too." Her head tilted. "Maybe I could break your curse, too."

The mere thought of it made his heart ache. The hope was painful, because he knew it wouldn't happen. "It would be lovely, but I won't get my hopes up." Fire ignited in her eyes, as a tiny line formed between her brows. There was something charming but naïve about her determination. And yet, it made him angry. Who was this young, foolish thing to think that she could do better than witches four times her age?

"Then maybe I'll surprise you," she shot back.

"Maybe you will, Miss York," he said. "Shall we play again? Herr Liszt could use our attention."

They spent another hour playing together, interspersed with conversation about her job, where she made overpriced coffee and baked muffins. He still couldn't understand why she worked for so little when she had such rare and valuable skills. He deftly avoided questions about himself, instead turning the conversation back to her work. Finally, she yawned and swore when she checked her phone to find it was past three in the morning.

"I lost track of time," she said with a yawn. "This was fun. Thank you."

"No, thank you, Miss York," he murmured.

"Alistair?"

"Yes?"

"If I get to call you Alistair, you should call me Shoshanna," she said.

"Shoshanna." It was music on his tongue. Her smile widened.

"I like that much better."

"As do I," he replied. "Good night."

She tilted her head in a little bow. "Good night."

Her light voice hummed as she walked away, retiring to her bedroom. He listened for her to go to sleep, her breathing slowing as the cat snuggled up to her. He left the piano to approach Lucia, his mind fluttering with possibilities.

"Lucia," he greeted. "This witch wishes to break your curse. All our efforts have been fruitless, but what harm is there in trying? If there is even a tiny chance to free you, then I would let her try."

He did not dare speak aloud Shoshanna's bold claim to break his curse. If he said it, he might curse it. And it wasn't as if she would succeed. But still...the mere thought of it made his heart soar.

THE NEXT EVENING, he rose after nine in the evening to find Shoshanna working in the sitting room again. Several large sheets of paper were taped together to create one massive drawing space. An intricate geometric design was taking shape under Shoshanna's careful hand. She was an artist, creating a masterpiece he couldn't begin to comprehend. Her competence was clear in each confident, precise stroke. Watching her was like watching a prima ballerina gliding over the stage.

Finally, he knocked gently on the door frame. "Oh my God," she blurted. "I must have silenced the alarm. Let me get your dinner. Breakfast? Which one is it?"

"Technically, breakfast," he said. "I'll get it."

"No, no," she muttered, tossing her pencils aside as she scrambled past him. With a little flicker of amusement, he rushed past her. He was at the refrigerator by the time she arrived in the kitchen. Her brow furrowed in a comical frown. "Vampire running is cheating."

"What do you mean?" he asked, taking out the bag. He squeezed it into a glass.

"I should..." She sighed and gestured broadly at the glass. "I'm supposed to do that for you."

"It's all right," he said. "Go back to your work. You were clearly engaged. I shouldn't have interrupted."

But she lingered, pulling out the double boiler and holding out her hand. "You can't drink it cold."

"I'm a grown man. I can drink whatever I like," he said dryly. But her stern look made him hand over the glass, and he watched with amusement as she dumped it into the pot. He wasn't sure if she was doing it because she needed the satisfaction of performing a task well, or if she wanted to care for him personally.

Both of them were endearing, and so he ignored his clawing hunger and watched her fussing over the pot. When her back was turned, he hastily squeezed the remaining drops from the bag into his mouth before she caught him. The taste of it turned his stomach but sanded the edges off his hunger.

"Do you know how long it might take for them to deal with this Casteron mess?" she asked quietly.

"You are safe here," he said. "Why are you so concerned?"

"Because I can't stay here forever," she said hotly. "And I got a call from my boss at the coffee shop this morning. She said a man came into the shop last night asking about me. It had to be Elliott. I'm afraid he's going to start hurting people to get to me."

"But you are safe here," he said.

She threw up her hands in frustration. "Why do I have to be the one to give up my normal life because he's being a psycho? I didn't do anything wrong, but I'm stuck here and he's out there doing whatever he wants."

"I'm sorry you are stuck here," he said.

Hurt filled her eyes. "I don't mean there's anything wrong with you. This has been—"

"I understand," he said abruptly. "Vampire politics are complicated. The Casteron are displaying poor etiquette by being in our territory, but they've not attacked our people directly. Until they directly act against us, it's in Eduardo's best interest to maintain peace."

Her shoulders slumped. "So I just wait."

"Eduardo did not become the Elder of the Auberon because he was weak or timid," he said. "He will put the Casteron in their place when he knows the pieces are arranged properly."

Her shoulders slumped as she turned away to stir his breakfast. Fingerprints still lingered on her skin, filling him with fury at this Elliott McAvoy. He was growing to enjoy her presence, but her light could brighten far bigger places than a lonely recluse's home.

Perhaps Eduardo could not act directly, but someone else might. A hunter, perhaps? Or someone who used a hunter's weapon of choice. If no one lived to tell their story, who would know the difference?

After checking the temperature with a thermometer, Shoshanna poured the heated blood into a steel cup. He frowned at it. "What's this?"

"It's insulated," she said primly. "It'll keep it warm longer."

He tilted his head. "Where did it come from?"

"I ordered it for you," she said. "The liner is plastic so it shouldn't affect the taste." Her nose wrinkled. "Not that I can verify the appropriate taste."

Despite himself, he smiled beneath the dark hood. To be on her mind even when he was out of sight...that was a lovely thought. He sipped and found it perfectly warmed. "Thank you for the gesture. It tastes quite good."

Her smile lit a fire in his chest. Then she sighed. "I'm going to get a little more work done before bed. Let me know if you need anything else."

"Of course," he murmured, watching her retreat.

With Shoshanna back at work, Alistair retreated to his bedroom to get his phone. He rarely had contact with the others, but he intended to change that tonight. He perused his list of contacts. Paris and Dominic were out, and Julian with them. And Nikko was too unpredictable; he might enjoy a good hunt off the clock, or he might take his duties seriously enough to rat him out. Sasha...he'd probably do it, but taking advantage of him was a line Alistair would not cross. That left Safira, who had a taste for violence and a lot of frustration to burn off.

Safira answered after two rings. "Well, hello, stranger," she purred. "What's wrong? Is the witch safe?"

"Nothing is wrong," he said. "I want to deal with a problem, and I want the others kept out of it."

"Secrets and mystery. You have my attention, Allie," she said. "What is it?"

"Find out what the Shroud knows about Elliott McAvoy," he said. "The vampire who attacked Shoshanna York."

"I'm on it," she said.

Upstairs, Shoshanna was listening to noisy electronic

music, oblivious to him. He changed clothes, exchanging his longer coat for something more form fitting, with a hood that drew tight around his face. After dressing, he contemplated the rack of weapons he'd accumulated over the centuries.

When he hunted humans, his bare hands and teeth were more than sufficient. But tonight, he would hunt his own. He strapped a harness to his back and secured two sharpened wooden stakes into it. The stakes were carved from white ash wood, which would incapacitate his prey long enough for a swift decapitation.

Once he was armed, he crept upstairs and drank another bag of blood to energize him. The rich taste of life spilling over his tongue put him on edge; an over-fed vampire was stronger, but more aggressive and volatile. All the better for hunting.

Safira texted with an address at just past one in the morning.

Safira: *Meet me in an hour.*

He frowned. He hadn't intended for her to join him on the hunt, but once Safira got an idea in her head, it would be impossible to shake it loose.

He listened for Shoshanna, who had since retired to her room. Water ran down the hall, and then it was quiet. He crept to her door and listened. Along with her quiet breathing, he heard light crunching sounds. A dry, pungent smell drifted toward him.

Cat food. A week ago, he'd have laughed at the thought of a witch and her black cat living under his roof. They'd be safe for a few hours, especially once he disposed of Elliott McAvoy.

Leaving the witch and her cat to their evening, he hurried

to the front door and locked it behind him. The balmy Atlanta evening was filled with the night chorus of humming insects and distant road noise. Half a mile down the road, he had an old car stashed in the parking lot of a twenty-four hour grocery store. Inside the musty car, he started his GPS and found that Safira's address was in Midtown.

As he drove, the thought of putting his hands on Elliott became more and more appealing. Then Shoshanna could get out of his house and back to her own life. And that was best for all of them.

But that wasn't it, was it? He didn't want her gone. Not even he believed that he was doing this to get rid of her. He wanted to rescue her, to be her hero. It was dangerously naïve; the same thoughts had resulted in his curse all those years ago.

But if he hadn't learned then, he never would.

The address brought him to a parking garage in Midtown. He drove in slow circles until he saw Safira standing in the harsh white light of a fluorescent bulb. Clad in black with her fiery hair braided tight to her skull, she was dressed to kill.

"Allie," she said as he got out.

"What are we doing here?"

She simply gestured for him to follow, then leaped from the third floor to the sidewalk. Her landing was graceful and silent, and he followed. Keeping to the shadows, she darted around a corner and down a dark street at a blistering speed. Worn brick and flickering neon blurred around him as he followed.

Soon, they arrived at the descending stairwell to a MARTA station. Several people slept on benches nearby, nestled into sleeping bags. He looked around to ensure he wasn't being watched, then took the stairs down in a single long leap.

The schedule signs were blank, though fluorescent lights still burned above the empty train platforms. The smell of burnt fuel, wet earth, and stale coffee hung in the air. Safira looked both ways, then hopped down to the lower platform. Alistair followed, his senses kicking into overdrive as they passed into a dark tunnel. After a minute or two, Safira halted in front of a door set into the tunnel wall. She opened it, then gestured broadly for him to enter.

"Just a bit further," she said.

Concrete stairs descended deeper underground. The scent of vampire blood greeted him at the bottom of the stairs. He grabbed one of his stakes to settle his crackling nerves.

The stairs ended in a narrow hallway. Safira brushed past him and led him to a large open room. Illuminated by a bare light bulb, trails of dried blood smeared the dingy tile beneath their feet. Three impaled corpses lay in the open area. Their heads had been severed, red eyes still staring in shock.

He covered his mouth. "What the hell, Safira?"

She cocked her head. Her eyes were blood red, and her fangs were descending as she spoke. "There are hunters in Atlanta, Allie."

"I'd heard."

"Then why are you worried about some asshole from Casteron?"

"I want to get Shoshanna out of my house," he growled.

Safira's red eyes rolled. "I'm sure it's a terrible burden."

"You have nothing on Elliott, do you?"

She sneered. "I'm Number Three of the Shroud, you presumptuous ass," she snapped. "I know everything from his high school mascot to his credit score. I also know that you called me because you think I'm too stupid to realize what you're up to."

"I don't think you're stupid," he replied.

Her teeth flashed as she glared at him. "Then why call me, and not your dearest Paris, who indulges your every whim?" Her brows arched. "Well, put me on whatever list he's on. I will not help you start a war with the Casteron."

He growled at her. "Then you've wasted my time. I'll find him myself."

"Good luck, Alistair," she said. "But while you're seeking your petty kicks, this is what we're dealing with." Her gaze snapped upward. "Listen."

Quiet voices echoed from above them. He closed his eyes to focus. There were two male voices somewhere nearby. One was tinged with a British accent, while the other was clearly American.

In and out quick.

We should wait for sunrise.

It won't matter underground. Let's just burn them and be done with it.

"Hunters. Presumably whoever made this mess," Safira said, gesturing to the bodies. Then her lips curled into a smile. "Perhaps you'll get the fight you were looking for."

He grinned beneath his hood. "Then this wasn't a wasted trip."

Her gaze darkened. "We enthrall them. Make them leave."

He threw up his hands. "Where are your teeth? What happened to the Guillotine of Auberon?"

A smile flickered across her lips, then faded into a somber expression. "These are different times, Alistair," she said. "Eduardo's command. If you violate it, I will not defend you to him."

He growled and pressed himself against the grimy wall. The hunters' footsteps crescendoed as they stalked down the hall. A glint of silver preceded the first of them, a stocky, well-built male with salt-and-pepper hair. The other was a wiry ginger with a wicked scar through his upper lip. Their black gear gave no clues about their affiliation. They both reeked of kerosene and sweat.

The bigger man stood in the center of the room, counting quietly. "All three are still here."

The ginger sneered. "I told you I checked," he snapped. He took two plastic sports bottles from his backpack and squirted a pungent liquid over the corpses. Safira shot out of the shadows and tackled him against a wall, knocking the bottles out of his hands. At the sound of his companion's surprised shout, the bigger man lunged at Safira with a wooden stake. Alistair pounced on his back and pulled him away.

They fought in a flurry of punches and kicks, and Alistair narrowly dodged a wooden stake that swung up toward his belly and caught the hem of his shirt. He twisted the hunter's wrist. Bones snapped. The man screamed and dropped his stake.

Thunder cracked in the small chamber, and Safira screamed.

He whirled to see Safira reeling with blood streaming from her side. A blonde woman stood in the doorway, holding a gun. Safira slammed the red-haired male into the nearest wall, and he fell to the ground unconscious. Glaring at the female hunter, Safira dug into the bullet wound and pulled a chunk of wood out. Her lip curled into a snarl as she sprinted after the blonde woman.

Alistair bore his prey to the ground, tearing open his own wrist with his teeth. With his prey pinned, he pressed the bleeding wound to the human's mouth. The big man writhed and yelled in protest.

"Just drink," Alistair ordered. With his free hand, he pinched the man's nose and calmly waited for him to run out of air. Finally, the man opened his mouth, but the bastard bit him hard enough to send pain lancing up his arm. He gritted his teeth and shoved his wrist deeper.

Soon, the hunter's struggles weakened. Then, his bite eased, and his lips closed on Alistair's wrist. A low groan vibrated against his skin. The euphoric sensation of vampire blood was washing over him now. Alistair pulled away, then flipped him over.

Alistair pulled his hood back to reveal his face, and the man's face twisted with terror. "Look at me," he ordered, pushing his compulsion through the power of the blood connection. He could feel the man's terror and revulsion, mixed with the strange magnetism that came from sharing blood. "Who are you from? *Le Bouclier?*"

"Shieldsmen," the man confirmed, his voice trembling. He hadn't seen their hunters in decades.

"And what is your name?" The man clamped his lips together, but Alistair leaned in closer to growl, "Tell me."

"Henry Marks," he spat, his face twisting with anguish. His fear started to overwhelm the connection, prickling at Alistair's nerves.

"And how many Auberon vampires have you killed, Henry Marks?"

"I don't know," he said. His brow furrowed. "A lot. Please don't kill me."

"Why did you kill these vampires?"

"Because we were ordered to clean up Atlanta," he said.

Alistair glanced up and saw that he was alone with the bodies. In the distance, he could hear Safira's rapid footsteps. Someone else was breathing hard, tiny sobs escaping with each breath. "Ordered by who?"

"The boss," he said. "There have been reports of dead bodies with bite marks. We watch for that kind of thing. I'm just doing my job."

Alistair leaned in. The red of his eyes glared back at him from the hunter's glassy gaze. "And I am doing mine. If it were up to me, I would rip your throat out and bathe in your blood. But for some reason, the Elder sees things differently. You and your murderous brethren are going to leave this city. If I encounter you again, I will not spare you. Do you understand?"

"I understand," he said.

Alistair eased off Henry, then hauled him up by his collar. "Leave and don't look back."

Henry's movements were halting and awkward as he fought back against the blood compulsion overpowering him.

Alistair snarled at him, then turned to the fallen hunter that Safira had left on the ground.

He found only an empty space and a flattened pile of cardboard boxes. No hunter.

Alistair spun on his heel and saw the wiry redhead lurching out of the shadows with a stake. He stepped to the side, but the stake came down hard on his shoulder and pierced behind his collarbone. Excruciating pain radiated down his arm.

The hunter flicked a lighter and dropped it, igniting one of the vampire corpses. Then he grabbed Henry's arm and ran out the door. Alistair started after him, but the potent wood toxins were already spreading through his veins. He fell to his knees, fingers curling against the dirty ground.

Behind him, the other corpses ignited. The foul stench of burning flesh filled the air. Alistair lurched out of the room and slammed the door behind him.

His muscles felt like lead, and his joints were coated in sandpaper. Leaning against the wall outside the burning room, he grabbed the stake and yanked it out. His roar of pain echoed in the hall.

As he dropped the bloody stake, Safira hurtled down the hall. Loops of silky red hair had been ripped out of her braid. Her lips were bloody. "What a mess. Oh shit, are you okay?"

He dropped the bloody stake and glared at her. She winced, though he wasn't sure if that look was for his exposed face or the bloody mess of his shoulder. "Bloody perfect. I enthralled the big one, but you left the other one here."

"He was unconscious," she protested.

"Was," he spat. "What about the woman?"

"Sabrina Milan. Hunter for the Shieldsmen," she said. "I took her driver's license and told her to leave town. I know where she lives now."

"We should have killed them all," he said. "Since when do we catch and release vampire hunters?"

"Since Eduardo told us not to kill them," she said.

He snarled at her. "I need to get home. Thank you for wasting my time and getting me staked."

"You got yourself staked," she snapped. "It's not my fault you're slow." Her tongue darted over her lip, catching a stray drop of blood. "Go home, Alistair. Drop this nonsense, and I won't tell Paris what you were up to."

"Are you blackmailing me, Edith?" he asked. Edith Brunner was the vampire Alistair had first known, but she'd changed her name many times over the years to suit her whims.

Her nose wrinkled in disgust. "Don't be a shit. I'm not going down for you."

He just growled at her, then retreated the way they'd come. Thankfully, she followed without speaking to him. He was angry and ashamed; he should have known Safira wouldn't break from the Court. It was easy to underestimate her, but there was a reason she answered only to Paris and Julian.

When they emerged into the open air, he bounded away from her, sprinted to his car, and got on the road back to Midnight Springs. His shoulder ached terribly, and he could feel the poison of the wood still seeping through his body. That was going to hurt for days.

Great.

It was just after four when he arrived home. He parked the

car at the grocery store again, then walked home. As he let himself into the house, he carefully stripped off his coat. Dried blood tore at his skin, reawakening the searing pain. "God-dammit," he swore.

A piercing scream rang out, and he snapped his head up to see Shoshanna in the living room, eyes wide. Then she raised her hand and shouted *"Mettrez à feu!* "

Her pointed fingers were like a gun shooting pure flame. An arrow of flame punched into his chest and knocked him off his feet. With a deep, rasping breath, she screamed, "Alistair! Get out!" She scrambled for the front door and threw it open, then slammed her hand against the door frame. "*Allumez!*"

A curtain of blinding light surged into existence in the doorway. "Shoshanna!" he roared. He lunged at the doorway, and the light seared his exposed face. Combined with the burnt wound in the middle of his chest, it was too much. He fell back and watched the guillotine fall on his nascent hope.

She had seen him. She had seen the monster, and now she knew the truth.

IO

Holy. Fuck.

Shoshanna's slippered feet were rooted to the ground as she gaped at the bloody gargoyle-like creature at the threshold. A charred hole ringed in flame pierced its belly. Blood splattered to the floor behind it, and it let out a deafening, wordless roar.

Instead of running out the front door, she sprinted for the garage, grabbing the car keys on her way. Her hand was on the doorknob when she realized her cat was still happily sleeping in her room. She kicked off her slippers and bolted across the house for him.

Despite the chaos, the opportunistic little cat was curled up on her pillow, which had only been vacant for a few minutes. She grabbed him by the scruff, prompting a yowl and a flurry of scratches. With him tucked under her shirt, she ran for the garage.

After sealing the door to the garage with another daylight sigil, she dove into the borrowed Escalade. The garage door was glacially slow, and she stared at the door the entire time. No sign of the monster.

As she squealed out of the private driveway, Magneto leaped into the back seat and let out a loud *meow*.

"Don't you dare angry pee in this car," she hissed.

Her heart thrummed as she sped down the deserted road, toward the faint glow of the suburbs. Out of this dangerous, crazy world of fangs and claws, and into the plain familiarity of humanity.

When that thing burst through the front door, she was certain that she was dreaming. It was a monster from her worst nightmares. Glowing veins like streams of lava glowed amidst stone-like gray skin. Twisted scar tissue overlaid dense muscle. And its face was a demon's visage, with fiery red eyes and short black horns that curled away from its brow.

But her fingers were singed from the fire spell. And she could smell the burnt flesh. That was no dream. That thing was real.

And she'd just left Alistair there alone with it. Despair washed over her. If he got hurt...

She let out a cry of fear and swerved into a gas station. She fumbled at her phone. In her frantic rush, she accidentally dialed *Papa Reynaldo's* for pizza. "Shit," she swore, hanging up and calling *Paris* instead.

The phone rang once before he answered. "You're up late. Feeling lonely or—"

"Something got into the house!" she blurted.

His tone changed immediately. "Hold on," he said. Loud music blared in the background. "Kitten, move or I'll move you, no matter how great your ass looks in that dress. Stop it. Touch me again and lose the hand, sweetheart."

And she'd just *left* Alistair in the house alone. Well, to be perfectly fair, he was the two-hundred-year-old vampire, and he had a far better chance of protecting himself from the burglar from Hell.

But Jesus Christ on a cracker, they were going to be pissed. Surely they'd take issue with her inability to keep a monster out of the house. And if they didn't protect her, then she was screwed.

The other end of the line went quiet. "Deep breath, *chérie*. Tell me what happened."

"Something got in the house," she said again. "I locked up before I went to bed, I swear. And I have some preliminary protections, but everything isn't finished because there was a shipping delay and I'm still waiting on my order of fluorite and—"

"Get to the point, Shoshanna," he said. "Why did you call?"

It took her a moment to catch her breath. "I got up for a glass of water and this creature came through the door. I know how crazy it sounds, but it looked like a demon. It came at me, but I blasted it and ran out through the garage."

"Fucking hell," Paris said. "Did you kill it?"

"No," she said. "I forgot the gun, so I used magic. I yelled for Alistair to get out of the house, but then I sealed it up, and now he's stuck in there. I'm so sorry, I just didn't know what else to do, and—"

"Okay," Paris said. "Stop talking."

"I'm just—"

"Shoshanna," he said sharply. "Go back to the house and wait for me."

"Are you going to kick me out?" Her throat clenched with fear. "Elliott is coming to my work, and I don't know where I can go that's safe. I'm really sorry. Please don't kick me out."

"Dear God, Shoshanna," Paris said. "You're not in trouble. But we have to talk. And this will be easier face to face. You're safe, I promise."

Her hands trembled as she made a U-turn in the middle of the empty road. It was still and quiet in Midnight Springs, with only the hazy glow of streetlights to cast a dreamlike veil over the dark landscape. The quiet darkness only made her feel more alone. When she reached the house again, she parked halfway down the driveway and kept the engine running.

That creature was still in there. God, she hoped Alistair was okay. Sure, he was a little aloof and moody, but she liked him. She certainly didn't want him getting ripped to shreds because she'd sealed him in with a horned demon on the rampage.

Thirty minutes later, a black BMW parked behind her in the driveway. Two well-dressed vampires climbed out, both glancing up at the sky. At nearly five in the morning, it was dangerously close to sunrise. Her heart thumped as she slid out and stared at the approaching vampires.

Paris's blue eyes swept over her, taking in her loose sushi pajamas and bare feet. "That's quite a look."

"Not funny," she said.

His head tilted, then his gaze flicked to Dominic. “He’s hurt. And pissed.”

“Alistair’s hurt?” Shoshanna asked. Her stomach lurched, sending a wave of guilt and despair through her. “You have to go help him!”

Dominic winced. “Alistair is in no danger.”

“But that thing is still in there!”

“That thing is Alistair,” Paris blurted. He took a silver flask from his jacket, took a sip, then offered it to Dominic. The other man gave him a dismissive gesture, and Paris shrugged. “Surprise.”

She frowned. “What the hell are you talking about?”

“Did this demon have dark gray skin? Glowing red eyes? Bulging veins?” Dominic asked.

Paris stuck his fingers up at his forehead. “Couple of twisty little horns? Shoshanna, was it ugly as fuck?” Paris asked. Dominic elbowed him hard enough to send him reeling. “What? He’d say it, too.”

“Oh, God,” she murmured. “I didn’t know.”

Dominic glared at Paris. “You should have told the truth from the beginning. Your lies only cause more trouble.”

Paris scowled back. “I was respecting his wishes.”

“As you so often do,” Dominic said.

“I’ll go check on him,” Paris said, approaching the door. When he touched the handle, he lurched back with a hiss. His once-smooth cheek was marred by a blistered red burn. “The fuck?”

“You wanted the house secured!” she said, tears welling up in her eyes. “It was in my contract!”

Clearly unconcerned with Paris, Dominic gave her an appreciative look. "That's quite impressive."

Pressing his hand to his cheek, Paris let out an explosive diatribe of filthy curses in French. His forced smile looked like a shark's grin. "Take it down so I can go inside."

Heart pounding, she touched the doorway. *"Tout va bien,"* she murmured, reaching out to pluck a tendril of magic free. Like untying a knot, the whole sigil loosened at her command. The bright light faded, and Paris took a step inside.

"Are there any other nasty little surprises I should know about?"

"No," she said quietly.

He sighed. "You stay here with Dominic. I'll deal with him."

"I should help," she said. "This is my fault."

"No, this is Paris's fault," Dominic interrupted. "Let him clean up his own mess."

Inside, there was a chorus of angry shouts in German, then a crash of breaking glass. This was utterly absurd, and yet it made perfect sense. She'd never heard of a vampire that couldn't handle normal light. Then again, she'd never heard of a vampire that had been cursed to be...well, what he was. She didn't know whether she was frightened, angry, sad, or maybe all of them. And just the tiniest bit guilty. Because the Alistair in her mind was breathtakingly beautiful, with graceful hands and a voice like a cello given words. The desperate desire she'd felt for him was now tinged in fear and regret that he was not what she dreamed.

Dominic grasped her wrist lightly. "Let's go inside. If this takes more than a few hours, we're going to be stuck here."

She headed back to the car to retrieve Magneto, who was curled up on the floorboard. He let out a pitiful *mrow* when she picked him up. "I know, buddy," she said. "I'm sorry. You can have extra treats tomorrow, okay?"

Holding him close to her chest, she returned to the house and tiptoed over the threshold. Bloody footprints formed a winding trail toward the basement. After closing the door tightly behind her, she released Magneto. There was a shout of pain from downstairs that sent the cat running.

"You staked him?" Dominic said. "Paris just pulled a couple of splinters out."

She shook her head. "I used my fire spell. I left the gun in my room and I didn't know what else to do."

"Then how did he get staked?"

"He was already torn up from something when he came in the door," Shoshanna said. "I couldn't tell what it was."

His brows lifted in a question. "When he came in the door?"

Her jaw dropped. Not only had she burned a hole right through him, she'd ratted him out. "Yes?"

"Interesting."

She busied herself in the kitchen. "Do you need a snack or something?"

"I ate. Paris will surely eat if you warm it up," he said. "But Alistair will certainly need to feed tonight. Live would be better, but a bag will do."

As she began preparing the double boiler to heat the blood, fear stitched through her with a twinkle of lust on its tail. Even knowing what he looked like, her body hummed to life at the thought of him feeding on her. "Are you suggesting..."

"Not you," he said. "Considering you hurt him, he might tear your throat out by accident."

"I didn't mean to!" she exclaimed.

He put up his hands. "I understand. Your instincts were good. But a wounded vampire is somewhat beyond logic."

"Is he going to hate me now?"

Dominic was quiet for a long stretch. "He won't hate you, but he'll probably be an asshole about it for a while." For once, the expression on his face wasn't a pronounced frown. It was the warmest he'd ever been around her. "It isn't your fault, but Alistair is sensitive. Before the curse, he was a pretty boy. Though I care for him as a brother, I have no qualms saying that he was an arrogant prick back then. Since the curse, he hates no one as much as himself. I would stake my life that he's humiliated that you saw him, not angry. I'm much more interested in why he was out of the house and how he got staked."

"Oh, thank God, I'm starving," Paris said. He brushed past Shoshanna and took down a glass. She was still stirring, but he took the pan from her and poured himself a full glass of blood. His tailored suit jacket had been discarded to reveal a blood-splattered white shirt. Rolled-up sleeves revealed tattoos of stylized swords on each lean forearm. "Did you stake him?"

"Jesus, no," she said.

He rinsed his hands in the sink, then took another long drink. "Someone did. Knew what they were doing, too. Smells like white ash. Nice and poisonous."

"Hunters?" Dominic asked.

"Probably," Paris said. "He's not talking." He pinched the

bridge of his nose. “Do you know how to brew a *nouvelle vie*? You mix it with fresh blood to help a vampire heal.”

“I’ve heard of it, but never made one,” she said. Her dad had made them constantly for the Casteron, and she had all of his old magic journals. “I can find out how. I think they’re pretty easy.”

“Do it today,” Paris said. He spoke quietly to Dominic, then poured another glass of blood, draining her pan. A few drops dripped onto the clean counter, but he ignored them.

Men.

“Um...are you going to explain what happened?” she said, grabbing a towel to clean up his mess.

He turned, his expression confused. As if they weren’t all avoiding the cursed elephant in the room. “What?”

“You lied to me about Alistair,” she said. “And I could have killed him by accident.”

“Don’t flatter yourself. Your aim isn’t that good,” Paris replied.

“Paris,” she said flatly.

The sky blue of his eyes had darkened to red from his feeding. He scowled. “You are not entitled to know our secrets.”

“We were all cursed,” Dominic said quietly. Paris spoke rapidly in German, but Dominic cut him off. “Enough! She has been dragged into our misery, and your pretending otherwise serves no one.” Maybe she’d been wrong in so quickly choosing Team Paris.

“Alistair told me that you were cursed by a Night Weaver,” she said.

Paris's eyebrows lifted. "Told you...meaning he spoke to you? Willingly?"

She nodded. "We've been playing the piano together," she said, cheeks warming. "Sometimes we chat. He wouldn't tell me much. He said it was your secret to tell."

Paris blinked rapidly, then glanced at Dominic. Then he shook himself. "He's right. No, we don't want to tell you."

"That's okay," she said. "But I want to try to break the curse. Starting with Lucia."

Paris's jaw dropped. "What do you know of Lucia?"

"Just that she was a woman who loved one of you," she said. "And that she doesn't deserve to be a statue."

Dominic scowled. "Your priority is protecting this place, not chasing flights of fancy."

"I can do both," she said.

"Better witches than you have tried," he said, taking a long stride toward her. He loomed over her, red eyes glaring down at her.

"Then you'll have to let them know when I do what they couldn't," she snapped. Dominic's eyes narrowed. She shook her head and stepped around him. "I need to go apologize to Alistair."

Paris headed her off. "Not a good idea. He's in pain, and he won't be happy to see you."

"So I just wait?"

"You just wait. There is plenty of work for you to do here while he nurses his wounded ego," Paris said. He glanced at his watch and swore. "We don't have time to get home. I'll call for a *veravin* for him tomorrow. He'll need to feed when he wakes up, and a blood bag won't do the job."

"I can do it," she blurted.

"Absolutely not," Paris said flatly. "Now, would you find us a room in this ridiculous house where we won't be deep-fried at sunrise?"

11

This was the second worst waking of Alistair Thorne's life. The first was the evening he woke after Armina's curse had run its course. Nearly a century ago, he woke from a days-long slumber to find that his agonizing transformation was not a nightmare, but his new hideous reality. With his leathery skin on fire and the realization that he had made an irreparable mistake, he had considered killing himself. He might have, if Paris had not been there to comfort him.

But this was a close second. His entire torso was a ragged knot of pain, with the wood toxins still crawling through his veins like biting ants. All he could do was stare up at the dark canopy over his bed and be miserable.

Even worse than was the physical pain was the memory of Shoshanna's face. There was horror and disgust there, just as he'd expected. And despite the knowledge that this terrible revelation was all but destined, his pessimistic mind could not anticipate how awful it would be. The wave of fear that rolled off her had filled the room with its scent, and he could swear it still lingered in the air.

When he woke, there was a bag of blood already lying on the pillow next to him, with a note in Paris's familiar scrawl.

Eat. Don't be an asshole.

He couldn't even muster a smile at Paris's unique flavor of concern. He drained the bag, lying back to let it course through him.

Upstairs, he could hear Shoshanna arguing with Dominic. Someone hadn't closed his bedroom door entirely. "Absolutely not," the vampire said flatly. "Brew the tonic."

"You're being unreasonable," Shoshanna replied. The sound of her voice made his chest ache. How could he even be in her presence again?

"That makes two of you," Paris said mildly. "If I need to tie you to a chair, I will. Do not test me, Shoshanna."

His lip curled at the sound of Paris speaking harshly to her. But after a muttered string of curses, he smelled the scent of herbs in the air. He drifted into a barely-conscious doze, and woke again to his door opening. Clawing at the bedpost for purchase, he hauled himself upright.

Low light spilled into his chambers from the hallway. Paris guided a blindfolded woman into the darkened room. "Here we are, *chérie*." A strong, medicinal smell surrounded her, though it didn't entirely mask the tantalizing scent of blood beneath her skin. Her heart thrummed.

"*Qu'est-ce que c'est?*" Alistair asked. *What is this?*

Paris raised an eyebrow. "She's a *veravin*. I told her that your face had been wounded," he said in French. "She's had a strong dose of *nouvelle vie*. Drink up." He guided the woman to the bed. Without being told, the curvy blonde sat on the bed, her face tilted up. Paris kissed her cheek lightly, then lightly tugged at her sheer sweater. Blue fabric slid down to expose creamy porcelain skin. The thin trace of blue outlined the flow of her lifeblood along her throat.

Even in the enveloping darkness, Alistair hated the sight of his mottled, gnarled hands against her lovely skin. But if she minded the feel of his rough skin, she didn't show it. Her long hair cascaded over her shoulder as her head tilted, revealing faint white bite scars along the curve of her shoulder. Her lips played into a faint smile, and Paris laid a line of light kisses along the other shoulder.

How many times had they fed together, then fallen into bed for their own amorous pursuits, the blood still fresh on their lips?

"All yours," Paris said. "I'll make sure she's happy." His other hand slid around to cup her breast gently, and she sighed happily.

Alistair grasped the woman's throat lightly, then sank his fangs into her neck. Hunger overwhelmed him, and he took a long, hard pull from her. She gasped, but he held her tight to keep her from pulling away. Her pulse thrummed beneath his fingertips, and the faintest whimper vibrated there.

Then his venom hit her system, prompting a whispering sigh. Her soft body relaxed. He could smell her desire, the burning of sheer physical pleasure.

With the *nouvelle vie* in her system, her blood tasted spicy and effervescent. It sent a crackling tingle through his body. And though she smelled entirely different, he could only think of Shoshanna. What he wouldn't give to touch her this way, to connect and taste her essence.

His gnawing hunger faded as he drank deep. The pain in his belly faded to a dull throb. He bit deeper, letting out a low growl. He was never satisfied, could never drink enough to truly be sated.

A firm hand squeezed his arm. "Enough," Paris said quietly. "Her heart."

He opened his eyes to see Paris gazing at him. The woman was still, though he could still feel her pulse under his fingers. It was irregular, a sign that he was taking too much. For a moment, he didn't care. He wanted to drink until he was gorged.

"Alistair," Paris said quietly. "She trusts us. There will be more."

The calm words broke through his desperate hunger. He reluctantly pulled away, licking his lips clean. Blood oozed from two punctures, but there were crescent-shaped imprints from his deep bite. Guilt twisted into a knot in his gut.

As soon as he released her, Paris pricked his thumb and pressed it to her neck. She slumped, her eyes heavy. He gently stroked her hair. "Thank you, *chérie.*" His gaze lifted to Alistair. "We'll get her home and make sure she's healthy. I'm leaving you with Shoshanna. Will you behave?"

"Don't patronize me," he snapped.

"The appropriate response was, 'yes, I'll behave. Thank you

for bringing me a meal.' I'll pretend that's what you said. How do you feel?"

"Better," he said.

Paris opened his mouth as if to speak again. His gaze held Alistair's for a long, uncomfortable stretch. Then he apparently thought better of it, and gently lifted the *veravin* into his arms. "Get some rest, Alistair."

He bit his tongue and watched Paris go. His friend sealed the door behind him, blocking out the noise of the house. Alone in the dark, he let out a heavy sigh. There was a maddening itch around the two wounds, and they were searing hot to the touch. Whatever the witch had given the *veravin*, it was working.

As lovely and competent as she was, he was haunted by the look in her eyes. How could he venture upstairs again? She would see only a monster now, as all of them did. Whether it was pity, disgust, or contempt, the eyes never lied.

1932 - Prague

"He doesn't want visitors," Paris protested, his muffled voice ringing throughout the house.

Alistair hadn't thought it possible, but his hearing was even more sensitive now, thanks to the witch's curse. As if being transformed into a horned monstrosity was not sufficient torture, his head had been pounding for days. Smells were more intense, and every little shift in the wind brought a cascade of fresh horrors, from unwashed bodies to sewage to rotting meat.

"He will wish to see me," an imperious voice rang out. "I am his Maker, you presumptuous dandy."

He sat bolt upright in bed. That was a voice he had not heard in decades. Feet thundered up the stairs, and he caught Paris's scent as he tried to block the door to Alistair's darkened chamber. "I said no."

Franziska Bauer, wretched harridan and demoness of the ill-fated Rubrum Court, drove her jeweled hand directly into Paris's chest. His knees buckled as he clutched at her wrist, letting out tiny choking sounds. "And I said get out of my way."

Even with her hand buried to the wrist in his lover's ribcage, Franziska was still as breathtaking as she had ever been. The fashions had changed, but she had not. Out of sheer instinct, his body stirred to life, but his soul cringed.

"Let him go," Alistair snarled, rising from the bed. The sheets fell away to reveal his leathery skin, the dim candlelight bringing the uneven planes into sharp relief.

Her hand wrenched free of Paris's chest with a horrific squelching sound, Crimson dripped from her long, elegant fingers. Her red eyes skimmed over him, and her face twisted in disgust. "My God," she murmured. "I had no idea it was this bad."

"Get out," Paris bit out, gripping the doorframe for balance. His white shirt was soaked through, but his eyes were filled with murder. He spat out a mouthful of blood and straightened even as his pale face contorted in pain. Scrubbing one hand across his lips, he lurched toward Franziska.

Franziska ignored him, drifting toward Alistair. Despite everything, his body remembered her, the sweetness of her kiss, the way her legs tightened around him when she made love to him. Her fingers, still bloody, traced the craggy landscape of his face. She made no attempt to hide her disgust. "She has ruined you, my sweet boy," she said. "What did you do to anger the witch so?"

Her scent was maddening, crawling along his senses and invading his mind. He slapped her hand away. "Did you only come to gloat?"

"You should have stayed with me," she said. "The Auberon have destroyed you."

"He's not destroyed," Paris said.

"And what curse did the witch bestow upon you?" she said. "Clearly not your face, nor the efficacy of your cock, judging by your thorough plundering of all of Europe." She cupped Alistair's face, forcing him to stare down at her. Even after years apart, the bond between a Maker and a Vessel was powerful. Her blood called to him, and he could not look away, even as he saw his hideous face reflected in her scarlet eyes. "Come with me. I will find this witch and peel her skin from her bones until she undoes this."

"I am still loyal to the Auberon," he said, fighting to get the words out.

"And are they loyal to you?" she asked. "Eduardo holds court while you hide here in the shadows. I hear he already has another fine entertainer. They are ashamed of you. They will forget you, despite all you have done. But I still love you, my sweet."

He tilted his head. "Have you lost your other playthings, Franziska? Is that why you must resort to begging for me?" He grinned, knowing how horrific his smile was.

She recoiled, but she recovered quickly. "You will always be mine. You were mine before any other knew you. Do you think this vain fool will care for you like I will?"

Snarling at her, Alistair said, "Leave. Consider yourself free of me."

Though his posture was hunched, and the smell of vampire blood filled the room, Paris stepped between them. "You heard him, Frau Bauer."

Her lip curled with disgust. "Then suffer together for eternity."

And with that, she flounced out of the room.

Paris grasped his face gently. "Are you all right?" The feeling of his hands, smooth and graceful and unmarred, awakened his lust and infuriated him. How could Paris, painfully flawless, bear to touch him?

He twisted out of the other man's grasp. "She's right. You should leave."

"She's right...have you gone mad?"

"You deserve better than me," he said.

Paris scowled at him. "I don't give a damn about your face, Alistair."

"Even you are not so good a liar," Alistair said. He pulled away. "Go back to the court. I will not drag you down with me."

"You don't mean that," Paris protested. "You are in pain, but it will pass. And we will find an answer. But you are still mine. No witch can take you from me."

He wanted to believe that. He wanted to trust that Paris could love him no matter what. But he had seen the look in his eyes when Alistair stumbled onto his doorstep with the witch's curse boiling in his veins. And as it progressed, taking over his body, Paris had grown distressed, even disgusted. He was a beautiful man, charming and witty and ferociously loyal, and he deserved someone who could stand at his side.

Not Alistair.

"I am not yours," Alistair said. "Please leave me."

"Allie—"

"Leave!" Alistair bellowed.

Paris gaped, and then his shock turned to anger. "You are in my home," he snapped. "You do not have to be alone, but if that is your choice, then you will be the one to leave. And when you find yourself utterly alone, remember that this is your doing. You didn't have to suffer this. I told you not to go."

His words were like a slap to the face. He was right. All of them had told him not to confront the witch. And they were right.

"I will be gone before sunrise," Alistair said.

Paris's lips parted, as if he wanted to speak, but he simply walked out of the room and left him alone, as he deserved.

A QUIET KNOCK at his door woke him from a tangle of unpleasant dreams and memories. He rose and inched down the hall and to the basement door. His hand brushed the knob as the second knock came. Her voice was quiet and tentative. "Alistair?"

He was silent. He wanted to be near her, to bask in that warmth again. But he didn't want her to see him ever again.

She knocked a third time. "I'm sorry to bother you," she said. "And um...I'm sorry about the fire. I didn't realize it was you. I want to talk to you face to face. Would you open the door?" She waited. "I know you can hear me with your super hearing." Another long pause. "Well, make sure you drink both glasses. The blue one is a healing tonic. It will help flush out the toxins from the stake."

Another long silence, then a sigh as she retreated. When she was down the hall, he opened the door, then grabbed the two large glasses sitting on a tray outside his door. After closing the door, he heard her footsteps, as if she'd run to see him. Then another heavy sigh. "Dammit."

Her disappointment made him feel oddly conflicted. All of this would have been easier if she just left him alone. But he liked her, and he liked even more that she was drawn to him.

The blue tonic tasted like vanilla and licorice, with the unpleasant edge of something unfamiliar. He drained it quickly and followed it with the warmed blood. While he drank his breakfast, he listened for the sounds of her moving around the house.

Since her arrival, he had learned the song of her evening; shower, then the intermittent bursts of water as she brushed her teeth. A little sing-song to the cat, who answered with chirps and meows. Then the long, satisfied sigh of sinking into bed. When the silence fell, he knew she was asleep.

When she retired for the night, he crept upstairs to speak to Lucia. Shoshanna's sweet scent hung in the alcove around the stone statue. A single sheet of paper with a dozen geometric drawings and scribbled notes lay on one of the cushioned benches in the bay window. The arcane drawings made no sense to him, but she had clearly been busy.

"Was the witch here?" he asked. "I apologize for not visiting you. There was...an incident."

He took his time to clean the stone, making up for his absence the previous night. After gently kissing her fingers, he settled down to read from the book of sonnets. Not wanting to risk an encounter with Shoshanna, he headed to bed early.

For the next few nights, their routine repeated. Shoshanna left him blood, heated to near-perfection, along with a glass of a sweet-tasting tonic that renewed his strength. On the third night, she left a hand-written note that said *Please come out and talk to me.*

He did not. It was not for lack of desire; he found himself at the door a dozen times, thwarted by the memory of her stricken face.

On the fourth night, he heard her practicing the piano. She played the top part of a Debussy suite for four hands. As the music rang out in the house, the empty spaces beckoned to him. There were incomplete chords, lines that went nowhere without him.

Still, he did not join her.

Paris visited twice more that week to check on him and inform him about Shoshanna's progress. A contractor would come during the day to take up the wood flooring in the living room, so she could place her central sigil on the concrete foundation. That was a sign that she would soon be done, and out of Alistair's hair. He supposed he should have been excited, but he felt only resignation.

Paris also informed Alistair of an upcoming celebration at Infinity, where they expected him to make an appearance.

"Eduardo has requested that you be there," he said. They shared a bottle of vintage wine in his study, but he knew Paris was not there out of politeness or concern.

"I don't do parties anymore."

"Let me rephrase," Paris said over the edge of his glass. "Eduardo has demanded that you be there. He wants to know how you got staked when you were supposed to be here protecting Shoshanna."

His blood ran cold. "I can explain."

"And you will. To Eduardo," Paris said. "You didn't want to tell me what happened, so I couldn't cover for you." He shrugged.

"And what of Shoshanna?"

"She will attend," Paris said. "Eduardo wants to speak to her in person about taking a retainer."

"Couldn't that be a phone call?"

"Probably, but she deserves to get out of the house," Paris snapped. "Its owner is being an absolute shit and making her stay miserable."

"She doesn't need to deal with me."

Paris arched his brow. "No, she doesn't. Not when you act like this." He drained his glass. "I have work. Consider being slightly less of a petulant little shit, would you?"

Alistair bit back on his retort, instead watching his old

friend gather his jacket and saunter out the door. Paris was right. He hated saying those words, but they were true.

The next night, he listened for Shoshanna at his door again. Quiet knock. Two *thunks* of glasses at his door. "Alistair, you need to come out. Pouting isn't helping," she said.

Anger flared up inside him. Who was pouting? Had Paris put her up to it?

He opened the door, thrusting his hand out to grab his dinner, when something tangled around his wrist. Tendrils of light erupted from the door frame, as if a spider web had surged into existence. It was hot, but didn't burn his skin. As he watched, thin strands of light crawled up his arm like vines, holding him even tighter.

The witch stared up at him with a triumphant gleam in her eyes. "Hi there," she said. "Are you going to talk to me now?"

12

The spell had actually worked. She wasn't sure if it came as more of a surprise to her or to Alistair, who was frozen in place. His face was uncovered, giving her a full view of his mottled gray skin. Black horns curled away from his face. He wore no shirt, exposing a muscled chest and the messy wounds in his shoulder and belly. New pink skin was slowly turning gray in blotches.

Dark lips curled back from his sharp white teeth. "Let me go," he snarled. His red eyes were filled with hellfire, not the ruby glow of normal vampires.

"Not until you talk to me," she said, crossing her arms.

Dull pain throbbed in her temples, and she could sense the spell nearing its limits. "Shoshanna, I'm warning you," he growled.

"I'll let you go when you talk to me," she said. The pain

intensified, and she felt a terrible scraping sensation in her head, like nails on a blackboard.

With an inhuman roar, he yanked his arm free. The tendrils popped with a sound like steel wire snapping. He lunged. His strong hands shoved her backward into the wall. One huge hand pinned her throat, squeezing just hard enough to send a message. There was no hiding his face now.

Thick veins on his jaw and down the corded lines of his neck glowed like molten lava in cracked gray earth. He looked like a nightmare that crawled out of hell itself, looking for foolish little witches to devour. Her reflection stared back at her from his glowing red eyes.

And even on the landscape of that monstrous face, she could see the pain, even humiliation. She didn't care what he looked like. He had to understand that. "Alistair, I just—"

She gasped as he whirled her around and pinned her to the wall, one arm tight in his grasp. Her vision was filled with dark, gilded wallpaper, and she wondered if the last thing she'd ever see were those gaudy gold swirls.

Shoshanna, what the fuck were you thinking?

There was nothing to stop the furious, hungry vampire from tearing out her throat and ridding himself of an annoying little pest. This was why the smarter part of her had been screaming to stay away since the day she arrived.

"What insanity has possessed you?" he growled in her ear. She wriggled against him, but his body was an immovable stone statue. "You are well paid to do a simple job. Is it too difficult for you to leave my meals and then fuck off?" There was an uncharacteristic meanness in his voice.

"I just wanted to talk to you," she murmured. "I wanted to apologize for hurting you."

"No need. You thought you were protecting me from the hideous beast before you." A hint of bitterness rang in his voice, making her unspeakably sad. At the same time, it annoyed her. He was acting like a moody teenager, and she was over it.

"If there's no need for an apology, why have you hidden in your room for nearly a week?"

"Because I don't want to see you and you can't take a bloody hint," he said.

She drew a deep breath. "Is that really it? Or is it that you don't want me to see you? You don't have to be embarrassed."

He leaned in closer. She didn't make a sound, for fear that it would be a whimper. "I have lived with this curse for nearly a century, you foolish creature. What qualifies you to diagnose me, little witch?"

"Because I know more about magic than you do," she said. "And until this happened, I was enjoying spending time with you. And don't call me *little witch,* you condescending jerk."

His grip on her arm tightened, and she let out the tiniest whimper. "Tread carefully, Shoshanna."

"Why? I'm not the one who's pitching a fit because I got my feelings hurt," she snapped, careful not to move. If she twitched wrong, her entire arm was taking a leave of absence from its socket. And she certainly couldn't stand her ground with the angry vampire if she was crying for mercy. "I was only frightened because I hadn't seen your real face yet. Because you and Paris lied to me. I thought something had come in to hurt us. I was scared for you, not of you. I yelled at you to get out.

Didn't you hear me?" He was silent for a long stretch, eerily quiet without the soft rhythm of breathing to betray his presence. "Would you please come and play the piano with me again? I miss playing with you."

There was a long silence. The pressure on her shoulder finally eased, though he didn't release her. His voice was quiet and deadly. "Now that you've aired your feelings, are you satisfied?"

"Are you going to speak to me now?"

"I am speaking to you. Listen closely, little witch." His fingers tightened on her arm with those words, as sharp and pointed as his teeth. "Leave me alone." There was the faintest prick of pain on the side of her throat. Sharp teeth grazed her skin, and icy air left a trail of goosebumps before he pulled away. "Do your job to the letter, or I'll drain you dry and tell Paris to find a more competent replacement after he disposes of you."

He released her and darted away. In an instant, he was gone, door slamming behind him.

She let out a shaky sigh.

Maybe it was for the best. Most of her shipments had arrived, and she'd begun the work on the primary sigil in the living room. It was fiddly, precise work, and the last thing she needed was a brooding vampire underfoot. Paris had delivered a crate of textbooks from her apartment, along with a pair of fuzzy cat slippers she was certain he'd grabbed only so he could make fun of her. She had her mind and her hands full with the task of untangling Lucia's curse.

And yet, she kept finding herself at that damned door, like

something was pulling her in. She needed things to be right. Idiotic meat machine that it was, her body was all aflutter with the memory of his teeth at her neck.

If anything, he'd proven she was right about vampires. He'd rebuffed her tentative kindness and punished her one attempt to be devious. So why couldn't she just let the stupid vampire disappear into the shadows?

THE FOLLOWING DAY, a delivery arrived with half a dozen dresses in red and black, all wrapped in garment bags. She was unsurprised to find that they were all her size. Pinned to the outside of one bag was a note from Safira that said *Pick something pretty for the party. I like the red.*

Ah, yes. Because vampires loved few things as much as their lavish parties. When Paris told her about the upcoming party at Infinity, she'd wanted to stay home. But except for her terrified flight, she hadn't left the house in nearly two weeks. And getting out of the house, where it was eerily quiet and full of tension from the brooding vampire downstairs...well, it had rapidly gained some appeal.

That night, she didn't bother to prepare Alistair's meal. If he wanted to be an asshole, he could fix his own damn dinner. Instead, she ate a salad while she read through an old treatise on curses.

Real curses were the domain of Night Weavers, a highly specialized cabal of *tisserande*. They used the art of Weaving as Shoshanna did, but they wove fate itself, binding powerful forces that could change the course of a life for eternity. Curses wove into a person's soul, until they were so tangled they could only be extricated by the one who placed it.

In a decade of training as a *tisserand*, one thing had been made abundantly clear to Shoshanna and her fellow trainees. They did not meddle in curses. They were not to manipulate fate, lest they bring ruin on themselves and all those around them.

But as she sat with Lucia hour after hour and stared at her with arcane sight until her head ached, she began to understand. The curse was complex, but not utterly incomprehensible. Furthermore, there was something unusual. Tangled there in the dark, bruised blue of the curse, there was a hint of pure, rose red. It pulsed slowly, like a heartbeat. She could barely glimpse it, and she didn't dare try to touch it yet. But she'd never seen such a thing. Alistair and Paris bore a similar bruise-colored energy, but there was no hint of this vibrant red.

A distant creak broke through her concentration. From the alcove, she could just see the piano in its new position. Quiet as a mouse, a familiar figure drifted across the uneven floor. Then there was the soft scrape of the wooden lid and the creak of the piano bench.

The gentle waterfall of Debussy cascaded from his fingers. Her heart thumped as she listened to him play. It took all of her mental fortitude to stay put, not to come running at the first hint of compromise. She was strong, dammit.

As he continued playing, she stared closely at Lucia again, trying to catch a glimpse of the pattern. The red thread was tangled through the curse, but she wasn't sure it was a part of it. Interesting.

Silence rang out. He cleared his throat, a quiet and rough sound. Then he began to play again, with an obvious gap where a partner would play. With centuries of practice and supernatural dexterity, he was easily capable of playing the missing part, but there was a ringing silence, an emptiness of an open chord and missing notes. Was it wishful thinking on her part, or was there an invitation in the emptiness?

He cleared his throat again, and switched to the bottom part, as they'd played the very first time. A smile crept over her lips, and she glanced up at Lucia. She could return.

Shoshanna set her notes aside and quietly walked into the living room, standing at the end of the piano to watch him play. He was dressed in dark clothes again, the shadowed hood pulled up over his face. This time, he did not wear the dark gloves. His bare fingers danced across the keys in a flurry of gray against white.

His head lifted and tilted ever so slightly. Without speaking, he slid to the left to make space. With a shaky breath, she sat down next to him and turned the page back to the beginning. He began to play again.

She wanted to speak and purge all this ugliness, but there was such simple joy in the music. The ink on the page outlined a conversation of chords and phrases that required no uncomfortable emotions, no hidden truths. It was simple and pure.

They played without speaking, page after page, melody after melody. When they finished the lengthy Debussy suite, she drew a breath to speak, but he simply folded the pages, put it aside, and opened another folio. Schubert this time, one of his favorites. He spoke only to murmur "D flat" when she missed a key change.

Halfway through their third suite, the antique doorbell rang. She froze. "It's so late. Are you expecting Paris?"

"Answer it," he replied. When she got up to answer the door, he continued to play, a quiet flurry of minor chords that sounded like a maelstrom.

With her heart thrumming, she peeked through the peep-hole to see a woman in a green Home Eats t-shirt. If he had ordered walking comfort food, she was going to kill him. Or get Paris to do it. She creaked the door open, ready to send the heavyset woman away.

"I have an order for Shayna," the woman said.

"Shoshanna?"

"Sure," she said, handing over a large paper bag. "It's paid up. Thanks for your order. Don't forget to rate us five stars."

"But I—" she trailed off as the woman disappeared down the long drive. *Didn't order anything.*

Peeking inside the heavy paper bag revealed an assortment of cardboard carry-out boxes. She frowned and locked the door. As she turned, Alistair was drifting into the kitchen.

"Did you order this?" she asked. He didn't answer, but instead uncorked a bottle of wine and poured a glass. "You don't eat. What's all this?"

In a wave of cool air that smelled faintly of soap and clean laundry, he brushed past her to unpack the bag. "I didn't know what you might like."

She took out one of the boxes and opened it to find a piece

of red velvet cake. Transit was unkind, judging by the flattened rosettes of cream cheese frosting. Warmth spread in her chest.

"It's ruined," he growled. "They'd better send another."

She chuckled and swiped a finger through the dense frosting smeared on the lid. "It's not ruined." She licked her finger clean and sighed at the rich, sweet taste.

Before she could plunge a plastic fork into the blood-red cake, he was there in a blur, snatching it away. In his hand was one of the gleaming silver forks she had polished the other day. "You will not eat cake with plastic in my house."

With a smile, she took the fork and took a small bite of the red velvet cake. His posture was stiff, leaning forward in anticipation. Beneath the dark hood, she could only see shadow and the faint gleam of his eyes.

"It's good," she said. Before she could take another bite, he took the box and handed her another. "Hey..."

"You should taste them all," he said gruffly. "I'd like to know which one is the best."

She watched him unpack another half dozen boxes. By the time he was done, there were eight takeout boxes strewn across the counter, along with an assortment of plasticware and napkins from different restaurants. "You do realize I don't have a vampire's metabolism."

"I have a refrigerator," he replied primly.

The next box held a thick slice of tiramisu covered in a dusting of chocolate shavings. Coffee and chocolate billowed out in an overpowering wave of rich sweetness. She took a bite and swooned. "Oh, my God," she murmured, leaning against the corner as she smiled. That was almost better than sex. He reached for the box, but she brandished the fork at him. "If you take this from me, I'll put this fork in your eye, big boy."

There was the tiniest chuffing sound from beneath the hood. If she didn't know better, she'd think Alistair Thorne laughed.

His hand still waited expectantly, so she reluctantly ate another bite of the tiramisu and handed it over. The next box revealed a slice of cheesecake dripping with strawberries and freshly whipped cream. After a big bite, she followed it with a sip of the sweet white wine. Finally, she broke the silence, surveying the decadent spread. "Are you going to watch me eat all night?"

"There are worse ways to spend an evening," he said. He paced at the end of the kitchen island, then finally planted his stone-like hands on the counter. "I should not have put my hands on you. You startled me, but I let my anger overtake me. I'm very sorry."

The memory of his teeth at her neck sent a shiver down her spine. "It's all right. To be fair, I probably shouldn't have used witchcraft on you to make you talk to me."

"You caused me no real harm," he said. "I was angry and I fully intended to frighten you. To hurt you, even. I should be better than that, but clearly I am not. I give you my word that I will never do that again."

"You know you didn't have to order dessert from every restaurant in town to say that," she said.

He stepped back from the counter. Just one stride felt like a mile, a chasm yawning open between them. "It was too much. I thought you would like it."

"No, no!" she blurted, stepping around the counter toward him. "God, I ruin everything. This is so sweet," she said. "Literally. I love this. I just meant that you don't have to earn the right to talk to me or apologize. Does that make sense?"

"I suppose," he said quietly. "Do you accept my apology?"

"I do," she said. "Please don't ever do it again."

"You have my word," he said. "Thank you for your grace. You are kinder than I deserve."

Something warm and lovely spread in her chest. This was not a vampire who wanted to hurt her. This was a man who wanted things to be right with her. He was reaching across a gap for her hand.

She eased a little closer to him. He retreated an inch, but she gained ground on him. "You know you don't have to hide your face from me anymore."

His posture stiffened again. "You saw me and your instinct was to kill me. You thought I was a monster, and understandably so."

"Because I didn't know," she said. "Now I do. Part of my contract was to keep unwanted things out of here, remember? Now you won't surprise me. Please. I'd rather talk to you than that hood."

He shook his head. "You mean well, but I cannot."

"Alistair—"

"Shoshanna," he said firmly. "Enjoy your dessert." There was an unspoken order there. *Don't ruin what has barely been repaired.*

"Fine," she said, forcing a smile. "Then I want you to make it up to me after all."

His arms folded over his chest. "What?"

"You have to sit here and talk to me while I eat," she said.

"Dreadful," he said, the faintest hint of humor in his voice.

"I know," she replied. She perused the spread, then opened another box to a colorful display of French macarons. She took a pink one and took a dainty bite of it. Sweet strawberry and champagne flooded her tastebuds. "Honestly, why don't I just have dessert for dinner all the time?"

"Why don't you?" he said.

"Because I would be the size of your house," she said with a laugh.

"You would be lovely no matter what," he said, the gruffness in his voice softening.

Her cheeks flushed. "Thank you." Popping the rest of the macaron into her mouth, she headed for the refrigerator. "Do you want me to make your dinner?"

"No," he said. "I am capable." He took a blood bag from the refrigerator, then dumped it into a glass and started drinking it cold.

"What happened to one hundred and ten degrees, Miss York?" she asked, mimicking his light accent.

His head tilted. "I hunger, Miss York."

A shiver ran down her spine. The words emerged from her memory, spoken by that beautiful man in her dream. Despite what she'd seen of his face, she knew somehow that she'd seen Alistair Thorne as he once was. The echo of those words stirred something in her, awakening the flame she'd felt when she woke from that dream. Knowing that his body was cursed did nothing to extinguish her desire for him.

"Then drink your fill, Mister Thorne."

His voice caught. "What did you say?"

"You heard me. Your hearing is perfect," she said quietly, emboldened by his unusual openness. She dared to take a step toward him.

"Is it now," he mused. "Tell me of yourself, Shoshanna."

"Oh, I'd much rather know about you," she said, settling onto one of the high-backed stools at the kitchen island. She dug into a piece of dense, dark chocolate cake. "Every time I ask you about yourself, you change the subject. Don't think I don't notice." She gestured with her fork. "And have a seat. You look like you want to bolt."

"I...I am not comfortable around people," he said.

"Because of your appearance?"

"Yes," he said, surprising her with his admission.

She shrugged. "How about this? I really don't care what you look like, but if you're happier, I won't bother you to uncover your face. In return, you don't run away for at least five minutes."

To her absolute relief, he relaxed. "That is reasonable."

"Get talking, Mister Thorne," she said.

"I come from Austria originally," he said.

"Really? Your accent sounds British."

He actually let out a tiny laugh. So far, he'd laughed more in ten minutes than in two weeks. "I'm over two hundred years old and I speak five languages fluently. Accents are relative," he said. "My English is perfect, but Paris says I speak French with an abominable German coarseness."

She laughed. "You two go way back?"

"We do," he said. "Our relationship is complicated. Over the centuries, we have been friends, enemies, lovers, and...whatever we are now."

"You were lovers?" she asked.

His head tilted. "For many years. Does that surprise you?"

"Given Paris? Not really," she said with a laugh. She raised her eyebrows. "He didn't break your heart, did he? I'll be glad to try out my next spells on him if so."

He was quiet for a while, and she kicked herself for poking a sore spot. But he finally spoke. "He was very good to me. Far better than I deserved. I pushed him away, and he eventually quit chasing. We did not speak for many years, but we have since come to an understanding. I suppose we are friends again, though it is something more than that, too."

"Did he turn you? Or vice versa?"

Alistair shook his head. "No, Paris had been a vampire for years before I was turned," he said. His hands splayed on the counter, fingers dancing slightly as if he was playing an unseen piano.

"Can I ask a really personal question?"

"I suppose," he said.

"Do you like only men? Or men and women?"

"Why do you ask?"

Her heart pounded. "Just curious."

"I like both men and women," he said. Her relief was immeasurable. "Intelligent, charming people come in all sorts of bodies." He leaned forward on his elbows, head tilting. It was the first sign that he wasn't trying to bolt. He tilted his head toward her. "Which do you like the best?"

She perused the spread of desserts. "So far, I'm Team Tiramisu," she said. "But I think we could have a dark horse in this peach cobbler here." She pushed the chocolate cake away and reached for the cobbler. "Tell me something else. What's the most interesting place you've lived?" She wanted to dive into the deep, gooey parts of him, but she'd stick to the superficial if he would just stay.

"I spent several years in Hong Kong before I was cursed," he said. "It was beautiful. The people were lovely, and though I couldn't eat, I could walk in the markets and smell it all for hours. Celebrating the lunar new year was a sheer delight. I wish I had visited when I was still human. But my favorite was Stockholm."

"Why? Beautiful blondes?"

"It's dark for twenty hours a day in the winter," he said with a chuckle. "Though Scandinavia is not a place for vampires."

"Why's that?"

"A particularly vicious band of hunters," he said. "Thanks to the Rodzina, no vampire court has resided in Scandinavia officially for as long as I have been a vampire. I spent only a year in Stockholm before I encountered a hunter. I hate to admit it, but I barely escaped with my life. I decided I valued my head more than the long nights and beautiful blondes." Before she could ask him another question, he pointed. "How's the peach?"

"It's amazing," she said. "But I think I'm going to die if I eat anything else."

"We certainly don't want that. That would be a tragedy."

She laughed and started to close the boxes, but Alistair moved toward her in a blur, pushing her hands out of the way. "Allow me. You take care of everything here." He reached around her, and for one brief moment, his chest pressed to her back.

She took a breath for courage, then pressed her hand over his, pinning it to the counter. He jolted, but didn't pull away. His skin was cool and rough beneath her fingers. "Thank you for all of this," she said, staring down at their joined hands. "I enjoyed spending this evening with you."

He gently withdrew his hand and touched her bare shoulder. A shiver rolled down her spine. "As did I, Miss York." Then his fingers left her skin. "I apologize."

"Don't. Don't apologize, I mean." Her cheeks flushed. "I like you touching me."

Fabric brushed her shoulder. "You are too lovely to be touched by these hands."

"Maybe that's not up to you," she said, trembling with anticipation. "Do you want to touch me?"

"More than I can express," he said.

Something warm and effervescent bubbled through her at the thought. Maybe it was the wine and all the sugar. Or a year long dry spell. Or the memory of how this two-century old vampire had rocked her world in a dream so thoroughly that she'd still felt it when she woke up.

Feather-light, so gentle she might have imagined it, his finger trailed from her bare shoulder, down to her hand. A thrill rocketed through her at the simple touch. Another finger joined the first, tracing up the back of her arm.

"Yes?" he murmured.

"Yes," she whispered. His touch was agonizingly slow, betraying a patience she certainly didn't share. There was a rustle behind her, and then cool lips pressed to the back of her neck. Her head lolled forward, and she suddenly grabbed his hand, pulling it to her stomach and sliding it up over her ribs, drifting closer and closer...

He pulled away slightly, chuckling against her fiery skin. "Patience, Shoshanna."

Patience was an impossibility, with that simple, fiery touch cascading all over her, igniting her nerve endings.

His fingers traced her spine idly, as if he wrote a secret message over the landscape of her back. Cool lips brushed the curve of her shoulder, then kissed the side of her throat. "Don't be afraid," he said. "I won't bite."

Why not?

His other hand roamed upward, cupping her breast. A bolt of heat shot straight down, and she instinctively pressed into his grasp. His soft chuckle rumbled at her back. Teeth pricked at her skin.

"Stop teasing me," she complained.

He chuckled. "You aren't ready."

A frown crossed her face, and she turned to him. Against the bright red of his irises, his pupils were dilated, lips curved into a smile. But when his eyes drifted down to see her, he recoiled and covered his face.

"Alistair, wait!" she protested. *Idiot,* she scolded herself.

"I've overstayed my welcome. Thank you for entertaining me," he said, his voice pinched. "Good night, Shoshanna."

And with that, he left her with a spread of desserts and an

insistent pulse pounding between her thighs. What kind of man left a girl hanging like that? She heard the creak of his footsteps heading downstairs.

And despite his best intentions, he'd left her a mess to clean up. Even with the frustration, she smiled as she closed the boxes and put them away.

He liked her. He *wanted* her.

Too bad it was going to take another century for him to really make a move. At this rate, she was going to have to hope someone turned her into a vampire so she'd be alive to see it.

13

He was a damned fool. Was it a greater curse to have this face, this body, or to be as goddamned stupid as he was?

To make matters worse, he wasn't sure if he was angry at himself for staying or leaving. Shoshanna's desire was palpable; it smelled like cinnamon and vanilla and it vibrated under her skin like an electric current. Her body thrilled to his touch, something he hadn't felt in many years. But when she turned to see his face, he'd run from her like a coward. And he never should have let it go so far.

He spent the rest of the night considering what he would tell Eduardo when he stood before him the next night. It was easy to forget everything else when he was with Shoshanna, but there was a world of trouble waiting for him outside this sanctuary.

His dreams were filled with soft brown skin and warm kisses. But every time he raised his head to look into her warm brown eyes, she screamed in terror. *Monster! No!*

He woke just after sunrise with a sick feeling in the pit of his stomach. The queasy weight of dusk hung on him as he rose and showered. He took care to shave and dress neatly. Though he would cover his face in the club, Eduardo would demand to see his face when he spoke.

Upstairs, he could hear faint music and the sound of water running. Dread rushed through him at the thought of facing Shoshanna after his hasty retreat the night before.

Drink your fill, Mister Thorne.

That had to be coincidence. With that echoing pause, the faint gleam in her eye that was somewhere between mischief and desire. Surely it was just his imagination, desperate as it was.

Trying to push the enticing image of the witch out of his mind, he dressed in a black suit that Paris had sent for him. The coat was well-tailored, though a little small in the shoulders. The heavy black cloak and hood that he wore over his face did not suit the refined ensemble, but he preferred stares at his odd fashion choices over stares at his monstrous face.

He headed upstairs and paced in the open living room. The court would send a car for them at ten. He was early, so he spent the time playing an improvisation in E-flat minor. Long ago, he'd dreamed of becoming a household name like Schubert, but he'd never done anything with the hundreds of sketches in his library.

The doorbell rang, startling him from his playing. Jason, one of the Court's regular drivers, waited at the door. "Sir," he greeted. "Are you ready?"

Alistair turned to call for Shoshanna, but she was already there, emerging from the dark hallway. Her silhouette was lit by the hazy glow of the lamp by his piano.

If he still breathed, he would have forgotten how. An elegant black gown hugged her body, accentuating her slender waist and curvy hips before erupting in a cascade of silky ruffles. Crimson jewels sparkled across her chest, with a matching antique comb holding her dark curls. Her simple beauty had been transformed into something transcendent.

Heat pooled in his groin, and he was suddenly even more glad for the fabric covering his face. "You look lovely," he said, as neutrally as he could. Lovely was an understatement that bordered on offensive.

She forced a smile. "Thank you. So do you." When she raised her hand to fiddle with one heavy earring, he noticed the twisted silver band around her wrist. The symbol of the Court's protection would keep curious vampires at bay during the party. He wished he had been the one to clasp it on her.

He wanted to speak to her. But he knew he had botched things so thoroughly that she would surely reject him. Instead, he offered his arm. "May I escort you?"

Her crimson-painted lips curved in a shy smile. "You may."

Half an hour later, Jason dropped them off at the nondescript building in Midtown. Other than the black-clad bouncers outside, the edifice of steel and tinted glass could have passed for any office building. One of the men nodded to them and gestured in welcome as the dark glass doors slid open.

Beyond the dark glass, a small lobby dripped with expensive marble and gilded décor. Passing over the threshold, Alistair saw the briefest flash of glowing shapes swirling around each other. His spine tingled, and then his vision returned to normal.

He stiffened. "Your work?" he asked quietly.

Shoshanna squeezed his arm, sending a shiver down his spine. "Did it tingle?"

"Indeed," he said, shaking off the strange sensation.

Several narrow hallways branched off of the ornately furnished lobby. Ahead of them, a pair of dark wood doors that led to the club proper were closed. Safira was there, along with a red-haired vampire he didn't know. The other woman held a tablet at the ready.

Safira smiled at them. "Alistair Thorne and Shoshanna York," she said to her companion. Her eyes slid over Shoshanna, her full brows lifting in a question. "I thought you might like the red."

Shoshanna smoothed the front of her dress. "I did, but I felt like this one really screamed 'bad witch in charge.' Thank you for sending them."

Safira laughed. "Then perhaps you'll have to wear the red for another party." She leaned over and kissed Shoshanna's cheeks, then gestured for her to enter. Her blue eyes swept over Alistair. "Allie."

"Safira," he said calmly. He wished he could make eye contact with her, to send a silent message. Instead, he lowered his voice and spoke in German. "What did you tell Eduardo?"

"The truth," she replied. "We dealt with hunters in the MARTA tunnels." Then she turned to a new arrival, her expression brightening. "Carmen! Don't you look stunning!"

With that, they were in. Beyond the big double doors was the main attraction of Infinity. Tonight, the intimate atmosphere was illuminated by twinkling golden lights that glowed like stars in the rafters. The club was filled with the smell of blood and lust. A string quartet played on the stage, accompanied by an electronic synthesizer with an eerie resonance.

His whole body was wound tight as they descended into the crowded club. There were at least a hundred vampires of the Blade of Auberon within the Atlanta area, and several hundred more in the surrounding states. These sorts of lavish parties had once been nightly occurrences, back when things were simpler in the old world.

Interspersed throughout the vampire guests were dozens of *veravin,* each wearing their flashes of blue. For certain Court events, no other humans would be permitted. Shoshanna clutched his forearm tightly, sending a warm thrill through him. He gently patted her hand. Even with the strangeness between them, he was pleased that he could make her feel safe.

As if he had been watching for their arrival, Paris emerged from the crowd and intercepted them. He greeted Shoshanna with a kiss on each cheek, then a clap on the back for Alistair. "Shoshanna, you look radiant. Like the sexy witch of the South. Don't worry. I'll ensure that no twit in tacky shoes comes along to drop a house on you."

Her dark-lined eyes gleamed bright as she laughed. He envied that sound, and the fact that it was Paris who could ignite that little spark of joy. "Thank you," she said.

Paris offered his hand to Shoshanna. "I'll take her off your hands now. I'm going to introduce her to Julian and see if she agrees with my ranking of which of you is the biggest, brooding cliche." His eyes flicked upward. "Eduardo is waiting for you upstairs."

"You're not coming?"

"He wanted to see you, not me," Paris said.

Dread gathered in his mind like thunderclouds. He slipped through the crowd, back to the lobby and up the spiral stairs to the upper floor. There was a big lounge area there, and he found Nikko sitting on one of the big leather couches with a file open on his lap. Though he wore a suit, there was no doubt that he was well-armed and would spring into action at the slightest provocation. With his long blonde hair tied off his neck, the swirling black lines of his curse were visible. It was only a matter of time before his curse took its terrible toll once again.

And to his surprise, there was Sasha across from him, quietly reading. A pang of sorrow stabbed through him at the sight of his brother.

"Alistair," Nikko greeted quietly. At the sound of his voice, Sasha looked up and frowned. The shift in his posture betrayed coiled muscle, an intent to strike. “He’s one of us, brother.”

Sasha’s pale green eyes drifted over him. The look of suspicion and unfamiliarity there was heartbreaking. Weeks after the full moon, he’d likely recovered some of his memory. Long ago, Alistair would have been there to help him remember, to be an anchor in the storm until the witch’s curse stole his memory again. But no longer. Alistair was a name in a book, if even that. “Show your face,” Sasha said coolly.

“No,” Alistair replied. “That won’t be necessary.” They’d once been close friends. He’d even saved Sasha’s life once, carrying him to safety when a hunter’s bomb left the other man broken and bleeding out. He was nothing more than a shadow crossing his path now.

“It’s fine,” Nikko said, nudging the other man’s foot. “Let him be.”

Sasha’s eyes narrowed as Alistair retreated, headed for his rebuke at Eduardo’s hands.

The narrow hallway to Eduardo’s office felt a thousand yards long. He had once been one of Eduardo’s favorites, and could do no wrong in the formidable Elder’s eyes. Things had clearly changed.

The Midnight War, when Alistair and his brothers were cursed, was not his first time crossing paths with the vicious hunters of the Shieldsmen. After Franziska turned him, she bound him into the Rubrum Court, a small and ruthless band of vampires residing in Austria. They were careless and messy, and they paid for it by falling under the stakes and swords of the Shieldsmen. As far as Alistair knew then, Franziska was dead, and good riddance.

When their Elder was slain, the Covenant binding the vampires of the court was broken. Few survived the blitz of the Shieldsmen. Those who did were scattered and struggled to survive. Suffering the blood lust and madness of a broken Covenant, Alistair and his comrade Sylvain fled Vienna for the safety of the Auberon Court in Switzerland.

They were nearly starved and half-mad when they arrived, but they made it to one of Eduardo's salons, where a younger and happier Julian Alcott nearly killed them on principle. Eventually, he and Paris allowed them to plead their case to Eduardo, who took them into the safety and security of his Covenant.

Alistair had quickly become one of Eduardo's favorite subjects. A virtuoso vampire pianist from Vienna was exquisite entertainment for Eduardo's parties, where he courted wealthy nobles in hopes of bringing them and their money into the court. And when the war began with a cowardly, unprovoked attack on the ball in Saarbrucken, Alistair had protected one of Eduardo's most beloved Vessels, Zephryine Lenoir.

But he feared that he had long worn out his goodwill with Eduardo. If he had not done so before now, his stunt with Safira would surely demolish what was left of their fond relationship.

Eduardo's severe secretary, Adeline, glanced up from her desk. Her dark eyes swept over him, thin brows arching. "He's waiting for you, Mister Thorne," she said archly.

The door was ajar, and Alistair crept forward. Inside the well-furnished office, Eduardo sat in a high-backed brown leather chair, long fingers steepled at his chin. His red eyes flicked to Hugo La Cour, the intimidating man that served as his Scythe. "You can go," he said quietly, his voice a low, jaguar's growl.

Hugo nodded to him, then left the room. Though he closed the door, Alistair was certain the other man was just on the other side. The pale, dead-eyed vampire had protected Eduardo for centuries. As the Scythe of the Court, he was Eduardo's closest protector, war advisor, and occasional executioner.

The pull of the Covenant was painful with Eduardo so close. Ancient magic bound the vampires of the Court to their Elder, and it was impossible to ignore. "Sir," Alistair, said, immediately kneeling on the plush carpet. Even with his immediate submission, he still felt Eduardo's anger searing his skin and prickling through his veins.

"Reveal your face," Eduardo said.

Without hesitating, he slid the hood back. The only thing that kept his chin high was the realization that he would offend Eduardo even further by refusing eye contact.

The Elder glared down at him, ruby eyes unblinking. "Are you well, Alistair?" he asked.

"Yes," he said.

The older vampire circled him slowly. "Do you find the home in Midnight Springs to your liking?"

"Yes. Very much so, sir."

"Did you understand the simple task you were given by Paris and Dominic?"

"Sir, I was—"

"Did you understand?" he said coldly. "Paris assures me

that the contract I approved was extraordinarily clear. I'll ask again. Did you understand the task you were given?"

"Yes, I understood," he said. "This is about what happened with the hunters, isn't it?"

"In part, but I'm more concerned about your failure to protect Shoshanna York," Eduardo said. "The *tisserand* is valuable to me. I want her in my service, but that will not happen if the Casteron get to her."

"She was always safe."

Eduardo leaned forward, eyes narrowing. He smiled, but it was an eerie, ominous expression. "Was she? How would you know when she was unattended? Why did you leave when your task was crystal clear?"

His knees ached, but he didn't budge. "I wanted to find the vampire that threatened her. Elliott McAvoy."

"And what did you intend to do with him?"

"I...I didn't really have a plan. I thought I might kill him and pin it on one of the hunters in town," he said. "I called Safira for information but she refused to help me. Don't blame her, please."

"I'm aware of Safira's involvement," Eduardo said. "Have you taken any further action against McAvoy?"

He shook his head. "No, sir. And I'm sorry."

Eduardo's head tilted. "Why would you act alone? Why did you not trust me to handle matters of my own territory? Do you think me incompetent?"

"No, sir. It was because..." He lowered his head. "The witch was afraid. He left his mark on her, and I was infuriated that he would touch her."

Never mind that he had nearly taken out his own anger on her, much to his shame.

Eduardo actually chuckled. "I have not heard you express anger over a lover in many years."

Despite his keen desire, he blurted, "She's not—"

"Regardless," Eduardo said. "This is unacceptable. Safira steered you clear of trouble, but your intentions were clear. Had you succeeded in your original plan, you might have brought war upon us. My people would be in danger because of your selfish desires." His eyes narrowed, and he rose, still glaring down. As his stare intensified, Alistair's blood heated. First, it was an uncomfortable tingle, then an unbearable needling pain that made him want to claw his skin off. "I am the Elder of this Court. Do you wish to sever your loyalty to me?"

"No, sir," he bit out, trying not to cry out as the agony crawled up his veins, down his spine, across his eyeballs. Through the blood bond, Eduardo's fury was palpable, pulsing like a heartbeat in his chest. "I'm sorry."

"You live a comfortable life at my expense. And when you are given a simple task, you will do it," he said. "If you wanted to go hunting, you should have stayed with the Shroud."

"But I—"

Needle-sharp pain lanced through his sinuses. He groaned, then bit his tongue hard enough to draw blood. Eduardo's voice was deadly calm when he spoke again. "I will forgive this indiscretion, but my mercy comes but once. If you meddle in my affairs without my permission again, you will beg for the more pleasant days of being cursed by a witch. Do you understand me?"

"I understand," he choked. "I'm sorry."

The terrible pain finally ceased. He felt as if he'd been scraped out, leaving a bloody husk. Eduardo's eyes were blazing red now, like flame burning behind stained glass. "I do not have to justify my orders to you," he said. "However, rest assured that I will deal with the Casteron vampires when I know that the fighting will not cost more than we can bear. Until then, you are to keep the witch from harm. Can you handle that?"

"Yes," he said.

"Good," Eduardo said. He gestured to Alistair, still scowling. "Leave."

He scrambled to his feet and out the door. Hugo's pale gaze followed as Alistair rushed past, covering his face in shame. Folding himself into the shadows, Alistair stalked around the upper floor until he reached the richly furnished lounge that overlooked the main floor. Just over a week ago, he'd gathered with the Shroud to drink and pretend that nothing had changed. In the dim expanse of the club below, dozens of vampires danced, drank, and debauched.

And there amidst the otherworldly creatures was a glowing flame. Entwined in Paris's arms was Shoshanna. Light played off her beautiful brown skin, turning it into gleaming bronze. Scarlet eyes followed her, but as long as she was with Paris, no one would make a move.

He descended the stairs, in hunt of a drink. Tucked into an alcove near the bottom of the stairs, a female vampire sat in the lap of a *veravin,* her teeth sunk into his throat. His head was thrown back, large hand under her short dress as she fed from him.

The quiet, wet sounds of feeding made him even hungrier. The combination of his hunger and Eduardo's power burning in his veins made a volatile mix. He felt barely contained by his ravaged skin, like his teeth were going to burst out of his jaw.

The club reeked of vampires and fresh blood. There was wine and whiskey in the air, threaded through with the musky scent of sex. And there, like a high note singing an octave above it all, was the sweet scent of one human witch. It grabbed him like a noose, and drew him toward the crowd against every instinct.

She was radiant, clearly something entirely other than the pale undead creatures around her. Her eyes gleamed as she gazed up at Paris.

In over two centuries, Alistair Thorne had never felt this writhing mess of emotions boiling up in his chest, threatening to burst from between his ribs, melting his skin. Paris's pale fingers were a stark contrast against the rich, rosy brown of Shoshanna's bare shoulder. As if he felt Alistair's glare upon them, Paris leaned to whisper in Shoshanna's ear, then spun her gracefully as he raised his head. His pale blue eyes found Alistair's and narrowed.

A light peal of laughter, a perfect melody that filled him with desperate hunger, rang out. At the sound of it, Paris' lips curved into a coy smile. Joy painted Shoshanna's features with a happy glow.

Of course she was happy with him. Who wouldn't be?

The feeling in his gut reminded him of the first days of his curse, when his body twisted and broke into something he did not recognize. There was rage, mixed with shame and regret. It needed to destroy something before it turned inward on himself. It was aimless and destructive and made no sense at all.

But as he watched Paris' hand drift lower on Shoshanna's waist, till it rested in that perfect curve of her hip, his rage solidified into something much simpler. Something primal. It was sheer, mindless possession.

With her sweet scent calling to him, he could have found her blindfolded amidst a crowd of thousands. He knew the way she moved, the way she breathed.

And Paris was fucking touching her. He felt her pulse beneath his fingertips. That delightful rhythm belonged to Alistair and no one else.

The animal rage that reared its ugly head was unfamiliar and strangely soothing. It was the most alive he'd felt in decades. His hearing was flooded with conflicting rhythms, and he realized that he heard the heartbeats of their dozen human *veravin*. The smell of blood was overpowering, almost sickening.

As he watched, Paris leaned in and murmured in her ear, so close that his lips had to be on her skin. And God, Alistair knew what that tasted like, from the soft, shy kiss he'd brushed on her neck. The thought of Paris having even a molecule of her made him want to snap his neck.

Then he broke away and beckoned to Dominic, who looked as sour as ever despite the lavish party. Dominic bowed slightly, then took Shoshanna's hand and guided her in a circle to resume dancing. His hands were gloved, protecting her from his curse.

His anger subsided slightly now that Paris had released her, but he couldn't help shifting some of it to Dominic. The sharp smell of blood drifted toward him, and he glanced to the side to see a pair of familiar blue eyes gleaming in the shadows.

Paris carried two slender flutes filled with blood and garnished with raspberries. He offered one. "Drink?"

Alistair simply stared out at the undulating crowd. If he dared look Paris in the eyes, he might tear the other man's head from his shoulders. And with the exception of a few tense decades, he generally enjoyed Paris's company. Someday—though not with the scent of Shoshanna still hanging in the air—he would regret a bloody massacre.

"Are you enjoying yourself, Alistair?" Paris asked.

"Walk away, Paris," he growled.

"Oh, look. Dominic is showing off again," Paris murmured. "Do you think Shoshanna would prefer me or Dominic?"

Paris had a silver tongue, but no one danced like Dominic Cattaneo. Shoshanna's wide gaze showed her dancing on the fine line between excitement and terror as he deftly whirled her around the floor. The faintest smile played on Dominic's lips, though Alistair was certain he was not pleased with Shoshanna, but rather enjoyed the small moment to show off his prowess.

"That's none of my concern," Alistair said quietly.

Paris sidled close enough that his arm touched Alistair's. His familiar scent awakened years of aching memories. He chuckled. "Well, you know Dominic can't fuck her. And I can't sleep with her. Perhaps we'll trade off."

Rage overwhelmed him. In a flash, he envisioned a dozen ways to kill Paris, finally settling on tearing his throat out with one hand.

Instead of acting on his fury, he darted down the narrow hallway to one of the private lounges. He came to a halt at the first open door. Inside the small chamber, two big settees invited hungry vampires and eager *veravin* to satisfy their dark appetites.

"Why are you running from me?" Paris said from behind him.

He whirled and balled his fists into Paris's coat, slamming him into the opposite wall. Fear flickered across his friend's face as his head smacked into the wall, but defiance took its place. The porcelain perfection of Paris's features made him even angrier. What could he offer to Shoshanna, when she could have Paris?

"I told you to walk away."

"Hard to do with you pinning me to a wall," Paris replied. "Why are you so angry, Allie? Unless this is foreplay, in which case you could have just asked."

"Is everything a game for you?" With him close, he could smell Shoshanna, like the shimmering echo of a choir in a cathedral. And that scent on Paris, on someone who had no right to touch her, enraged him.

"Most things," Paris replied. "Not everything."

"You could have anyone you want," Alistair said. "Why her?"

"Why not?" His eyes narrowed. "Why not, Alistair? Tell me why I shouldn't seduce her. You know better than most that I am very generous. She's never had anything like what I could give her." He chuckled, and a nasty sneer curled his lip. "God, can you imagine what she tastes like? What she looks like when she comes?"

Rage boiled up in his chest. Her scent was stronger now, though he was certain it was his anger, his sheer need for her that swirled it into a maddening feedback loop. He leaned in close to Paris. "Because she is mine," he growled. "Not yours."

He wasn't sure what he expected from Paris, but it wasn't the toothy grin, and certainly not the ripple of laughter. His laughter stopped abruptly when Alistair grabbed his throat and lifted him off the ground.

His friend's eyes went wide as they darkened to a warning red. "Say it again," Paris said, his voice rough.

"She is *mine,*" Alistair growled.

"Then fucking act like it," Paris said. He drove his fist into Alistair's chest hard enough to crack bone. As Alistair reeled, Paris pounced and shoved him into the cushioned settee. It was all too easy to let Paris's charm lull him into a sense of complacency, forgetting that he was Second of the Shroud for a good reason. Looming over him, Paris's pretty face had turned into something frightening and lethal. "I promised Shoshanna that she would never be left alone here. Nothing more."

"Then why the games?"

"Because you're going to ruin this," Paris snapped. "I've got no intention of claiming her."

"And Dominic?"

"I bet him a thousand dollars that I could get you to punch me before the night was over," Paris said. "I was—*fuck,*" he swore as Alistair obliged on his bet. Blood streamed from his nose.

"You were saying?"

"Goddammit, Alistair," Paris swore. His voice was nasal as he pinched his nose. "In the face?"

"You shouldn't have been so familiar with her," he replied.

"And you shouldn't be hiding in the shadows when a woman like that is drifting around without you."

"She deserves better than me," he said.

"That's debatable," Paris said. "But she deserves better than you making decisions about what she wants. And if you want her, then you're doing a shit job of showing it."

He hesitated. "What if she ends up like Lucia?"

"This is not Lucia, and you are not Kova," Paris said. "The goddamned Night Weaver is on the other side of the world. Who you fuck in the privacy of your home is your business." He dabbed at his nose again, then smiled faintly. "I haven't seen you like this in a long time."

"Like what?"

"Awake," he said. "Alive. Doing incredibly stupid things for someone you care about."

"I don't..." As he trailed off, Paris's smile widened. "I do care for her."

"As you should," Paris said. "I like her. We should keep her."

"Then what do I do?"

"Alistair Thorne, are you asking me for love advice?"

"It's been nearly a century," he said. "Since you. And we both know I handled it poorly."

Paris's expression softened from his broad, mischievous grin to an affection smile. "Open a door for her rather than slamming it in her face. Then you must trust her and welcome her if she walks through."

14

Being the belle of the vampire ball was good for a girl's ego, but Shoshanna wasn't sure whether the vampires watching her wanted to meet her or eat her. Though she felt well-protected with both of her vampire companions, she kept searching the shadowed corners of Infinity for Alistair. Considering he'd hidden from her within the privacy of his own home, it shouldn't have surprised her that he was nowhere to be found amidst the crowd.

When she asked Paris about him, he just gave her a knowing smile. "He's a recluse under the best of circumstances." There was a strangely wistful cast to his eyes. "He used to be the life of the party. Second to me, of course."

"Of course," she said with a laugh.

"Do you really think you can break the curse?" he asked as he twirled her, letting her fluffy skirt spin around her like every little girl's Disney dream.

She hesitated. "I'm making progress on Lucia. I think I understand the basics of how the Night Weaver built the curses. I need to spend time studying Alistair to understand how his works, but I would assume it's the same at its core."

"That's not what I asked," Paris said. "Yes or no?"

"I really don't know," she said. "It won't be for lack of trying." He still looked dubious. "I am very good at what I do."

His brow arched. "Confident, are we?"

"That's not a bad thing," she said. "But this isn't in my books. It may take time, but I'm going to keep at it."

He nodded. "I hope you can do it. He was not meant to hide away in the shadows forever."

"You really care for him, don't you?" she said.

Paris gave her a cocky smile as he whispered in her ear. "Don't tell anyone. You'll shatter the illusion if anyone knows I've got feelings." His gaze lifted, then he brushed a light kiss on her cheek. "Dear Dominic would like a turn," he said. "Don't take his piss-poor attitude to heart. His demeanor has nothing to do with you."

Her heart thumped as Paris held her hand and turned her around, where Dominic waited. He bowed, then took her hand firmly and spun her around the floor. It was odd, but he wore smooth leather gloves that made her wonder if he planned to carry out an assassination between dances.

Unlike Paris, he did not speak. It was a challenge to keep up with him, but his powerful lead made it impossible to misstep. Eventually, her feet began to ache, and she hesitantly patted his shoulder. "Excuse me, but could we take a break to rest my feet? High heels."

His brow furrowed. "I do not understand such painful fashion." He held her hand lightly and guided her off the dance floor and to the bar for a drink.

A lovely woman with glossy black hair sidled up to her. "Miss York," she greeted. "A drink?"

"Just water, please," she said.

The vampire woman looked a little disappointed. "I have an excellent selection of liquors if you'd like. Our bar is stocked for human guests."

"No, thank you," she said politely. "I don't want to get dehydrated. Part of my skincare routine." That, and she wanted to be stone-cold sober in the den of vampires.

The woman shrugged and brought her a glass of ice water, garnished with a neat slice of lime. "Sir?" she asked.

"No," he said flatly.

Dominic leaned against the bar, watching the crowd silently. She stole a glance at him. He had a strong profile, with a nose that might have been too much on a less handsome face. Like Paris, he wore a well-tailored suit, though he wore a dapper black vest and black shirt underneath. But it wasn't his sartorial choices that interested her; it was the tension on his face. There were fine lines at the corners of his eyes, and the hint of a vein rising on his forehead.

She sipped her water and closed her eyes, letting her arcane sight take over. Deep blue-black energy tangled around him in thick, knotted ropes, a marked contrast to the finer threads of crimson that marked the other vampires. And his seemed to be pulsing, as if it was aggravated by something around them.

She dared to touch his arm. He startled and pulled away. "I'm sorry," she murmured. "Are you okay?"

His brow furrowed. "What do you mean?"

"Your curse," she said. "I can't help noticing it."

"It's none of your business," he said. "Concern yourself with your contract."

Her cheeks heated. "I was just—"

Dominic straightened suddenly. She followed his gaze to see the dancers parting like the blood-drinking sea before vampire Moses.

Eduardo Alazan, Elder of the Blade of Auberon, vampire king of Atlanta, and her current employer, drifted across the black and white tile like a king making his gambit. Behind him were his three advisors; she recognized Violette, the Gilded Hand, and Hugo, the Scythe. The third was the Veil, though she had not yet met the man. The music continued, but people bowed their heads politely to Eduardo as he passed through the gauntlet. A woman in a conservative black dress hurried in front of him, guiding the way to the elevated platform at the far end of the nightclub.

Hugo broke from the pack to beckon to Shoshanna. With her heart pounding, she took his offered arm and followed him to the raised dais.

A low wall surrounded a small, cozy lounge with black leather couches. A petite woman with gaudy blue jewelry waited there, her hands folded neatly in her lap. Her strapless dress left her neck and shoulders bare, inviting sharp white teeth. Eduardo sat on one of the couches and gestured to Shoshanna. "Miss York," he said. "Sit."

She tucked her dress under her and perched on the edge of the couch opposite him. "Sir." Her hands were clammy and trembling.

"I hear that the protections on Mr. Thorne's home are quite strong," he said. "I hear something about a sunlight wall."

"Yes, sir. It's created from—" His eyes narrowed slightly, and she froze. "Not what you asked."

"Are you close to finishing the work on Mr. Thorne's home?"

"About halfway done," she said. "I should finish in another week or so. I hope that's okay."

He nodded. "Take the time you need. Sooner is better, but I prefer well-done to quickly done. When you're finished, you'll recreate the same protections in my home. I also want this daylight spell added to the doorways in Infinity."

His casual presumption of control over her schedule sparked her temper. "Sir, with all due respect, I have to get back to my life."

"Why do you want to return to a life where you scrape by with..." He glanced at Violette.

"Twenty-six thousand dollars a year," she said archly. "Your skills are much more valuable than that."

"It's honest work," Shoshanna said. And what the hell? Did they have her tax returns or something? It wouldn't surprise her, but it felt like they'd found nudes from her phone and projected them for the entire club to ogle.

"We value you more than that," Eduardo said.

"And I value my freedom," she said.

"Freedom?" he scoffed. "I do not intend to chain you in a

basement, Miss York. You're free to live your life and collect a generous paycheck. No different than what you're doing now, and you can stay in your own home if you like."

"And answer when you call."

"That goes without saying," he said.

"And when you ask me to do something I can't stomach?"

"Does this have to do with your father?" Hugo asked.

Her stomach plunged into the floor. "What do you know about him?"

"We know that he worked for the Casteron of upstate New York until his death," Hugo said, staring evenly at her. "And that they paid a hefty sum to your family after his death."

"To my mother and brother. I refused their money," she said.

"That was foolish," Violette said.

She wasn't wrong. "That was my choice," Shoshanna said. "If you'll excuse me—"

"I do not excuse you," Eduardo said sharply. He glanced at Violette, raising a hand to quiet her. "Given what you've accomplished in a short time at my club and Mr. Thorne's home, I find your potential quite promising. Furthermore, unlike the so-called Barons of Casteron, I would not send a human witch to do my bloody work. There are many sharp blades within my reach that are far more effective and less prone to fits of conscience. While I do not share your delicate sense of morality, I do respect it. Would it affect your decision if I tell you that you can say no to my requests within reason?"

She hesitated. "And if I decide to end the contract, I walk away from you."

He glanced at Hugo, who scowled. "With certain agreements."

"Such as?"

"Most important, if you were to use your knowledge of my court and its workings against me, your life would be forfeit," he said. Her stomach twisted in a knot; how was he so casual about an execution clause? "But yes. I agree. You may end your contract with me at any time. Do we have an arrangement?"

"I want to think about it," she said.

Hugo started to speak, but Eduardo held up a hand to cut him off. "Agreed. When your work at the Thorne house is done, I'll expect an answer."

"That's fair," she said. She bowed her head slightly. "Thank you for being reasonable."

"You can go," Eduardo said, waving his hand. She quickly gathered up her skirt and practically ran down the stairs, where Paris was waiting for her with his arm out.

"You heard all that, I assume," she said.

"Every bit," he replied, guiding her through the crowd. "You should really consider it. Just think, if you became our witch, you could spend even more time with me."

"Shouldn't you be convincing me to accept, not run away?" she teased.

He laughed. "You'll come to see that I am an utter delight."

She frowned, lightly fingering the sharp collar of his crisp white shirt. "Is that blood?"

"Clumsy eater," he said smoothly. He tilted his head toward the bar. "Come. Let's get you something that came from grapes instead of a lovely housewife."

Around three o'clock, some of the crowd had already trickled out, headed for wherever vampires went for after-parties. Half of the raised booths were occupied by pairs and trios of vampires feeding on *veravin.*

She had long given up on dancing in favor of sitting at a corner table where she could see the entire club. Paris and Dominic had taken turns keeping her company throughout the night. Safira had dropped by to chat for a few minutes, revealing that the Shroud was building a file on Elliott McAvoy. Then she demanded a dance with Dominic, and Paris took over babysitting duty. One by one, he pointed out different vampires and told her interesting tidbits.

One of the men across the club, with his teeth buried in a middle-aged man's throat, had been turned into a vampire by his mother in an attempt to keep him from being drafted in World War II. "He's been a mama's boy for eighty years," Paris griped.

There were dozens of interesting stories in the court, though she sensed Paris was being very careful about what he told her. Eventually, the driver who'd brought them to Infinity approached the table and bowed his head to Paris. "Sir, Mr. Thorne has informed me that he's ready to leave."

Paris glanced at Shoshanna. "I'll walk you out."

Her feet throbbed when she rose and put weight on them again. No more high heels for her. "Thanks for keeping me company," she said.

He nodded, resting his hand at the small of her back as he

guided her to the lobby and out the glass doors. "Dominic and I are the envy of quite a few guests," he said. He gently kissed her cheeks. "Good night, Miss York."

"Good night, Paris," she replied. With his help, she climbed into the SUV, where Alistair already waited.

As soon as her door was closed, Jason pulled away and turned up quiet music. If working for Eduardo meant that someone would drive her everywhere, she was going to have a hard time saying no.

Alistair was quiet for a long while, staring out the window. The red of his eyes reflected from the dark glass. They were nearing the interstate when he finally spoke. "Did you enjoy yourself?"

"It was interesting," she said. "But I'd rather be at home with you, Magneto, and the piano."

His shoulders lifted, as if he'd let out the tiniest laugh. "As would I. How did your meeting with Eduardo go?"

"Thought-provoking," she said. "Yours?"

"Humbling."

He was quiet for the rest of the drive home. She kicked off her shoes and let out a soft sigh of relief. Next time, she'd wear more reasonable shoes that weren't picked out by someone who barely felt pain. She was ready to scrub her makeup off, eat a midnight snack that qualified as a Thanksgiving meal, and fall into bed.

Ahead of them, the dim lights on Alistair's house were a beacon in the night. Jason entered the security code at the gate, then drove around the curved driveway to drop them right at the front door. When she went to open her door, Alistair covered her hand and said, "Wait."

He got out, opened her door, then said, "May I?"

When she tilted her head in confusion, he leaned in and scooped her into his arms. "Oh!" she exclaimed with a peal of laughter. "What are you doing?"

His feet crunched in the layer of dried leaves on the steps. Shifting her carefully, he entered the code on the door and carried her inside. "Your feet were bothering you."

"I didn't say that," she said.

"I watched you at Infinity," he replied. "And you made a face of sheer relief when you took off your shoes. I know that face." He paused at the threshold. "Shall I take you to your room?"

"Kitchen first," she said. "I'm starving." In weeks of living under his roof, Alistair had barely touched her. It thrilled her to have him close, carrying her across the treacherous expanse of cold tile floor.

He set her on the counter and turned away to open the refrigerator. "What would you like to eat?"

"Alistair, I can take care of myself," she said.

"I know you are capable, but you don't always have to," he replied. He pulled out the bowl of fruit salad she'd made yesterday. "How's this? Or something more substantial?"

"This time of night, that's the safest bet. Hand it over," she said. He handed her the big bowl, and she waited patiently. "A fork, please?" He retrieved a fork and offered it. She let her fingers brush over his gloved hand as she took it. "Thank you."

"I'll leave you to it," he said. "Good—"

"Don't leave," she interrupted. She speared a piece of pineapple from the rainbow medley. "I didn't see you all night."

"Well, you seemed to have a fine time with Paris and Dominic," he said, his voice low and rough.

Was he jealous? She hoped so. "You saw?"

"I enjoyed watching you," he replied.

Her cheeks flushed as she bit into a strawberry. "You watched me?"

"Of course," he replied. "How could I not?"

"I wish you would have joined me," she said, plunging into the frightening depths. She was tired of pretending that she didn't want him. "Instead of just watching me."

"I would not have subjected you to such humiliation," he said. "Believe me, I wish I could have joined you."

She set the heavy glass bowl aside and slid off the counter. Staring over the long stone island at him, she beckoned with both hands. "Then dance with me now."

"What?"

"You heard me. Do you want to or not?" The question hung in the air for a painfully long time. She braced herself for yet another rejection.

"Yes," he blurted. He stalked around the island, staring at her with those fiery red eyes cloaked in shadow. After a stiff bow, he offered one hand. She smiled and grasped it tight. His other hand pressed to her back, pulling her in close. That was more like it.

It was a bit odd to dance with him, faceless and cloaked in black. But she knew who he was now, and it wasn't the frightening gray-skinned demon, nor even the beautiful man of her dreams. In her mind, she didn't see a face, but she felt his shape and the powerful magnetism that pulled her close to him. His presence was a lovely blend of safety, elegance, and comfort.

Dominic could keep his fancy moves, and Paris his charm. She was blissfully happy as she danced with Alistair in the moonlight. There was no music except her heartbeat and the rustle of her skirt. With a little squeeze of his hand, he pushed her away, spun her around, then brought her in even closer. His arm tightened around her waist. There was something quiet but clear in that possessive gesture.

Mine.

He released her hand, then traced a soft line from her wrist to her shoulder. His strong fingers grasped her chin and tilted her face up. Her breath caught in her throat. "Close your eyes, Shoshanna."

It was not an order, but a promise, a whispered midnight deal at a moonlit crossroads. *Give me this, and you can have whatever you want.* And wasn't that a small compromise? She closed her eyes and breathed deep.

There was a rustle of fabric in the darkness, then a tingle as he drew close. The first brush of his lips drove all thoughts out of her head. His vampiric energy tangled around her, like a shimmering cloud of energy, a rich scent that awakened her arcane sight in an explosion of fireworks in red and pink.

A faint growl rumbled in his chest, but it only stoked the fire burning in her. She pressed herself tighter to him, welcoming the hungry kiss. His tongue danced with hers, teasing and tasting, pulling her deeper into him before he responded in a dizzying counterpoint. As he kissed her, his hands slid down to her waist, over her hips, then pulled at the fabric of her skirt. He made a sound of frustration and broke away. "The bloody thing never ends," he growled.

She laughed and went to help, but he batted lightly at her hand. Instead, he knelt and slid his hands up her legs. A shiver rippled down her spine as he made his way up under her skirts and lifted her by the waist. Then there was the bump of the countertop and the kiss of cold stone against her bare thighs. "Don't ruin my dress," she said playfully as she gathered the skirt around her waist to make room for him.

He nipped at her throat, then licked her lower lip. "I'll buy you another." Before he could take over, she hooked her legs around his waist, pulling him in tight. "Are you sure?"

"About?"

"That you want me to kiss you," he said. "To touch you."

"I wished for it before I even met you," she said sheepishly. "Are you sure?"

He chuckled and gently turned her head to the side. His cool lips brushed against her throat in a soft kiss. He took his time there, covering her neck in a thousand kisses that left her dizzy. "You make me feel things I have not felt in decades. Perhaps ever. I nearly tore Paris's throat out because I thought he was trying to seduce you."

She burst out laughing. "That's why there was blood on his shirt." With the echo of his lips burning on her neck, the question bubbled up before she could stop herself. "Why didn't you bite me before? The night I grabbed you in the hall."

"Because you weren't ready," he said.

"You think I can't handle it?"

"That's not what I mean." His hand slid down her shoulder, leaving a blazing trail over her skin. "Some of us prefer to drink when our prey is...seasoned."

"Seasoned?"

"Some vampires like the taste of fear or pain," he said. He whispered in her ear. "I prefer arousal. Lust. The dreamy haze after orgasm when your soul has not found its way back to your body."

"Damn, Alistair," she murmured. Fire blazed to life between her legs. "I was plenty afraid then."

"Which is why I wouldn't have bitten you." He kissed the curve of her shoulder, then her neck. "I would taste you at your sweetest."

She shivered. "Then what about now?"

His lips brushed her ear. "It's tempting."

"Then why not? I give you permission." Even with his desire laid bare, she feared his rejection again.

"There is only an hour until sunrise," he said. "And I would need more than an hour to have my way with you. It would be a shame to rush."

"Then I suppose we should both go to bed." Or better, into the shower to deal with this situation he'd just begun. She started to slide off the counter, but he held her waist firmly, keeping her in place.

"I said nothing of the sort. There are plenty of ways to spend an hour, Shoshanna, without going our separate ways to be frustrated," he said indignantly. His nimble fingers searched at her back. "Where are the bloody ties on this thing?"

She let out a laugh. "Can I open my eyes?"

He froze. "I'd rather you didn't. I...I'm sorry."

Even as his hands lingered on her skin, she felt the distance yawning between them once more. She gripped his narrow waist to keep him from fleeing again. "It's okay." She lifted her right arm to let him undress her. "This is a modern dress. No ties. Zipper down the side. Nope, further back."

His fingers grazed her breast, sending a shiver over her as he unzipped the side of the snug bustier. Then with a little chuckle, he lifted her up easily and shook the dress off her like it was a pesky bit of debris. "There we are," he said. Then he carried her...into the living room, by the sound of his feet across the wood floor. Then there was the soft tread of his feet on carpet, and the familiar smell of her perfume and soap in her bedroom.

When the door closed behind them, she heard a familiar purr. She stole a peek and saw Magneto in the middle of her neatly made bed. His yellow eyes glared up at them as he turned sideways. His tail fluffed in his best menacing display.

"Oh, hello, sir," Alistair greeted jovially. "I'm about to put your mum to bed. Go find something interesting to knock over." There was a *thump* as the cat left the bed, then a rattle of him nosing in his food dish.

She laughed as Alistair laid her on the bed and kissed her again. He made quick work of her strapless bra, exposing her to the cool air. She held her breath, wishing she could see the look in his eyes.

"*Mein Gott,*" he murmured. His lips brushed over her breast, then his tongue swirled around her nipple, teasing it into a peak. "You are so beautiful. Sheer perfection."

“Stop it,” she muttered.

His head lifted. “Oh?”

“Don’t stop that,” she scolded. She felt him smile against her as he returned his attention to the tight bud. His touch was like finally getting a drink on a scorching summer day. “I just—”

“Shoshanna,” he said against her tingling skin. “Enough talking. Shall I occupy your mouth instead?”

“That would be quite lovely,” she said, mimicking his accent. He chuckled, then lowered his head to kiss her.

His cool lips sealed to hers, and she forgot her own name as he showed her what a kiss could be. The men before him had smashed their lips to hers and used their tongues in a clumsy stumble. Kissing Alistair was a song and dance that made her dizzy and delighted.

He broke away long enough to kiss the side of her throat, as if to mark the spot where he would someday drink.

Someday. Wasn’t that a strange thought? To think that this might not be some strange dream borne of a little too much wine and adrenaline?

The thought of him biting her sent a shudder of pleasure through her, and she hiked her leg over his. He pulled her thigh up, one strong hand holding her to him while he kissed her neck. He was hard beneath his tailored trousers, and his hips undulated slightly as he ground against her.

She lost track of time as he explored her, his lips marking every inch of her with soft kisses. His fingers walked up the inside of her thigh until they settled at the warmth of her sex. She gasped, hips bucking at his touch.

"I hate to leave you unsatisfied," he purred in her ear. His fingers stroked at her in tandem with his tongue in her mouth. He broke away, leaving her breathless. "Sunrise isn't far. Shall I leave you with something to remember me by?"

She nodded eagerly, and his hands left her. When he touched her again, his gloves were gone. His cool fingers slid up her thigh and under her panties. She let out a soft moan as he stroked and circled slowly.

The way he made her feel was so strange; she felt safe and secure. Even with her eyes closed, her body completely exposed to this powerful, predatory creature, she had no fear. Wonderful tension tightened between her thighs as he mastered her body with the same deft confidence as the grand piano.

His fingers quickened as the first fluttering spasms rippled through her. His mouth was at her throat, tongue flicking against her skin. "You smell divine," he growled. He kissed her, closing his teeth just enough to scrape over the vein.

At that touch of his fangs, the hint of what was to come, something twisted in her core and drew every cell of her body in tight. She arched into him, her mouth open in a silent gasp. His strong arm slid under her, and he lowered her gently to kiss her lips.

"Every bit as beautiful as I imagined," he said roughly.

"Thank you," she murmured. She let out a soft laugh. "That was incredible."

"I'm glad." His lips brushed her brow. "Thank you."

"For what? I think you did all the work."

He laughed softly. "For not giving up on me when I was so unpleasant."

"I think you made your case with the red velvet cake," she teased. Though she couldn't see him, his body was practically wrapped around her. It was the best she'd felt in ages.

"So the red velvet was your favorite? I suspected as much," he said.

"Hands down," she said. "I ate the rest of it for breakfast." Sliding her hand flat, she found the curve of his neck, then a stray lock of hair. Despite his harsh features and rough skin, his hair was thick and silky soft. "But I'll take this after dinner over cake any day."

"You're being too kind."

Still twining that lovely hair around her finger, she hesitated. "Maybe six days a week. Cake one night. The red velvet was pretty damn good."

At that, he actually laughed, a full-throated sound that filled her with a bubbling joy. A shrill beep interrupted her dreamy haze. He kissed her brow again, then eased away. "I'm afraid it's time for me to retire."

She groaned. "Can't we just pull the curtains? I want you to stay."

"I wish it were that convenient. When daylight comes, I'll be weak, and I'd prefer to give you my best," he said. His fingers splayed over her thigh, holding her tight to him as he kissed her neck again. "I will dream of you. And when night falls again, I will come to you."

"That's a promise?"

"A promise."

15

When the sun set and the first gentle chimes of his alarm roused Alistair Thorne from his rest, he was reluctant to shake off his blissful dream. He and Shoshanna wandered through a lush vineyard, with her long white dress billowing behind her. The sun shone on both of them, and he felt the warmth of her presence, the warmth of daylight so clearly that he could have sworn it was real. And just as he lifted her off her feet, laying her in a soft field of grass to make love to her, the sound of technology ruined it.

He groaned as reality set in. Slowly, his eyes focused on his dark bedroom and the dim lamp in the hall. Instead of the usual scents of laundry and soap, the air smelled faintly of vanilla. Shoshanna's scent still clung to him. The realization energized him, like a shot of sheer adrenaline. The dream had been lovely, but there was the witch in flesh and blood, somewhere above him. He could still taste her on his lips.

His cock twitched at the mere thought of her. He took a long, hot shower, careful to scrub every inch of himself so that she would find him appealing. But his anticipation turned to loathing when he caught a glimpse of his reflection in the glass doors of the shower. *She ruined you,* Franziska's voice echoed. *She made a monster of you.*

But instead of turning away, he raised his head and glared at the red-eyed creature. Perhaps he was a monster, but Shoshanna wanted him.

Mine, he'd told Paris, as if he had the right to claim her. And Paris, who he had long trusted and loved, had told him to make his move. Many years ago, Paris had told him Franziska was trouble, and he was right. Paris had told Alistair he was an idiot to push him away, and he was right about that, too.

And he wanted Paris to be right this time, that he couldn't be sure what Shoshanna wanted. That maybe he was worthy of her regard.

Somehow, Shoshanna saw something else. And whatever she thought of him, her desire was pure honesty. Her lust for him crackled like electricity in the air. That kind of hunger was something he had not experienced in many years.

He hesitated with a hooded shirt. Did he dare show himself? That was an act of bravery he could not handle just yet.

He growled and yanked the shirt over his head, tugging the hood up. Fear stitched through him as he ascended the stairs. Her warm scent grew stronger as he climbed the stairs and approached Lucia's alcove. Shoshanna sat on a cushion at her feet, completely absorbed in her work.

A loose black shirt hung off one shoulder, baring the lovely brown skin to the hazy lamplight. Her bouncy curls were barely tamed by a headband, and a pencil was stuck behind her ear.

He was content to watch her from the shadows. Geometric designs covered several large pieces of paper on the floor. Next to the drawings were strands of black string lying in piles. As she worked, she turned to her side to examine a square panel of light wood. Dozens of tiny nails were already hammered into its surface, with tangles of string connecting them in a strange pattern.

She placed a nail, then hammered it in with a few sharp raps. He jolted at the sudden noise, then watched her carefully wind a strand of string around the nail. She pulled it into place beneath another string, then cursed.

"Shit," she murmured, unwinding it. She made a series of gestures over the panel, as if she was weaving invisible threads. Then she moved the thread, twisting it around two other threads before securing it. "Hmm."

Her intelligence was absolutely ferocious. He could practically see the fire burning in her brain as she wrestled with the stubborn spell. It was that combination of steel and smarts that had turned his front door into a flaming portal and then snared him in a web of magic. She was a force to be reckoned with.

And she wanted him. It was unbelievable.

She set the hammer aside and leaned back against Lucia's statue. Her bare toes curled as she stretched out her shapely legs. "Listen, honey, we're going to figure this out. It's gotta suck being made of stone. I hope you're comfortable, at least. Maybe having nice dreams."

His heart ached as he watched her. She scrubbed at her eyes, then glanced at her phone. Her brow furrowed, and she looked over her shoulder. At the sight of him, she yelped in surprise. "Jesus, Alistair, you're sneaky."

"Good evening," he said.

"Come over here," she said.

"So quickly?" He eagerly swooped in, ready to pull her clothes off, but she swept some of her drawings aside to make a space for him on the floor. "What's this?"

"I need to look at you," she said. "Sit."

"What? I'd rather—"

"No, not look at you look at you," she said. "I mean, I'd like that, but...I need to look at your curse."

"Oh," he said, lowering himself into the open space she'd indicated. Nerves tickled at his chest. "Shoshanna, did I misunderstand you last night?"

"What, about the part where you need more than an hour to have your way with me?" she said with a playful perk to her brow.

"Yes, that."

"You understood perfectly well," she said, squeezing his hands. A delightful flush rose on her cheeks. "And we are going to do that thing, but I need to make some progress on this first. Because I really hope that once we get in bed, I'm not going anywhere else for a while. So I have to chase this rabbit all the way down its hole before I forget."

Fierce desire rolled through him. He wasn't sure he'd manage to wait, but he nodded. "I understand. What do you need?"

She smiled. "I'm going to examine you. It won't hurt, but you might feel a tingle. Is that okay?"

"Of course," he replied. She slid closer and pushed up his sleeve. He recoiled as his mottled gray skin was exposed to the light. Glowing red veins pulsed along his forearms. "I'm sorry, I'd rather..." He settled himself. She did not hate him, no matter how much he hated himself. This was a small thing, and he had to stop being a coward. "Do what you must."

She nodded solemnly. "I know that it's difficult. I appreciate you pushing through it. This is important to me." Her hands closed around his wrists. "You can hold mine." He cupped her arms gently, linking them together. Her pulse was a steady, soft current beneath his fingertips.

An electric tingle washed over him, and he suddenly felt as if a thousand tiny needles prickled across his skin, down his spine, into his groin, to the tips of his toes. Then there was a searing heat, focused as an arrow straight to his core. It was as if she was caressing him, one finger running along his spine.

Flashes of erotic splendor rushed through his mind. Shoshanna's eyes, heavy-lidded and filled with satisfaction. Her perfect breasts, gleaming with a sheen of sweat as her back arched in a graceful curve. The perfect rosy flower of her sex, holding him tight as he made love to her. The sharp scent of desire filled the air, and she cleared her throat. "Are you doing something?"

"I'm thinking rather pleasant thoughts of you," he said with a note of amusement.

"Stop it," she said.

"I can't help it. Your energy is all over me, and it's very appealing."

She squeezed his arms. "Alistair, please." He sighed, pushing the thoughts aside. *Soon.* He tried to focus on the importance of her work. Though he did not dare hope that she could break his curse, if she could free Lucia, then this was worth doing.

"There," she said, squeezing his arms tight. That same heated feeling speared through him again, like a shooting star that settled in his groin. No matter how intently he thought of dull gray paint and dry deserts, he was filled with raw desire. "Huh."

"What?"

"I must not have seen it before," she murmured, suddenly letting him go.

Though the feeling of her magic subsided, the throbbing ache in his groin did not. When he opened his eyes, he found her scrawling on a blank sheet. He leaned over her, gently touching her neck. Goosebumps followed the trail of his finger. Decades of shame and hatred melted away at that simple thing, to see her respond with need instead of revulsion.

"Wait," she said, grabbing his hand. "Please, I can't think straight when you touch me."

"I'll take that as a compliment."

She just chuckled, then fixed her gaze on her work. He left her to it, going to the kitchen to drink his breakfast. After biting into the bag of A-negative, he returned and found her still drawing. A large circle was filled with several smaller circles, connected with a series of spirals and triangles. And in the center of it, she had drawn a small spot of red.

"Is this me?" he asked.

"It's the curse on you. And this part," she said, tapping the red. "I looked at you before, and this wasn't there. Or I didn't see it."

"What does it mean?"

"I don't know." She flipped through one of the big sketch pads to show him another diagram. They looked similar to his untrained eye, though this one had a red line that formed a full circle, intersecting a series of triangles. "This is Lucia's curse."

"I don't understand."

She sat back on her heels. "If you understood it at a glance, I'd think that my years of studying magic were fairly useless," she said. "Night Weavers use the same basic art that I do, but they play with souls and destiny, which is dangerous. Still, at its core, Weaving is Weaving, whether you're shielding a home from intruders or turning an innocent woman into stone." She traced the sketch of his curse. "If I can understand exactly how she wove the curse, I might be able to untangle it. But this red worries me. I looked at Paris, and he doesn't have this. Or maybe it's hidden like yours. Maybe he can come over and let me look at him." Her eyes lifted to him. "Tomorrow."

He spared a smile, even though he knew she couldn't see. "Can I help you somehow?"

"Not unless you have a library full of Night Weaver books," she said with a sigh. "Only *tisserand* masters can look at them, and even that's highly restricted. I'm doing everything from scratch."

"We both know someone who's killed a few Night Weavers, and is a bit of a hoarder," he said. Paris had wiped out a coven of Night Weavers in France, giving them each the opportunity to break Armina's curse before he killed them. They had it coming, he'd said, though Alistair even flinched at the bloodshed. Somehow he doubted Paris's claim that he'd made it quick.

Her jaw dropped. "Dominic?"

He shook his head. "Paris killed several of Armina's apprentices trying to learn how to break the curses she put on us," he said. "And he took all of the books he could find, hoping that eventually someone would find a solution. But we never had a witch who was both clever enough and willing to help us."

"And now you have both," she said. "I hope. Can you call him?"

"I will."

She sighed. "I'm sorry. I ruined our moment. I just get so fixated on things, and—"

He gently put his finger to her lips. "You have ruined nothing," he said. "I admire your tenacity. Particularly considering you're working to end someone's suffering. Lucia is lucky to have you on her side." She smiled at him, and the sense of gentle admiration and peace there sent a warm rush through him. There would be time for them. "I'll call Paris now. Do whatever you need to do."

Leaving Shoshanna to her work, he retrieved his phone to call Paris. He answered after two rings, with booming music in the background. He had to be at one of their human clubs. "*Bonne nuit,*" Paris greeted.

Alistair glanced at Shoshanna, who was back to drawing. "*Gute nacht,*" he responded, continuing the conversation in German. He explained Shoshanna's predicament. "Can you bring us the books you took from Armina's apprentices?"

"Right now?"

"God, no," he said. "I intend to be otherwise occupied after I get off the phone with you."

"With...Alistair Thorne," Paris said. "Tell her I'm terribly busy tonight, but I'll bring them tomorrow. It'll take me some time to gather them all."

"Thank you," he said. "She also wants to examine you."

"Examine me?"

"Something about the curse," he said. He hesitated. "I think she might actually pull this off."

"That is a dangerous hope. But for your sake, I hope she can." Then his tone shifted. "Why are you still talking to me? Get the witch to bed. And while you're there, give her a little smack on the ass. I think she'd—"

"Good night, Paris," Alistair interrupted.

He prepared himself to wait for hours while Shoshanna worked, but when he left his library, he found her already walking his way. "Any luck?" she asked.

"Paris is busy, but he'll gather the books and bring them for you tomorrow. He says you can examine him as well." He tilted his head. "Are you done for the night?"

"All done," she said. Before she could say another word, he scooped her into his arms. She laughed and pushed against his chest. "Wait! I need a minute. I have cute lingerie and everything."

"Don't bother," he said. "I plan to peel it off you instantly."

"Mr. Thorne," she teased.

He carried her down the hall, down the darkened stairs and into his chambers. Her eyes were wide as she took in the dark chamber. A single low light cast the richly furnished room in a warm glow. "This is so much nicer than I pictured," she murmured. "I was imagining a grimy dungeon."

"Honestly, I'm offended," he said. His room was meticulously neat and furnished with exquisite furniture he'd collected over the years to remind him of the better days back in Europe.

"Well, I'm glad I was wrong," she said.

He settled into a plush chaise with her in his lap. It was one thing to dream of her, but another to be faced with the reality of showing himself to her at last. Her hand drifted up, fingering the edge of the hood over his face. One sweep of her hand, and his entire face would be shown.

Even as lust and need raged through him, fear held him back. He caught her wrist and gently pulled. "Shoshanna, I—"

"Please don't send me away," she said. "Unless you truly don't want me."

"Don't be absurd." He gripped her hips, pulling her tighter to him until she was nestled against his cock. Her soft warmth was tantalizing, and she pressed tight to him instead of recoiling. It was a marvel. "I have dreamed of you every night since you arrived."

To his surprise, her lips curved into a smile. "I might have dreamed of you." She ran her hands over his chest. "You can see in the dark, can't you?"

"I can," he said.

Then she sprang off his lap and hurried to his bathroom, where she paused. "Damn, your bathroom is even nicer than mine." Then the lights turned off. She crept toward the door that led to the stairs and closed it firmly. The seal around it prevented any stray light from upstairs from coming in. Then she flipped the switch, plunging the room into pitch darkness. "Oh, dammit. I didn't think about that." There was a bump, and she laughed. "Shit."

He chuckled and hurried toward her. Thanks to his curse, there was a faint reddish glow from his bulging veins that cast enough light for him to see. He could see her in the doorway, eyes wide, heart thrumming. He grabbed her by the waist and carried her to his bed. "Are you ready, Miss York?"

"I've been ready for days," she replied with a delightful laugh.

In the safety of the shadows, he tugged off his shirt and exposed his face. He took his time tracing the planes of her face, cupping the full curve of her cheeks before he kissed her. Her soft moan of agreement electrified him, and he realized that he would not have the patience to merely kiss her for hours.

Her pulse accelerated as their tongues tangled. He could taste the blood just beneath the soft skin of her lips. Breaking away, he slid his hands under her loose shirt. Her skin was so warm to the touch, like sun-kissed sand. She wriggled out of the shirt and lay back, her small breasts exposed.

"God, you're beautiful," he murmured. Resting his head

against her chest, he slowly teased at her, watching in rapt fascination as her nipple tightened into a sweet dark gem. His tongue darted out to tease it, and she gasped.

Her warm hands found his shoulders, and he tensed. Surely she would push him away. She had changed her mind. She would run away, leaving him alone.

But her fingers curled into him, pulling him closer. With a smile, he rose again to kiss her neck. She drew a shuddering breath. "Are you going to bite me?"

"Not yet," he said. "Have patience."

"It's hard when you do that," she said.

"I am immortal, and I am in no rush," he said. He grasped her hands, then lightly pinned them to either side of her. Then he took control of her, allowing his hunger to emerge as he kissed her full lips. The welcoming warmth of her mouth embraced him, tongue searching for his.

Veiled in darkness, he could almost forget what he was. His only purpose was to please her. He lowered his head and kissed his way down to the soft curve of her stomach. Then her body tensed as he tugged at her loose pants. As he pulled them off, she was already wriggling out of her silky black panties. He finished the job for her and tossed them aside.

"I'm going to taste you now, Miss York," he growled against her thigh. Her hips rose at his mere words, bolstering his confidence. With a little growl, he hauled her toward the edge of the bed and knelt between her legs.

She was already flushed and slick with need. He kissed the inside of her thigh, prompting a shiver. Then he took his first taste, savoring the explosion of Shoshanna that flooded his senses.

She was perfection. The smell of her, the taste of her, the way her soft, pliable body melted under him; it was the purest, sweetest thing he'd ever experienced. He spread her wide, hands splayed over her thighs. He could feel her heartbeat on his tongue as he licked and lavished her.

A quiet whimper burst from her, followed by a manic giggle. "Oh my God," she panted. Her graceful fingers fisted into the covers, and her back arched, threatening to pull her away from him.

That would certainly not do.

"You're not going anywhere," he teased. He growled against her and hauled her back, fingers splaying her open as he licked and sucked. As Shoshanna would come to learn, vampire hunger was not just for blood. He hungered for vengeance, for justice, for love, and in this moment, for her pleasure. He was insatiable, and the only thing greater than her need to come was his need to give it to her.

She tasted earthy and sweet, and he could have lapped at her for days, savoring the nectar that exploded on his tongue. He would have been happy to draw it out, to tease her until she was on the brink of madness. But there would be time for more. He wanted her to know that he was a man of his word, and that he could deliver exactly what she needed.

His lips sealed to her, and he gently sucked that sweet bundle of nerves into his mouth. His tongue flicked across her clit. As if he'd touched a live wire to her, she let out a clipped cry.

He couldn't see her face, but he could feel the heat in her blood. He could feel the warm wetness on his face, slicking her thighs. And just below that velvet-soft skin, there was a lovely vein full of crimson that would taste like the finest wine.

Not yet, but soon. He was almost afraid to taste her.

Once he did, he was done for.

16

In the space of fifteen seconds, Shoshanna York saw the solution to everything, the very fabric of the universe, and then forgot it all in an obliterating haze as her mind completely shut down. Every fiber of her being gathered into one single cell, a singularity of want and desperate need that answered only to Alistair Thorne.

His sharp teeth grazed the inside of her thigh, and she nearly shot off the bed as the electric sensation rocketed through her. But he placed a kiss on her hip, then gently kissed his way up her body until he reached her throat. "I need you, Shoshanna," he said. "I want to drown in you."

Without her sight, she was hyper-focused on the delightful roughness of his hands and the wet sounds of him feasting upon her. She could smell his rich, masculine scent all around her. His red eyes glowed slightly, letting her glimpse the outline of his face. She dared to reach up to him, but he grabbed her wrist and traced the veins with his tongue.

Before she could get her hands on him, he turned her over easily. His strong hands gripped her hips and pulled her back to let his cock rub against her. He was thick and hard as steel. "Do you want me, Shoshanna?"

"I do," she breathed, leaning back against him and arching her back. The darkness stripped away her inhibitions. She didn't care about making unflattering faces, nor what her breasts looked like, or how she tasted. Here in the shadows, she was free to feel and feed without shame.

His hands gripped her hips tight, and then he was pushing at her entrance. There was a split second of pain as he breached her, but he made short, shallow thrusts as her body stretched to embrace him.

"More," she demanded. God, he felt so good. Feeling just that first inch of him made her feel empty and indignant at being denied more.

"You can have everything, but I'm going to savor this," he said. He kissed her spine, and she tried to push back into him to demand more. But he held her hips firmly, controlling her as he pushed further into her, deeper and deeper until he filled her completely. "*Scheisse,*" he swore. His hands traced circles on her back as he lingered, engulfed in her.

She breathed hard as her body warmed to him. Just as he promised, he savored it. With each slow stroke, he nearly withdrew, then slid back into her until he bottomed out again. Her whole body fluttered around him, her fingers fisting into the soft sheets.

"More," she whimpered, squeezing him tight.

"Patience," he said. "We've waited this long."

"Which is all the more reason to speed it up, Mister Thorne," she teased.

He palmed her ass cheek and gave it a tight squeeze. "Careful, Miss York, or I'll have to take control."

"Maybe you should," she said. He stilled, then there was the faintest chuckle as he withdrew. "Not like that!"

Then he lifted her and placed her on her knees on soft pillows. "Hands up in front of you," he said calmly.

At the sound of his calm command, her entire body tied in a knot around that pulsing core between her legs. Her hands came up to find smooth wood. Drifting down, she found the firm edge of a headboard under her palms. Then he entered her again, sinking all the way in. When he was buried deep, he grabbed her thighs and spread them wider.

She was utterly under his spell. The darkness was a dangerous place to be with him. No one else was here to see her face, to hear the obscene noises that crawled up from her throat as he rocked into her.

Her fingers curled around the headboard as he dragged himself slowly out of her, then drove back in. His hands pushed her forward, then pulled her back to meet him, intensifying each stroke until she forgot to breathe.

"Is this more to your liking, Miss York?" he said, his voice strained.

She whimpered, hoping there was a *sweet God, yes* somewhere in the nonsense.

"You are a work of perfection," he crooned, quickening his

pace, a clear desperation overtaking his movements. His cool skin smacked against her thighs with each hard stroke.

She was dizzy with pleasure, so close again to that mind-shattering place where it was nothing but a sensation without shape and name. Suddenly, his strong arms encircled her and pulled her back to his chest. With her caged in his arms, he still thrust in slow, rhythmic strokes. One hand slid over her belly, down to her clit and stroked gently. She jolted in surprise, but he held her fast. He spoke in a low, rough voice. "Are you going to come?"

"Yes," she panted.

"With me inside you?"

"Yes," she repeated, pushing her hips to meet his hand. "Almost there."

Still barely moving, he gently gripped her hair and pulled her head to one side. Her chest heaved in anticipation as he licked her neck, marking the place where he would drink. "May I drink?"

"Yes," she blurted. "Will it hurt?"

"Only for a moment. And then it will be sweet beyond your wildest imagination," he said. His sharp teeth grazed her skin, igniting the nerve endings along her throat. Then there was a split second of sharp pain. His fingers rolled across her clit and drew her attention away from the pain and down to the gathering inferno.

With the first pull at her throat, the pain evaporated into a dizzy blur. Her skin tingled, every inch aflame as if she lay in warm sand. That was nice, and then—

His fangs were a lightning rod for pleasure; white-hot

sensation ripped through her from throat to thighs. She let out a sharp gasp and went rigid against him. Still, he held her fast, pinned against his body as he made love to her and drank his fill, penetrating and piercing until he was running through her like electricity. She felt like she was falling and flying and all she could do was grip his wrists tight, as he took her deep into the shadows.

Her body tensed as orgasm exploded through her. She let out a wordless cry of pleasure. This didn't fade, but took hold, as if she'd leaped from a precipice only to catch a powerful current that carried her up and out into oblivion. Black pressed in around her vision, and she slumped against Alistair in a dreamy haze. She was only vaguely aware when his hips twitched behind her, muscles clenching as he came.

He held her, lips still pressed to her neck, until she breathed easier. Then he withdrew slowly, both above and below. One finger pressed to her neck, and it went pleasantly numb. He gently stroked her brow and pulled her back down to lie with him.

She instinctively rolled over to look for him, but his arms folded around her and pulled her close. Dizzy euphoria still clung to her, as if she had fallen into bed after drinking a bottle of wine. She wanted to speak, but her brain had shut down. All she managed was a quiet, happy sigh.

"Shoshanna?" he asked quietly. "Are you all right?"

"Mmm," she said, wiggling her hips back into him. His arms tightened around her. "You?"

"I feel as though this is a dream," he said. "It seems impossible that I could be here with you."

"I dreamed about you, too," she said, her voice sounding far away. "The first night I was here."

He laughed, a rich, full-throated sound that vibrated into her chest. "And I dreamed of you."

"This was better than my dream," she said. Her fingers drifted to her neck. "What did I taste like?"

"Perfection," he said. "The sweetness of vanilla and honey. The warmth of fine whiskey. The richness of the finest red wine. I could live my whole life and never taste better." His lips nuzzled against her. "Lie here. I'll be back."

There was a faint blur of red as he climbed out of bed, leaving her alone. In his absence, she stretched lazily and let out a happy sigh. She'd had a few meaningless hook-ups in her life. Each had been followed by an immediate rush of shame and regret, like *what did I just do?* This time, she just felt satisfied.

"I just banged a vampire," she said to herself, then let out a peal of laughter.

"Yes, you did," he announced as he walked back in. She caught the briefest glimpse of him before the door closed again and plunged her into darkness.

Her cheeks flushed. "God, with the hearing!"

He laughed and climbed back into bed. Once he was settled, he pulled her against his chest, then pressed a glass into her hand. "Drink."

"What is it?"

"Orange juice," he said. He kissed her neck. "I don't want you to feel any pain because I fed on you."

She sipped the juice. Everything felt better in the afterglow of sex, particularly with him. Generic brand juice tasted like fresh-squeezed tropical sunshine. "I could get used to this."

"I certainly hope so," he said, his deep voice a pleasant rumble at her back. He kissed her neck again, as if he was looking for a last drop.

"Are you still hungry?"

"I am always hungry," he said.

"Do you want to feed again?"

"I do," he said. "I could drain you dry and never get enough of you. But I would not risk hurting you. I am capable of controlling my urges." His tongue flicked at her ear. "Even when they are nearly irresistible."

"Is it harder to have a human lover than a vampire?" she asked. "I mean, do vampires bite each other?"

"No," he said. "We bleed, but our blood is unappetizing. It lacks the essence that human blood carries. You may find it strange, but you are my first human lover since I was turned."

"Really?"

"Indeed," he said. "I have fed on *veravin*, and occasionally given them pleasure while drinking, but no sex. Not like this."

"Then I'm special, I suppose," she said.

"That you are," he said. "May I ask you about your life?"

She gave his arm a squeeze. "Considering what we just did, you don't need permission," she said wryly.

"Politeness is never out of place," he said, kissing her ear. "If you prefer to lie here in sated silence, I would happily accommodate that as well."

"Yes, you can ask."

"I...I hardly know what to ask," he said. "Tell me of your family."

"My mother and brother live in New York," she said. Her chest tightened. "My father passed about nine years ago."

"I'm very sorry," he said gently. "May I ask what happened?"

"He worked for vampires for my entire life, but ironically, it was cancer," she said. "The most normal thing you could imagine." And there hadn't been a damned thing she could do about it.

"Your father worked for vampires? The Vasilieva, I'm assuming?"

She shook her head. "The Casteron. And I'm assuming that's how Elliott ended up here looking for me."

"Did he not consider being turned?" Alistair asked. "That's how—" He paused, as if to hold back a secret. "Some vampires turn in order to escape human frailty."

Her breath caught in her chest. "I know they offered, but he refused for some reason. I wish he had. I miss him." Her eyes stung, and she pushed back into him. "Can we talk about something else?"

"Of course," he said. "I'm sorry to bring up painful memories." He gently rubbed her temples, strong fingers spiraling in tight circles.

She groaned in delight. "Keep doing that," she said. "Ask anything you want."

"Am I your first vampire lover?"

"Yep," she said. "And you set a high bar."

His chuckle rumbled through her. "I'm pleased. What do you want?"

"Right now?"

"In general," he said. "When Elliott is no longer a problem and your contract is complete, what would you do?"

The question stunned her. Crossing his threshold had been like stepping through the looking-glass. She'd nearly forgotten her life outside these walls. "I want to finish my *grand travail.* Maybe go and study magic further."

"And then?"

She laughed. "I don't know. Just getting that far would be a good first step," she said. "I'd like to keep studying magic so I can build more spells like the ones I'm working on here. Maybe stronger ones. Honestly, I'd just like to be comfortable and happy."

His hands stilled, and he gently kissed her temple. "If I can do anything to make that possible, then I will."

"You're very sweet," she said.

He scoffed. "I am not sweet. I am terrifying."

"Sweet as pie," she teased. "You're every bit as sweet and delicious as that cream cheese frosting."

In a blur, he pushed her onto her back and pinned her lightly. He kissed her ferociously, until she had to push him away to catch her breath. "I am not sweet, Miss York."

"You're not convincing me," she teased. "Perhaps if you kiss me some more, I might believe you."

He let out a little growl and set out to do that, and quite a bit more. By the time he was done making his argument, she was wrung out and exhausted, her chest heaving as the echoes of climax rippled through her.

He lay flat on his back next to her, fingers entwined with hers. "Have I convinced you?"

"Not yet," she said. "Maybe tomorrow." Her heart pounded as she squeezed his hand. "Alistair?"

"Mm?"

"Thank you for tonight," she said. "I want you to know that I feel really good with you. Not just the sex, although that is crazy good."

"I agree," he rasped.

"But you make me feel safe," she said. "I don't know if that means anything to you, but it's important to me."

He was quiet for a while, and she wondered if she'd stepped in it. She wasn't usually so direct, but she usually didn't bang two hundred year old vampires either. This was different than anything she'd ever experienced. His voice was rough when he finally spoke. "That is very important to me, too. It pleases me to know that you enjoy my company so much. My...my appearance does not bother you?"

She shook her head. "Even if I could see it, no," she said. "It seems like you think it's...a shell. Like a turtle."

"I am a turtle?"

With a laugh, she hooked her leg over his. Thanks to their exertions, his skin was warmer than usual. His muscular thigh was broad and solid beneath hers. "No, silly. But turtles are covered entirely by their shells, right?"

"I suppose."

"But you're not a turtle. You're more like a diamond," she

said. He was quiet. "Your appearance is one facet of you. Maybe it's the only one you see in the mirror, because you can't bring yourself to turn it any other way. But I see the other parts of you, too. You're thoughtful and talented. Intelligent. Generous. Protective. Very good in bed." He chuckled. "There may be a facet you don't like, but the entire diamond is something I like very much."

He clasped her hand and brought it to his lips, kissing her fingers lightly. "Thank you. It is very encouraging to hear you say such things."

"And I know you don't believe me," she said archly.

"I didn't say that."

"Oh, I'm well acquainted with accepting a compliment you don't believe," she teased. She pulled his hand to her and kissed it, gently stroking the rough skin. "Maybe you'll believe me eventually. I'm patient." Then she yawned and rose. "I need a snack. Come upstairs with me."

She got up and flipped on the low light. He growled, but she said, "I'm not looking."

"I am," he said in a low, rough voice.

She shimmied her hips and headed up the stairs, naked as the day she was born. There was a noisy rustle, then heavy footfalls as he chased after her.

Alistair Thorne was *hers*.

THE NEXT DAY, Shoshanna woke with a pleasant ache between her legs, and the faintest soreness at her neck. Her fingers drifted up to her throat and found two raised welts. His blood had healed the bites considerably, leaving her skin cool to the touch. Just the brush of her fingers ignited a searing heat that seemed to radiate from her heart down to her fingertips.

With a jaw-cracking yawn, she fumbled for her phone. It was already one in the afternoon. Spending her time with a vampire was playing hell on her sleep schedule. But last night was completely worth it.

She scrubbed at her eyes and sat up to check her phone. Along with several missed calls, she had a text from her boss, Jolene, at Average Joe's.

Jolene: *call me when you get a chance*

She sat bolt upright and braced herself on the nightstand as the world began to spin. After taking a quick shower, she dressed in comfy clothes and clicked her tongue to call Magneto. He had not been pleased at her long absence last night, so she was making up for it this morning with some wet food and some special treats.

With her heart thumping, she called Jolene. The familiar, noisy clank of dishes in the background reminded her of being at work. That world seemed so far away now, as her entire life had become this small place that was somehow so huge.

"Hey Jo, it's me," she said. "Is now okay?"

"Yeah. The lunch rush is winding down," Jolene said. "Just a second, honey." There was a pause, then it went quiet. "Stepped outside. I'm not gonna beat around the bush. I know you told me you had some personal things you needed to take care of. Life happens. But I need to know if you're coming back anytime soon."

Her stomach plunged. "I was planning on it," she said automatically, though as soon as she said it, she realized it wasn't true. In the last week, she barely remembered what it felt like to scrub out chocolate-crusted mugs and swipe debit cards and force smiles for rude customers who treated strangers' dogs better than human baristas. "Why?"

"Well, if you're gonna be out much longer, I've got to get some extra help, or promote Janie to full time. I also..." Jolene let out a heavy sigh. "I can't have men coming to the shop looking for you every other night."

"What?" Shoshanna spluttered.

"That good-looking guy I told you about has come by several times since I last talked to you," she said. "I told him I couldn't give out your information, but he won't take a hint. Last night, I saw him sitting in his car across the street watching us, so I called the police. Then he left."

The floor spun beneath her. Of course Elliott had to ruin the good thing she'd dared to enjoy. The lovely floating sensation of her night with Alistair evaporated, bringing her crashing back to Earth.

With her mouth going dry, Shoshanna said, "I hate to do this to you, but go ahead and hire someone else. If he comes in again, tell him that I quit."

Jolene was quiet for a while before she said, "Are you going to be all right, Sho? If you're in trouble, I can help. My sister's got a rental place out in Blue Ridge if you need a place to go."

Her heart ached as she imagined Jolene's kindly smile. "I'm okay right now," Shoshanna said. "I'll explain when I can. I don't want him to bother you anymore, but I also can't come back to work yet."

"Okay," Jolene said hesitantly. "You promise me that you'll keep in touch and let me know that you're okay. I'll switch you to seasonal so you can still come back if you change your mind."

"Okay," Shoshanna said, her throat closing off. "Thanks."

As she hung up, she realized she had just crossed another threshold from which she couldn't return. First it was taking the devilish deal that Paris offered on behalf of the Court, then falling into bed with Alistair and letting him bite her. And this was a hair's breadth from admitting defeat; it was only a matter of time until she took Eduardo Alazan's hand and became another asset in his portfolio.

And the most upsetting part of it was that it felt right. A few days ago, this whole situation was a glitch in her otherwise reliable and predictable life. She was just another human scraping by in the sweltering metropolis of Atlanta, with the occasional foray into the shadowy underworld of vampires and magic. And now, she was attending vampire parties and as of twelve hours ago, getting her world rocked up one side and down the other by cursed vampires.

But now, getting up at one in the afternoon with the mark of a vampire on her neck didn't feel strange. Her morning—now early afternoon—routine was to clean the house a bit, check her emails, and work on the spells she'd been constructing. Her main sigil, the power source, was holding strong and entering the reservoir state, where it would replenish itself from the earth's power and no longer need her to dump energy into it. She had a meticulous spreadsheet laying out where she'd work each day. When that was done and she was off the clock for the Auberon, she would spend a while analyzing Lucia's curse. Then she'd prepare Alistair's meal, and greet him for the evening, and see where his hunger took them.

This life was starting to fit. Maybe the old one had never quite fit, or maybe she'd changed. Either way, it was exhilarating and terrifying to think that she might have crossed the point of no return. Even if she could go back, did she want to?

She squinted at the bright sun pouring through the window of her bedroom, then closed the curtains. Her eyes were still bleary, so she splashed cool water on her face, then headed out to begin her work. In her rush to call Jolene, she'd overlooked a text from Paris, sent around five this morning.

Paris: *I'll have you know I passed on a late-night rendezvous with a pair of enthusiastic redheads. I sacrifice so much for you.*

Paris: *I've got the books Allie requested. And if you'd like to examine me very closely, I'll be over at 11:00. If you're naked...well, don't warn me. ;) I like a surprise.*

She laughed and shook her head. As she straightened the kitchen and scrubbed down the counters, she called Ruby. Her friend answered after the third ring. "Girl, I miss you! When are you going to be off vampire lockdown so we can get Mexican?"

"Soon, I hope," she said. "I have to tell you something, because I know you'll kill me if I wait."

"Let me guess. You banged the vampire."

"Ruby!" she spluttered.

"Am I right?"

"Yes," she said. "Several times."

Ruby let out a whoop of victory. "I knew it. I could feel the disturbance in the Force when you got laid. Tell me everything. Did he bite you? Was it amazing? Tell me about his dick. Wait, don't. Yes, do."

She burst out laughing. "It was...it was amazing."

"You can do so much better," Ruby said. "I need details. I told you all about that thing that Blonde John did with the chocolate syrup, so you have to spill."

"That's because you have no filter and no shame," Shoshanna said.

"Nor should I," Ruby said. "What's to be ashamed of? I'm a goddess in bed and people should know about it."

"I'll fill you in next time I see you," Shoshanna said. "But it was mind-blowing. And the rumors are true. The biting thing...unbelievable." She opened the refrigerator, mentally counting the bags of blood and adding it to her shopping list. "Hey, have you heard from Elliott again?"

"Not since the last time I talked to you," she said. "Why?"

"Just wondering. He's been showing up at the coffee shop. Just be careful," she said.

Ruby chuckled. "I'll let the others know. Auntie K keeps a loaded gun under the counter. She would be thrilled to use it."

"I'm serious. Be careful," Shoshanna said.

"I will," Ruby said.

"One other thing. What do you know about curses?"

"I know that you shouldn't be fucking with people's lives like that because the universe will always pay you back for it," Ruby said sharply. Her gleeful tone had completely evaporated. "What are they asking you to do?"

"I'm not trying to make one," Shoshanna said. "I'm trying to break one."

"That's your field, friend. Way beyond what I do," Ruby said. "Come to me if you need a tea to get your man hard."

"Not a problem," Shoshanna said. She shivered at the memory of him sliding against her and clenched her thighs together. "Definitely not."

"I hate you!" Ruby said. "But seriously, be careful. You know the rules. Never mess with things you don't understand."

"I know," she said. "I'll be careful."

Shoshanna spent the next few hours inscribing sigils on the window frames of the ground floor, each intended to strengthen the glass and ignite a daylight shield like the one she'd deployed against Alistair. They required little magic energy, just a lot of patience and meticulous measuring. She completed half of the bottom floor, then carefully began tying the threads of loose magic to the central sigil in the living room. When she was done, their house would be a fortress.

Their house.

The thought had felt so natural, but it was shocking. Why had she instinctively thought of it as theirs? His house. It didn't quite fit when she thought of it that way.

She shook it off as she went to make herself a salad for a late lunch, which she carried to Lucia's alcove. Bright light poured through the open window, casting a harsh white glow on the stone surface. She winced, shielding her eyes as she closed the curtain. Even with the window closed, there were still pulsing spots in her vision like she'd stared at a camera flash.

She opened her large sketchpad and reacquainted herself with Lucia's magical signature. As a *tisserand,* Shoshanna had been trained to observe the flow of magic in all things living and otherwise. Different creatures had patterns and flows that could be represented with the large geometric sigils she drew. As Madame du Mourier, one of her novice trainers, explained, the sigils were useful tools that gave their minds a way to comprehend the incomprehensible. Magic did not actually flow in such precise shapes, but it gave them a way to handle the ephemeral, mysterious power.

Most humans had similar patterns, with only minute variations. Vampires were different from humans, though quite similar to each other. And on the heels of a fifty-year research project, several *tisserande* had recently discovered that the longer a witch studied and practiced magic, the more her pattern diverged from that of a normal human. As far as Shoshanna could tell, Lucia wasn't a human or a vampire, but she certainly wasn't a witch.

Like choking vines, the dark blue-black energy of Lucia's curse radiated throughout her entire body, entangling her true essence. And there was that strange red thread that made no sense.

Her arcane sight didn't reveal the mercurial changes in emotion, though there were witches who could read emotions. This red wasn't something Lucia had once felt, but something much more powerful.

Vampires showed signatures of red, but it was typically a dark crimson, not a lively, glowing fiery red like this. Was this an element of the Night Weaver's magic? She wasn't certain if it even mattered, but she'd learned that it was better to find useless information than to act on ignorance.

After four hours of intense work, she had sketched the entirety of Lucia's curse. She couldn't begin to guess at the elements used to create the curse, nor the rituals the Weaver would have used to put it in place. This was less reverse engineering and more defusing a bomb. The longer she worked, the more certain she became that she could unravel it. The question was whether it would blow up in her face, and what effect it would have on Lucia. There was no point in breaking the curse if it killed the poor woman in the process.

Around nine fifteen, she took a break to prepare Alistair's breakfast. She hummed lightly to herself as a pleasant warmth ignited between her legs. The mere thought of him made her heart race.

As she stirred, a pair of arms slipped around her waist, and lips pressed to her cheek. She smiled and wriggled back against the solid body. "Good evening."

"Good evening," he said. "Did you sleep well?"

"Like a rock," she said. "You?"

"I slept well, but I would much rather have been with you," he replied. He reached around her to dip a finger into the pan. "I'm starved."

She tilted her head. "Do you want..."

"At least a day between," he said, squeezing her waist gently. "It's lovely of you to offer, but you need time to heal each time." He kissed her neck. She turned slowly, looking up to see his face concealed by the dark hood. Red eyes glowed faintly within the shadows. "You've got sixty seconds to put that in a glass."

Her stomach churned at his firm tone. "Why?"

"Because that's how long I'm going to wait before I carry you off somewhere to put my hands all over this body," he said.

She laughed. "Maybe I have things to do."

"Indeed you do. I'm one of them. Fifty-seven."

"Alistair!"

"Pour, Shoshanna," he teased.

With a nervous laugh, she grabbed the insulated cup she'd bought him and carefully poured the warm blood in. He reached around her, took a long drink of it, then hauled her up over his shoulder with a grunt of effort. "That wasn't even sixty seconds!" she protested.

"I'm a musician, not a mathematician," he replied gruffly. He carried her into her bedroom, and she shivered in anticipation. He hit the lights, and the room was plunged into near-darkness.

"You should know Paris is coming over tonight," she said. "With books."

"So?" His hands slid under her shirt, cupping her breasts. She sank into him as his fingers pinched lightly, teasing her nipples into hard peaks quickly. Her body sang at his command.

"So unless you're planning to invite him to join, we either have to make this fast or wait," she said.

"Call him and cancel," he murmured, burying his lips in her neck.

"It's important," she said, writhing against him. His hands

slid over her hips, and she felt the hard length of him pressing against her. "But you make a good point."

"How long do I have to make my point?"

"Ninety minutes."

"I can manage," he growled.

17

The knock on the door came just four minutes after Alistair surged out of the shower, still toweling his hair dry. Upstairs, he heard the frantic patter of feet as Shoshanna yelled, "I'm coming!"

"That was earlier," he muttered to himself. The room still smelled of sex, of Shoshanna's rich, earthy smell and the sweetness of her skin. There was something she put in her hair that drove him wild, a mix of flowers and vanilla that made her smell of pure sunshine and light. When he held her, he remembered what it was like to walk in the sun.

He dressed quickly, donning a light hooded shirt to cover his face. *One day,* he told himself. But today was not that day.

After sliding on his shoes, he darted upstairs to find Paris carrying a polished wooden chest across the living room. The sharp smell of blood was in the air, and he peeked around the corner to see Shoshanna in the kitchen. Her hips swished back and forth, like she was dancing to music only she could hear.

Paris smirked and said, "I hope you didn't hurry on my behalf."

"No talking in German!" Shoshanna yelled from the kitchen. "I know that means you're talking about me or keeping secrets."

"Je suis désolé, ma sorcière," Paris yelled back. "I was telling Alistair that I'd hoped to find you cleaning house in lingerie."

"You missed it by five minutes," she deadpanned. "Every day I vacuum in a French maid costume, complete with thong and thigh-highs."

"Merde," he drawled. Then he glanced at Alistair and mouthed, *really?* Alistair shrugged, savoring the awestruck look on Paris's face. Though she was teasing, the image of Shoshanna in black and white lace was enough to stir his cock to life again.

A few minutes later, she brought both of them a glass of warmed blood. "Can I see now?"

"This weighs more than you," Paris said. "Bring those to the library." Alistair ran his fingers down Shoshanna's back, then pushed her lightly down the hall to his library. There, Paris opened the big wooden chest to reveal a carefully packed array of books. The smell of dried paper and old leather drifted out.

Shoshanna's eyes lit up as she examined the books. "I can have all of these?"

"You may borrow all of these," Paris said. "Technically, they belong to the Court. But, if you think you can help Lucia, then you may use them as long as you need." He leaned over and pulled out several of the books. “These are the oldest. This is hardly my area of expertise, but these are likely closest to the source. These came from Armina’s right hand, Karlotta.” He shuddered. “Unpleasant little wench.”

Her brow furrowed as she opened one of the books. “What language is this?”

Paris turned the page. “Czech,” he said. “Do you read it?”

Her expression was incredulous. “No, do you?”

“Obviously,” he said. One by one, he placed the book in neat stacks and told her where they’d come from. “I got these from a shop in Zurich a few years ago. They’re journals, not grimoires, but I bought anything that seemed useful.”

She was quiet as she surveyed the impressive display of books. Her eyes were somber when she looked up. “Paris, how many witches did you kill to get these?”

He gave her a toothy smile. “More than a few,” he replied. “Rest assured, I gave them all ample opportunity to simply hand them over without violence.”

“That doesn’t make it right,” she said.

His eyes narrowed. “You don’t know what they did.” His eyes drifted to Alistair. “Perhaps some of us deserved our fates, but Lucia certainly didn’t.”

She took a tentative step back. “I think it’s time you guys tell me what actually happened. If I’m going to undo this, I need to understand what she did.”

“That sounds a convenient reason to nose about our business,” Paris said sharply.

“Paris,” Alistair growled.

Despite the warning in his voice, Paris’s mouth pulled up in a mischievous smile. "You might want to pour a cup of tea, little witch. This could take a while."

And so they settled into the plush chairs of the library, and began to reveal the truth of their curses. Nearly two hundred years ago, the Blade of Auberon held its seat of power in Europe, with Eduardo holding court in Switzerland and Germany. They enjoyed their lavish, decadent parties where the lords and ladies of the court danced and drank their fill from willing, starry-eyed humans.

From the shadows, the warriors of the Shroud ensured that their way of life was not threatened by hunters. Vampires like Dominic, Paris, and even Alistair once upon a time, had hunted and killed to keep their secrets safe and their blood-bound family protected.

With a dozen Courts scattered across the world, vampires were able to carve out their own territory, so long as they had a modicum of respect for one another. Unfortunately, as Alistair came to learn, not all vampires could manage the tiniest shred of civility. After being forcibly turned by Franziska Bauer, he had become a part of the Rubrum Court, who flaunted their status and left dead humans in their wake.

It was not long until the reckless libertines of the Rubrum drew the attention of hunters. Fueled by religious fervor, *Le Bouclier d'Argent,* or the Shieldsmen, had targeted the Rubrum for eradication. After picking off dozens of individual vampires, they struck a mighty blow and killed the Rubrum Elder, shattering his hold over his court.

Emboldened by their victory, the Shieldsmen continued to hunt the survivors of the Rubrum court. And when they could find no more, they turned their attention to the Blade of Auberon. Though Eduardo had always prided himself on a policy of secrecy, willing to cast out and prune "poisonous fruit," the Shieldsmen would not suffer the Auberon to live. And thus began the Midnight War, with over a decade of secretive attacks. Every time they ferreted out some tiny cell of the Shieldsmen, thinking the problem was eradicated, another would pop up.

"They were like fucking cockroaches," Paris said. "Or herpes." He gave Shoshanna a lascivious grin. "Not that vampires have that problem."

She shook her head. "Good to know."

"Nothing is so dangerous as a man who believes he is on a mission from God," Alistair said.

"But you were killing them, too," Shoshanna said.

"They left us no choice," Alistair said sharply. "The final days of it began when they struck us at a private party. There was no one there who was not willing. Every human there was like the *veravin* at Infinity. Willing thralls, eager to be fed upon and enjoy what we offered. Some were ready to be turned. And the Shieldsmen blindsided us and firebombed us. Dozens of innocent people died, many humans among them. I barely escaped."

"Trust me," Paris said. "Unlike the Casteron, we were devoted to secrecy. We wanted none of the witch hunts and pitchforks our brethren had faced. Eduardo had tried to keep the peace, but no longer. After the attack in Saarbrucken, he ordered the Shroud to eradicate the Shieldsmen. But we found that they were much stronger than the hunters we had faced for years before. They had Armina on their side. And dozens of dhampir."

"The dhampir hunted you, too? Seems like a betrayal."

"Some of them chose their human side over their vampire side," Paris said. "After the attack, we hunted the hunters. Eventually, we found their leaders and gave them a simple choice: surrender or die. They chose poorly."

Shoshanna looked stricken. "Then how did they curse you?"

Paris's lip curled. "Armina was one of the most clever witches we ever encountered. If she had not been systematically blacklisted by the rest of her kind, she might have gone down as one of the best of them."

"I've never even heard of her," Shoshanna said. One would think that she would have learned about a witch with such power.

"Because even the Night Weavers washed their hands of her, lest she bring war to their doorstep," Alistair said. "Her name is likely still whispered among their inner circles."

"Armina designed death curses," Paris said. "She and her apprentices knew that they might eventually fall. And not just to vampires, but to anyone who took issue with their spells and hexes. It had not been so long since the witch hunts, after all. They cast curses upon themselves that would be triggered upon their deaths. Whoever killed them would reap the bloody cost."

"And that's what happened to you two?"

"Well, to me. Safira, too, as well as some of our brothers that you haven't met yet," Paris said. His eyes drifted to Alistair.

"Allie was different." He shook his head. "As were Dominic and Julian. She concocted something special for them. Bespoke torture, as it were."

"Lucky me," Alistair said archly.

"And what about Lucia? What did she do to Armina?"

"She did nothing," Paris said, averting his gaze as his fingers drummed on the wooden arms of his chair. "She was a sweet dhampir girl who fell in love with Kova. She was the sun to him. She never hurt anyone. Never even crossed the witch's path, and still Armina took her from us. And he could not bear it, so he took himself from us, too."

Alistair's heart ached with the memory, when they realized that all they had left of their brother was his last journal. The words of that final entry dripped with guilt, begging them to forgive him for leaving. "When he was gone, I swore to take care of her, in case something ever changed."

"If you can fix any of this, you fix her first. She is innocent and far better than any of us," Paris said firmly. He gripped Shoshanna's wrist tightly. "Do you understand?"

Her eyes shone with tears. "I will." Her hand closed on Paris's arm, but her eyes drifted to Alistair. "And when."

"What?"

"When I fix this," she said. "Not if."

His lips curved into a sad smile. "I envy your confidence."

She set her jaw. "I need to look at you," she said. "And the others, when we can. The more I know, the better."

"Naked or otherwise?" Paris quipped.

Shoshanna smiled. "Ah, that's better," she said. "Serious Paris was very confusing. You can keep your pants on."

"A pity," he said, shedding his jacket and tossing it over a chair. Shoshanna bustled out of the room in a rush of warm air. Her feet pattered across the house.

"Thank you for not telling her everything," Alistair said.

"You can tell her what you wish in your own time," he said. His gaze drifted up again, and his expression brightened. "How would you like me?"

"Sitting in that chair," she said primly.

Alistair watched as she scooted closer to Paris and took his hands the way she had taken his before. He bristled at the memory, the way that primal animal lust had roared through him. That was for *him,* not for Paris. Sure enough, it was as if Shoshanna flipped a switch in Paris. He sat bolt upright, blue eyes shifting to red as they widened. But there was no lust in his old friend's gaze; there was only sheer terror.

"It's all right," Shoshanna said quietly. "I'm not going to hurt you." Her peaceful expression was a marked contrast to the tension on Paris's face, the veins standing out on his neck. Finally, she opened her eyes. "That's strange."

"What is?" Paris asked.

"No red," she said, looking from Alistair to Paris. "What's different? Maybe it's the death curse. You said Alistair's was different." She almost seemed to be talking to herself rather than looking for answers from them.

She began sketching with her right hand. As she drew, she held out her left hand for Paris. He went rigid again as her power swept over him, and she continued to draw in bursts. After nearly an hour, Paris was pale and drawn, and Shoshanna had a full rendering of whatever she saw.

"Did this help?" he asked, running a hand through his disheveled hair. Alistair had not seen him look so distressed in a very long time.

"I don't know yet," she said, staring at the arcane drawing. "I don't understand why you have no red. Alistair does, and Lucia definitely does."

"What does the red mean?" Paris asked.

"I don't know," she said. Her brow furrowed. "Do you think Dominic would let me look at him?"

Paris glanced at him. "I'll ask. But I'd suggest you have more to go on beforehand. Dominic is no fan of magic, and if what you just did is any indicator, he's not going to have a good time."

Her jaw dropped. "Did I hurt you? I'm so sorry."

"Not at all," he said, gently holding her hands. "But it stirred up some things I'd rather forget."

"Paris, I—"

"Shoshanna," he said sharply. "I would let you do far worse to me if it means that Lucia would be free. I'll speak to Dominic. If you can gain something from it, then I will ensure that he helps."

She nodded eagerly. "Thank you."

He nodded to her, forcing a smile. "Alistair can translate much of this for you," he said. "I have business to attend to this evening, but I can return later this week if you need me." He put his coat on and nodded to Alistair. "Walk with me."

They left Shoshanna poring over the books, and Paris walked with him out of the house. "What was that?" Alistair asked quietly.

"It's as if she triggered my curse," he said. "I saw things. You know."

His throat tightened. "I'm sorry. Are you all right?"

"Fine now," he said absently. The way his gaze skimmed away from Alistair's gave away his lie. "I won't put Dominic through that until we know it helps. What happened to you?"

"It was...it was different for me," he said. How odd that her power had made him feel so good, while it had terrorized Paris with his waking nightmares.

Paris glanced back at the house. "Do you really think she can do it?"

"I think she has a better chance than anyone we've ever known," he replied. "And I'll help her as much as I can."

"And that fact that you're fucking her doesn't influence you a bit?" Paris said.

"You encouraged me," he said indignantly.

"Of course I did. Look at her," Paris said. "It doesn't change my question."

"I don't know what she's capable of," he said. "But it won't be for lack of effort."

Paris nodded thoughtfully. "I hope for all of our sakes that she can pull it off." He clapped Alistair on the back. "I'll leave you to your business."

He returned inside and found Shoshanna making neat stacks of books in the library. Each stack was labeled with sticky notes. He gently rubbed her shoulders, then kissed the back of her neck. She made a little humming sound, almost like a cat's purr. "What are these?"

She didn't look up, just tapped each stack in turn. "English.

French. German. No clue. I hope you speak more languages than I do."

"I speak quite a few," he said. "Tell me what to look for, and I can skim the German and Czech for you."

She combed her fingers through her soft curls and let out a sigh of exasperation. "That's the problem. I don't know. Something about red? That seems so vague that it's got to be useless. Curses, I guess?"

"Red and curses," he said. "I can do that."

She took a deep breath, then turned to gaze up at him. Her brown eyes were warm and wide. "You don't have to tell me if you don't want to, but if I'm going to break the curse, it could help. Why are you different?"

"What?"

"Paris said that he and Safira and some of the others were affected by death curses," she said. "I haven't met them so I don't know why that's important. But he said you and Dominic and Julian are all different. That she made the curse especially for you. Why?"

He hesitated. Then he crossed the room, poured himself a generous glass of whiskey, and settled onto the couch. When she joined him, he scooped her legs into his lap and stroked her calf idly. He enjoyed the energy that thrummed beneath her warm brown skin. "I was not part of the attack on Stillerwald. Armina was bound to a hunter named Tobias. As one of the leaders of the Shieldsmen, Tobias was the one orchestrating the attacks on our people, and they wanted to take him out and find the upper leadership. I remained behind to help protect Eduardo and some of the others. I felt like a coward."

"Did he order you to stay?"

He nodded. "I had previously protected several of his most precious Vessels, Zephyrine and Valentin. Zephyrine demanded that I stay close to protect her."

"Were you...together?"

Was that jealousy in her voice? He smiled within the confining shadows of his hood. "We were not. She was simply attached to me. At Eduardo's command, I remained there to protect them."

Her shoulders relaxed. "Then you don't need to feel like a coward. You did what your boss asked," she said. "So how did you end up cursed?"

His chest tightened, and he distracted himself by rubbing her slender foot, savoring the way a wave of relaxation rippled up her body, and she sank further into the couch. Her brown eyes followed him, a faint smile on her lips.

"The others didn't realize right away that they were cursed. Paris thought he was merely having nightmares as first."

"What exactly is his curse?"

"It is not for me to tell," he said, shaking his head. "It was only when Sasha lost his memory for the first time that we realized something had happened."

"I haven't met him," she said.

He shook his head again. "You likely won't. Every full moon, his memory fails. He forgets everything."

"That's terrible," Shoshanna murmured.

It was heartbreaking to see the formidable assassin as lost and frightened as a child, over and over again. "The Shroud watches over him to ensure that no one takes advantage of him, and that he is not a danger to others. Introducing you would only make things more confusing." He smiled sadly. "And knowing you, it would break your heart when he forgot you. Dominic and Julian didn't kill witches. Or at least, that wasn't how they were cursed. They killed Tobias for information, and Armina designed curses specifically for them, far nastier than the others."

"And you? I thought you weren't there."

"I was an idiot," he said flatly. "When I saw the way my brothers suffered, I was angry. Julian almost killed himself on multiple occasions. It took both Paris and I to stop him, and he nearly killed us both to get through us. They all suffered terribly, and when we lost Lucia and Kova, I had enough of standing by. Paris had been hunting down the Night Weavers for seventy years, and I joined him on the hunt. But he never found Armina. I was certain that I could."

"But you were wrong?"

"Oh, I was right," he said. "I found one of Armina's apprentices and took her to bed. I believed that my masterful seduction would be more than sufficient to turn her against Armina. And when she gave up Armina's location, I was cocky. I thought I would bargain for a cure, that I would succeed where the others had failed." His chest tightened. How many times had his brothers warned him against pursuing the witch?

"And she cursed you," Shoshanna said quietly.

"She knew I was coming. Her apprentice played me, letting me believe I had turned her against Armina, when in fact she had set up a trap for me," he said. "I was a damned fool to think that I would sway her. And I might have gotten away with it, but I taunted her, thinking I had nothing to lose. My mouth ran away with me, and I offered to fill the void that her lover had left." Shame boiled in his gut. "She cursed me. At first I thought it was merely pain. My skin felt like it was burning and turning to stone. I fled, and by the time I reached home in Prague, I was the monster you saw. I am this way because I was a fool. There was no reason for me to suffer. The others told me not to bother, not to risk myself, and I did it anyway." He pushed her feet away and drained the rest of the whiskey, resting his head in his hands. "You must think me a terrible fool."

She was quiet, and then there was the quiet shift of fabric and creaking leather as she shifted closer, her warm body resting against his. Despite his shame, her touch was a balm. She rested her head on his shoulder and stroked his hand. He fought the urge to pull away, so she could not see the ugly, twisted flesh. "I don't think you're a fool."

"It's a sweet lie, but you don't have to coddle me."

"Can't you hear my heartbeat?"

"Yes, of course."

"Does it sound like I'm lying?"

Her pulse was steady and slow. "Go on."

"I think you cared for your friends," she said, still stroking his hand. "The family you built. And you did something a little crazy to help them. Why would I think anything but kindly of you for that? I'm going to figure this out. And when I do, you won't have to hide anymore. And Paris won't have to...well, whatever is wrong with him, too. I'm going to do it, Alistair."

"Your confidence is endearing." Her weight shifted, and she punched him in the arm. "Ouch!"

"That didn't hurt."

"Not really," he admitted. She did it again, this time hard enough to send a fleeting spike of pain up his arm. "Shoshanna!"

"Look at me," she said. He turned, though he didn't pull back his hood. "You don't know how persistent I am."

"I know that you bespelled a trap on my bedroom door to force me to talk to you when you wanted to apologize," he said drily.

Her smile was dazzling. "I did, didn't I?" Then her brow furrowed. "I have worked my ass off since I was seventeen. My mom wanted me to stay in New York and go to school with Casteron money, and I refused. I took out my own loans and I paid them. I'm still paying them. So maybe we're both idiots," she said with a wince. "And I underwent *tisserand* training even though I didn't have generations of legacy, only a dad with a bad reputation for his affiliation with the Casteron. I've lived here on my own for over a decade. I have a lot to be proud of, and I've earned it."

"Would it be demeaning to your accomplishments if I told you that your speech just made you even sexier?"

"Only a little, but I'll allow it," she said, a mischievous gleam in her eyes. "Maybe you and your fanged friends think that I'm just going to tinker around and give up after a few days, but I'm not. You know all those spells I put on Infinity and here in your house? I didn't learn them from a book. I built them myself. If there's a question, there's always an answer. And I can find it if I work at it."

He tipped her chin up. "I believe you."

"You do?"

He wasn't certain that he did. It was not that Shoshanna lacked intelligence or skill, nor the persistence necessary. She had all of those things in spades. But she was kind, with integrity that shone bright. Armina and her apprentices had a knack for torment, for cruel vengeance that would spiral across time and space. Julian and Sasha had paid for their sins a thousand times over. Nikko, too. The loss of her lover had long been repaid, and still, they suffered without relief.

How could Shoshanna combat that kind of darkness? He wanted her to remain the warm beacon of light that she was, not immerse herself in Armina's dark arts. But he also wanted Lucia to walk in the sun again. And if he could be so selfish, he wanted to face the world again. He wanted Paris to sleep through the night and for Nikko to have some peace at last.

"I do," he said.

"Good," she said with a nod. "Then let's get to work."

18

Weeks into her unplanned stay at Chateau Vampire, Shoshanna York was elbows-deep in a practical exam unlike any she'd faced in her *tisserand* training. She'd transformed Lucia's neat little alcove into a lab, with drawings laid across the floor and into the hallway. Bags of spell reagents were strewn all around. Her housekeeping left something to be desired, but her witchcraft was on point.

Crawling on her hands and knees, she carefully measured a grounding circle around Lucia. At five points of the circle, she placed chunks of hematite, then carefully lined the outer perimeter with black salt. The coarse sea salt was mixed with iron shavings and a handful of graveyard dirt to absorb the negative energy from the curse, like rubber grips to prevent an electric shock.

"This should be no different than deconstructing a sigil,"

she told herself. She wasn't sure if she was reassuring herself or the phantom voices of her instructors, who would likely shit a refined French brick if they knew she was toying with curses.

With a deep breath, she settled onto a cushioned stool and closed her eyes, breathing deeply to a slow, measured count. "Sweet mother of the earth, bless me with the strength of your ground. Good spirits of the sky, fill my lungs with the energy and resolve of the air," she murmured. As she went through the calming ritual, she visualized glowing gold roots that stretched from her spine down into the earth. Warmth surrounded her. "Spirits, search my heart and know that my intentions are pure. I seek to undo harm, not to cause it. I seek to end the suffering of a living creature. Please guide my words and my will."

Without opening her eyes, she opened her arcane sight and let Lucia's essence flood into her mind. It felt like she dove into icy water. She gasped in surprise, then reached for the first thread, as she'd planned in her days of analyzing. When she grasped the thread, a shock ran up her arm, like she'd grabbed an electrical wire. She tried to pluck the thread free, but it was far stronger than she expected. Where her magic was constructed of thin spider-web silk, this was a fat steel cable under such tension that she could barely budge it. Gritting her teeth, she pushed her power into it, using the same explosive energy that she'd used to burn Alistair a week earlier.

It snapped back on her, vibrating through her whole body. She frowned and moved to the next thread she'd chosen. It was just as tense as the first. As she tested the threads, the burning red thread flamed brighter. It was entangled around Lucia, casting a lurid, purple glow on the blue threads of the curse.

Overcome by curiosity, she grabbed the red thread and pulled gently. Energy like she'd never felt surged over her like a boiling wave. A woman's scream echoed in her head. A powerful force pressed all around her, crushing her. As her vision faded, she saw a handsome man with red eyes bellowing in rage at her feet.

Then it was cold and dark.

Shoshanna gasped and pulled away. The spiraling whorls and tangles of the curse flashed in her vision. As she sat upright, excruciating pain squeezed her temples like a vise. "Shit," she muttered. She'd been so fixated on untangling the threads in the correct order and how to diffuse the negative energy that she hadn't even considered that she wouldn't be able to break them.

Black pressed in around her blurry vision. She eased to her feet and gently squeezed Lucia's shoulder. "I'm gonna get this," she told her. "And I'm really sorry if I hurt you just now. Just give me more time."

She headed to the kitchen for a snack. Carbs helped her think. As she crunched on buttery crackers, she paced around the island and fretted over her experiment. It should have worked. Maybe she just hadn't put enough muscle behind it. She helped herself to some orange juice straight from the carton, then stormed back to Lucia.

"One more time," she said. She was about to open up, but she paused. Eduardo's words echoed in her mind. Well done was better than quickly done. She took the time to breathe evenly, then invoke the protection of nature. When she was settled, she opened her arcane sight and braced herself. This time, she coiled up her energy, like stretching a rubber band to its breaking point. When she caught the first thread, she unleashed the gathered power.

Gravity inverted. Her head thumped against the floor. She opened her eyes to see the blurry outline of Lucia's outstretched hand overhead. With a groan, she hauled herself upright using the statue's arm for balance.

If all that power wasn't enough to snap the thread, then she was missing something. Either she needed to juice herself up, or she had to weaken the threads. But for now, she needed a break. The mother of all headaches was blooming like blood in water. After retrieving some aspirin, she laid on the couch in the living room and called Ruby.

Deafening music burst from the phone. She heard Ruby cursing, then the music went quiet. "Hey babe, what's up?" Ruby said.

"Sorry to bug you," Shoshanna said. "Can you tell me how to make that headache tea, or maybe have Miles deliver some out here? I'll pay him cash. Tell him to name his price." When he wasn't trying to make it big as a professional gamer, Miles also worked as an Uber driver.

"Do you need it now? I'll bring it to you," Ruby said.

"No, it's not that bad," Shoshanna said, immediately feeling guilty.

Ruby scoffed. "You wouldn't have called me for help if it wasn't really bad. You have to be careful with your vampire boyfriend drinking your blood while you bang."

"Ruby," Shoshanna said drily. "For your information, it has nothing to do with that. He only did it once. Bit me, I mean."

"But he banged you more than once?"

"Way more than once," she said with a laugh. Then she groaned as the quick muscle contraction sent a stabbing pain between her temples. "I'm supposed to be keeping this place a secret."

"Who am I gonna tell?" Ruby asked. "Send me the address."

"Good point," she said. "Do you think you can bring it tonight?"

"I had a really important date tonight with a kinky book and a battery-operated device, but for you I can postpone."

"That's how I know you love me," she said. "You're the best."

While she waited, Shoshanna gathered her sketches and spread out in the library to analyze her work. Her vision swam as she stared at the drawings. The lines seemed to slither together, making it impossible to see where she'd gone wrong. Out of sheer stubbornness, she continued to glare at the drawings as if she could intimidate them into spilling their secrets.

By the time alarm rang to make Alistair's breakfast, she had accomplished nothing but making herself angry at her inability to figure this out. She stomped into the kitchen. The harsh LED inside the fridge made her wince, and she actually missed on her attempt to grab the blood bag. Everything was blurry and moving, as if she was staring at it through water.

It had to be magic overload. She simply wasn't accustomed to this kind of heavy work. One of the first things she'd learned in her adept training was the importance of rest and being mindful of her body and its limitations. An exhausted witch was not only ineffective, but dangerous. There was a good reason she'd told Eduardo her work here could take weeks.

She gritted her teeth and leaned in close to the fridge, getting so close that her nose nearly bumped the shelf. Guiding herself with her hands along the counter and the shelves, she managed to get out the double boiler and begin preparing Alistair's meal.

The water had just begun to boil when her phone rang. "Hey, it's me," Ruby said. "I can't come in the gate."

Shoshanna hurried to the front door and pushed the button on the keypad to open the security gate. A few minutes later, Ruby's little red car pulled up to the small porch. Her glossy black ponytail swung as she bounced up to the house. Her eyes lit up, and she came in hot for a hug. "Uh, you failed to mention that you were living in a mansion."

"It's pretty nice," she admitted, leaning into the hug. Maybe it was best friend mojo or something about Ruby's magic, but her hugs were the best around. The savory smell of fried noodles smacked into Shoshanna as Ruby followed her into the house. "Did you cook?"

"I love you but not that much," Ruby said. "Auntie K was cooking so I stopped by to get us something to eat. She says hello and to come over soon so she can find you a boyfriend." Ruby raised an eyebrow. "I didn't tell her about Hottie McFangs."

Shoshanna laughed. "Thanks."

Ruby nodded. "That was as much for me as for you. I didn't want to be there all night explaining why a pretty witch like you was shacking up with a bloodsucking undead monster," she said. "That would be her reaction, I'm assuming. Anyway, you should eat before you drink this tea or it'll make you puke." She froze as they walked into the kitchen. "Hi."

Alistair stood at the end of the stone island, his face in shadow. "Who are you?"

"Oh!" Shoshanna exclaimed. "This is my best friend, Ruby Wang." She gestured to Alistair. "This is Alistair Thorne."

Ruby gave him a stern look, which was no doubt matched as Alistair gave her an appraising look. Though she couldn't see his eyes, there was no mistaking the way his head dipped and rose again.

"I wasn't aware we expected guests," he said mildly.

"I had a bad headache," Shoshanna said. "Ruby is a top-notch green witch. The Wangs are the best in Atlanta."

"Did you tell anyone where you were going?" Alistair said.

Clearly unfazed by Alistair, she said, "Yeah, I put an ad on Facebook and invited everyone I know for a sex party. I hope that's not a problem." She rolled her eyes and set the bag on the countertop. "I'm not an idiot."

While Ruby took out plastic dishes stuffed with homemade food, Shoshanna brushed past her to get to the cabinet. Her fingers slid off the closest glass, and it toppled onto the hardwood floor. Glass shattered, and she jumped out of the way. "Shit!"

"Let me get it. You sit and eat," Ruby said.

"There's a broom in the closet around the corner," Shoshanna said, fumbling for another glass. Alistair gently pushed her out of the way and took the glass. But he set it aside, ignoring his meal.

His cool hand tipped up her chin. "What's wrong? Your heart rate is elevated, and your pupils are dilated."

She shrugged. "I started working on Lucia's curse, and it didn't go well. I just overdid it a little, that's all."

"Armina was extremely powerful. You must be careful." He squeezed her arm gently. "Can you trust this friend?"

"She's my best friend," Shoshanna said. "I trust her more than anyone I know."

He hesitated, then gently took her arm and guided her away from the glass and onto one of the barstools. A minute later, Ruby returned and swept up the broken glass. Shoshanna watched with dread turning in her stomach. She couldn't see the pieces of glass, even as she heard them scraping against the tile. It had to be this headache. In the past, she'd had ocular migraines that caused pulsing auras in her vision.

When Ruby was done, she found plates and dished out a massive pile of thin fried noodles with vegetables. It smelled heavenly. She glanced at Alistair. "You don't eat, right?"

"Correct," he said coolly.

Ruby nodded. "Good. You can find me a teapot while we eat."

Shoshanna wished she could see the expression on his face at being ordered around, but the little huff was satisfying in itself. While he got up to follow Ruby's orders, Shoshanna took a pair of chopsticks and ate a tangled knot of noodles. The burst of flavor made her swoon. Much better than the quick salads she'd been eating between work sessions. "This curse is serious," she said. "I thought I could just untangle it like a normal sigil, but it's really strong."

"Makes sense," Ruby said. "And it's old, yeah?"

Shoshanna nodded. "Is there some way I can...God, this sounds stupid. Can I power myself up somehow? I grabbed one of the threads and it just about knocked me out."

"You did what?" Alistair said sharply.

She ignored him and gestured with her chopsticks. "And there's something strange there. There's this red thread through it all. Until now, I'd never seen it." She glanced at Alistair, then closed her mouth. It wasn't her place to tell his business.

Ruby scoffed. "Maybe it's a fate thread. Auntie K said I must have gotten mine tangled on some guy's bedpost and that's why I can't find a husband." Alistair nearly spit out a mouthful of blood in a violent cough. Ruby glanced at him. "I'm not shy."

"I can tell," he said roughly.

"Wait, what? A fate thread?" Shoshanna asked.

Ruby swallowed a big mouthful of noodles, then held up her pinky finger. "Yeah. The red thread of fate. It connects you and your soulmate. It's just a folklore thing. Auntie K is full of shit."

"As far as most people are concerned, everything we do is a folklore thing," Shoshanna said. She stood up abruptly and left her plate as she dashed into the alcove. Standing in front of Lucia, she closed her eyes and used her arcane sight to look for the red thread.

The red current circulated through her essence, like arteries and veins. As Shoshanna looked closer, she noticed a brighter tangle around her hand. But when she shifted perspective to follow Lucia's gaze, she could see the red thread extending far beyond her grasp. It faded in the distance, rigid and straight like it was pulled taut.

Shoshanna hesitated, then pulled gently on the thread. It sent another powerful surge of heat up her arm, and again, she saw the anguished face of a dark-haired man. A hooked scar intersected his red eye. Bloody tears streamed down his face as he fell at her feet.

She had only a moment to catch her breath before the ground dropped from beneath her, and everything went black.

19

Foolish, stubborn, wonderful witch. Alistair saw her knees buckling and dove to catch her before her head struck the floor. Her dark curls draped over his arm as he cradled her. He rushed into her bedroom and laid her on the neatly made bed. The veins stood out on her forehead, and her right palm was singed as if she'd touched an open flame.

Ruby scurried after him, lingering at his shoulder. "You better not have bitten her too much," she said.

Fury flared to life in his chest. He was no angel, but he had shown the restraint of a saint with Shoshanna. "Exactly who do you think you are?"

"I'm her best friend and I know how to brew a poison that will put a vampire in a coma," the other witch said calmly. "From there, decapitation is easy."

"Are you threatening me?"

"I'm telling you that you'll only get an opportunity to hurt her once," Ruby said. As Alistair gently stroked Shoshanna's cheek, the little black cat emerged from under her bed and leaped into Ruby's arms. She gave him a faint smirk. "Hi, buddy."

Despite her harsh words, he found Ruby's protective streak endearing. "Is she strong enough to break a curse?"

"Maybe, but she shouldn't even be trying," Ruby said. "She's smart, but she's too stubborn. I'm not a *tisserand,* but even I know this is high-level stuff. She could seriously hurt herself."

He nodded. "That's what I'm afraid of."

"You stay here," Ruby said. While she hurried back to the kitchen, Alistair perched on the edge of the bed. He'd awoken with visions of taking her to bed and worshipping every inch of her until she wore that ridiculous, sunny smile and could speak only in soft moans and giggles. And instead, she was suffering because she was determined to break their curses.

Shoshanna jolted violently, and her eyes flew open. "Oh, shit," she muttered, frowning up at him. "Did I fall out?"

"Yes," he said. She tried to get up, but he pushed gently against her chest. "That's enough magic for today."

"But I figured something out," she said. Then she clapped her hand to her forehead and squeezed her eyes shut. Pain etched lines into her pretty face, and he was angry all over again. "Okay, you win. My head is going to explode." Ruby bustled into the room with a cup of foul-smelling tea. He held it while Shoshanna slowly sipped it. "Ugh, it's disgusting. No offense."

"None taken. It's nasty," Ruby said. "But it works. Drink at least half of it and lie down. In half an hour, you'll be as good as new." Ruby shot Alistair a pointed look, then walked out of the room. From the kitchen, he heard a box rustling, then a quiet voice. "You need to make her rest. Absolutely no biting. Play along with what I say, and I'll stall her for a few days." She returned with a box of wheat crackers and handed Shoshanna a few. "That'll cut the taste. Just don't eat too many or you'll neutralize the active ingredients."

"Thanks," Shoshanna said sheepishly. "I hate that you guys are fawning over me."

"That's what friends and vampire roommates are for," Ruby said smoothly. She glanced at Alistair, and he nodded to her. Her lips curved into a smile. "Promise me that you'll give this thing a rest for a few days."

Shoshanna shook her head emphatically. "I have to work on this," she said. "That statue is a person. She's suffering."

Alistair gently squeezed her hand. "I mean no disrespect, but Lucia has been a statue for over a century. A few days more will not matter."

"But—"

"And I'll talk to Auntie K," Ruby said. "She can probably juice you up. Hell, she probably knows someone who can break a curse. I'll talk to her and have her make some calls tomorrow."

"Okay," Shoshanna agreed. "I'll wait."

Ruby sighed. "Good. Now you need to rest. If your head still hurts tomorrow, drink another batch and then go back to bed. I left you a whole tin in the kitchen."

Shoshanna held out her arms and embraced Ruby. "Thank you."

"I love you," she said. "Don't be stupid."

Shoshanna laughed. "I'll try."

Ruby gave him another stern look and walked out of the room. He heard the rustle of her gathering her things, then the crunch of her feet on the gravel outside. "I know you can still hear me," she said quietly. "I meant what I said. She trusts you, so I'm trusting you to take care of her. But if you hurt my friend, your curse will be the best thing to ever happen to you."

He just smiled. Maybe they weren't friends, but he liked Ruby Wang very much. When the other witch was gone, he gazed down at Shoshanna. Her eyes were closed, but her pulse had slowed. He laid next to her, then carefully turned her over. With a gentle touch, he rubbed her back in slow, soft circles. She let out a happy groan and stretched like a cat. "Thanks," she murmured.

"I mean what I said," he said. "Your commitment to help Lucia is honorable, but she has been in this state for a long time. I want to help her, too, but not at your expense. And I will not let you hurt yourself to fix me. Nor would Paris or any of the others."

"Maybe it's not up to you," she said.

Now it was not anger, but fear that rolled through him. Her stubbornness might be the end of her, and she would not let him protect her. "Shoshanna," he said in a warning tone.

But she was undeterred. "Alistair, do you believe in destiny? in fate?"

"What does that have to do with anything?"

"Soulmates," she said.

He felt as if she'd punched him in the gut. "Maybe. I believe that people can love each other so intensely that they become like one. And should one of them fall, it would ruin the other. Is that what you mean?"

"Maybe," she said, frowning. He slid his hand up to her neck, gently massaging the tension out of her muscles. Her clammy skin felt feverish beneath his fingers. "Have you ever seen it?"

"Julian," he said immediately. "Not long after the Midnight War ended, he met a woman named Brigitte. She was perfect for him in every way." They had all adored her, sometimes teasing him that she had only loved him because she saw him first.

"What happened to her?"

"The curse took her from him," he said. "And he nearly died of heartbreak. Paris and I had to fight him many times to stop him from ending his own life."

And at the time, he had not understood. He had experienced heartbreak when love fizzled away. Even though he had been the one to drive Paris away, he'd still drunk himself into a stupor for months, mourning what he had lost.

But even in that darkness, he did not understand what could drive Armina to seek such wicked revenge. Lovers left. They died or fell out of love or betrayed, and the world went on its grim march even so.

Even when he watched Julian wailing over Brigitte's body that first time, screaming at the heavens, he had not understood. Grief made sense, but this was madness. He and Paris had once fought him so hard that Paris lost an eye, Alistair took three stakes to his half-shattered ribcage, and Julian ended up chained in the bowels of a French castle with half his limbs broken because it was the only way they could keep him from immolating himself. How could someone as strong and wise as Julian be so destroyed by loss?

It was incomprehensible then, but no longer. Watching his beautiful witch with pain all over her face, he started to understand. If someone laid a finger on her, he would become a beast of pure fury and madness. Just the thought that she would endanger herself made him furious, and it was only his concern for her that kept him from shouting at her. How could she be so careless with herself, when she was so uniquely precious?

Yes, he could understand that madness very well now.

He combed the hair away from her neck then leaned over to kiss her shoulder. "Can we talk of more pleasant things?"

She nodded. "My head feels a lot better already," she said. She rolled over and stroked his arm gently. "Did you eat?"

"I will when you rest," he said. "And when you speak to her again, please reassure your friend that I will not hurt you by feeding on you."

"She's a lot. I'm sorry."

"Don't apologize," he said. "We should all be so lucky to have such protective loved ones." He gently placed his hand on her stomach. Her pulse was steady beneath his fingertips. "Did you work all day?"

"Yeah," she said.

"Then no more working," he said.

"But I wanted to translate," she complained.

"No," he said firmly. He slid his hand further up, cupping her breast. Her back arched slightly as a faint smile curved her lips. He was learning his own magic with her as his medium. "Shall I tire you out in other ways?"

"Will you read for me after I go to sleep?"

He walked his fingers over her chest, relishing the way her body reacted to his touch. "I will read and translate if you go to sleep and do not attempt to break the curse for at least a week."

"Two days."

"Stubborn girl. Five. "

"Four," she said. "Final offer."

He sighed. "Deal."

As if he'd flipped a switch, she grinned and grabbed a thin strip of black fabric from her nightstand. With a wicked smile, she pulled the mask over her eyes. He straddled her and peeled her shirt off quickly. "Did you get that for me?" he asked.

"Maybe," she said. Her hands slid under his loose shirt. He froze as her warm hands covered his scarred, leathery skin. It made his skin crawl with dread, even as her touch awakened a desperate need in him. "Is it okay for me to touch?"

"It is not pleasant to the touch," he said, peeling his hooded shirt off.

"But I like the way you feel. It's you, so I like it," she said. He loved the words, but he could not accept them. He gently held her wrists and pinned them to her sides. She let out a throaty laugh. "And that's an option, too."

He chuckled in response and lowered his head to kiss her. Her legs parted for him, making a place for him to nestle into her. Her hands strained slightly as she pressed her hips up to him. "Be patient, little witch," he growled against her lips. "I am in no hurry." He kissed the palms of her hands gently. "Now you must be patient. No touching."

"Alistair," she complained.

He released her, waiting to see what she would do. When she left her hands where he'd placed them, he grinned to himself and slid down her body. If only she would be so compliant when it came to keeping herself safe.

With a feather light touch, he traced her collarbones, trailing to the hollow of her throat. Her rich brown skin danced beneath his fingertips, tiny muscles twitching and goosebumps rising. He gently kissed her belly, slowly working down to her thigh.

His cock strained at his trousers, but he ignored it. This was not for him to plunge into her warmth, no matter how sweet and decadent it was. This was an act of gratitude and devotion. He could sense the way her body warmed, the perfume of desire as that strange alchemy turned her blood to the sweetest wine. That smell was loud and clear, and he had not imagined that he would ever see such a thing again.

"You're just keeping me here so I don't work," she said.

"Obviously," he growled. She laughed, and he made his way down the inner curve of her thigh. "It's working, isn't it?"

"Yes," she said. "Obviously."

"And just how disciplined can you be?" he asked, making his way back up her thigh, to that warm perfection between her legs. Watching her shiver with desire made him smile.

"What do you mean?" she asked.

"You're going to let me do whatever I like," he said matter-of-factly. "And you may not touch or hurry me."

"That's very bossy of you," she said. "But I accept."

"Good." And with that, he kept his promise to take excellent care of Shoshanna York.

NEARLY AN HOUR LATER, Shoshanna was asleep with a blissful smile on her face. Alistair took it upon himself to scoop out the foul-smelling dry chunks for her pacing tomcat, then trudged to visit Lucia.

Slowly circling the statue, he said, "I'm sorry for the delay. You know that I cared for you, too. I hope that you'll understand why I can't let Shoshanna risk herself for you. If the cost was mine to pay, I would do it gladly. But not her."

Guilt gripped him. Lucia had suffered for Kova, just as Shoshanna was ready to suffer for...for him. He knew that she cared for Lucia, but he was no fool. She wanted to break his curse, too. Did she want to break the curse so badly because she needed to prove herself? Or was it to make him into something that she could bear to love? The question filled him with a squirming sensation of doubt.

He shook himself and gently kissed Lucia's outstretched fingers. "I'll play for you this evening while she sleeps."

After gulping down the lukewarm remains of his breakfast, he returned to the piano to play quietly. He played a Liszt etude from memory, letting his mind drift away on the intricate melodies and cascading flurries of notes.

His playing was interrupted by a phone call from Paris. He answered gruffly. "Hello?"

"Allie, I do hope I'm not interrupting," he said. "If I were you, I'd have my face between Shoshanna's thighs as often as possible."

"You know me well," Alistair said. "I just put her to sleep."

Paris laughed. "I'm proud of you. You were always good with your mouth." He sighed. "I'm afraid I didn't call for tales of your amorous exploits, though I'm certainly pleased that you're both enjoying the carnal rewards of this little arrangement. Just a while ago, I met with a representative from the Casteron. I told them that Shoshanna York was ours, but they refused to acknowledge it without a blood bond to Eduardo."

He was silent. "Then what does that mean?"

"That means that she's fair game as far as they're concerned," he said. "They will take no action against Elliott McAvoy until Shoshanna is bonded to us."

"Which she has repeatedly refused," Alistair said quietly. "Stubborn witch."

"That fiery personality will be the end of her," Paris said.

You have no idea. "And what are we doing about Elliott?"

"That's just it," Paris said. "If Shoshanna was ours, then I would be the first to remove his testicles for laying a hand on her. But she's neutral. And as far as vampire law is concerned, she is not our territory. Therefore, our hands are tied. And Eduardo was very clear about rogue action."

"Then I must convince her to swear loyalty to us," he said.

"Keep her in bed for a few more nights, and she'll be addicted to you," Paris said.

He chuckled. "I don't think I'm quite that charming."

"You underestimate yourself, Mister Thorne," Paris said. "Has she had any luck with the curse?"

"She's making progress," Alistair said. "But I fear that her efforts are going to kill her. And I would carry the curse forever to protect her."

"*Oui,*" Paris agreed. "I will not let her hurt herself for me, and no offense, but not for you either."

"Agreed," he said. "It may be a futile hope."

"We have lived with it this long. We will survive."

After his conversation with Paris, he returned to playing the piano. Soon, he heard a low moan and a yawn, then the soft shuffle of Shoshanna's feet. Her floral scent, mixed with the rich, warm scent of her desire, drifted into the room just ahead of her. It was the sweetest perfume he'd ever smelled. She sat on the bench next to him and rested her head on his shoulder.

Sex with Shoshanna was incredible. But he liked these quiet moments almost as much. She was comfortable with him, something he had never imagined possible. Given the run of this huge house, she wanted to be in this tiny real estate next to him. Until she had come along, he hadn't realized just how much he missed simple closeness.

"Did I wake you?" he asked, leaning his head against hers.

"Sort of, but I wanted to play with you," she said.

He squeezed her thigh gently, then reached across her to change the music to one of their duets. As he arranged the pages, he hesitated. "Paris called. He spoke with a representative of the Casteron."

Her brow lifted. "And?"

"And they still consider you fair game," he said reluctantly. "Until you are bloodbound to the Auberon, they consider you neutral territory."

She sighed. "I'm not territory or property. I'm a person."

"I understand," he said. "And as long as you are under my roof, an act of violence against you is an act against the court."

"But if I want my normal life back, then I'm a sitting duck," she said, shaking her head. "This is so unfair." Her breath hitched. "I had to quit my job at the coffee shop. Elliott was showing up there."

Anger roared through him. "Did he hurt anyone?"

"I don't think so," she said. "So when this is done, I'm back to square one."

"Why?" he asked. Her head cocked. "Why do you have to start over? I have more money than you could earn in a lifetime, and Eduardo has made you a generous offer to do exactly the kind of work you're already doing."

"I don't want to be owned," she retorted.

The vehement response felt like a punch to the gut. It was a reminder that this was only temporary, and soon her light would be gone. He wanted to recoil and hide again, but he felt such a powerful pull that he couldn't. Even if she refused him, she deserved comfort and safety. "You would not be owned," he said. "The Court is a family. Protection, shelter, fellowship."

"And obligation, debt, and servitude."

"Will you go through your whole life refusing to commit to anything?" he asked. "Will you stubbornly fight alone just on principle?"

"I have so far," she snapped.

He shook his head. "Shoshanna, when you were afraid, you called Dominic for help. When you thought I was in trouble, you called Paris. You already seek the support of the Court when it suits you."

She slid away from him slightly. Only a hand's breadth separated them, but it felt like miles. "Can we just play?"

"Certainly," he said quietly. He flipped the page to an arrangement of the waltz from Tchaikovsksy's *Sleeping Beauty*. "Would you like to be on top?"

Her lips quirked into a smile, and it warmed his heart to see that the crude innuendo would still please her. "Slowly," she said, scanning the page. He was genuinely impressed with her musical skill. Though she had not taken lessons in a few years, she had a natural sense of musicality. They played slowly through the first few pages.

She struck a discordant note and swore. "Sorry," she said. She squinted and leaned in to look at the page. After tinkling through the passage she'd missed, she shook her head. "One more time."

They played it again, and she missed another series of notes. He glanced over and caught her scrubbing at her eyes. "Are you all right?"

"I think my eyes are just strained from staring at my drawings for so long," she said.

"Hmm," he said. He closed the sheet music and started a playlist of quiet piano music on his phone. Then he grasped her hand and pulled her to her feet to dance. "Then I shall entertain you."

She smiled and joined him, leaning her head against his

chest. The lovely warmth soothed his nerves, washing away the tension between them. "I suppose this will do."

"You suppose?" he said wryly.

Her laugh rumbled into his chest. "I suppose. I just want you to know that I'm thinking very dirty thoughts about you."

His cock twitched. "Are you now? Then perhaps you should tell me a few of them. I assure you, I am all ears."

20

As Shoshanna made her first cup of coffee at two in the afternoon, she realized that Alistair Thorne was a virtuoso at more than the piano. Last night, he'd taken her to bed, worn her out, then rubbed her back until she fell asleep. It wasn't until she woke to a beam of sunlight across her bed that she realized she'd fallen asleep without telling him good night.

Despite their growing affection, she was always a little wistful to awaken in the morning with no one else there. Or at least, no one that didn't have four paws and fish breath. Alistair could not join her here because of the morning sun, and he would not let her sleep with him downstairs. But being held at a distance still stung, even if she knew it wasn't about her. No matter what he thought, she could handle his appearance.

His fear only motivated her further to break the curse. That would set him free, just like it would set Lucia free.

And that was why she was going to keep the caffeine flowing for as long as it took. The bright sunlight was making her blurry vision even worse. The tiny fill lines on the coffee pot were nearly impossible to see. Putting her face close to the glass carafe, she pressed one finger to mark the spot and filled it with water.

She'd managed to convince herself that her poor vision was strain from overusing her magic. Maybe it was connected to the monster headache she'd had yesterday. But it hadn't gotten better; in fact, it had only gotten worse since last night. She wondered if this was revenge for trying to free Lucia. When she tugged on that red thread, had Armina felt it and dished back a dose of magic?

That was insane. And yet, this witch had managed to curse half a dozen powerful vampires with curses that had lasted over two centuries. Who knew what she could do?

For the first time since she'd arrived at the mansion, Shoshanna considered calling Vivienne, her mentor from the Grand Guild. But if Vivienne knew what she was tinkering with, she'd be furious. It would be one thing to approach the Grand Guild with proof that she'd untangled a complex curse. It would be quite another to come to them helpless and suffering the consequences of dealing with forbidden magic.

Instead, she decided to get back to work. Once she freed Lucia, she could untangle the issue of her eyesight. People dealt with bad vision all the time. When she ordered her next grocery delivery, she'd add a pair of reading glasses to get her by.

Armed with a fresh cup of coffee, she headed to the library to read. Alistair had kept his promise last night by translating for her. Bright blue sticky notes burst from the pages. His handwriting was beautiful, a flowing script with precise loops and swirls. Atop the stack of books was a note:

Please don't overwork yourself. I'll read whatever you need this evening.

Yours-

A

"Mine," she murmured. She smiled as she pictured him writing the word *yours* in that lovely, precise script. It had probably been a mere formality, but it felt weighty and significant to her.

Last night, she'd seriously contemplated what it would mean to be with Alistair. He'd let slip that hard mask when he had offered to care for her. It should have been thrilling; a wealthy vampire with a big library and a taste for witches was practically a dream come true. And though she'd rejected the offer instinctively, she was more frightened at how much she liked the idea.

She liked the idea of taking what Alistair offered, of spending her days working on advanced magic while he did whatever rich vampires did to entertain themselves. She liked the idea of greeting him with dinner, whether it was in a glass or from her throat. And she loved the idea of dancing with him in the moonlight, of being held tight and adored forever.

It was beautiful and terrifying, and she was afraid to take a step in either direction for fear of falling.

She tried to put it out of her head. At the moment, she had more pressing matters, like helping Lucia. Upon opening the first of the witch journals, she found that Alistair had marked dozens of pages, writing a short summary of what he found in each passage. Several referred to red stones or red flowers being used as a reagent to create passion or anger in a target. Several more spoke of threads, but that was like reading about cells in a biology book. Virtually everything *tisserande* did involved threads of magic.

In a book that looked like Russian, one particular note caught her attention.

I'm not certain of the translation here, but the phrase seems to refer to the wives' thread. It talks about a binding that cannot be broken except through death.

The wives' thread. And Ruby spoke of the red thread of fate connecting soulmates. Shoshanna had always thought of soulmates as fairy tale nonsense that sounded better on paper than in reality. But she couldn't deny that there was something unique in Lucia's aura, something that she now saw in Alistair. Those were facts, not folklore.

But if soulmates were real, wouldn't there be more talk of it? She hesitated, then called Maya, one of her classmates from her last summer course. They'd shared a cottage and grown to be friendly, if not exactly friends. The older woman answered after two rings. "Hello?"

"Hi Maya, it's Shoshanna York. From the summer intensive," she said. "Sorry to bother you, but I had a craft question."

"Oh, lovely," she said in her sweet, smoky voice. There was a clatter in the background. "I was just helping my daughter bake cupcakes. Can I call you back?"

She bit her lip. "It'll just take a moment, if you don't mind.

Have you ever come across anything about soulmates? Or a lovers' thread?"

"Not exactly soulmates," Maya said. "But I remember reading a book that talked about how powerful bonds can be between family and lovers. I wish I knew more. Maybe Vivienne would know."

"I'll try her," Shoshanna lied. "Thank you."

She rustled through the textbooks she'd brought, but they were mostly useless. As a *tisserand,* her focus was primarily on inanimate objects. She put spells on doorways and buildings, or on small objects that would be worn on one's person. She didn't toy with the threads of someone's essence.

It took hours of skimming through the books, but she finally struck gold—or red, rather—in one of the French journals Paris had brought. She searched for the word *rouge*, finally finding what looked like a set of lecture notes, based on the date and neatly listed bullet points. Some of the grammar was unfamiliar, but she managed to get a rough idea of the translation.

Strong bonds appear within one's aura as brighter and thicker threads. These threads can be manipulated by a skilled Night Weaver, empowering the work and anchoring powerful spells. Of note are bonds between a mother and daughter, a father and son, twin siblings, and lovers. Perhaps most significant, though rarely seen, is the red thread that binds lovers. If any of these soul threads are altered or broken, the energy released is incredibly potent and destructive.

Shoshanna sat back and took a deep breath. She even

grabbed her phone to check the translation of *âme*. It immediately popped up: *soul.*

That only seemed to confirm what she'd learned. A "red thread that binds lovers" had to be the mark of a soulmate. Her best guess was that Armina had used the power of the soulmate bond to strengthen her curse.

So did this mean that she had to break the thread to break the curse? That seemed impossible, even if she would want to. Why would she want to break Lucia's bond to her soulmate?

She flipped through the book, but the rest was filled with meticulously drawn diagrams and lists of reagents. Her stomach turned when she found that the last quarter of the journal was blank except for splatters of blood across one half-filled page. A chill prickled down her spine at the thought of Paris striking down its owner with a smile on his face.

With a sigh, she set the book aside to take a break. She took a walk around the house, took some aspirin for her headache, and refilled her coffee. When she returned, she turned her focus to grounding agents and building a better protective sigil. The backlash when she messed with Lucia had likely been because she was holding the thread, like slicing into a live wire with metal shears. Her grounding sigil had been a good start, but she needed something that would absorb as soon as she touched it, not only when she broke the curse.

For the next few hours, she skimmed her books and drew a new diagram. Still, as she went through the steps, she couldn't shake the thought of that red thread. This was not just any spell. She had to understand what to do about that thread before she could break Lucia's curse.

She was still working when she heard the soft shuffle of Alistair's feet. She jumped up. "I'm sorry, I didn't make your breakfast yet."

He chuckled. "I cared for myself for many years before you arrived. While I appreciate the concern, I can manage."

She bumped into the table and cursed. "I know, but considering I'm living rent free..."

"Your company is payment enough," he said. He brought his other hand from behind the door frame to show the full glass of blood. "You're not working too much, are you?" He tilted up her chin. "Come take a break."

"I think I've found something," she said.

"Then come sit and tell me about it," he said, taking her hand gently.

She pulled her hand back. "You're being distracting."

"That was my intent," he said. "But I truly do want to hear what you've learned." He took her hand and pulled lightly, guiding her out to the living room. A break did sound nice.

"Your notes were helpful," she said. As she told him what she'd found, she wished she could see his face. "I think soulmates are a real thing, Alistair."

He was silent for a while. "People who are in love? Of course."

"No. It's not just a poetic thing," she said. "Something you can see and measure, almost."

He tilted his head and sat at the piano, picking up the Tchaikovsky waltz they'd played yesterday. His deft hands danced over the keys. He improvised, combining the two parts to make a single, solo part.

"Show off," she said.

"I have much to show off," he said.

As he played the haunting, familiar tune, she focused intently on him. The impact on her vision hadn't altered her magical sight, and she could see the threads of magic surrounding him as clearly as ever. The fragment of red had grown, like a seedling taking root. Tendrils of bright, pulsing red radiated from a small core. When opened her eyes, letting her mundane sight and arcane sight overlap, she could see the flicker of red at the base of his hand. A thin thread extended from him and across the open space.

While he continued to play, she raised her left hand. A pulsing core of red wrapped around her little finger like a ring with a fat ruby setting. Her heart thumped against her ribs. She got up, slowly moving toward him. A wispy tendril of red extended toward Alistair, and when she was within arms' length, they met, intertwining.

A warm, satisfied sensation washed over her. She could feel a distinct tug at her wrist, as if he was touching her. "Oh God," she murmured.

"What's wrong?" he asked.

"Nothing," she blurted.

Thanks to melodramatic TV shows, she'd had plenty of expectations from pop culture for losing her virginity. In magazines, there were guides on "What to Expect When You're Expecting" and "Top Ten Signs Your Man is Cheating." But nothing in her twenty-nine years had prepared her to discover in the space of a single day that there was a very real, perceptible proof of the existence of soulmates, and that hers was a cursed vampire.

Soulmates.

What would he think? Would he want her to be his forever? Did she want him to be hers forever? Was this some cruel trick of fate? Her mind was spinning, and he was still staring up at her, or at least she assumed he was because his damned face was still covered.

"Shoshanna?"

She pressed her hands to his shoulders, resting her chin atop his head. "Keep playing. It helps me think." He hesitated, then continued to play. She hummed along to the melody.

"What's that you're singing?" he asked, without missing a note. His head tilted to brush against her hand. "Your voice is lovely."

"It's from the movie," she said. "You know, Sleeping Beauty. They dance in the woods after he kisses her to break the spell, and..." She froze as the idea hit her like a slap in the face. "Did Lucia meet Kova before or after he was cursed?"

"After," he said.

"And Julian and Brigitte?"

"After," he said. "Why?"

She plopped onto the couch, turning her gaze inward. They'd spent many hours in training learning their own auras, tracing the unique patterns of their own essence. It felt like staring at her face to put on makeup, with every crevice and pore familiar. When she examined the knot of red around her hand, it was surrounded in a tangled web of bluish-purple, like the one that covered Lucia.

She was cursed. And it was connected to the red thread.

If this was what she suspected, then the curse was only going to worsen. Would she go blind entirely? Perhaps turn to stone like Lucia? Maybe Lucia had started to lose her sight, too. She jumped up from the couch and knocked something over in her hurry. The piano stopped suddenly. "Shoshanna, are you all right?"

"I have to get back to work," she blurted. She bumped into a table as she stumbled across the living room. Using the walls to guide her, she hurried back to Lucia's alcove, to the growing fortress of books and papers.

Alistair was already there before she could sit down. "What's going on with you?"

"I'm fine," she insisted.

"You must rest, Shoshanna," he said, slipping one hand to her hip.

She gently pushed it away. "I can't now. I have to finish this."

"I told you before that Lucia can wait," he said. "And I can wait. You're exhausted. I can see it on your face."

She mustered a weak laugh. "Mister Thorne, didn't you know you should never tell a girl she looks tired?"

"Come sit with me a while," he said. He gently tugged at her hand. "I can think of things that need your attention."

Irritation sparked through her and spread through her frazzled mind like a brushfire. She knew exactly how he planned to distract her, and while her body thrilled at the thought of it, it was almost insulting. Apparently he thought she was so simple-minded that she would put orgasms above everything else. She pulled away from him. “This is important.”

“As is your health.”

She gave him an arch look, imitating his dry delivery. “While I appreciate your concern, I have taken care of myself for quite a while.”

He let out a growl of frustration. “Then what will make this go faster?”

“You not arguing with me every step of the way,” she replied, plopping down amidst her papers. She squinted at one of the diagrams, then closed her eyes to visualize a modified version. She’d always been good at geometry, at turning shapes back and forth in her mind. Now that she knew the red thread was bound into the curse but not part of it, that changed things. The journal had mentioned that soul threads released a large amount of energy. Perhaps she could somehow channel that power and turn it outward to shatter the curse. “Will you write for me?”

“I suppose,” he said, though he sounded annoyed at being put on secretarial duty.

“I need two large amethysts. A good batch of graveyard dirt. Iron shavings,” she said, continuing with a long list of reagents. She winced. The edges of her vision shimmered through a dark halo. “Did you know Lucia when this happened to her?”

“I did,” he said. “We were all in Vienna then, enjoying the peace that came with the end of our war with the Shieldsmen.”

She was careful in her words. “How long did it take her to turn into stone like this?”

“I’m not certain. Kova told us that she was ill perhaps a

week before it happened. I saw her a few days before, and she was bedridden. She had difficulty breathing, as if..." he hesitated. "As if she had begun to change from the inside."

Shoshanna took a deep breath. Surely the tightness in her chest was paranoia. "Were there any other symptoms? Body temperature, aches, maybe her vision?"

He tilted his head. "Why?"

"I just want to know as much as I can," she lied. "Every detail helps."

"I don't know the specifics," he said. "Kova only told us that she had become ill. We tried giving her vampire blood, but it did not cure her. We brought in doctors, even a blood witch from the Court of Thanatos, and no one could help. The blood witch knew she was cursed, but could not break it." He suddenly gripped her chin. "Shoshanna, are you ill?"

"No," she said. She tried to pull away, but he held her firmly. "I'm just wondering."

"Your heart is pounding, and your eyes just flicked away from me. You're lying." He released her and shook his head. "I would rather you tell me something unpleasant than lie to me. Why are you asking me all these questions?"

She took a deep breath, gazing at him through her blurry, shimmering vision. "Because I think whatever happened to Lucia is happening to me."

Her words were a splintered stake through his heart. "What are you saying?"

Staring down at her, he could see the change to her eyes. A cloudy sheen covered the whites and closed in around the rich, oak brown of her irises. She looked down, then reached for his ungloved left hand. He resisted the urge to pull away. Her touch was a warm flame that prickled up his arm, making him feel welcome and safe despite his self-loathing and revulsion at the sight of his hands. She hooked her pinky around his. "I can't believe I'm about to say this, but we're soulmates."

He stiffened. "That's not possible."

"I can see it. The same red thread that runs through Lucia is running between you and me. It wasn't here before I met you, and now it is," she said. She put her hand to his chest. A flood of warmth swept over him. He felt a distinct pull from his finger, straight to the base of his spine. "Do you feel it?"

Soulmate.

It was impossible, but he knew it was true as sure as he knew his own name. The thought filled him with hope and terror at the same time. How could he, inadequate fool that he was, be entrusted with such a treasure? "I certainly care for you, Shoshanna, but how is this possible?"

Her head tilted, a flicker of hurt in her eyes. "I don't know. It just is. And it's connected to the curse on me."

The warmth of her touch turned to icy cold in the pit of his stomach. "Curse on you? What do you mean?"

She nodded grimly. "I don't fully understand how, but I've been cursed sometime in the last week or two," she said. "I think what happened to Lucia after she met Kova is happening to me."

Confusion and shame swept over him. He couldn't help staring at Lucia, frozen in her eternal silent sorrow. The thought of Shoshanna's skin turning gray and cold was enough to make him despair. He had done this to her. If he had kept his distance and resisted his base urges, she would be safe. "Then you must stop this before it gets any worse. We will get you help."

"From who? The witch who placed the curse?" she said with a sad smile. "I don't think she's inclined to help either of us. You said yourself that you've been trying for a century to fix it and no one has been able to."

He shook his head. "But how could she possibly know about you? Unless you've kept something from me, you haven't left this house except for the party at Infinity. And we were never together there. Did you leave without telling me?"

"No," she said. "My best guess is that she's still connected to the curses somehow, so maybe she felt it when I was messing with Lucia. But honestly, how she did it isn't really important right now. My vision has been getting worse and worse every day."

"Why didn't you tell me?" he said sharply. She pulled her hand away, and he regretted his sharp tone.

"I thought it was just strain from working so much," she said. "Until I read those journals, I didn't put it all together."

He gripped her wrists. "Then you must stop. Lucia can wait."

Her springy curls bobbed as she shook her head. "That's just it. I think it's going to get worse and worse. If I don't figure out how to save Lucia, then I'm going to be right here with her," she said quietly. Though her face was set with grim resolve, her accelerating heartbeat betrayed her fear. "I have to finish before it's too late."

A wave of despair washed over him. "I won't allow it. I will not see you here next to her." He tore away. "I have ruined you, Shoshanna. I'm so sorry."

Her brow furrowed. "Alistair, this is not about you and your self-loathing right now. I need to finish this work. And I need you to help."

He shook his head and gently extricated his hand from hers. "I will not hasten your demise, Shoshanna," he said sharply. "I forbid you to work on this further."

Her eyes widened. "You forbid me?"

He drew himself up to his full height. While he lacked Julian's towering stature, he still dwarfed Shoshanna. "This is my house, and—"

"And I am a grown-ass woman," she said, raising her voice. "And while destiny may have some plans for us, it sure as hell didn't grant you authority over me. Don't think for a second that you get to make decisions for me because of this little red thread." Her eyes gleamed as she grabbed his hands and held them tight. "Please help me. I don't know how long I have before I...before I can't."

He felt wrenched in two, utterly helpless. He was helpless when Julian was ripped apart by anguish after Brigitte died in front of him, again and again. He was helpless to watch Paris in the throes of his curse, enmeshed in his inescapable night-mares. And now, he would know the unique torment that Kova felt, the same pain that drove him to destroy himself rather than suffer any longer. He would not have Julian's strength to survive for two centuries with his mate torn away.

He wanted to turn back the clock and keep her at arm's length, to have never laid his touch upon her. Perhaps she would have been spared such an ugly fate. It was beyond cruel to discover that destiny itself had brought them together only for him to see her snatched away because of the sins of his past.

But her resolve in the face of fear shamed him. Wallowing in his misery in a luxurious little cage was a coward's way. If this fragile human would fight to the end, then what excuse did he have? And if destiny itself had bound them together, then surely he bore the sacred duty of standing by her side.

"What must I do to help?"

Her gaze softened. "Thank you." She folded her arms around him and rested her head against his silent heart. Even with the divine warmth of her body and her sweet scent, he already felt the specter of grief looming over them. He could see Shoshanna standing here in this lonely alcove, eyes turned up to him as if to ask *Why did you let this happen to me?*

When she tried to pull away, he held her tighter. If he could have stopped this through sheer willpower, it would already be done. A small chuckle vibrated against his chest. "We have to work."

He reluctantly released her. "Tell me what I should do."

For the next few hours, they worked on Shoshanna's spellcrafting. Rather, she gave orders, and he carefully sorted through her ingredients and weighed them on a small digital scale. He obediently followed her directions, but he was plagued with worry as he watched her fumble around the small bags and bottles several times. It was such a stark contrast to the graceful and precise dance of her fingers across piano keys.

After an escalating series of yawns, he finally set a tiny bundle of herbs aside. "You should rest."

To his surprise, she nodded her agreement. He helped her up and guided her back to her bedroom, trying not to think about the implications of her growing dependence on him. He waited as she washed up, scrubbing her face clean and leaving a pleasant flush on her full cheeks. She perched on the edge of her bed, holding her arms out. "Will you lay with me until I go to sleep?"

"You didn't even have to ask," he said. Still, he was pleased that she did. Every little expression of desire bolstered him. He lay down and wrapped his arms around her. "Promise you'll rest and not keep working when you wake."

"Hmm," she said.

"Shoshanna," he said.

"Just lie with me," she said quietly. "Thank you for helping me tonight." Her hands slid to his, holding his left hand tightly. He could feel the tug of that thread again, and a strange tension around his pinky finger, as if he wore a tight ring.

"Of course," he murmured. "I will do whatever I must to keep you safe."

There was a thump, then a puzzled *mrow?* as the little black cat padded down the length of the bed. It tilted its head, then carefully climbed onto Alistair's leg and walked up to lie atop his ribs. The cat's tail flicked in his face. "Your cat objects to my presence, it seems."

"It's fine, little man," Shoshanna said with a laugh. "You're going to have to get used to him."

A smile crossed his lips. "Will he?"

"Indeed," she said. "Unless you object to being in bed with me."

"And here I thought you were clever," he said.

She chuckled and said, "Besides, he's purring. That means he likes you. I know I do."

"And I you," he said. He swept back his hood and kissed the back of her neck. "When I sleep, I will dream of you."

"Naked?"

"I was trying to be romantic, and you're so crass," he teased.

She laughed. "I apologize."

"But now that you've said so, I'm sure nudity will be involved at some point," he said. She laughed again, a full-bodied sound that broke through his gloom for a moment. "What does it mean for us? That we are soulmates. I thought it was a poetic notion, not a concrete reality."

"I don't know," she said. "Maybe when this is done, I'll be able to study it more. With you." She wriggled her hips back against him, stoking a low flame. "I wonder if I...if I feel the way I do for you because of the bond, or if the bond began because of my feelings for you. Did it happen because we are in this situation, or did fate bring me to your door? Which came first?"

"The questions of a wise philosopher," he said solemnly. He stroked her arm, then reluctantly pulled away. She gave him a quizzical look, but he began to rub her shoulders, squeezing out the knots of tension. A smile spread on her lips as she shifted to lie on her belly, resting her head on her folded arms. "Go to sleep. I'll be here until you're in the land of Nod, as they say."

She sighed happily and said, "Alistair?"

"Yes?"

"I'm sorry I snapped at you earlier," she said. "I know you only want to protect me."

"It's all right," he said.

"I just don't want to go to sleep with that hanging between us," she said.

"Consider the air cleared," he said. "You can sleep easy, sweet little witch."

As her eyes closed again, words of power tried to crawl from the safe silence of his mouth. He fought to keep them there, where they could do no harm. Even with her revelation, he feared that the mystical thread would dissolve if he was clumsy.

I love you. I would do anything for you.

And in his silence, she fell asleep. Her breathing slowed, and the tension flowed out of her as he rubbed her shoulders. When she was deeply asleep, he slowly stroked her back, occasionally toying with one of those silky curls. As fierce and intelligent as she was, she was so vulnerable and fragile.

He waited as late as possible to leave. His phone tweeted an alarm from across the house, but he ignored it, slowly extricating himself and pulling the blanket up to her shoulders. He laid a feather-light kiss on her cheek and murmured, "Good night, my love."

What would he do if he woke to find her encased in stone like Lucia? He had to talk her out of this. She was so determined to fix every damned thing that she would doom herself. He would gladly live with his curse for all eternity if it meant she stayed safe.

"I will do whatever I must," he said again quietly.

With the words lingering on his tongue, he hurried downstairs to sleep. The sun's approach had him feeling achy and lethargic. He drew the curtains around his bed, plunging himself into deep darkness. "I love you," he murmured, hoping the words would find their way into her dreams.

THOUGH HE HAD HOPED for pleasant dreams of Shoshanna, he was plagued with nightmares. She cursed his name as her beautiful brown skin turned to gray stone. Diamond tears glittered on her stone cheeks as she silently pleaded, her final cries echoing in his ears for eternity.

When he woke, he shot out of bed and listened for Shoshanna. The house was quiet, but his hackles were raised when he caught the scent of blood and smoke. He hurtled up the stairs and found it quiet and undisturbed.

Shoshanna lay on the couch in the living room, her bare feet propped up and a damp washcloth on her brow. There was blood on her shirt, and he caught the scent of the pungent tea Ruby had brought days earlier.

Anger prickled through him as he stormed to Lucia's alcove, where the smell of smoke was stronger. The neat containers he'd weighed and labeled were empty. White chalk lines surrounded the rippling stone hem of Lucia's dress. The intricate design seemed to match what he'd seen Shoshanna drawing over the last few days. At various points in the diagram were piles of ash, some colored and some pitch black. And there was blood on the floor, with tiny droplets that trailed toward Shoshanna's room.

He shook his head. This had to stop, or she would burst her own brain before the curse took hold. Moving quietly, he rolled up the drawings, then carefully placed all her reagents and tools back in their box. Fueled by desperation and a bit of anger, he managed to clean the whole mess up in fifteen minutes and hide it downstairs in his armory.

When he was ready, he strode into the living room and knelt next to her. He gently touched her brow, fearful that she would not wake. But her eyes fluttered open. "Hi there," she murmured.

"Hello," he said coolly. "Shoshanna, I told you not to keep working on this."

She sighed and sat up. Pain creased her eyes, but she glared at him. The gentle waking was over, just like that. "And I told you that you are not an authority over me." She pushed past him and stormed into Lucia's alcove, then froze. "Where are my things?"

"I got rid of them," he said.

Her jaw dropped as she whirled to glare at him. Her brown eyes were a pale café au lait color thanks to the curse. He would be surprised if she could see more than a black shadow where he stood. "You did what?"

"If you will not listen to reason, then I will make you," he said.

"I know what I'm doing," she said. "Give me back my things."

"No," he said calmly.

"Alistair!" she protested. Then she brushed past him, headed for the hall that led down to his bedroom. "Did you hide it down there?" Pain stabbed through his chest as he watched her veer to the side and bump into the wall.

"I'm not going to tell you," he said. "I will not stand by while you kill yourself for this."

"And I told you yesterday that I have to," she said. "Would you rather stand by while I turn to stone?"

"Call your witch friends," he said. "Ask for help."

"They can't help. Ruby said Auntie K is working on something. Even if she can help, it'll be too late," she said. "I just need to finish. I broke Lucia's curse, and I know how to do it for you and me now."

"What are you talking about? Because I can actually see, and Lucia is still the same cold stone she has been for a century," he snapped.

Her face fell. "Maybe it takes a while. I know it worked."

"No, it didn't," he said sharply. "Who are you to think that you could outsmart someone like Armina? Do you think you are the only clever witch to try such a thing? Many have tried and failed."

"Why are you being this way?" she said. The anguish on her face broke something open in him. It was the look that Paris had given him when Alistair rejected him.

"Because you didn't have to suffer this!" he roared. "I warned you. I should have never touched you. And now you are ruined. And because you will not listen to reason, you will force me to watch you die or turn to stone."

"Only you could take this and make it about yourself," she said, her voice cracking. "You've known me for less than a month, but you think you know better than me what I'm capable of, and it's so damned small. Meanwhile you can't even show me your face. You are a coward, Alistair, but I am not."

She could have staked him in the heart and hurt him less.

The pain was made worse by the realization that she was right. "Shoshanna," he said quietly.

"You're not going to talk me down," she said. "I am so much more than you believe I am. I am capable of breaking this curse. And I am capable of loving you just as you are, even if you are incapable of believing in me. Now where the hell are my things?"

He was silent, struck dumb by her harsh rebuke.

"Fine," she said, returning toward her room. Using her hands to find the walls, she crept down the hall. "I've spent so much time on it, I can still see it in my mind. You're not going to stop me."

"Like hell I'm not," he said. "If I have to lock you up, I will." She ducked into her room and slammed the door, but he pounded his fist against it. "Shoshanna, don't make me do this." He didn't know what he was going to do, but he sure as hell wasn't letting her do another spell that would probably kill her.

A burst of heat surged from the door, and he cringed away, shielding his eyes as a bright sigil flared yellow-white in the center of the doorway. Sunlight. His clothing protected him, but it was blinding.

She opened the door, but the sigil still hovered in the air, casting a warm glow on her face. "I'm sorry," she said, tears flowing freely.

"I can't lose you," he said. "You have to stop this."

"You're going to lose me if I don't keep going," she said.

"Drop the magic," he said, raising his voice.

She shook her head. "No. It breaks my heart to say this, but I don't trust you."

The heat of the sigil seared his face, even beneath the hood. "None of this had to happen."

"But it did," she said. "And instead of trusting me, you destroyed my work. I can do this. I can set you free."

"I've lived with this curse for over a century," he replied. "I would rather live it with it for eternity than watch you suffer."

"I believe you," she said. "But that's not the choice before you now. One last chance. Give me back my things."

"I burned it all," he replied. Better for her to hate him than to kill herself.

Her face fell. Tears pricked her eyes, and she let out one single whimper before setting her jaw. She nodded, then shut the door in his face.

Despair wracked him. He had half a mind to tear through the barrier. If he couldn't go through her door, he'd simply break through the wall. He had to make her understand that this was because he loved her. How could he stand by and watch her destroy herself?

Fuck destiny, and fuck fate. Why would they torture him so by giving this gift only to snatch it away?

He braced himself for the pain and pounded on her door. The stench of burnt flesh filled his nose as the sunlight scorched his exposed hands. "Shoshanna!"

"Go away," she said.

"Not until you speak to me."

"Then you'll be waiting a long time," she said.

"Shoshanna, please," he said, his eyes stinging. "What happened to not going to sleep angry?"

Silence. Then he heard the patter of water in the shower, and the soft sound of crying.

He truly was a monster.

22

Shoshanna's eyes were a burning desert when she woke to her chirping phone alarm. She'd only slept for a few hours, just long enough to be certain that Alistair was asleep. As soon as she woke, she texted Ruby, holding the phone close to her face to see the blurry letters.

I need your help. Emergency.

Her heart thumped with fear as she contemplated her day.

How long would the curse take to be complete? She'd barely slept, for fear that she wouldn't wake up, and she'd end up a stone corpse in this bed forever. And it hadn't helped that Alistair had lingered until nearly dawn, quietly asking for her forgiveness. Every time he spoke, she felt a faint tug up her left arm that reminded her of the supernatural bond between them. Even in her fury, she wanted to go to him and find comfort in his arms. Her body and soul wanted him more than anything else.

But he'd proven that he would do anything to get his way. He'd destroyed her work, and she had no doubt that he'd lock her in a closet like some twisted fairy tale princess if that meant he didn't have to feel guilty for her suffering. She supposed on some level he thought he was protecting her, but he was only making it worse.

So much for soulmates. Maybe their threads had gotten tangled somewhere along the way.

Her phone rang as she climbed out of bed. She grabbed it and shuffled into the bathroom. "Hey."

Ruby's voice was full of righteous fury. "What did he do? I'll fucking kill him. I told him I would. Go ahead and tell him I'm on my way with a stake."

"It's okay," Shoshanna said. "I mean, it's not." She burst into tears and sank to the floor. "I'm in trouble. I messed with this curse and I think the magic snapped back on me or something. Maybe the Night Weaver got me. Either way, I don't know how long I have until I end up like Lucia and turn to stone, or—"

"Whoa, honey, take a breath," Ruby said. There was a thump, then a muffled curse. "Gotta find my glasses and get dressed, then I'm coming to you. What do you need me to bring? Should I get Auntie K to come? My cousin Lucy is out of town but if I tell her it's family, she'll be here in a couple hours."

Her heart swelled. "Thank you. Just you, but if Auntie K can help, then I'll take it. Maybe we can go to your place to stay."

"Okay," Ruby said. "Are you safe at his place right now?"

"Yeah, he's asleep," Shoshanna said. Ruby started to

protest. "He's not going to hurt me. We had a fight, but this isn't about him." Well, it was actually entirely about him. But that wasn't what Ruby needed to know.

Five minutes later, Ruby hung up with a promise to be here in an hour. Shoshanna hesitated, then released the sunlight sigil on her bedroom door. She peeked outside and found the hallway empty. A folded piece of paper fluttered to the floor, silently landing on the carpet in front of her. She knelt on the plush carpet and unfolded it, hands shaking.

Dear Shoshanna-

I understand your anger with me. It is what I deserve. But I hope that you understand I only wish to protect you from a terrible fate. I cannot stand by while you destroy yourself for my sake or Lucia's. She would not want that for you. It goes without saying that I do not want that for you. Your perseverance is admirable, and your skills formidable. This world is far better with you to brighten it. Please do not mistake my insistence for an insult to your competence. It is my affection for you that forces me to interfere.

Please do not give up on me. On us. I will fight this with you, if you only let me.

Love-

Alistair

Her heard thumped as she traced the letters in *love*.

One hundred years of being a self-imposed hermit had left him with a strange notion of love. His fear of suffering had condemned her to Lucia's fate.

She quickly packed a bag with her notebook, which thankfully hadn't been with all her diagrams, and the few reagents that hadn't been with her workspace near Lucia. Using an open can of cat food, she coaxed Magneto out from under the bed and wrestled him into his carrier. She stuffed a change of clothes into her oversized purse and left everything else.

One hand slid along the textured wallpaper as she crept down the hall. She headed to the kitchen to wait for Ruby. Magneto let out a mournful *meow* from his perch on the counter, while she crept to Lucia's alcove.

The stone was still cool and hard as ever, but she could feel the lingering heat of magic flowing through Lucia like an electric current. Alistair didn't know what the hell he was talking about. She'd managed to do *something* here.

"Yeah, and it's not enough," she said to herself. Creating a magical circuit was first year *tisserand* work. It was hardly groundbreaking. But she'd been so sure she'd done something, directing magic into the red thread and prying apart the curse. Every bit of it had been structurally sound. She didn't understand what had gone wrong.

She closed her eyes and felt for Lucia's essence. Compared to the dim blur of her normal vision, her arcane sight was remarkably sharp and clear. The dark blue of the curse remained, but the red thread seemed to be brighter. Tendrils branched from it, wrapping around Lucia like roots. When she brushed her mind over the red thread, a woman's scream filled her ears. She wrenched away.

What if her work had hurt Lucia? Had she awakened the poor woman to some terrible pain that she couldn't escape, because her body was immobile stone? She shook her head. "I'm so sorry," she said. "I will fix this. I promise."

The doorbell rang, prompting a metallic clatter as Magneto

jolted inside his carrier. She hurried past him and opened the front door to find Ruby waiting. Dark glasses covered her eyes, a sure sign that she was hung over. She held out a cup of coffee. A smudged ink stamp was still on the back of her hand. "You sounded like crap on the phone," she said, her voice rough.

Shoshanna just threw her arms around her friend, inhaling the clean herbal smell that always clung to Ruby. There was also the lingering hint of stale cigarette smoke, like she'd been at a bar. A red silk scarf was looped around her neck, an odd choice of accessories. "Thank you so much for coming. Okay, so—"

"Listen, honey, I want to hear everything," Ruby said. "But let's do it somewhere else that doesn't have bloodsuckers, okay?" She glanced around. "He's asleep?"

"Yeah, he's basically comatose during the day," Shoshanna said. She took a long drag of the coffee and winced at the bitter aftertaste. "Yikes."

"Not good? Geez, I told them to go easy on the cinnamon," Ruby said. "They use the artificial stuff and those sweeteners have such a funky aftertaste. I know you use all the real stuff at the shop."

She shook her head, not wanting to appear ungrateful. "It's fine. Thank you." She took another big drink and headed back to the kitchen to retrieve her bag. As she stepped across the threshold, a strange, dizzy sensation washed over her. She gripped the counter as her legs buckled.

"Uh oh," Ruby said calmly. She grabbed Shoshanna's arm and pulled her up. A heavy, dull sensation weighed Shoshanna down. "That was fast."

"Huh?" Shoshanna murmured. Her head felt thick and foggy. Then Ruby, all of five foot two and a hundred and ten pounds, swept her up like they'd just gotten married and carried her out the front door. Her limbs felt far away as she reached for the open doorway, but Ruby kicked it closed behind her. "What are you doing?"

"I'm really sorry," Ruby said. The trunk of her car was open and cleared of its usual clutter. Shoshanna's instincts finally tore through the fog, and she kicked wildly as Ruby deposited her in the trunk. She grabbed the scarf, but it slipped from Ruby's neck and into her hands. Two bruised punctures marked the side of her throat.

"Did someone bite you?" Shoshanna asked.

Ignoring her question, Ruby took a vial from her pocket and flipped off the cap. Her fingers dug into Shoshanna's jaw, forcing her mouth open, and a few drops of foul-tasting liquid trickled onto her tongue. "Bottoms up. Pretend it's a birthday tequila shot."

She gagged at the taste and tried to spit it out, but it was already working. Her tongue went numb, and the odd sensation quickly spread down her throat.

Ruby pushed up her sunglasses and sighed. "I really didn't want to do this," she said. Even with her blurry vision, Shoshanna could see the faint red glint to Ruby's eyes. "But Elliott wants you, and I have to do it."

Horror washed over Shoshanna. "Ruby, please don't do this." But her words were garbled mush, and she felt her eyes closing against her will.

"He's not going to hurt you," Ruby said. "He promised. Now, I have to keep my promise."

SHOSHANNA WOKE SLOWLY, with the foul taste of licorice and battery acid on her tongue. She opened her eyes to a blurry, dark room. Fear erupted in her chest as she lurched to her feet, only to find her hands tied to the arms of a chair. Her ankles were tied to the legs of the chair, and she managed only to bump her hips a few inches out of the chair.

"Hey!" she bellowed into the darkness. She squinted around her, barely making out the boxy shape of some piece of furniture. Under her bare feet, she found the rough grain of carpet. The room smelled of a familiar blend of herbs and Calvin Klein perfume. That was Ruby's smell.

The last thing she remembered was Ruby carrying her out of Alistair's house and talking about Elliott. Had they turned her into a vampire?

No. She walked in the sun, so Elliott had to have enthralled her by giving her blood. She should have known he would try something insane. He knew where Ruby worked, and where half of Shoshanna's friends and family members lived. And she'd just been playing house with Alistair like there was nothing else going on.

Her head pounded. She tried to shake off the drugged haze. If Elliott came in here for her, she'd incinerate him just like she did in her apartment. She twisted awkwardly, trying to direct the palms of her hands toward the tight bindings. She had decent aim when she could actually see, but this was less than ideal. There was a good chance she'd light herself on fire.

Then again, a little pain was better than ending up in Elliott's possession. Burns would heal, and she could survive with one useable hand, even if it meant never playing the piano with Alistair again.

Straining against the bindings on her wrist, she twisted her right hand, trying to work up the nerve. *Mettrez à feu,* she recited in her head, not quite working up the nerve to say it aloud. Her fingers tingled with the gathering energy, ready to answer her call. She'd get maybe three shots before she passed out, so she had to make it count.

"Shoshanna?" Ruby said quietly. The electronic glow of her smart watch cast a bluish glow on her face. Her form was blurry, but Shoshanna could make out the gleam of light reflecting from her eyes. "Are you okay?"

"Ruby, what the hell? You've got to let me out of here," Shoshanna said, pulling against the bindings. "Please."

A lamp flicked on, casting a warm yellow light around the room. Shoshanna squinted, trying to take in her surroundings all at once. Small bedroom, probably in an apartment. The sparse furnishings and plain dark bedspread confirmed that she wasn't in Ruby's eclectic apartment.

A wad of fabric shoved at her lips, and she gasped in surprise. Ruby pushed the gag into her mouth, then quickly tied a strip of cloth around her head and tied it tight. Shoshanna coughed and tried to shove it out with her tongue, but it was tight enough to tug painfully at the corners of her lips. "Sorry, honey. He didn't want to risk you burning him again." She slid her finger under the ropes on Shoshanna's wrists and tugged lightly. "This isn't cutting off your circulation, is it?"

Shoshanna let out a muffled sound of indignation. Ruby stepped aside, then said, "It's safe."

Footsteps shuffled behind her, and she craned her neck to see Elliott circling her. "Shoshanna York," he said, sitting down on the bed across from her. Though she could barely make out his features, she would recognize that smug drawl anywhere. "I'm glad to see you again."

"Fuck you," she said. Her words were garbled, but she imagined that the harsh consonants and fury made her intent perfectly clear. She lurched in the seat, managing to scoot it forward an inch before it jolted up her spine. Elliott planted one foot on the edge of the chair, between her legs.

"Tied up and gagged is a nice look for you," he said. "Maybe we'll get to that later. When you're feeling more agreeable." Disgust rolled over her like a wave of steam, leaving her feeling sticky and filthy. "You've made this incredibly difficult, you know. I made you a great offer, and you snubbed me for a dusty old court that's still stuck in the eighteenth century."

She mumbled at him. Elliott sighed. "This is very unsatisfying. I've changed my mind. Ruby, untie that thing and then come sit with me."

Ruby untied the gag, pulling at Shoshanna's hair. She hurried around Shoshanna as she struggled to spit out the offending cloth, then settled into Elliott's lap. There was a little whimper, but Elliott chuckled. "You like this, don't you, Ruby?"

"Yes," she said calmly. The flat voice was so un-Ruby that it made Shoshanna want to scream in fury.

Shoshanna squinted, trying to make out Ruby's features. Both of them were both a featureless blur; Elliott a wash of alabaster and Ruby a faint golden streak. "What did you do to her?"

"I gave her my blood and made her my thrall," Elliott said. "And she's been very appreciative. If it makes you feel better, she was very resistant about coming to get you. But with enough blood in her system, she really doesn't have a choice, do you, sweetheart?"

"No," Ruby said.

"You better not have touched her," Shoshanna said.

"Or what? What will you do, little witch?" Elliott said. "Your scary alpha vampires aren't here to swing their dicks this time."

"She has nothing to do with this," Shoshanna said.

"She's here because you forced my hand," Elliott said. "I told Cristiano I could deliver a witch, and you made me look like a fool."

"You made yourself look like a fool," she said. "You know I work for the Auberon now. When they find out what you've done, there are half a dozen vampires that are going to fight over who gets to tear your face off."

"Will they, now? Because the last I heard, you were committed to being a free agent. Not blood bound or anything," he said. He sniffed the air. "I just smell grade-A witch. Though it smells like you've been fucking a vampire. Tsk, tsk." He patted Ruby's thigh with a noisy smack. "And now I'll have two pet witches. First we'll take out Cristiano, and then the Auberon. It won't be particularly hard, considering you can unravel all the security at Infinity."

Horror prickled through her. "You can't be serious."

"I'm serious," he said. "Don't you remember how I was voted mostly likely to succeed in high school? I'm going to be the Baron of Atlanta before I turn thirty."

She wanted to laugh in his face. Even as an immortal vampire, he was still hung up on the past. But as foolish as it was, this was very real. She held back her derisive laugh and softened her voice. "You don't have to do this," she said. "Please, just let me go. What if I offered to help you? We can make a deal."

He shook his head, then dashed out of sight. Ruby squawked in protest as she stumbled and hit the floor like discarded garbage.

Cold hands squeezed her upper arms as his lips grazed the back of her neck. She squeezed her eyes shut, tamping down her revulsion. "You had your chance to do this the easy way. You know those wonderful action movies, where the villain gives a big speech so the hero has time to escape and thwart his plan? "

She was silent, fighting to breathe evenly. Even though he could surely hear her racing heart and smell the fear on her, it made her feel better to control what little she could.

"I'm not that stupid," he said. His grip tightened, and suddenly, there was the coppery bite of blood in the air. Hot warmth pressed to her lips.

Fury flooded through her at the violation. She bit him as

hard as she could. It was horrifying to sink her teeth into pliable, living flesh, through the thick resistance of skin and muscle.

"Fuck," he growled, still not breaking his grasp.

Vampire blood spilled over her tongue. The taste turned her stomach at first, but it quickly transformed into something intoxicating. It was the darkest chocolate, the richest coffee, hot and cold, numbing her mouth and igniting a flame in her core. Even as the last fragment of resistance screamed *don't!* her lips sealed to his skin and drank.

"That's one way to get a taste," he said. He still held her firmly as she drank.

Her will meant nothing. The taste of him turned her to a primal creature of hunger. He released her hair and stroked her head instead.

"That's it," he said gently. There was a strange ripple as his muscles flexed, and he pulled his arm away.

She was wheezing and gasping for air, but she wanted more even as the warm red dripped down her chin. "More."

"No. Too much and I'll be weak tonight," he said. Then he slowly circled her and knelt in front of her. He tilted her face up and wiped the blood from her lip. "What's wrong with your eyes?"

"I'm cursed," she said. "I need to break it before I turn to stone."

"Turn to stone..." he said absently. "Never mind." He gently touched her cheeks and brought his face close to hers. "Look in my eyes."

Through the intoxicating haze, she felt the sense of alarm,

that she was about to fall into something far worse. She closed her eyes and turned her head away. Elliott gripped her chin and spoke again. His voice reverberated down her spine, as if she was the clapper in a massive church bell. "Shoshanna. Look into my eyes." Her eyes opened slowly. His red eyes were just inches away. "You're mine now. Just like it always should have been."

At the words *you're mine,* it felt as if he reached into her chest and gripped her heart. Suddenly her thoughts of escape, of despair and fear, were no more than pesky afterthoughts. She had one thing in mind right now, and that was to please Elliott. Her tongue darted over her lip to catch a lingering drop of his blood. It tasted sweet beyond description, with the decadent satisfaction of melted chocolate and fresh whipped cream. It sent a shock of warmth down her spine to settle between her thighs. The flicker of arousal reminded her of Alistair.

In a rush of warmth rising in her chest, he pushed through the ponderous weight of Elliott's control. Alistair wouldn't do this to her. And he would be homicidally furious with Elliott. Despite the command in his blood, she didn't want to serve Elliott. She wanted to be home with Alistair.

She shook her head and took a shuddering breath. "Not yours," she managed to say. The words seemed to fight her, but she spat them out finally.

Elliott gripped her throat. The warm rumble of satisfaction in his voice turned to a sharp edge. "You are mine," he said slowly. "Bound to me by blood." There was a strange swelling in her chest that radiated down her arms and legs. "Tell me who you belong to."

Alistair's face, burning red eyes and bony horns and all, faded into a red haze, leaving Elliott's face in her mind. He was crystal clear in front of her. How had she never noticed how beautiful he was? His eyes were the color of roses in deep shade, framed in thick, dark lashes. She could stare into his eyes forever.

"I'm yours," she said in an awed voice.

"Good girl," he said. "Now, we have a lot of work to do."

23

Twilight still hung thick and heavy as Alistair awoke with the heavy weight of regret upon his chest. His alarm had not rung, but his racing mind would not let him sleep any longer. He growled and staggered to the door to listen for sounds of Shoshanna moving about the house. It was eerily silent.

He feared the worst. He was all but certain that he would find her sprawled on the floor. Would she be unmoving stone like Lucia? Or would she be dead and cold, having given herself an aneurysm with too much magic?

He threw the door open and lurched up the stairs. Relief washed over him when he heard the insistent thrum of a heartbeat. He followed the sound, then paused, frozen in place. There was no smell of blood in the air. Then again, after the way they'd shouted at one another, he hardly expected her to have a meal waiting for him. But the air was too still and stagnant. Usually he rose to the smell of coffee and something savory in the air, the remnants of whatever she had eaten for dinner.

Furthermore, he smelled a feline. On the granite island where he'd first dared to touch Shoshanna, there was a blue plastic crate.

And it was purring.

He frowned. "Magneto?"

The cat let out a mournful yowl. He crept closer to see baleful yellow eyes peering at him through a lattice of bars. The feline butted its head against the door, rattling the cage.

"Shoshanna?" he called.

No answer.

After another unsuccessful attempt to use its skull as a battering ram, the cat let out a pitiful *mrow*. He hesitated, then opened the door. In a blur of black, the cat leapt down and bolted for Shoshanna's room. "Shoshanna?" he asked again, hurrying toward the sound of the heartbeat. Grim relief swept over him. He could deal with her ignoring him if she was alive.

The heartbeat was coming from the direction of his library. He growled in frustration. Perhaps she had called his bluff and went searching for her things. He stormed across the living room, then froze when he rounded the corner.

Lucia's alcove was empty. The curtains were open, and one of the windows stood open, letting in a balmy breeze. Dirty smudges marked the otherwise pristine windowsill. A trail of mud outlined small footsteps down the hall, toward the library. And strangest of all, a plain gray dress lay piled on the floor. It was intact, as if someone had simply stepped out of it. It took him a solid ten seconds to wrap his mind around what he was seeing.

"What in God's name..." he murmured. He darted down the hall, toward the library. The source of the heartbeat huddled in the corner, blue eyes wide as saucers. He froze. "Lucia?"

Blonde hair was plastered to her corpse-pale skin. The woman screamed and scampered back into the corner, babbling in Czech. The smell of smoke and sweat filled the air. She was naked as the day she was born. She spoke so fast he could barely keep up, but he understood, *help me God. Save me.*

"Lucia," he said, running toward her. She screamed in fright, but he gently touched her arms. "It's me, Alistair Thorne," he said in Czech. It was rusty, but he could manage introducing himself. Without thinking, he swept the hood from his face. Her eyes widened. "Fuck," he muttered. The poor creature really was going to think she'd woken up in Hell.

She screamed and kicked at him, catching him in the chest. Alistair backed away, protesting, "Lucia, it's me! Please. Listen!" He dodged another kick, then caught her arm and spun her to his chest, holding her tight. Her entire body trembled with terror as she screamed in protest. Her words disintegrated into wordless sobs. "I know I look frightening," he said. "It's me, Alistair."

In her weakened state, her struggles were fruitless. He kissed the top of her head, wrinkling his nose at the smell of unwashed skin. It was hardly fair to judge her hygiene considering she'd been a stone statue for more than a century. There was also a fresher smell of dirt. Combined with the footprints, he guessed she must have gone out the window in her confusion, then returned to the safety of the house.

"You know me. I was cursed like Kova," he said.

At the sound of Kova's name, she stilled. "Am I dreaming?"

"You are not dreaming," he said gently. "You are here."

"Where is Kova?"

"He is not here," he said, thankful that she could not see the wince on his face. He gently stroked her matted hair. "I will care for you until he returns. I cannot imagine how you must feel."

"Cold. Hungry," she said, trembling.

He nodded, then gently pulled away from her, sweeping his hood over his face again with one hand. She cowered. "I'll be back. I'll find you some clothes and food. Yes?"

She just stared up at him, terror still etched on her beautiful face. Her breaths were quick and raspy, betraying her panic.

He hurried out of the room and shouted, "Shoshanna! Your anger must wait. You were right. You did it, but I need you to help her." He hurried to Shoshanna's room and found her bed neatly made, her things still strewn about. The black cat was curled up on her pillow and gave him a strange look. "Where is your human?"

It meowed, then twisted awkwardly to lick its back. Useless beast.

He hurried through the house, looking into each room. "Shoshanna?" he asked, dread swelling in his chest. The only heartbeats in the house belonged to Lucia and the little feline. If she was here...

No. He would not entertain such thoughts.

Still, he searched from room to room, calling her name and sniffing the air. Despair gripped him as he returned to the kitchen. In his rush to find the source of the heartbeat, he hadn't seen Shoshanna's phone laying on the kitchen island. He tapped the screen to see a text notification.

Ruby: *i'm outside with coffee! let me in!*

It had arrived at eleven that morning, not long after he had gone to sleep. He ran to the front door and yanked it open, as if he would magically find them there ten hours later. It was still and quiet, the expanse of the manicured lawn dark and untouched. A faint scent of herbs lingered in the air, a smell that had wreathed Ruby when she visited before.

He tried to swipe at Shoshanna's phone to call Ruby, but the message cleared, then asked for a passcode. "Fuck," he growled.

"Alistair?" a rough voice called. "*Kde jsi?*"

This made no sense. He hurried back into the house, then looked into the garage. The black vehicle that Paris had loaned to Shoshanna was still there. He paced in the kitchen, then dashed downstairs for his own phone. He grabbed a bathrobe and hurried back upstairs as he called Paris. When his charming voice said, "Leave a message," Alistair growled and hung up. He texted as he bounded up the stairs.

Answer your phone. It's an emergency. Shoshanna is gone.

He was halfway down the hall when Paris called back, his voice all business. "The fuck do you mean Shoshanna is gone?"

"I don't know what happened," he said. "I just woke up and she was gone."

"Maybe she stepped out." Paris sounded utterly unconcerned.

"The car is here, as is her phone and her cat. Furthermore, she broke the curse on Lucia. So I have a very confused dhampir in my house, and no witch."

"Am I hallucinating? Did you just say she broke the curse? As in Lucia is no longer a very lovely stone woman?"

"That's what I'm saying," he said. "And I need to find Shoshanna. Something's wrong."

"Fuck," Paris said. "I'll be there as soon as I can."

Alistair found Lucia standing in the doorway of his library, arms folded over her naked frame. He shook his head guiltily and held out the bathrobe. "Come here, love," he said gently, holding out the robe for her. He pointedly turned his head away while she shakily put one arm into the sleeve. When she was bundled in, he gently picked her up and cradled her frail body to his chest. He was afraid to ask too much about the effects of the curse and what she might have suffered. He carried her to the couch and set her down gently, then shook out a blanket over her legs. Her breathing had slowed, though her eyes were still wide and terrified.

He ignited the electric fireplace, which filled the room with sweltering heat. She gasped in surprise. He groaned inwardly. She was going to have a lot of catching up to do. "*Voda, prosim*?" she asked, her voice dry and rough.

"God, yes, you must be parched," he said in English. What would Shoshanna do? The fact that Lucia was staring up at him was evidence that something bad had happened. If Shoshanna knew that her magic had worked, she would have been here with a warm meal, and most likely a well-deserved *I told you so.*

He hurried into the kitchen and poured Lucia a glass of water, then rifled through the cabinets to find some of Shoshanna's crackers. He took the food and water to Lucia, then knelt at her feet. With him holding the glass for her, she drained the water in seconds. While he refilled her glass, she tore into the crackers. The poor thing must have been starved.

"I'll arrange for a proper meal for you right away," he said gently. He had a thousand questions, but the selfish part of him only cared about Shoshanna. "Did you see anyone when you woke? Perhaps a pretty woman with brown skin?"

"The witch?" Lucia asked.

Hope sprang up in his chest. "Yes, the witch. Did you see her?"

Lucia shook her head, then tapped her temple. "In my long dream, I saw her many times." She looked around, craning her neck. "Where is Kova?"

"He is not here now," he said. He was certainly not prepared to tell her that her beloved was dead. "I will notify him at once."

Her nostrils flared as she sniffed, then looked around slowly. "Where are we, Alistair? This is not your home, nor Kova's. And when were you cursed? I don't remember that."

He lowered his head. "Lucia, it's been a very long time since you...since you fell asleep."

Her brow furrowed. "How long?"

How was he supposed to tell her that she had awoken more than a hundred and fifty years after being turned to stone? That she was in a world she would no longer recognize, and worse, she was there without the man she loved? "Well...what year was it when you and Kova—"

Tires rumbled, and he heard several sets of feet hurrying across the lawn. He rose, ready to attack. The front door swung open, and he rushed to find Paris storming in with Nikko and Dominic close behind. Before Alistair could speak, the other three men pushed past him. Nikko froze at the doorway, his pale eyes wide. "Impossible."

"She did it," Paris breathed. "She said she would and she did." Lucia's brow lifted, a faint smile on her face at the sight of the familiar men.

"She doesn't know about Kova yet," Alistair said quietly in English. "Don't tell her yet. We have to find Shoshanna. Lucia can wait."

Dominic nodded grimly, but his expression softened as he pushed past Alistair to join Lucia. "*Halo,* Lucia," he said gently.

"Dominic," she greeted warmly. "Is Kova with you?"

"He is on his way. He was traveling but I know he will return soon, especially when he hears word of your recovery," Dominic said smoothly. Of all of them, Dominic had been the closest to Kova, and thus to Lucia. At his words, he heard her heart slow. Her voice warmed as she spoke to him, complimenting his strange but handsome haircut.

While Dominic kept Lucia busy, Paris pulled Alistair into the kitchen. Nikko seemed torn between the wonder of Lucia's recovery and the grim business of Shoshanna's disappearance. He finally turned to Alistair, planting his hands on the granite counter. His short sleeves revealed the dark marks that inched toward his hands. He was due for a bad night. "I want to help."

Alistair nodded. "Thank you."

"Julian was with Eduardo," Paris said. "He has business, but told me to update him if he can help. Obviously, the Shroud is at our disposal. Violette's checking Shoshanna's credit card for any recent transactions." His eyes narrowed. "What happened?"

"We had a falling out last night. I..." He lowered his head. "I broke her trust."

"What did you do?" Paris said sharply.

"She was hurting herself to break Lucia's curse," he blurted. "Her vision is failing, and she will turn to stone just as Lucia did. Because she and I are...soulmates. And she is cursed because of me."

"Soulmates?" Nikko said incredulously. "There's no such thing."

"You know there is," Alistair said. "How else can you explain Kova or Julian?"

"Guilt and grief," Nikko snapped. "It is nothing so poetic."

"Are you serious?" Paris said to Alistair. Then he shook his head emphatically. "It doesn't matter. What does that have to do with her leaving?"

"I told her that I destroyed her work," he said. "I drove her away."

"You did what?" Paris spluttered. He gestured to Lucia. "The witch did it, you fucking idiot. And you destroyed our only chance at ridding ourselves of this nightmare?"

"I didn't destroy it," he snapped. "I'm not a monster. I

simply hid it to delay her for a few days while she rested. I feared that she would hurt herself trying to fix Lucia. But I may have doomed her. And worst of all, she was right." He gestured broadly. "She said she could do it, and she did."

"How did she do it?" Nikko said. One hand absently skimmed over the marks on his arm, his mind clearly on his own curse.

"I don't know," Alistair said. "She's been working at it for weeks. She's brilliant. As smart as she is beautiful. And I've ruined her."

Paris clapped him on the back. "For once in your bloody life, you're not going to wallow in self-pity." Despite the sharp tone, there was a gentleness in his eyes. "Because we will find her. Dominic told her it couldn't be done, and I'd love to see the look on his face when he has to eat his words."

"I heard that," Dominic said mildly from the living room.

"I wasn't being secretive," Paris responded.

"What can we do?" Nikko asked. His wonder at Lucia's transformation had dissolved, leaving behind his shrewd, incisive nature. This was the Nikko that they needed on the hunt. "Do you think she was taken, or did she leave intentionally?"

"I think she intended to leave," he said, with a pang of sorrow piercing through him. He gestured to the plastic carrier. "But something happened before she left. She adores that foolish creature, and it was caged when I woke up. She would never leave it locked up without food. And there was a text from her friend saying she had arrived."

"Which friend?"

"Ruby," Alistair said. "She's a—"

"Ruby Wang. Green witch, thirty-one, works at the Jade Breeze health shop in Midtown. Part of the Wang family network of practitioners," Nikko interrupted. "I know who she is."

He stared at Nikko. "And you know this how?"

"We all have our jobs," Nikko said with a shrug. "Before she ever set foot near Eduardo, I compiled a file on Shoshanna and her known contacts."

"We need that file," Paris said. "Is it in your office?"

Nikko snorted in derision. "It's the twenty-first century, Phillippe," he said derisively. Paris scowled at the use of his real name. "It's all in the cloud." He pulled out his phone and typed rapidly. "I shared it with you. Check your email."

"Do you think this could be the Casteron?" Alistair said. "Elliott McAvoy was after her, which is why she was staying here."

"It's possible," Nikko said. "We've been keeping tabs on him but he hasn't yet made a move that warrants action by the Shroud. Ruby is our most concrete lead. We start there and then move on, yes?"

Alistair nodded. Paris nodded and flicked his eyes to Alistair. "Let's go. Nikko, you go to the shop and see what you can find. We'll go to Ruby's address and see if Shoshanna's with her. If not, we'll find that little Casteron fuck and twist his nutsack off if we must."

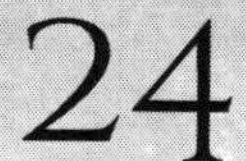

"You look hot," Ruby said appreciatively.

With her eyesight failing, she would have to take Ruby's word for it. In the full-length mirror, Shoshanna's reflection was nothing more than a blur. Her friend had fussed and primped over her makeup, as if they were just going out for a normal girls' night instead of being mind-controlled arm candy for a power-hungry vampire.

She smoothed her hands over her stomach, feeling as if a puppetmaster operated her limbs. Somewhere inside her, a tiny voice was screaming in protest, but Elliott had commanded her to get dressed for the occasion. Therefore, she got dressed.

After Elliott enthralled her, he had freed her hands and left her with Ruby. When Ruby guided her to the kitchen for delivery tacos, Shoshanna caught a glimpse of the rest of the townhouse. It was clean and sparsely furnished, as if he'd rented a model unit without bringing any of his own belongings.

Blackout curtains covered all the windows, rendering it vampire-friendly. Elliott hovered nearby, but she was free to walk around. Even under his control, she still had her own thoughts and desires; she wanted to be back in the safety of Alistair's home, preferably while someone cut off Elliott's head.

But her objections were vague thoughts, rendered unimportant by her burning desire to please Elliott. It was like driving in Atlanta rush hour traffic and realizing she needed to pick up milk at the grocery store. A valid concern, but all of her attention would be devoted to keeping herself alive until she escaped the tangle of interstates.

While Shoshanna tore into a chicken taco, Elliott sidled up to Ruby and bit into her neck with no warning. Ruby whimpered faintly, and Shoshanna glared at him. "Hey. Don't bite her," she snapped.

"She likes it," Elliott said, pulling away. "Don't you?"

"Yes," Ruby said flatly. Shoshanna watched in blank horror, the food suddenly turning her stomach. How far would Elliott push his power over them?

After dinner, he ordered Ruby to get ready for their evening plans. Pressing a paper towel to her bloody neck like it was simply a cut from shaving, Ruby had led her back to their shared room and pointed out the bathroom. Hanging in the closet were several dresses from Shoshanna's closet. She felt a vague dismay at the thought of Ruby and Elliott in her apartment, pawing through her things. She'd pushed a short black dress into Shoshanna's hands. "He likes this one."

An hour later, they were dressed for a formal cocktail hour, complete with uncomfortably high heels and glittering jewelry. She might have enjoyed the glamour if she was headed to Infinity with Alistair, but her stomach churned with dread at the thought of Elliott's plans for them.

Her voice was quiet and shaky as she turned to face Ruby, clad in a sparkling silver dress. "Don't you want to leave?"

"Of course," Ruby said, though her intonation was flat and dead. "But we have to stay. That's what Elliott wants."

"How did this happen?" Shoshanna asked.

Ruby was eerily calm. "He caught me coming home the day after I came to bring you tea. He forced me to drink and brought me here. He made me show him my texts and found out where you were staying."

Revulsion boiled in her gut, followed by the nauseating rush of shame. "I'm so sorry," Shoshanna said. "Did he...did he force you to do anything?"

Ruby glanced back at her. "Did he make me fuck him?" It felt as if gravity doubled in that pause. "No," she said. "He wants you. He's obsessed with making you his queen. He planned to come and get you last night, but put me up to it instead when you called for my help."

Shoshanna stared at her, trying to make out her expression with her blurred, dim vision. If she hadn't been so stubborn and accepted Eduardo's offer weeks ago, this would have never happened. "Ruby, I'm so sorry about this," she said softly.

"It's not your fault," Ruby replied. "Come on, I have to get you ready."

"You don't want to be here, do you?" Shoshanna asked.

Ruby shrugged. "No, but he does. And I can't fight it." She approached, gently wrapping a curl around her finger to smooth it out. "What's wrong with your eyes?"

"I'm cursed. I have to break it, or I'm going to end up like that statue in Alistair's house," Shoshanna said.

"If we ask him, maybe he'll let you," Ruby said. Using her fingers, she gently combed Shoshanna's hair away from one side of her face and secured it with a heavy metal comb. "But we have a big party tonight. It'll have to wait. His priorities come first."

The door creaked open, and she whirled to see Elliott's lanky figure approaching. He touched her chin and smiled. "Don't you look beautiful. Come with me." He gripped her hand and led her out of the room. Her legs seemed to operate on their own. Even the subtle command of *come with me* resonated through her.

As they walked, she tugged on his hand. "Elliott, I need to break the curse."

"It can wait," he said.

"I don't know if it can," she said. "Please."

He whirled and grabbed her throat. His hand squeezed tight enough to send a warning as he brought her close, red eyes flaring. "If I tell you it can wait, it can wait. Do you understand me?"

Fear prickled through her. "I understand. It can wait."

Up close, she could see his scowl shift into a smile. "Good girl," he said. He released her and gave her a once-over. "There's no need for that look. You're so much prettier when you smile."

She fixed a bland smile on her face and followed him to his car parked out front. The moon hung heavy and silver overhead, and the world was a dark blur around her. Though Elliott's power still held, her will was awakening again. Maybe it was time, and maybe it was a heavy meal of tacos soaking up his blood like Waffle House after tequila shots. Either way, she was glad for it.

How could she break free? How long would it take for his blood to wear off? She regretted that she hadn't quizzed Alistair on every aspect of vampire physiology. Despite growing up around vampires, working for them, and now sharing a bed with one, she'd never had much experience with thralls. But if his power was based on her ingesting his blood, then it had to eventually weaken enough for her to resist.

"Have you explained what she needs to do?" Elliott asked. He drove, while Ruby and Shoshanna shared the back seat.

"Elliott says you used a fireball on him when he visited your apartment," Ruby said.

"Something like that," Shoshanna said. "When he broke in and assaulted me."

"If you would have listened to reason, it would have been a much more pleasant visit," he said.

"You'll use that power again tonight," Ruby said. "When Elliott tells you."

She shook her head. "I keep telling you that I can't see."

"Ruby will help you aim," Elliott said. "Do whatever you need to prepare before we get there, so you're ready at my word. Don't let me down, or the consequences will be dire."

Her heart thumped. "What are you going to do?"

"I told you already," he said. "I'm going to be the king."

DREAD POOLED in her stomach like ice as Elliott drove up to a gated compound. Beyond the wrought-iron gates, she could just glimpse the blurry outline of a massive house cast in warm, glowing lights. After a brief conversation with a security guard, the gates opened to allow them to drive in.

Once they pulled around the driveway, a man in a suit opened her door and helped her out. Before she could take a step further, Elliott grabbed her hand and set it on his arm. Ruby joined him on the other side, and he left the vehicle with a valet.

The front doors opened to a dimly lit mansion, where music and conversation mingled into a low blur of noise. Elliott led them across a pale expanse of marble floor. Her heels clicked noisily as she hurried to keep up.

Couches and tables were situated all around a huge sitting room, but in the low light, she could barely see. A man approached them and greeted Elliott. "Mr. McAvoy, good evening," he said in a clipped British accent. "I see you've brought some delightful guests. Will you be sharing?"

"Perhaps you can have a taste later," he said.

She shrank back, hoping he wasn't about to lay her out as a feast for his vampire friends. A waitress in a skimpy red outfit walked up to them with a tray of glasses filled halfway with blood. Her head bowed as she offered the tray to Elliott.

Elliott took one, drained it, then plunked it back on the tray without a word. Shoshanna glanced up. There was an upper floor to this massive room, and she could see the vague outlines of people upstairs looking down.

And there at the back of the room were two raised chairs, like thrones upon a dais. She didn't have to wonder for much longer what Elliott was up to. With both witches still clinging to his arms, he strode up to the two thrones. Up closer, Shoshanna could see a man on the left, with a slender, shirtless man laid across his lap. His wrist was in the vampire's mouth, and several thin trickles of blood ran down his pale arm.

"Baron Moretti, I issue a challenge," Elliott said boldly.

As if someone had flicked a switch, the conversations all around the room stopped. The pulsing electronic music went silent a few seconds later.

Though the crowd was a featureless blur, Shoshanna felt the weight of eyes upon her as the silence filled the air like smoke. She wanted to scream *I'm not with him. Please don't eat me.*

There was a boisterous laugh. "You wish to challenge me?" the man's rich voice boomed. This had to be Baron Moretti. "This is not the way."

"This is the way of the Casteron," Elliott replied. "A Baron will defend his title if he wishes to keep it."

"A dull-fanged fool will defend his head if he wishes to keep it," a woman said. The voice seemed to come from the woman on the other throne. All Shoshanna could see of her was a red sparkle from her dress.

"This is the way," Elliott repeated. "And if I'm not mistaken, Cristiano, this is how you became a Baron, is it not?"

"More than a hundred years ago. Before you were even born, little boy," the Baron replied. "I'll advise you to think carefully. If you wish to keep your head upon your shoulders, you should leave immediately. Leave this house, leave the city, and never look back. Perhaps you should leave the continent to be safe."

"I don't think I will," Elliott said. He took a tentative step forward. "I've read the codex of our laws. Contracts are sacred, and if you choose to ignore the law for your own benefit, then all of our laws are meaningless."

"Our laws," the woman's voice scoffed. "You have been one of us less than a decade. You have scarcely earned the right to call them your own."

"Am I wrong?" Elliott said sharply.

A noisy buzz of conversation rose around them. Shoshanna instinctively squeezed Elliott's arm. There had to be at least fifty vampires here, all of them watching rapt. As she listened to the men argue, horror dawned on her. Elliott was going to use her as the executioner's axe, and if it failed, then there would be a whole clan of vampires furious with her. They would tear her to shreds before she could blink an eye. And there wasn't a damned thing she could do about it, because she had no choice but to follow his orders.

Cristiano Moretti chuckled. He released the wrist of his human meal. "You've interrupted my party, boy," he said, his warm, jovial tone sharpening. "You insult my hospitality. You insult my guests. So I will entertain them by painting the floor with your entrails and mounting your head on my wall. You will have your duel, and I'm sad to say, you won't be alive long enough to regret it."

He rose, letting the half-dazed human tumble off his lap unceremoniously. At that, there was a flurry of activity all around them. Furniture scraped over the marble floors, and glasses clinked.

What had been a dance floor only minutes ago, alive with the shimmering movement of dancing and revelry, had became a battle arena. All around was a buzz of excitement, with whispers of *not a chance* and *what's he thinking?*

Elliott gripped her chin, then leaned in to kiss her on the lips. She recoiled, but he held her firm. The taste of his blood spread on her tongue. Hating herself for it, she drew a mouthful, swallowing it like a shot of whiskey. When he broke away, he smiled. "Remember what you have to do." His eyes flicked to Ruby. "Help her."

He was careful of his words, knowing that every vampire in the room would hear him. Her eyes widened, as she realized her way out.

"I'm—"

He grabbed her jaw and hissed, "You will not say a word until Ruby gives you permission."

She mouthed *please.*

"Soon enough, you'll be my queen," he said. Then he shed his jacket and handed it to Shoshanna. He raised his voice. "If you'd prefer, you can hand me your throne and I'll let you walk away."

"If you choose to insult my honor further, I'll make your

death take days," Cristiano growled. "It's been a long time since I flayed someone."

A gruff voice with a thick Scottish accent spoke. "In accordance with the laws of the Casteron, any vampire may challenge a Baron for control of their clan, through a trial of their choice. Elliott McAvoy has challenged Baron Cristiano Moretti. The trial will end only when one man is dead. Do you accept?"

Elliott chuckled. "I accept."

"I accept," Cristiano said.

"Choose your weapons," the Scottish man said.

"I choose the hand of my lovely mate," Elliott said. She cringed at the word *mate*.

Cristiano laughed. "And I shall choose my own hand. That is all I will need to put you in your place. Vanessa, take note. I will rip out his heart for you, then pull his spine out for a trophy. Mark my words, love."

Ruby held Shoshanna's hand and guided her to the edge of the makeshift arena. Her legs were trembling and rubbery. Ruby's lips pressed close to her ear. "Get ready."

Elliott's command was fresh, with the coppery tang of his blood still fresh on her tongue. And so, as she knew that her own life hung in the balance, she closed her eyes to envision the simple geometric sigil of fire, laser-focused and explosive. Her fingers tingled with power, and the taste of blood intensified. Energy crackled down her spine, as if the vampire blood was super-charging her. It would be much more powerful than when she'd used it on Elliott and Alistair. It might even kill him outright.

"Begin!" the gruff voice shouted.

The crowd erupted in jeers and shouts all around them. At once, the cultured, sophisticated crowd was screaming for blood. She heard the thick, meaty sound of fists. One of the men bellowed in pain, and shoes squeaked against the floor. They moved in an impossibly fast blur.

Ruby squeezed her wrist, then suddenly yanked her arm up. "Now," she snapped. "You have permission."

"*Mettrez à feu,*" Shoshanna spat, wishing she could stuff the words back into her mouth. It felt like vomiting, her whole body retching as she spat the words. Fire peeled away from her fingers and coalesced into a flaming arrow. Cristiano let out a piercing shout of pain.

"Cheater!" the woman's voice screamed. More shouts erupted. "No! Stop him!"

Just feet away, Shoshanna saw Elliott straddling the other man, his hand buried in his chest as Cristiano tried to in vain to fight him off. Smoke curled up from the smoldering ruin of his chest. The stench of burning meat filled the air. She saw a spray of red, then closed her eyes and buried her face in Ruby's shoulder. There was a loud crack of bone, then a horrific squelch followed by a noisy *thump*. Her mind painted the grotesque details that her eyes could not.

Stunned silence overtook the crowd. Firm hands grabbed Shoshanna's shoulders, and voices rang out in a furious cacophony. "Witch! He cheated!"

She shook her head, struggling to get away, but their hands were iron shackles, squeezing tight enough to bruise. Voices snarled around her. They were going to rip her apart.

"Release her!" Elliott bellowed. "The witches are mine."

Still, the furious Casteron vampires closed in, more hands grabbing her. "By our laws, I am your Baron now. And if you do not release her, you will face the fate he did."

Suddenly, they released her and shoved her forward. Her legs went weak as the crowd parted. Elliott's figure loomed as he strode toward them. She let her eyes drift up to the few lights so she couldn't see the hateful stares or Cristiano's bloody remains. *I'm so sorry,* she thought desperately.

As it turned out, she didn't need to see it. She had used the spell on Alistair and saw the messy wreckage it left. Her mind painted a gory picture of a headless vampire with his chest blown open. The guilt was immeasurable.

A woman's screams rang out. "Cristiano! *Tesoro!*" Her cries of anguish stabbed through Shoshanna. There was a clatter of heels over the floor, then wordless wails of despair.

The gruff man's voice rang out over the woman's sobs. "By the laws of the Casteron, Elliott McAvoy is now your Baron. All hail."

There was another long silence, then a few voices rang out. "All hail."

"Sit, my dears. Shoshanna, I believe you've earned a throne," Elliott said, gesturing broadly. Ruby held her arm as she settled into the plush chair. Once she was seated, Ruby sat on Elliott's lap.

The woman who'd been weeping over Alessandro had gone quiet. "You fucking bastard," she swore. "I challenge you—"

"Think carefully, Vanessa," Elliott said. "Do you wish to end up like him?"

"Vanessa," a quiet male voice said. "We will not let this stand."

"I hear treasonous talk," Elliott said. "The Casteron live and die by their laws, do they not?" He gripped Shoshanna's hand, entwining his fingers with hers as she shuddered. "Vanessa, because I am gracious, I will grant you the opportunity to leave in peace. I wish you no ill will."

"The other Barons will hear of this," she said.

"I welcome it," Elliott said. "Your man agreed to my challenge."

"And you cheated."

"I told him exactly the weapon I planned to use," Elliott said calmly. "As I said, you may leave in peace, or you will be removed."

The woman sneered and backed away. As she went, Shoshanna could see several other figures following her. But to her surprise, the majority of them remained. There was a nervous buzz in the air.

Elliott gestured. "Nordan, have this cleaned up. And resume the music."

"Y-yes, sir," the Scottish man said. "Lads, you heard the Baron." He stumbled on the word *baron.*

Within minutes, the furniture had been moved again, and music played. The boisterous atmosphere had given way to quiet conversation, but there was no indication that there had just been a brutal fight to the death.

Elliott leaned closer to her and brushed a kiss on the back of her hand. "I told you that you would serve a king. And I have grand plans for us."

25

Paris knocked, waited two seconds, then broke the doorknob on Ruby's door. As he threw open the door, there was a questioning squawk from inside the apartment. Alistair sniffed, catching the scent of a human male, and the rhythmic sound of flesh. There were tinny erotic sounds, as if someone was watching a video.

Feet clambered across hardwood, and a wiry young man bolted down the hall with a baseball bat. Loose red shorts were tented over an erection, while the noisy sounds of theatrically exaggerated fucking rang out from a room down the hall.

"Get the fuck out of my house!" he bellowed.

"Whoa there," Paris said, approaching slowly. "Let's just—"

Alistair darted forward and snatched the bat as the man swung it. "Where's Ruby?"

The man screamed and scrambled backward. His foot

caught on the shaggy purple rug, but Paris caught him by the arm before he fell on his ass. "*Mon ami,* we don't want to hurt you or steal from you," he said calmly. "We just need to know where Ruby is."

"Why? You gonna hurt her?" he asked.

With a growl, Alistair broke the baseball bat in half. The wiry man's face expression faltered, his eyes comically wide in fear. "And what will you do to stop us?"

Paris swore in French. "We're not here to hurt you. We're looking for our friend Shoshanna, and the last we heard, she was with Ruby. Tell us everything you know, and then you can resume masturbating."

His cheeks colored. "I wasn't m-mast—"

"Focus!" Paris snapped. "Shoshanna and Ruby."

The man's face creased. "I haven't seen Shoshanna in a while. She used to come over every week and make some bombass nachos for movie night. Like with little jalapenos and—"

Alistair lunged in and grabbed the man's throat. He was five seconds from taking down his hood and letting him think the Devil himself had come to call. "What about Ruby?"

"She's been gone a couple days," the man said, batting at Alistair's arm to escape. "She was hooking up with this new guy. Eric, or Edward, or something."

"Elliott?" Alistair asked.

"Yeah, that was it," he said, nodding frantically. His dark eyes were comically wide. "He was here a few nights ago. I didn't like him, but Ruby said I was jealous. I'm not fuckin' jealous of that douche. Besides, Ruby's my cousin."

"Shut up," Alistair said, giving the man's throat a warning squeeze.

"Yep," he squeaked. In the background, a whining female voice was begging someone to stick it in. Charming.

Paris shot him a look. "Then this is the Casteron."

"I'm going to fucking kill him," Alistair replied. Eduardo be damned. He should have hunted the bastard down a week ago.

"Don't kill me, man," the man protested. "I told you everything!"

"Not you," they replied in unison. Alistair released the trembling man, and he clambered backward with a whimper.

Paris wrinkled his nose. "Go back to your entertainment. And for God's sake, get an air freshener. It smells like farts and sweaty testicles in here."

The man's face flushed, and he bolted down the hall like a rabbit at a race track. As they left the apartment, Paris called Nikko. "No Ruby here. Roommate said she was hooking up with Elliott and hasn't been home in a few days. Sounds like he's got her. Maybe used her to get to Shoshanna."

Alistair could hear Nikko on the other end. "Same here," he said. "The Wang shop is closed, but I had Safira call Ruby's mother and pretend to be Shoshanna looking for her. She said Ruby wasn't at work today, and that she's been talking to some new guy. She didn't know his name, but she said, and I quote, if Shoshanna talks to Ruby, to tell her that she's in big fucking trouble."

"We're going to Elliott's," Paris said. "Meet us there."

As they climbed back into car and pulled onto the interstate, Alistair felt as if he would burst out of his skin. "If he touched her, I'm going to kill him. Scratch that. I'll kill him regardless. But if he touched her, I'll make it take a decade."

"Alistair." Paris's voice was eerily calm.

"He was warned," Alistair seethed. "I will flay him. Peel his fucking skin off centimeter by centimeter."

"Alistair, calm down," Paris said.

"This is Shoshanna," he retorted.

Paris shook his head. "If you kill him outright, you will ignite a war with the Casteron."

"I don't care," he said. "Let them come to war."

"I care," Paris said. "As does Eduardo. Everyone else in the court will care when they are thrust into war because of your impulsivity."

"I cannot sit by while he hurts her," he said. "She is mine now, and it is my responsibility to protect her." A responsibility that he had failed twice now.

"I'm not asking you to," Paris said. "Just use your head for a moment. Elliott had sufficient opportunity to kill Shoshanna. That's clearly not what he wants. He wants her power."

"But if he touched her," he said quietly. "If he violated her..." As a disgruntled ex-boyfriend, there was no telling how the vampire version of Elliott might take out his old complaints on a vulnerable Shoshanna.

Paris was silent. "I know. He will pay for this."

"I will not let Eduardo sideline me this time," he said. "He cannot remain neutral."

Paris gave him a look, eyebrows arched. "I'm on it already." Alistair just tilted his head. "Circumstances have changed slightly. Shoshanna isn't blood bonded to the court, but she's bonded to you, and that surely counts for something. Second, Shoshanna can untangle the security at Infinity. Eduardo isn't going to leave her in the wind and jeopardize the entire court."

"It's somewhat less than encouraging that he values her as a security risk more than a person," Alistair said.

"It's business," Paris replied. "And Eduardo will see it that way when we tell him as much."

At nearly two in the morning, the traffic was minimal. It took half an hour to reach the address Nikko had sent them. His sporty black car was already parked outside, and the faint blue glow of a phone screen illuminated his face. Elliott McAvoy lived in a small townhome in a row of identical units. Most of the windows were dark, with a single home at the end of the street illuminated in the flickering blue light of a TV.

Paris and Alistair stormed up the sidewalk while Nikko darted around the back of the house. Alistair and Paris silently crept to the front door. They were both still and silent, listening carefully. Though Alistair heard the whir of several air conditioning units and a loud conversation in the house next door, there was silence from within Elliott's house. Paris tapped lightly on the door, then moved to open it.

Alistair gripped his arm. "If he made her…" he sighed. "If he made her use her magic, she might have trapped the door. Let me." He broke the door handle and braced himself for the scorching burn of Shoshanna's sunlight sigil. But there was nothing, just the lingering smell of vampire and something spicy. Was that tacos?

"Elliott McAvoy?" Paris asked quietly. "Delivery for you."

Inside the home, the air was crawling with the smell of a vampire. Mixed with it, he detected two familiar scents. There was the leafy, herbal scent that surrounded Ruby, and the vanilla-sage smell of Shoshanna. He also smelled both human and vampire blood. "Shoshanna?" he called.

He didn't know if smelling her here was a comfort or a pain. He wanted to believe that she was somewhere burying her feelings in a piece of cheesecake while crying about what a wretched excuse for a lover he was. Then she would be safe. Knowing that she'd been here opened his imagination to a whole new avenue of dread.

Despite finding her scent relatively fresh, he knew they would find nothing. Nikko had since joined them, and they silently moved through the house, inspecting each room. He heard Nikko and Paris saying, "Nothing," as they searched rooms.

Upstairs, he found one large bedroom lit only with a table lamp. Blackout curtains were taped to the walls with shiny silver tape. A single cup crusted with dried blood sat on the nightstand. He wrinkled his nose at the inelegant setup.

The room across the hall was sparsely furnished, and Shoshanna's scent was stronger here. His stomach lurched at the sight of her clothes, discarded across the bed. He lowered himself slowly to smell the bedclothes. They smelled a little musty, like fabric that had been stored for a long time. There was no hint of sex, nothing of the impossibly rich scent of

Shoshanna's body. Relief washed over him. Tucked against the far wall was a big pink duffel bag, and he checked the tag to find *Ruby Wang* on the label.

Paris sauntered in, then picked up a pink plastic tube from the dresser. "Looks like someone was getting pretty. Makeup and perfume." He patted his pocket and took out his phone. "Shit, it's Julian." He answered and set the phone on the dresser. "You're on speaker."

"Good," Julian's rich voice said. "I have information for you, but whatever you're doing, do not make a move on Elliott McAvoy."

They exchanged looks. Paris smirked. "We're in his house right now. Uninvited, if that matters."

"Then get out," Julian said. "I'll meet you at Alistair's house. Get there now."

"But we need to find Shoshanna," Alistair protested.

"I know where she is," Julian said. "We'll get her back, but not tonight. Get to Midnight Springs."

They left the apartment quickly, pulling the door closed. "He'll know we were here," Alistair said.

"All he'll know is that a couple of vampires were here," Paris said. "What's he going to do about it?"

Paris and Alistair were nearly silent on the way back to Midnight Springs. Streetlights zipped past them in a glowing blur as miles of interstate rolled by. Between this futile search and his disastrous hunt with Safira, this was the most he'd left home in decades, and with nothing but simmering anger and despair to show for it.

Alistair wanted to voice his frustrations, but how many

ways could he say *I need her back?* He had to apologize for the ways he'd failed her, most of all for failing to believe in her. If she was correct, and they were soulmates, then perhaps there was hope. He had to trust that there was a chance she would forgive him.

But he knew well that being bound by such a powerful love didn't guarantee a happy future. Julian and Lucia were proof of that. He squirmed, digging his dark nails into his palms until they broke the skin. The pain only made him angrier.

He should have been out there, hunting her down. What if she thought he was so wrapped up in himself that he had abandoned her to a terrible fate? She had to know better. Though he could not see the magic that Shoshanna saw, he tried to imagine a red ribbon winding around their hands, alive and pulsing like blood through an artery.

I promise that I'm coming. I love you. Stay alive for me.

It was Paris that broke the silence just before he exited the interstate to drive into Midnight Springs. He spoke in his native French, as he often did when he was feeling particularly introspective. "Is this soulmate thing real?"

"Shoshanna believes it is," he said quietly. "She believes that Kova and Lucia were soulmates. She noticed something in Lucia that led her to breaking the curse. And that's how she saw it in herself and in me."

He was quiet. "And me? When she looked at my aura or whatever she called it?"

His heart sank. He wished he could lie, but his silence would say everything Paris didn't want to hear. "She said you were different," he said. "But I don't know what that means."

Paris forced a bitter laugh. He knew when the other man's smile was faked to hide pain. "Of course I am. I imagine I'm too much for one person to handle." He glanced at Alistair. "I care for her, too."

"I know."

He chuckled. "Would you be angry if I told you I thought about seducing her when we first met?"

"I would think you were blind if you had not considered it," he said. "Or that you had struck your head."

Paris nodded solemnly. "She adores you, Allie. She's brought you back to life. So if destiny intends for you to have her, then I will make sure destiny has her way. You have my word."

"Thank you," Alistair said. "You have given me much more grace than I deserve. I am lucky to have you." Using the present tense felt dangerous; did he, in fact, still have Paris?

He chuckled again as they pulled into the private drive. "I certainly have, and you certainly are." The other man's agreement was a relief.

Another black car was parked in the drive, right in front of the house. Paris parked in the garage, next to the vehicle he had loaned to Shoshanna. Before getting out, he simply squeezed Alistair's hand. "We'll get her back, *mon ami*."

Inside the house, he found a house full of vampires crowded around Lucia, who was bundled in blankets on the couch. The house was sweltering with the fireplace still going and the heat running. She wore a bright pink bathrobe that had to be the work of Safira, who was gently brushing her damp blonde hair and weaving it into an intricate braid.

The smell of warm food filled the house, reminding him of Shoshanna. Several large paper bags were strewn across the stone countertop. There had to be enough food for an army.

Lucia clutched a bowl with a spoon, but she appeared preoccupied with the black cat who was purring noisily as he kneaded the pile of blankets over her lap. He wasn't sure if the opportunistic feline was attracted to the strange new woman, who had a heartbeat and warm blood like his mistress, or if he smelled her food.

Traitor, he thought. As pleased as he was to see Lucia alive and well, he wanted only Shoshanna.

Julian had made himself at home, sitting at Alistair's piano bench. He lifted his eyes to Alistair and nodded, then gestured to the living room as if he was giving him permission to sit in his own house. Alistair suppressed a comment and settled into the chair across from him. As his weight pressed into the cushion, the scent of Shoshanna billowed up from it, making his heart ache. Julian nodded to Safira. "Will you take her to bed? She should rest."

Safira took the bowl from her, and stood aside as Dominic gently lifted Lucia. He spoke in Czech, his voice unusually gentle. "Little bird, you need to rest," he said.

"Will Kova be here soon? I can wait," she asked.

"It'll be a few days," he said. "He has a long way to travel."

"I see," Lucia said. She pointed back to the couch. "Will the cat come?"

Safira chuckled and scooped up the black cat, following behind them to put Lucia to bed.

Nikko watched her go. His grim look echoed Alistair's own thoughts. "Someone has to tell her soon."

"After she's had a chance to rest and recuperate a while," Julian said. "I hate lying to her, but she will need a gentle hand. This is already a tremendous shock." He crossed his legs and leaned back against the piano. "Our contact in the Casteron court called tonight. Elliott McAvoy just killed Cristiano Moretti."

"Are you fucking serious?" Paris asked. "Did they tear his head off?"

"No," Julian said calmly. "He challenged Cristiano for the throne. Cristiano accepted a challenge by combat, and he lost. Elliott is now the Baron of all the Casteron vampires here in Atlanta."

"What about the Covenant?" Alistair asked. The last thing they needed was a clan of feral vampires driven mad by the broken binding.

"If the Baron is defeated in combat, his challenger drinks from him to anchor the Covenant. If it is not already official, it will be before sunrise," Julian said grimly.

"Good God," Alistair breathed. "And Shoshanna?"

"Elliott used her as his weapon," he said. "She incapacitated Cristiano, and Elliot dealt the final blow. Natalia wasn't certain, but she believes the two witches are enthralled to him. They flank him on the throne now."

He buried his head in his hands. "If he lays a hand on her..."

"We must tread carefully," Julian said. "There were some who were clearly loyal to Cristiano, and they left with Vanessa. But the majority remained. Like it or not, Elliott is now a rightful Baron. He speaks for the Casteron here in Atlanta."

"And he now holds the key to unraveling all the security at Infinity," Paris said mildly.

"I'm aware," Julian replied. "That still does not give us a right to simply go in and kill him."

"Then I'll challenge him," Alistair said. "And when I kill him, I'll reclaim what he stole."

"It's not that simple," Julian said. "You're not from their court."

He shook his head. "Is that a requirement? How specific are their laws?"

Julian opened his mouth to protest, then tilted his head. "An interesting point. I don't know."

Dominic returned. The stern expression he usually wore had replaced the gentle affection for Lucia. "And what will you do if you win? Declare yourself Baron of Atlanta?" He scoffed. "You've scarcely left this house in decades, why would—"

Alistair snarled at him. "While my social skills may be lacking, I am more than capable of tearing Elliott McAvoy's head from his shoulders."

"Dominic has a point," Nikko said. "Assuming you win, what would you do? Rule over the Casteron? What's to say that one of them doesn't immediately challenge you and kill you?"

"It wouldn't be that easy," he said. Nikko's lips pursed.

"Hear me out," Paris said, pacing across the plush carpet. His eyes were alight with a devious gleam. "Alistair becomes the Baron. Obviously, he's still loyal to Eduardo. Now the Blade of Auberon effectively controls all of Atlanta."

"You know as well as I do that the other Barons would never let that stand," Julian said. "You will have a target on your back."

"Let them come for me," Alistair said. "If that's what it takes to get her back, that's what I'll do."

"We should wait it out," Julian said. "I would all but guarantee someone else challenges Elliott within a month."

"A month," Alistair spluttered. "I will not leave her with him for another day, let alone a month."

"Why does this human witch matter so much?" Julian asked. "What is your rush?"

"He says she's his soulmate," Nikko said derisively.

Despite the harsh mockery in Nikko's tone, something changed in Julian's expression. His eyes were haunted, as if he heard something else entirely. "Is this true?"

"Shoshanna says it is, and I believe her," Alistair said. "Whether there is some magical thread binding us or simply my devotion, I love her. And I will not let her remain in his grasp for another day, whether I have your support or not."

Julian nodded. "And you believe she can break our curses?"

"You saw Lucia," Alistair said. "I know she can."

"I have an idea," he said. He flicked his eyes to Nikko. "Are you up for a fast run to Infinity and back?"

The wiry man grinned. "What do you need?"

26

Her hopes that she would awake to find herself in the cozy confines of the house in Midnight Springs were dashed when Shoshanna woke amidst a nest of pillows in a luxurious guest room in the Casteron mansion. It smelled all wrong.

Ruby was already puttering around the room. The smell of coffee filled the air. Shoshanna groaned and sat up. Her vision was a blurry wash of color, with a glaring white spot that had to be a window.

It was with a start that she realized she hadn't seen much of the sun in the last month of her life. As her schedule shifted to accommodate Alistair, she'd become used to the dark of night. Her evenings were lit by the moon and the hazy glow of candlelight. And now, that had changed again, as if to remind her how far she was from her safe refuge.

As she sat up and tried to make sense of her surroundings,

she checked in with her body. She wasn't a statue, so that was a good sign. Her limbs felt normal, if a little achy from the uncomfortably soft bed.

"Good, you're up," Ruby said. "We have work to do today. Elliott expects us to be ready for court tonight."

She squinted to bring Ruby slightly into focus. "We should leave. He's probably sleeping right now."

Ruby sat on the edge of the bed. "I want to. I keep telling myself to walk out the door, but I can't. I tried and made it halfway down the hall before my legs wouldn't even move. I just know that's not what he wants." She gently took Shoshanna's hand. "Do you think Alistair is looking for us?"

She nodded. "Yes. And Elliott's not exactly being subtle. He has to know where we are now."

But she had to wonder. They'd been insistent that they couldn't take action against Elliott before because of the potential for conflict. Now things were even worse, with Elliott sitting on the throne instead of being a nobody.

Ruby nodded, then threw her arms around Shoshanna. Her chest heaved. "I'm so sorry I got you into this."

Tears pricked Shoshanna's eyes. "This is one hundred percent not your fault."

"But I should have been better prepared to fight him off," Ruby protested.

"No," Shoshanna interrupted. She pulled away and cupped Ruby's cheeks, trying to focus on her dark eyes through the dark blur of her failing eyesight. "You're amazing and gorgeous, but he only came after you was because he was trying to get to me through you. This is my fault, and I'm going to make it up to you when this is over."

"It's his fault," Ruby said. "Because he's a stupid dick." Her eyes suddenly flicked to the door. "I feel bad saying that. Do you think you he heard it?"

Shoshanna shook her head. "No way."

Ruby sighed. "Okay. Up and at 'em, sleepyhead."

Shoshanna showered in the posh bathroom. As she stood under the warm spray, panic threatened to well up in her. Though she still felt that strange empty-headed serenity of Elliott's enthrallment, she knew she was in a very bad situation.

Just run, she told herself. *Just one step.*

But as soon as she imagined herself running into the safety of the sunlight, her muscles turned to concrete. She growled in frustration, but her body simply wouldn't respond.

After her shower, she was leaning close to the mirror and trying to tame her curls when a strange blonde woman walked into the bathroom behind her. She screamed in fright and scrambled for a towel.

"My name is Victoria," she said in a soft, high voice. "I work for Baron McAvoy." A tattoo of two red dots marked her collarbone. "You have work to do today."

"Do you mind? I'm kind of naked," Shoshanna said.

"You have work to do," Victoria repeated. "Get dressed, and I'll give you your itinerary."

Shoshanna grumbled and put on a bathrobe, then followed her back into the bedroom. Half a dozen shopping bags were strewn across the bed, and Ruby was pawing through them. "What's all this?"

"The Baron requested that his two witches have appropriate clothing to fit his status," Victoria replied. "In twenty minutes, I will return to bring you to your work. You will need your witchcraft supplies."

"Oh, nice," Ruby said as she pulled out a glittering red dress.

"Focus," Shoshanna said. "Is there anything that's not skintight?"

"The Baron would like you to present yourself and your best assets," Victoria said.

Shoshanna glared at her. "Considering why he wants me so badly, I think we both know my boobs aren't my best assets."

Victoria's head tilted. "You will hold a position of great respect in the Baron's court. The least you can do is dress respectfully."

She bit her tongue and nodded. "Fine. Can you leave?"

With a little *tsk,* Victoria left them, and Shoshanna pawed through the clothing. She found a pair of tight black pants and a sheer black top that looked slightly more comfortable—and easy to run in—than one of the short, skintight cocktail dresses. Not only was Elliott a gross, mind-violating bloodsucker, but he was sexist as hell.

All of the shoes were high heels, so she went barefoot to meet Victoria at the door. The blonde woman glanced down. "You will not walk into the Court barefoot. Put on your shoes."

"You're not Elliott," she replied. "Lead the way."

The tiny victory felt monumental after being ordered

around for the last twenty-four hours. Behind her, Ruby was hurrying to keep up in the short red dress and matching shoes.

Victoria led them downstairs to the open room where Elliott had killed Cristiano the night before. Though she couldn't make out details, Shoshanna could still see the massive pool of blood in her mind's eye.

Blurry figures worked around the room. Glass clinked, like someone was putting away barware, and there was the quiet hum of a vacuum cleaner. Rhythmic pounding and breaking tile signaled someone tearing up part of the floor, just as they had in Infinity.

"The Baron wishes you to create protections around the club, of the sort you created for the Auberon vampires at Infinity," Victoria said. "You'll focus at the front doors and the perimeter of his throne first."

Shoshanna surveyed the area. "That's going to be a problem."

"Why?" Victoria asked.

"Because, as I told Elliott yesterday, I'm cursed," she said. "My vision is getting worse every day, and I don't think I can see well enough to draw the sigils. I also don't have all my—" Her stomach plunged, and she caught the words before they could spill out of her mouth. *My books. They're at Alistair's house.* "I don't have all my supplies."

If she said she needed books, Elliott could pry out of her where they were. And then he might send his people to kill Alistair. While she was certain that Alistair could tear Elliott apart, she wasn't so certain about his odds if he had humans that were under his thrall that attacked the house in broad daylight. He would be helpless.

"What supplies do you need? Make a list, and someone will fetch what you need," Victoria said.

Her mouth was dry as she swallowed. "I can tell you. But I still can't see very well."

"You'll have to make do," Victoria said. "The Baron will allow you to attend to your own matters after this is done."

"That could be too late."

"Then it behooves you to work quickly, doesn't it?" she asked.

She took a tentative step toward the petite blonde. "Do you really want to be doing this? Or did he make you do it too?"

Her brow arched. "Of course I want to be here," she said. "It is a great honor to be a human assistant to the Casteron."

"And he didn't enthrall you?"

"He gives me power," she replied. "Just as Cristiano did before him."

"What does that mean?" Shoshanna asked.

Victoria shook her head and gripped her forearm. Her grip was powerful as she guided Shoshanna across the tiled floor. "I did not bring you here to answer all your questions. Get to work. Ruby will help you draw as needed."

Once someone delivered a box of chalk and an assortment of rulers, Shoshanna worked for hours. As they had done in Infinity, several workers broke up the tile around the elevated dais where the Baron sat. Kneeling on the hard concrete subfloor, Shoshanna crouched with her face just inches from the floor as she measured out the points of a circle. It was slow work with her vision fading. Elliott hadn't said how fast he wanted the work done, so she thought she might stretch it out over months. But as she purposely started to draw slower, she found herself resisting.

This isn't what he wants, she thought. *I can do better.*

Instead, she worked as quickly as she could with her limited sight and working only from memory. Heavy curtains covered all the windows, giving her no sense of the time. She only realized that it had been hours when her stomach growled. Sometime later, Victoria delivered them neatly packaged salads. She had only eaten a few bites when the human woman grabbed the food. "You've barely done anything."

"This takes time," Shoshanna replied. "It took me a week to do all the work at Infinity."

"The Baron wants this complete by tonight," she said.

Shoshanna laughed. "That's not going to happen."

"Then you can tell him as much," Victoria said. "He will not be pleased."

A chill prickled down her spine. The woman kept her dinner, and she knew she wasn't going to find any stashed snacks here in a vampire den. Her knees had begun to ache, and her hands were covered in chalk dust when she heard a deep male voice say, "Good evening, sir."

Dread pooled in her growling stomach as she raised her head to see a dark-clad male figure coming her way. "Good evening," Elliott said calmly. His legs were all Shoshanna could see as he stopped to survey her work. "I expected this to be complete. I told Victoria as much. Why is it incomplete?"

"It takes a long time to do," she replied. "I told her that when I did this at Infinity, it took me a week."

"Is that true?" he said, gently gripping her chin. "Tell me why you're working so slowly."

"I can barely see," she said, her voice trembling.

"And?"

The truth pushed up like vomit. "And I don't have all my books."

"Where are your books?"

She clamped her lips shut, but Elliott pressed his finger to her lips. The taste of his blood was warm and sharp, and she involuntarily opened her mouth to let it trickle over her tongue. Shame pulled tight around her as her need for it rose. He gently touched her lips, then tipped her chin up. "Where are they, Shoshanna?"

The power he held was stronger now, and there was no resistance. "At Alistair's house. Everything is there."

"We'll send someone for them tomorrow, then," he said. "That wasn't so hard. Have you tried your best to complete this work otherwise?"

She nodded. She hated him, but she desperately wanted his approval.

"Good girl," he said. "I forgive you." The relief that washed over her was sickening.

The deep male voice that had greeted him spoke up. Nordan, if she remembered correctly. "Sir, may I offer a word of caution."

"You may offer it," Elliott responded.

"You have given the humans quite a lot of blood since

yesterday. The scent of it is quite strong," he said. "Too much will damage their minds."

"They're strong," Elliott snapped. "And I need them cooperative."

"I understand, sir," Nordan said. His placating tone reminded Shoshanna of when she had to talk down an angry customer at Average Joe's. She hoped he wasn't going to lose his head, too. "But if you want witches who can use their power on your behalf and not mindless bloodbags, tread carefully."

"Duly noted," Elliott said. "Is the security team ready with new orders for this evening?"

"Yes, sir," Nordan replied. "I politely request that you to allow me to appear in your place tonight."

Elliott's voice rose. "Do you think me weak? Is it wise to insult your new Baron?"

The other man cleared his throat. "No, sir. But the Casteron tradition of trial by combat is rarely used anymore. It is likely that this will be a rocky transition, and you may have other challengers who wish to take advantage of you being new to the throne. Baron Cristiano faced several challengers in his first year of leadership, and he was generally favored to take the throne over his predecessor."

There was a long silence. "What is your implication?"

"I imply nothing, sir," Nordan said mildly. "Simply that as your steward, I am concerned for your safety."

"Your concern is noted," Elliot said. "Let them come."

Despite Elliott's cocky dismissal of his steward's warning, he revealed his fear when he came to fetch Shoshanna and Ruby from their shared bedroom upstairs. At Victoria's order, they'd dressed in red for the night's events.

Clearly dissatisfied with her sartorial choices, Victoria had chosen a criminally short red dress for Shoshanna. When he arrived at the door of their suite, his red eyes drifted over her. She stiffened as he leaned in and kissed her cheeks. "Since you were unable to complete my protections, I will trust you to defend me as you did yesterday."

"I don't want to hurt anyone else," she protested. "Please."

He squeezed her wrist tight and brought her close. His red eyes gleamed as he glared down at her. "You will do exactly as you're told."

"What are you trying to accomplish?" she asked quietly. "Are you just going to keep me enthralled forever?"

His brow furrowed. "I want you to be my queen. We were so good together before."

"We were kids," she said. "People change."

"That they do. Now I am the king of Atlanta, and you could be my queen," he said. He slid one hand down to her hip, his thumb stroking lightly over her stomach. "I can give you anything you want. Everything you need."

Dread prickled down her spine. "But I don't want that."

His grip tightened until little darts of pain shot from his fingers. "You don't mean that. Eventually, you'll come around. And until then, you'll do as you're told," he said, kissing the side of her neck. His teeth scraped the sensitive skin, reminding her of Alistair's bite. She hated the instant hunger that awakened in her. Elliott growled in her ear, "Now, finish getting ready."

An hour later, they descended the stairs with Elliott. As far as she could tell, the gated mansion was essentially the Casteron Baron's castle. Ruby had noticed the rolling hills of a golf course beyond the gates, making them think they might be in one of Atlanta's ritzier neighborhoods.

The music and noise of the gathered court was disorienting. Hazy red illuminated the elevated throne across the large gathering space. Voices chattered all around them in a dozen languages, and though Elliott was the source of her worst fear, she gripped his arm tighter.

"Don't worry," he said. "No one will touch you."

Her throat was dry as he rose to the throne, holding her hand as she settled onto a cushioned stool next to him. Someone approached and offered Elliott a glass. After he took it, someone pressed a glass into her hand.

"Enjoy," Elliott said. He raised his glass. "To the might of the Casteron!"

There was a halfhearted cheer from the crowd, then the music resumed. Huge sprays of dark red roses upon gold pedestals were arranged around the dais, covering the broken tile where her incomplete sigils lay. People approached, offering introductions and congratulations to Elliott upon his ascension. Some sounded sincere, but a few clearly spoke with obligatory politeness.

Shoshanna kept herself occupied by taking tiny sips of her champagne. Though it was tempting to gulp down the bubbly wine and make it through tonight in a drunken haze, she wanted her wits sharp. She glanced up at Elliott. "They're going to know you're enthralling us."

His hand slid down to grip hers, but his fingers dug painfully into the fleshy pad between her thumb and forefinger. "There are ears everywhere, Shoshanna," he said. "Sit here and be a silent beauty until you're told otherwise."

She drew a breath to argue, but the words dried up on her tongue. Surely people would figure out eventually that he had two unwilling slaves, not two eager companions.

The night passed in a blur of simpering vampires greeting Elliott. Eventually, a human woman presented herself, and Elliott drank deep from her as she moaned lasciviously.

He had just sent the woozy woman on her way when a shout of protest rippled through the crowd. "You are not welcome!" a woman's voice shouted.

She heard a chorus of inhuman snarls, then a male voice shouting, "Stop!"

A broad male stepped onto the dais with her, though he positioned himself in front of Elliott. "Sir, we will remove you."

"What is this?" Elliott demanded.

"Interlopers from Auberon," the man said.

Her heart soared. Was this it?

"Who let them in?" Elliott said.

"I don't know," he said. "They didn't come in the front door. One of them says he's here to issue a challenge to you."

Her jaw dropped, and she squinted to see Elliott's face. His voice took on a whiny edge of indignation. "They can't do that. They're not Casteron."

"Where is Elliott McAvoy?" a familiar voice boomed,

clipped with a faint accent. Her body warmed, and she felt the familiar tug on her hand as their bond resonated. She knew that voice, and the stubborn ferocity behind it.

"What are you doing here?" Elliott snapped. "This is a private party. Leave while you still can."

"I am here to challenge you," Alistair announced, his voice carrying in the quiet room. "Prove that you are worthy to hold the title of Baron."

"Only the Casteron can challenge me," Elliott replied.

Alistair chuckled, a smug sound that made her smile. "I'm afraid not. Your laws allow for any vampire to make a challenge."

"And who are you?"

A gasp rippled through the crowd, and she knew he had uncovered his face. She heard a few *what the fuck?* from the gathered vampires. "Alistair Thorne," he replied. "Soon to be Baron Alistair Thorne."

"Jesus, what are you?"

"Your executioner," Alistair replied. "Unless you'd like to concede before I kill you."

"I don't think so," Elliott said. He shed his coat and tossed it into Shoshanna's lap. He glanced at Ruby. "Be ready to aim her."

"Ah, Mr. McAvoy," Alistair said. "As the challenger, I will choose the weapon. We will fight with our hands, and only our hands. Further treachery with the witch will be an act of dishonor."

Elliott was silent for a moment. "Can he do that?" he asked quietly.

"He can," Nordan said. His amusement was barely concealed. "You can refuse, but if he will not renegotiate, you forfeit the throne."

"I accept," Elliott said loudly. He stepped down from the dais. "And when I kill you, would you prefer your head to be thrown in the garbage or returned to your Elder?"

Alistair laughed. "You can do whatever you like with it. I'm here for one thing only." Again, she heard the scraping of furniture as the vampires made way for a bloody fight. For the first time, she was grateful for her poor vision. Though she was thankful Alistair was here, she didn't want to see him hurt.

When both men were facing each other on the stone floor, Nordan shouted, "Begin!"

Screams erupted amidst the crowd. A body slammed into her, and she felt herself rise in the air amidst a chorus of shouts. Her feet dangled dangerously, and she clung hard to the broad forearm wrapped around her ribs. They landed hard, and the body pulled her back into a dark alcove. Warm lips brushed her ear as a hand covered her mouth. "Don't worry," he said. "It's your other favorite vampire."

A broad smile crossed her face. She nodded, and Paris removed his hand. She turned to find his red eyes staring down at her. "I want to help him. Point me at Elliott, and I'll light him up."

Paris shook his head emphatically. "If you interfere, the Casteron will retaliate. We're doing this by their laws so we don't ignite a war. If he pulls this off, we all walk away clean."

"And if he loses?"

"We must pray he doesn't."

Catching that first glimpse of Shoshanna clad in a revealing red dress that revealed most of her body ignited a righteous fury like he'd never felt. He was relieved to see her alive and whole, with no sign of serious injury. But to see her treated like a glittering accessory for that pompous fool infuriated him. Furthermore, even through the cataract-like film on her eyes, he could see the red tint that betrayed the power of Elliott's blood.

That was his soulmate, chosen for him by destiny itself. This was more than a promise of lust fulfilled, of love returned. He had been given a sacred responsibility to protect her and see that she walked safely through this world. And he had failed once, but no more. Elliott McAvoy would pay for what he had done with his life. If the Casteron tore him to shreds after, so be it.

When the steward gave the order to begin, Alistair hesitated for a split second to let Paris run past him. When he looked up to see Shoshanna's seat now vacant, he bared his teeth and lunged at Elliott. They tussled in a flurry of blows, bare hands balled into fists. Alistair held nothing back. He unleashed the rage that had simmered in him for nearly a century.

The rage of Franziska stealing his dreams simply to have a plaything that would amuse her forever. The rage of the Shieldsmen igniting a war that would kill hundreds for no reason. The rage of watching everyone he cared for fall to Armina's curses, bearing punishments for which they more than paid.

And most of all, the rage that he had lost so much of his life to this ugliness. And that this bastard, this fucking fool, would touch what was his.

Though it had been decades since he had fought with the Shroud under Julian's command, his body had no hesitation. He blocked Elliott's blows easily, barely even thinking as he shifted and danced around the other man. He feinted and let Elliott in close enough to strike, then threw a bone-cracking punch into his shoulder.

Elliott screamed in pain, eyes brilliant red. "Ruby!" he bellowed.

"She's gone!" Ruby yelled back.

"You can't cheat this time," Alistair snarled. "She belongs to me."

Elliot bared his teeth and came up, driving something thin and sharp up into his chest. Acidic heat spread from the small puncture, and he looked down to see just an inch of thin wood protruding from his ribs. Then Elliot yanked his hand back, taking the slender stake with him.

Treacherous bastard. Weakness radiated from the wound, and one leg threatened to buckle.

Elliott shouted, "Shoshanna! Answer me!"

Alistair punched him hard, but they both froze and looked up at the sound of her voice. "I'm here."

"No," he murmured. Paris was behind her, but his face was blistered, and he was frantically trying to put out the fire on his jacket. "Get her out!"

At that, a pair of vampires grabbed Paris and yanked him back, snarling and fighting. He heard a body thump twice in rapid succession, thrown up to the ceiling before crashing to the floor.

"Do it, Shoshanna!" Elliott ordered. His eyes flared red, and Alistair recognized the pressurized pulse of power.

Her eyes drifted downward. Though her vision was failing, he knew she was looking right at him, the thread connecting them pulsing like a heartbeat. "Alistair?"

The sound of her voice pushed away the pain. "I'm right here," he said. "No matter what happens, I love you. I know it's not your fault."

The tug on his hand was powerful, as if something was trying to pull them together. He could imagine the way she'd described that little thread, looped around his little finger. He wanted to weep at the beauty of that bond, of feeling connected to her so profoundly.

Elliott barked a bitter laugh. "You love her?" Then his eyes widened. “Ruby told me she was fucking the vampire who protected her. You? Disgusting.”

“Think what that says about you if she prefers me,” he replied, baring his teeth.

“Shoshanna!” Elliott yelled again.

“No,” she said in a clear voice. Something vibrated through him, like a plucked string.

“No?” Elliott said, comically indignant. While he stared up at Shoshanna, Alistair pounced. Alistair bore him to the ground, shattering the tile beneath them as he hit the floor. The frenzied crowd bellowed, apparently more vested in a bloody finale than a particular winner. He even heard a few shouts of *kill him!*

Alistair twisted Elliott’s arm up and planted one knee on his back. “People of the Casteron, your Baron has a choice,” he shouted. “I will grant you mercy if you wish it, but you will be severed from the Court and banished from the city. Refuse to yield, and I will kill you.”

Elliott squirmed. His voice was wheedling and thin as he cried, “I yield!”

Of course he would, the coward. For good measure, Alistair leaned on his arm, shattering his shoulder joint. Ignoring his cries of pain, Alistair raised his head to see the silver-haired man at the dais. The steward shouted, “Alistair Thorne has claimed the seat of the Baron.”

There were surprising shouts of joy, though he heard the whispers about his appearance. Let them think that that he had crawled from Hell itself. He cared for only one person, who stared down at him with Paris holding her hand gently. His old friend nodded to him. Then his handsome face twisted as he raised a hand to point.

Alistair had just enough time to turn before a stake slammed into his chest. He grabbed Elliott's wrist as the weapon buried itself between his ribs. His vision went white, and his muscles went weak. "Fuck," he groaned.

"I don't lose," Elliott said.

His eyes widened as Alistair grabbed his wrist and pulled the stake free. A gout of blood sprayed from the wound. Pure rage powered him now. "I'm glad you did that, because I wanted to do this." With a growl, he swept Elliott's legs from under him, then twisted his head around. In a haze of red, he tore the other man's head from his shoulders and tossed it across the room. It hit the ground with a wet thump and rolled into the crowd. Bloodthirsty roars surrounded him.

Heels clattered, and he turned to find Shoshanna running for him. He swept her into his arms. The smell of her soothed his rage. Every beat of her heart was a gentle whisper that all was well. "I'm so sorry," he said. "For everything."

"I know," she said. "Me too."

"I need you to know—"

"Alistair Thorne, I challenge you to the throne," a female voice announced.

Shoshanna grabbed his arm. Her eyes were wide with fear. "You can't."

He kissed her forehead. "Don't worry." He still held Shoshanna's hand as he turned to see his challenger. "And who challenges me?"

"Vanessa Moretti," the elegant woman said, stepping

neatly over Elliott's body. An organized formation of well-dressed bodyguards fanned out behind her, but none of them moved toward him. Though she wore a modern black dress and simple diamond jewelry, she had the regal bearing of a queen.

"And how do you wish to challenge me?" he asked.

"Combat befitting vampires of the twenty-first century," she replied. "A vote will do."

"Very well," he replied, sparing a faint smile. "All who wish for me, Alistair Thorne, to be your Baron, speak now."

"Oi, let the ugly fucker do it!" someone shouted.

"Seamus, shut the fuck up," a woman yelled from upstairs. "Bloody arsehole."

"And those who wish for me, paramour to your rightful ruler, who was slain by this treacherous upstart, who has known and loved the Casteron for over two hundred years?" The crowd roared their approval. "What do you say, Mister Thorne?"

"I yield to the will of the court," Alistair said, bowing his head.

"By the laws of the Casteron, Vanessa Moretti is the Baron of this court," Nordan shouted.

The raven-haired woman stepped up to the throne. "As my first act as your Baron, I pardon the human witches, Shoshanna York and Ruby Wang. They were enthralled against their will and weaponized against your rightful Baron. I will abide no retaliation against them." Her eyes drifted to Alistair, and he nodded in recognition. That had been a critical point of their negotiations. Vanessa's scarlet eyes scanned the crowd. "Victoria Beck."

A petite blonde woman took a shaky step forward. "Ma'am."

"Is your loyalty to the Casteron or to Elliott McAvoy?"

Her head dipped, and the woman knelt, just inches from Elliott's decapitated body. "To the Casteron."

"Should I hear so much as a whisper to the contrary, your life is forfeit," Vanessa said. Her eyes lifted to Alistair. "Our guests from the Auberon may leave. There is court business that needs my attention." She snapped her fingers, and a trio of her bodyguards approached Alistair. One gestured broadly toward the exit, and he took the hint.

Paris joined them, holding Ruby's hand. The other woman stared up at him with sheer wonder in her eyes. Shoshanna clung tightly to his hand, her whole body trembling. He wanted to trust Vanessa's word, but he was no fool. He wouldn't rest easy until they were out of the court and back home.

When they reached the lobby, Vanessa's guards led them out, and pointedly slammed the doors behind them. Outside in the moonlight, he grabbed Shoshanna's face and kissed her. "Are you all right?"

"I am now," she said, gently cupping his cheek. Though her eyes were cloudy, he could see his own hideous reflection. For once, he didn't turn away. He didn't want to miss a second. "I knew you'd be here."

He kissed the tip of her nose. "A fight to the death and a five-minute monarchy have worn me out. What do you say? May I escort you home, Miss York?"

"I would like nothing more, Mister Thorne."

PARIS DROVE them back to the house in Midnight Springs. The entire way home, Shoshanna's friend Ruby talked about the fight and quizzed Paris about how long it would take for her vampire blood to wear off. "Shit!" she exclaimed when they neared the exit to Midnight Springs.

"What's wrong?" Paris asked, looking at her warily.

"That asshole bought us like ten grand worth of clothes," she complained. "I should have gotten to keep it."

"I am not getting paid enough for this," Paris complained.

Shoshanna just chuckled, holding Alistair's hand as she rested her head on his shoulder.

"Are you taking me home?" Ruby asked.

"You'll stay at Alistair's home for a few days," Paris said. "Until Elliott's blood has worn off, we want you two under supervision. By the way, your mother says you're in big fucking trouble."

Ruby sighed. At her request, Paris took them to an all-night drivethrough, since Elliott had "no fucking clue how to keep humans alive." Once both witches were settled with their meals, they returned to the welcoming glow of Alistair's home.

Paris escorted Ruby inside, leaving Alistair and Shoshanna at the door. The big house loomed over them, with its darkened window and the soft murmur of conversation inside. This quiet place, which had only been his for so many years, was theirs now. Something had changed forever when she arrived, and it had been set right with her return.

Before he took her inside, Alistair paused and grasped her

hand. "I need to apologize to you. I am sorry that I ever doubted you."

She sighed. "No, you were right. I thought it worked, and—"

"Bloody hell," he muttered. He laughed and pressed his forehead to hers as she stared up him in confusion. "There was no way to tell you. It worked. Lucia is alive."

Her brown eyes widened, her lips curving into a smile. "Are you serious?"

"I rarely joke, and this would not be the time to start," he replied. "Come in. Just know that she doesn't know about Kova yet. If she asks, he's traveling."

She nodded solemnly. "I understand."

When they walked into the house, they were greeted by a flurry of conversation. He heard Dominic's low voice say, "She's back." He rounded the corner to find Lucia at the counter, wringing her hands. Dominic sat at the kitchen island reading a book and sipping from a glass of blood. He glanced up. "Welcome back, your majesty," he said drily.

"You missed your opportunity to show fealty," Alistair replied. Dominic just raised an eyebrow and folded his arms, watching as Lucia dashed for Shoshanna.

Lucia spoke rapidly in Czech. "I saw you in my dreams!" She threw her arms around Shoshanna and lifted her off her feet as she hugged her. "Oh, bless you and your kindness!"

Shoshanna laughed. "I don't understand you. I'm so sorry, but I think you're happy."

"She says thank you," Dominic said. "And that she saw you in her dreams and knew that someone would save her." He spared the faintest smile as he watched Lucia's effervescent joy.

"You're welcome," Shoshanna said. She gently grasped Lucia's shoulders and smiled. "I'm so happy that it worked."

Dominic nodded to them. "I've made myself at home down the hall. Paris will stay tonight as well to ensure that your friend is safe. Both of you need to stay in for a few days until the blood is out of your system."

Her brow furrowed. "How long does that take?"

"Without any further influence from Elliott, you should be fine in a few days," he said.

With a quiet patter, a blur of black barreled down the hallway and leaped at Shoshanna. Shrill meows pierced her laughter as Magneto rubbed against her legs. Tears streamed down her cheeks as she picked him up. "Oh, buddy," she said, pressing her face to him. "I'm so sorry. Were you good? Did they feed you?"

"He was thoroughly cared for," Dominic said. "Lucia saw to it."

Shoshanna kissed the top of the cat's head, snuggling him close as she spoke in soft, cooing tones. "I love you, little man," she murmured. "I won't leave you again, okay?" Eventually, she let him go and glanced up at Alistair. "I need you to help me in the library."

"Surely you need to rest after all of this," he said, already fearing the standoff to come.

She shook her head. "I need to break this curse before it's too late," she said. "I have to redo everything that you destroyed."

He shook his head. "Shoshanna...I didn't destroy it," he said. "I would never destroy what you worked so hard on."

Her brow furrowed. "But you told me..."

"I told you that to protect you," he said. "To slow you down so you didn't kill yourself."

Her sad smile sent a spike of guilt through his heart. "You were very convincing."

"I'm so sorry," he said. He extended his hand. "Come with me."

He guided her carefully down the stairs to the basement and into the sparsely furnished training gym. While she waited, he brought out her rolled-up drawings and supplies from the locked armory. He might have been pleased with the expression of relief on her face if he had not been the cause of her grief. "It's all here," he said, averting his gaze.

She sank to her knees, spreading out the drawings. Her eyes glistened. "I should have known you wouldn't destroy it."

He shook his head and joined her on the floor. "No, you shouldn't have. I was awful to you about this. And I am truly sorry."

"I forgive you," she said. "I'm sorry for using the sunlight on you."

"It was warranted," he replied. "Are you sure you want to do this now?"

She drew a shaky breath. "No. But I'm afraid if I wait, I'll end up like Lucia."

"We asked her about her symptoms," he said. "She didn't remember losing her sight until the very end. Does that change anything?"

Shoshanna shook her head. "I can't take the chance," she said. "Every day I wait is a risk."

A lump rose in his throat. "I won't stop you if you believe it's the right thing. But don't hurt yourself for me." He shook his head. "I can live with my appearance if it means you're still here. Promise me that you'll put yourself first."

Her clouded eyes gleamed. "I promise. Me first. Then you. And I will break yours, along with the others eventually."

"I know you will," he said, cupping her cheek. He froze as her warm hand brushed his cheek, tracing the ridged lines. He wanted to hide, but he held steady, leaning into her touch.

"You're not hiding from me," she said, smiling.

"Never again. If you see something you like, then who am I to question it?" he replied.

She smirked, that wonderful mischievous gleam in her eyes. "It's about time."

He leaned in for a kiss. Her lips parted for him, and she made her way into his lap, letting him embrace her as they kissed, long and sweet. He could taste the blood of the other vampire on her, but he resolved to let his passion for her burn it all away.

She broke away, tracing his brow. "I love you, Alistair," she said. "More than I ever knew I was capable of."

"And I love you," he replied. "I will spend my eternity proving that I am worthy of what destiny has given me."

Her brow lifted. "You're a poet."

"Do you like it?"

"I do," she said with a chuckle. She kissed his brow. "I might need your help with this."

Following her guidance, he helped her draw the intricate lines and spirals of the spell on the wood floor. As he had before, he measured out ingredients for her, placing each pile of herbs or crystals where she directed. He could hear her pulse accelerating as they completed the process.

They were nearing dawn when she took a deep breath. "I think it's done."

"Should I leave?"

She shook her head. "I need you here," she said. "I didn't realize until I was working on Lucia how important her soul-mate bond was. I think that's where the curse came from, but it was also how I broke it." She rooted through the box and came up with a piece of red string. She clasped his hand, then wrapped their hands in red.

He listened in awe as she recited a ritual in French, invoking the power of the earth and the air. Her voice seemed to vibrate in his bones. It seemed like standard ritual stuff, until she came to something unexpected. "Threads of destiny, red as blood, bindings break and poisons purify. As it is spoken, let it be done."

The ground shuddered beneath them, and a powerful wave of heat rolled up his spine. Desire roared to life within him. She gripped his shoulders painfully tight, and he claimed her lips in a hungry kiss, devouring her. It took every ounce of willpower not to bite her, with those sweet arteries pounding like drums.

Fire surged from his hand, up his arm, and into his still heart. Every muscle in his body tensed. It felt as if he would split in half, with pain rampaging up one side of him and mindless pleasure rolling down the other. He was breaking, shattering, and melting all at once.

Suddenly, he was falling into the black, unmoored as he floated into oblivion. He was curiously numb.

"Shoshanna?" he murmured. He was all alone. The world was deep, fathomless black, with fireblooms of blue and purple igniting like fireworks.

A pale woman clad only in bluish light emerged from the shadows. "Cursed one," she said, her voice coming from all around him. Thunder rolled, then blue lightning burst across the void. In its afterglow, he saw millions of tiny threads in a thousand shades of gray.

"Who are you?" he asked. His voice was thin and flat, barely a whisper compared to the woman's thunderous voice.

"Are you worthy of her?" the figure asked.

He froze. "I do not know. I hope so. I love her."

"You have a choice," the woman said. "Bear your curse forever, and she will live. Break your curse, and she will die." Her head tilted, alien eyes narrowing. Lightning illuminated her again. In that flash of sickly blue light, he could have sworn he saw the body of a spider, long legs clinging to the web of threads around them. "What is your choice?"

"It is no choice," he replied firmly. "I will bear my curse. Let her live."

"You have cursed the Night Weaver's name for nearly a hundred years," the female figure said. The spider's body was no more, leaving only the lithe, slender woman's figure. "One human, a mere flicker in eternity...is she worth such a trade?"

He growled and surged forward. "I would bear this curse for millennia for her. For the rest of time if that's what it takes."

The alien figure smiled, baring impossibly long, sharp canines. Her eerie silver eyes reflected his monstrous face. "Very well. You have chosen."

Lightning flashed again, and the ground rumbled beneath him.

The dull numbness was gone, and he plunged into a fiery pit of agony.

I love you, he thought as he fell into the darkness. *Please let me see her again.*

28

Glowing threads of bruise purple and midnight blue surrounded Shoshanna, as if she was a tiny fly snared in a monstrous spider's web. Screams on the icy wind bellowed her name, cursing her in languages she could not comprehend. It hadn't been like this with Lucia, and she feared that she wouldn't survive this time.

No.

She had not fought her way through this witch's curse, then survived Elliott's indignities just to die in a damned spider's web inside her own mind. There was a soulmate and a whole lifetime of possibility waiting for her, and she would not give it up without a hell of a fight.

Raising her left hand felt like lifting a mountain. Wrapped around her wrist was a red sash, its tail whipping in the vicious wind. It unraveled slowly, threatening to escape her grasp. But as she clenched her fist firmly, the ribbon tightened around her wrist. Soon it, streamed up her arm, then split into a thousand brilliant strands that tangled into the bruise-like web. The web resisted her, sending a painful shock back into her body.

This was too much power. So much malice was woven into Alistair's curse, and thus, the curse that had afflicted her. Gazing at the massive display of Armina's power, she understood what the Night Weaver had done. Looking up, she could see a mirror image of the web below her. This was a curse upon a curse, unleashed upon the one Alistair dared to love with all his heart. It was the soulmate bond that had triggered her curse, and it was that same bond that would break it.

Somewhere in the distance, she heard Alistair scream, an inhuman sound of agony. Despair wracked her, and she clawed to get free. She had to protect him. There was no point to all of this without him.

I love you, she thought, feeling the warmth of him all through her, surging through her veins, sparkling and crackling on every nerve ending.

The gravity of the Night Weaver's power pulled her down into the web. But the red ribbon around her wrist pulled taut, wrenching her upward. She reached for the ribbon and plucked it like a harp string. The deafening sound threatened to vibrate her entire body into subatomic particles. A shockwave rumbled across the web.

"With love's bond, be broken!" she bellowed into the void.

Light exploded across her vision, and then she was sinking, holding onto the burning red thread with her fading strength. Though she clawed upward, she sank deeper and deeper into the consuming dark.

Her descent slowed, and she found herself standing on a dark, foggy expanse. A strange creature emerged from the darkness. At first, she thought it was a woman riding on a huge spider's back, but she soon realized the woman and the spider were one. The creature's upper body was that of an ethereal, pale woman with bright silver eyes, while her lower body was the gleaming black body of a spider. White tendrils formed her hair, floating around her angular face as if she was sinking underwater.

Shoshanna recoiled, but the creature closed the distance quickly. In a voice like the humming of crickets, the creature said, "What demands do you make of me now, witch?"

"I make no demands," she said calmly. "Who are you?"

Silver eyes skimmed over her, and she did her best to maintain an even gaze. Finally, the spider creature nodded and said, "Your intentions are good. The one who came before called me *fati aranaeum,* but this name means nothing to me."

"Do you have your own name?" Shoshanna dared to ask. "I'm Shoshanna."

The spider creature's head tilted slightly. Her expression wasn't quite a smile, but it was somehow inviting. "My full name would take hours of your mortal time to hear, and you would not be able to pronounce it with your human voice. Would you like to pick a name that sounds pleasant?"

Staring at the creature with those eight gleaming onyx legs, Shoshanna could only picture Ursula, which she'd always thought was a beautiful name despite its association with a voice-stealing sea witch. "Do you like Ursula?"

The way the creature repeated it was closer to *Orr-soo-lah,* but her expression was a genuine smile now. "This has a pleasant sound. You may call me this, Shoshanna. I thank you for this name," she said. Her hands lifted, displaying two tattered ribbons of dark blue, the exact color of the curse that had bound Lucia and Alistair. "You have broken these spells."

"Were they yours?" she asked.

"Never," Ursula said. She sighed. "But when a contract is made, a contract is honored. And when one such as me is bound, I must obey."

"Did the Night Weaver bind you?" Shoshanna asked.

"This is truth," Ursula said, releasing the ribbons. They dissipated in a dust that shimmered faintly before fading away. "And now I am free. I may return to the webs, to weave fate."

"Oh," Shoshanna said. "So you didn't intend to hurt Alistair or me?"

"No," Ursula said. "But it was demanded. And when a contract is forged, a contact is honored."

The spider woman started to turn away, but Shoshanna took a step forward and blurted, "Wait, please. Can you tell me anything else? I know there are others that are cursed. Did your contract include them?"

Ursula shook her head. "These are not my contracts," it said. "Therefore I do not know their rules."

"Could you help me break the others? Maybe I could release your friends if they're trapped."

"One such as me has no friends," it said. "Only duty." Her stomach sank, but Ursula's head tilted. "But this binding defies fate. It would drive apart those who fates wishes to bind together. It is improper for weavers to be bound in webs."

Ursula stepped closer and took Shoshanna's hand. Her skin was ice cold and eerily smooth.

Searing heat burst in Shoshanna's palm as an incandescent white thread burst from her hand. A firm tug rippled down her arm and to her spine. Lightning illuminated the dark canvas, displaying an impossibly intricate web. One single glance made Shoshanna dizzy, but she tried to follow the bright white thread. Her eyes closed involuntarily, and then it was dark again.

"I see that your thread is woven through many others," Ursula said. "It is important for you to continue." With a little flourish, she turned over her hand to show a gleaming silver ring. She slid it onto Shoshanna's right ring finger. "You show respect by giving me a pleasant name, and you show respect to fate by untangling this knot that has long disrupted the flow. In return, I will give you knowledge."

Shoshanna stared at the glowing ring. This was getting wild, even by witch standards. "What knowledge?"

"You will have insight when the time is appropriate," Ursula said. Thunder rolled across the sky, and Shoshanna felt the ground shaking beneath her. "Now you must rest and regain your strength."

"Wait—"

But Ursula was already gone, climbing a gleaming strand to that beautiful, dizzying web stretched across the darkness. And then it was all gone, and there was only black.

This was the worst hangover of her life. Her head felt like it would split in two. She didn't remember drinking, but only cheap wine or cheaper tequila could make her feel this crappy.

Shoshanna opened her eyes and immediately closed them. The glow of her phone was meteor-bright, leaving glowing spots on the comforting dark of her eyelids. A furry tail flicked against her face. Without opening her eyes, she felt for the cat and scratched his back, prompting a purr. He flopped over and pushed his little bean-like toes into her cheek. Very dignified.

"Mags, I feel terrible," she croaked. Her lips felt stuck together, and she half-wondered if he had used her face as a litter box. She slowly opened her eyes and surveyed the room around her. The dark fabric stretched overhead was unfamiliar at first, but she soon recognized the scarlet bedclothes, and the woody, clean smell of Alistair in the room. Only a single low lamp burned in the corner of the room, casting a soft, warm glow.

She'd never woken here, but it felt like home. When she reached across the bed, she found it empty. There was a folded note propped up in front of the other pillow. It read:

Drink when you wake. -A

Rolling over, she found a glass of water on the nightstand. Her vision was still a bit blurred, but she could see the outlines of her fingers as they wrapped around the glass. It was a vast improvement over the last few days.

Maybe she'd done it.

She took a long drink of water, which tasted bitter and ever so slightly of dirty socks. It had to be one of Ruby's concoctions, or something had gone terribly wrong in the house's pipes. But she was grateful for the funky taste as a warm feeling spread down her shoulders and up the back of her neck, easing the wicked ache.

Magic had been one hell of a party drug. She'd had dreams of spider ladies and fate and magic glowing rings. On a whim, she lifted her right hand and gasped. While there was no ring, thin inked lines formed an intricate, spiraling web around her ring finger, with several delicate tendrils across the back of her hand.

It was real. And if she could trust her own memory, she'd gained a hint of favor with a creature that seemed to think it was responsible for weaving fate itself.

The light tinkle of the piano from upstairs broke through her spinning thoughts. There would be time to ponder exactly what she'd experienced. For now, she needed to see that Alistair was safe. After checking that she was sufficiently dressed in a loose nightgown, she trudged up the stairs. Reaching the ground floor felt like running a marathon.

A familiar hooded figure sat at the piano, hands flying across the keys. It was one of her favorites, a Schumann fantasy. She drew a breath to call his name, but he turned before she spoke.

Her breath caught in her throat at the sight of his hands, splayed across the polished wood of the piano bench. She'd barely noticed while he played; the pale, unblemished skin had almost blended into the ivory keys at a distance. As he stood, he shook his head to let the hood fall back from the face she had seen only in her dreams.

Her eyes widened. "I know you," she murmured. The man

before her was impossibly beautiful, with thick, dark hair that fell in messy curls over his brow. Lovely blue-green eyes followed her, twinkling with mischief as she approached. A dusting of dark scruff clung to his broad jaw. His lips were flushed and full, as if he'd just fed.

He was the man she had seen in her dreams, the first night she was here. Despite his magnetic beauty, she felt the tiniest ache of regret that the other version of Alistair was no more. She had not hated it the way Alistair had, and had come to like him, rough gray hands and hoods and all.

"Excuse me, but what have you done with my soulmate?" she said, fighting back tears.

His brow furrowed. "Shoshanna, it's me," he said, clearly hurt. He cleared his throat. "Is my voice...is it different?"

She gasped and shook her head. "Oh, I was kidding. I'm sorry!"

His lips spread into a smile, and he darted for her, lifting her up by the waist. He gazed up at her. "I'm afraid I'll have to do in his place."

She laughed and ran her palms over his smooth cheeks. "How did this happen? I was focused on myself. I didn't try to break your curse at all."

"I think you said it yourself," he replied. "Your curse was bound to mine. When you broke one, you broke the other."

She touched his brow, where there had once been curled black horns. His brow was smooth, his skin cool to the touch. His eyes closed, his obvious satisfaction reminiscent of Magneto getting his ears scratched. "How do you feel?"

"I won't lie to you," he said. "I had a rather unpleasant evening. Imagine a snake peeling out of its old skin."

"Gross," she said.

He nodded. "Extraordinarily so. But now you have returned to me, and I have everything I could possibly want." His head cocked, and a mischievous smile spread on his lips. "Almost everything."

In a blur, he carried her downstairs and deposited her on the sumptuous expanse of his bed. She marveled at him as he knelt over her. The simple pleasure of seeing him in the light was incredible. "I need a shower," she complained as he lavished her with kisses, awakening the heat of desire. "How long was I asleep?"

"Two days," he said. "I don't care. I need you."

"Considering how good your senses are, I care," she said. She pressed one finger to his lips to silence his protests. "You can shower with me."

He tilted his head, considering her offer. "Fair enough."

He could barely keep his hands off her as she stripped down, and he was still half-clothed when he stumbled into the shower with her. As the warm water burst from the shower, he pressed her to the cool tile and kissed her thoroughly, tongue claiming her mouth. She gave up and let him scrub her clean with a sweet, floral soap that made her think of springtime and flowers bursting open.

Warm water cascaded over her back as he scrubbed her, kissing her shoulders, then in a line down her spine. She shivered with anticipation as he rose again, his cock hard against her. She turned to him and stared in wonder at his face. For the first time, she saw the desperate hunger in his eyes as he gazed at her, finally unafraid to be seen.

"My brilliant, beautiful mate," he murmured. He kissed her lips, sliding one hand down between them to stroke her. She rose on her toes, giggling against his lips as pleasure flickered through her.

"I like the sound of that," she replied, tracing the broad expanse of his shoulders. He grinned and hiked her thighs up around his waist, then carried her out of the shower. She squealed with surprise at the cool air, but he snagged a towel and tossed it around her. "It's cold!"

"I'll warm you up," he growled, kissing the side of her neck. He gently placed her on the bed and knelt so that he was on eye level. His blue-green eyes were utterly riveting. "What would you like from me? I am entirely yours."

"I want to look at you," she replied, pulling him to the bed with her. She gently pushed on his chest, guiding him to lie back. A gentle smile spread on his handsome face as she braced herself against his chest, undulating her hips back against his hard length.

"I certainly cannot complain about the view," he drawled. His hands caressed her, sliding down to rest on her hips. "Are you pleased with what you see?"

"I was always pleased with what I saw," she said. He scowled, but she tapped his nose lightly. "I saw you as you were from the beginning. I always knew you were beautiful. No curse could hide that. But I like seeing your smile. I like that you're not afraid anymore."

She expected him to argue, but his eyes gleamed. "I was

afraid. But no more. I love you, Shoshanna York. More than anything I have ever known. I want nothing more than to spend my eternity making you happy."

With a smile, she bent and helped herself to a long, lazy kiss. His hand tangled into her hair, holding her until she was breathless and dizzy. She broke away to gaze down at him. "And I love you, Alistair Thorne. I want to spend my eternity letting you make me happy."

He laughed, rumbling through her body. "Easy enough." Then he growled and flipped her onto her back. "Shall I begin making you happy?" His cock nudged at her, and she shifted her hips to welcome him. Warmth slid up her spine as he pushed into her, his gaze never breaking from her. Watching his eyes flutter made her clench tight around him. She saw his hunger taking hold, as the blue-green turned to purple-red of wine, then the bright red of a ruby in sunlight.

Something resonated throughout her body, centered at her chest. Though she'd enjoyed sex with him before, it was nothing compared to this as the power of the soulmate bond echoed around them. Her whole body trembled as he moved in her.

Something snapped taut between them. His eyes widened, making it clear that he felt it too. "Shoshanna," he panted, quickening his thrusts.

She just nodded breathlessly, circling her hips to meet him, holding tight to his broad shoulders. "I know," she breathed. "I know."

Fiery desperation tightened in a metal band around her core, pulling tighter and tighter to where their bodies met, melding together into one pulsing heart. Her fingers tangled in his thick hair, pulling him down as she threw her head back in invitation. He kissed her neck, sucking at the soft hollow before his teeth pierced the skin. Pain faded quickly into nameless pleasure, so intense it overwhelmed her.

The world was a trillion threads of magic wrapping around her. It was better than magic, better than chocolate, better than sex itself. This was the soulmate bond, made reality. Two bodies, two hearts, so thoroughly entwined that she could not remember what it was like before she knew Alistair's touch, that there was ever a time before his lips were at her throat.

She let out a clipped cry of relief and sheer delight as orgasm exploded through her, fireworks of red and pink and white that pulled her body in a tight arch. Alistair caught her, crushing her to his chest as he finished with a triumphant shout. His lips were wet and red with her blood, and he lowered his head to kiss her. "Shoshanna," he murmured, pressing his forehead to hers. "My God."

"Alistair," she replied, wiggling her hips beneath him. He groaned, withdrawing slowly as he flopped onto his back and gave her a glorious view of his body, naked and gleaming with sweat. As she caught her breath, she simply marveled at him, tracing the soft curve of muscle on his shoulder, down to the hollow of his elbow where a single vein stood out against his lean forearm. Then she kissed the inside of his wrist and sat up. "You know, all this time, it's been very unfair."

"Hmm?"

"You've gotten to look at me naked a dozen times, and this

is my first time," she said with mock anger. "You've kept all this concealed."

"Well, by all means, look as you will," he said, propping one arm under his head.

She traced one finger along his lower ribs, then down his hipbone and lower. She watched with delight as the muscles in his thigh twitched, chasing the grazing touch of her fingers. When her hand drifted up to his chest, he gently grasped her right hand, fingers tracing the new, dark lines. "What is this?"

"It's so strange," she said. "But I had a vision when I broke the curse." She told him about Ursula, and to her surprise, he didn't look skeptical.

"I saw something as well," he said quietly. "It challenged me on whether I was worthy of you. It didn't look quite the same, but I caught flashes of a spider." His strong fingers massaged her hand lightly, sending shivers down her spine. "So what arcane knowledge did your new friend give you?"

"I don't know. She said I would have insight," she said. "I wonder if I might be able to call on her for help with the others." She shook her head. "It's a lot to figure out. I'll start researching. She called herself *fati arana...*"

"*Aranaeum*?" he asked. "Makes sense. Spider of fate, I think."

She raised an eyebrow. "Of course you know that." He rewarded her with a dazzling smile. "But we have time for that later." She withdrew her hand and resumed her gentle exploration, tracing every soft curve and hard edge of his body. "You realize this is the first time I've seen your cock, right?"

He laughed, a wonderfully light sound. "Really?"

"Mmhmm," she replied. She kissed his inner thigh. "I have plans for that later."

His red eyes gleamed. "I look forward to it."

"Do the others know?"

"That you're mine to make love to forever? Yes, of course," he said. "What you plan to do with my cock, I certainly hope not. Some things should be mysterious, Shoshanna."

She laughed shook her head. "No, silly. That your curse is broken."

He shook his head. "Not yet. I've kept them at bay until I knew you were well. As soon as I call, they're all going to show up here. They've been texting nonstop to check on you."

Her eyes widened. "Oh, my God. I'm the worst friend ever," she said. "What about Ruby?"

"She's fine," he said gently. "Nikko took her home last night, but I was given strict orders that you are to call her when you wake up, after you finished fucking your vampire boyfriend." His brow arched. "That's a direct quote."

"Shit, I should call her," she said, but as soon as she leaned over for her phone, he let out a play growl and pounced her.

She laughed as he rolled her over, kissing her neck, her chest, all over as if he was afraid she would melt away. "Who said you were finished with me?"

As Alistair had warned, his vampire brothers were insistent upon visiting before the night was over. After another hour spent in bed and a shower that threatened to upend their plans, they both dressed and prepared for their guests. While Alistair pulled out several good bottles of Scotch and blood bags, Shoshanna called Ruby to let her know that she was awake and alive.

"Thanks for the headache tea," she said.

"I broke my fingers off in that one," Ruby said. "Hopefully it's a little milder than the last one."

"It was amazing. What about you? Any lingering issues from Elliott?" Shoshanna said.

Her friend was uncharacteristically quiet for a while. "I don't know. Physically, I'm fine. But my head's a mess, and I probably need therapy. But what am I supposed to say? A vampire with no respect for consent used me to kidnap my best friend?"

"I'm so sorry," Shoshanna said.

Ruby chuckled, but it was a strained sound. "It's not your fault. I'll figure it out."

"Not by yourself," Shoshanna said. "Now that he's out of the way, we have several weeks of girl's nights to catch up on."

"That would be nice," Ruby said. "Mexican?"

"Absolutely."

They chatted for a while, until she heard the first car pull up outside. After making plans for Ruby to come over in a few nights, Shoshanna hung up and checked the refrigerator. Hopefully, Alistair's frat squad of cursed vampires were bringing their own stash of blood.

Before she could answer the door, it swung open. Paris crowed, "Honey, I'm home!"

She greeted him at the door and raised an eyebrow. "Are you talking to me or Alistair?"

"It depends on who has a snack for me." He smirked at her. "You look quite refreshed. Satisfied, even." He leaned in to kiss her cheeks, and his hands lingered at her shoulders for a while. When he pulled away, his face was unusually somber. "I'm pleased to see that you're all right."

She threw her arms around him, hugging him tightly. He stiffened in her grasp. "Thank you for helping Alistair," she said. "And me, of course."

He kissed the top of her head. "Only for you, *ma sorcière.* I have a soft spot for cute witches, but you mustn't tell."

She heard the telltale click of heels as Safira waltzed in, with an unfamiliar blond man trailing behind her. While Safira gave her a hug, Dominic simply nodded to her. He carried a big black cooler, from which he unpacked several dark glass bottles of champagne and a stack of blood bags. She wrinkled her nose, did a quick head count, and retrieved glasses from the liquor cabinet in Alistair's study.

"Where's—" Safira asked. Then she clapped her hand over her mouth as Alistair rounded the corner, buttoning up a crisp white shirt. "Holy shit."

The others froze and watched as Alistair stepped into the big kitchen, where the low light reflected from his blood-red eyes. Pride swelled in her chest as she watched the vampires crowd around him, like small children enrapt with wonder.

One man she hadn't met stayed at a distance, staring with cold intensity at Shoshanna. "What did it cost, witch?"

Alistair's eyes narrowed. "Watch your tone, Julian."

"Nothing," Shoshanna said. "It was difficult but it was just good magic." She drew a deep breath. "We're soulmates. As far as I can tell, that's the key."

The blond man's shoulders slumped. "Then you can't break ours, can you?" He shook his head. "I'm Nikko, by the way."

"Nice to meet you, Nikko," she said. "And I'm going to try."

"Well, I hate to break it to you, but most of us are over two hundred years old and haven't been so lucky to find a soulmate," Paris said. His gaze shifted to Julian. His lips parted, then sealed again as if he'd thought better of making a comment.

Her cheeks heated, but Alistair gently gripped her hand. "This woman looked you two in the eye and told you she would break Lucia's curse, then mine. It took her less than a month to make good on her word. Are you such a fool that you would doubt her now?"

A twinkle lit in Paris's eye. "Shoshanna, I will gladly be proven wrong."

Safira shook her head and deftly opened one of the bottles of champagne. "Unlike these brooding dicks, I'm here to celebrate," she said. "Even if I didn't get to participate, there was an epic ass-kicking. Alistair was king—"

"For less than three minutes," Alistair said.

"And Shoshanna just did something none of us could have pulled off. And now Alistair can party with us again," she said. "This is cause for celebration."

"Hear, hear," Paris said. They quickly distributed glasses of blood and champagne.

"To my mate," Alistair said, eyes fixed on her. After they clinked glasses, he leaned in to kiss her lips.

When they all had full glasses, they retired to the living room and settled into the comfy couches and chairs. The house was even more beautiful with guests. Though most of them were only her acquaintances, if that, they were Alistair's chosen family. It filled her with pride to see him among them, smiling and chatting.

"I hate to bring the mood down," Julian said, setting his glass aside.

Paris rolled his eyes and said, "No, you don't. You love to bring the mood down." Safira chuckled, then hid her smile behind her glass.

The older man shot him a glare. "We must tell Lucia the truth."

"What truth?" Shoshanna asked. They had taken Lucia to a vampire hospital to give her a thorough checkup. She hadn't heard the final reports yet.

"That Kova is dead," Julian said. "Eventually the excuse that he is travelling will wear thin."

She cocked her head in confusion. "Kova was her soulmate, right?" Julian nodded. "He's not dead."

They were strangely silent, staring at her like she was a poor, helpless idiot. Alistair squeezed her hand lightly. "I assure you he is."

"I assure you he's not," she replied. "Did you see him die?" He shook his head, and she scanned the gathered vampires. All of them frowned, glancing at the others. "Any of you?"

Julian set his glass down. "He left a note apologizing for

leaving us," he said. "And he left. We assumed he killed himself, an assumption that was borne out by his absence for more than a hundred years."

"You assumed? Did any of you ever see his body?" she said archly. Their silence was the only answer she needed. "I used the soulmate bond to break the curse on Lucia. There was something on the other end of her fate thread." They began to shift nervously, so she put up her hands. "I'm learning this as I go. There's a chance I'm wrong, but—"

"If there is the tiniest chance you're right, then you must give her hope," Dominic said sternly.

"But if he's not dead, where is he?" Safira said. "That would mean he lied and left us for over a hundred years. Why?"

Half a dozen pairs of red eyes turned to Shoshanna as she said, "That's your drama, not mine. But I'll do what I can to figure it out. I know you've all been through a lot, and I won't promise something I can't deliver. But I promise you that I'm going to do what I can to help all of you."

There was a strange, fraught moment, eyes full of unspoken fears and hopes. Then Paris cleared his throat. "Well, I for one am glad that Alistair should be doing seventy-five percent less pouting than he has done for the last century."

"Fuck off," Alistair said with a chuckle.

"It's true," Safira said. "You have a lot of birthdays to catch up on."

The tension passed, and the night eventually turned to nostalgia. They were almost like parents trying to embarrass Alistair, telling her stories of his silliest moments. He shut them up by playing the piano, eventually coaxing her to join. Though

Alistair was clearly happy, she could see the deep longing behind his friends' eyes as they saw him finally freed.

When their guests eventually left, she watched them driving away, headlights fading into the night. "I'm going to help them," she said to Alistair, wrapping her arms around his waist.

He kissed the top of her head. "I know you are. Will you let me help?"

"Obviously," she teased. "You're my manservant."

"Yes, I am," he said. His hand slid down to pinch her bottom. "How may I serve, my lady?"

Twenty-nine days after his curse was lifted, Alistair Thorne had not yet tired of watching Shoshanna cross a room or pour a drink or do the most mundane tasks. He was increasingly certain that he never would. He was enchanted by the hypnotic rhythm of her steps and intoxicated by her warm scent. When he woke in the encroaching dark of twilight, he opened his eyes to a world where inexplicably, fate had chosen the most beautiful, brilliant woman in the world to be his beloved.

Though he had convinced Eduardo to not make an announcement of his return to court, it was clear that word had spread of the curse being broken. The ballroom of Eduardo's grand home was filled with the upper echelon of the Blade of Auberon. While dozens of them had flitted by the grand piano, where he had provided entertainment for the last hour, he had eyes only for Shoshanna, who always had one of his brothers at her side or on her arm. Though he knew none of them would dare seduce her, he still felt a flicker of jealousy when Paris touched her and prompted one of those delightful smiles.

Since breaking his curse, Shoshanna had spent weeks poring over the texts that Paris had brought. Together, they painstakingly translated every page. Though his brothers tempered their hope with cynicism and practicality, Shoshanna was determined to solve their problems and break their curses. Her optimism was infectious. He'd noticed the unusual warmth in Nikko's voice when he mentioned "the witch", and the way Paris's eyes lingered on them.

Still, she had a Herculean task ahead. Unless she was able to find destiny's perfect match for each of them, she would have to find another way. But even with the insurmountable odds, they were far closer than they had ever been.

Just after midnight, Eduardo's Scythe, Hugo, came to fetch them both for the bonding ceremony. He could hear Shoshanna's heart racing as he joined her, lightly grasping her hand to take her into the inner sanctuary of Eduardo's home. They did not speak, but exchanged a series of quiet glances and smiles.

The familiar tingle of Shoshanna's magic clung to the house, evidence of the security measures she'd created for the Elder. Even he had never seen Eduardo's innermost sanctum. Past a wine cellar and a library that smelled of old books and dust, a heavy wooden door led into the small, temple-like room.

Walled in dark gray stone, it was silent as the tomb, with an ornate silver altar along one wall. Dressed in all black, with a small silver pin bearing the sword and rose crest,

Eduardo stood in front of the altar. Eduardo's advisors, the Scythe, the Veil, and the Gilded Hand, flanked him. "Miss York," he said politely. "On behalf of the Blade of Auberon, I offer sanctuary and protection from all threats. I offer the sharp bite of my fangs, the dark shield of the Shroud, the financial comforts of my kingdom, and the eternal power of my blood. In exchange, I require your loyalty. When your power and knowledge may serve the greater good of my court, you will use it in service of those who protect you. Do you accept?"

Her hand tightened on Alistair's, and she exchanged a look with him. Then she raised her chin to look up at Eduardo. "I accept your offer and give my loyalty in exchange."

Hugo took her hand, then drew a sharp stiletto from his coat. Alistair tensed instinctively. He knew there was no danger, but it was hard to watch the deadliest vampire in the court wielding a blade at his beloved.

The Scythe pricked the soft pad of her thumb, but Shoshanna remained calm. He nodded and placed the blade on the altar, then beckoned for her to come closer. Eduardo brought her hand to his lips. With a light brush of his lips, he drew her blood into his mouth. The smell of it awakened a raging hunger in Alistair, and an accompanying, primal fury that anyone else dared taste it.

But Eduardo's gesture was largely symbolic, and he surely drank no more than a thimbleful of her blood before finishing. At his other side, Violette poured a dark wine into a ruby-adorned goblet, handing it to Shoshanna. She took a drink, then passed it back. Finally, Stefan Varga held out a silver bracelet, a far more intricate and bejeweled version of one that Dominic had loaned her months ago.

Eduardo placed the bracelet around her wrist. The solid silver bangle was entwined with vine-like strands of platinum and silver that tangled around a silver rose flecked with ruby and garnet. "We once granted these to patrons and sympathetic humans who were kind to us," he said. "This is a sign of my favor."

"Thank you," Shoshanna said, touching it lightly. "I am very grateful."

"I will return your mate to you shortly," Eduardo said, tipping his head to Shoshanna. "Good evening, Miss York. Please enjoy our hospitality."

When she left the room, her scent lingered. Thanks to their soulmate bond, he still felt her presence nearby, a gentle pulse at the base of his spine. She had quite literally become his heart, reminding him that he lived, rather than simply lurking in the shadows.

Eduardo was silent for a while after Shoshanna left, but he finally raised his eyes to Alistair. "Destiny has a strange way of carrying out its will, does it not?"

"Indeed," he said.

"I have considered your request, and I will grant it," Eduardo said. "You have been reinstated to the Shroud, and you will report to Julian tomorrow."

A warm sense of pride filled him. "Thank you, sir."

His eyebrows arched. "I fear that we will need you sooner rather than later. The continued turmoil of the Casteron will bring trouble to our door." He spared a faint smile. "Perhaps you should have remained their king and gotten them in line before handing over your throne."

"Perhaps," he said drily. "And perhaps another foolish upstart would have beheaded me before I had a chance to make reforms."

Eduardo chuckled. "A far more likely scenario. In either case, your primary responsibility is to protect this witch. She will make us powerful, but she may also make us a target," he said. "And if these hunters return, we will need all capable hands to protect our people."

"I will take the responsibility," Alistair said.

He nodded. "I am pleased for your happiness, Alistair. I have not forgotten what you and your brothers have suffered to protect this court. I hope for their sakes, that she can free all of them from their curses."

He nodded. "As do I," he said. "Thank you, sir."

Eduardo nodded and gestured his dismissal.

When Alistair climbed the stairs, he found Shoshanna sitting on a plush settee with Lucia, dressed in an elegant purple dress. She managed a smile and carried on conversation in halting English. She had wept bitterly when they finally told her how long it had been, and how long Kova had been away. But just as Shoshanna claimed to have sensed something, Lucia swore she could feel that Kova was alive. He only hoped that it was not false hope. Given what Shoshanna had accomplished, he believed that her sheer force of will might bring him back. When she wanted something, the universe would reorder itself to make it so.

In his absence, someone had taken over the music. A string

quartet played a romantic waltz, reminding him of when he was young. He swept by, grasped Shoshanna's arm, and led her to the floor. She just smiled up at him, eyes twinkling with joy as he led her around the floor. "*Je t'aime,*" he said quietly.

"*Je t'aime,*" she replied.

He kissed her forehead, then spun her dramatically. Her skirt twirled around as she returned to him, body pressed tightly to his. "I will never tire of dancing with you."

Over her shoulder, he saw Dominic speaking to Lucia and coaxing her to dance. Her somber expression melted away into a gleeful smile as he guided her around the floor.

They whirled and spun, occasionally trading off partners. He danced with Lucia, marveling at her grace, while Dominic took Shoshanna around the floor in a whirl of scarlet skirts.

Eventually, Shoshanna whispered, "I'm hungry. Break time." On their way back to a private corner, he gestured to one of the waitresses. After glancing at Shoshanna, the woman nodded eagerly. She promptly returned with a silver tray of neatly sliced fruit, crackers, and cheeses. Shoshanna smiled. "Thank you," she said. "Did you sneak food in for me?"

"Violette asked me for what you liked," he said. "A sure sign that you are someone of importance to the Court."

She chuckled. "And to you?"

"Oh, you are the person of the greatest importance to me," he replied earnestly. He stroked her arm. "Have you thought about what I asked yesterday?"

Her smile faded, sending a ripple of fear through him. "Yes."

Fool. He should have waited, when the turmoil of vampire

politics was not fresh on her mind. He shook his head. "We don't have to—"

"Of course I'll turn to be with you," she said. "I can see that worry on your face, Mister Thorne. You stop that right now."

Relief bubbled through him. "I feared the worst."

"Because you're a worrier," she said, lightly touching his noise. "Not yet. A few more years, at least. I want to see a few more sunsets before I say goodbye to it forever. Hawaii and Fiji, for sure. But definitely before my hair starts turning gray."

He was struck with a pang of sorrow. "You would give up the sun for me?"

"If it means I get to be with you, then yes. What good is it to be soulmates if we don't get to enjoy it together?" she said. "You'll keep me warm and safe, won't you?"

He smiled and leaned in for a kiss. "I will be your light forever."

"Forever is a long time," she said, giving him a mock serious expression. "What if you get tired of me singing in the shower?"

"I would not," he said with earnest seriousness. "But if I did, I'm sure earplugs would suffice. What if you tire of my melancholy moods?"

She leaned in and kissed his cheek, letting her warm hand rest on his thigh. Warmth pulsed through their bond, making him feel like he'd submerged into warm water. "Good thing I know how to cure your melancholy moods."

He laughed. "You do, indeed." Furthermore, his melancholy moods were quite rare with her in his life.

"Are you going to make good on your promise? To spend our time making me happy?" she asked.

"It is all I want to do," he said.

"Then who needs the sun?" she said. "You are what I need and what I want."

"Then you will want for nothing for the rest of time."

CURSED BLOOD will continue with *The Hunter's Curse,* featuring Nikko Baudelaire and a human woman determined to rescue her sister from the Casteron vampires. Keep reading for a sneak peek!

AND IF YOU can't get enough of Alistair and Shoshanna, I've got an extra treat for you. Get a glimpse of life - and a well-spent night - with these destined mates in a special bonus scene only for subscribers!

THE HUNTER'S CURSE: A SNEAK PEEK

A mournful jazz singer crooned a haunting lullaby as Olivia Pierce crossed the dance floor to a distinguished gentleman who sat alone. She offered her hand and said, "Mr. Boyd, may I have this dance?"

Eddie's silver-blue eyes were partially obscured by bushy gray eyebrows that rose in surprise. Gripping his cane tightly, he stood up and grinned. "I thought you would never ask. As long as you don't mind my assistant, Biltmore." He shook his cane at her with a little laugh.

"Mr. Biltmore may join too," she said. She let Eddie hold her arm for balance as she took him a few steps out to the dance floor, then placed her hand on his shoulder.

He cleared his throat. "Oh, Miss Pierce, is it all right? I don't want to overstep."

With a smile, she gently guided his hand to her waist. His hand barely brushed her, as if he was afraid to offend. "Yes, sir," she said. "And I truly appreciate you asking first. You are truly a gentleman."

His eyes closed as he swayed. He was a little out of time, carefully leaning on his cane for balance. A partial stroke a few years ago had weakened Eddie's left side, but he was as quick-witted as ever. "My Jeannie would sing to me every morning when she cooked breakfast," he said, a wistful hint in his voice. "I used to tell her she could have sung with Duke Ellington or Glenn Miller if she'd been born a little earlier."

"I bet that was wonderful," she said. "What was her favorite song?"

He pondered. "She used to love Paper Moon. Sometimes she'd sing Cheek to Cheek, but then I'd try to sing like Louis Armstrong and she'd laugh so hard she cried." His eyes glistened with tears as he said, "I wish she could be here."

"I know," she said, her throat clenching tight. "After book club tomorrow, would you like to go for a walk and tell me more about her?"

"Ah, you don't want to hear an old man rambling," he said.

"No, I don't," she said, squeezing his shoulder gently. "But I do want to chat with my new friend about his wonderful wife. If you have some pictures, I'd love to see them."

Eddie laughed a little and brushed a trickle of tears against his shirt sleeve. "I think that would be nice. It's a date." As the song came to a halt, he kissed the back of her hand. "Thank you for the dance, Miss Pierce."

"It was my pleasure, Mister Boyd," she said, giving him a little curtsy before guiding him back to his seat.

The main room of the activity center at Fernbrook

Commons had been transformed into a ballroom for the night, with gold tinsel streamers and silver stars decorating the beige walls. A buffet table held trays with scraps of the meat and cheese trays and finger sandwiches, while a few of the residents were laughing like teenagers in the photo booth. The elaborate photo booth had eaten up a good chunk of her budget and left her decorations looking like a half-assed high school prom. But there had been a line all night as the guests printed pictures of themselves in silly hats and glasses. Money well spent, as far as she was concerned.

Her coworker, Desmond, grabbed the karaoke microphone and tapped it lightly. “Attention to our party guests. It’s last call, so if you want a little something for the road, head over to the buffet table. We’ve got the photo booth until eleven o’clock tomorrow morning, so anyone who missed their chance can pop in at breakfast tomorrow.”

She met Desmond at the buffet table, where they’d already prepared a stack of to-go boxes and cups. After their first few parties, they’d learned to send their guests home with the leftover snacks. Olivia had nearly perfected the art of ordering just enough to keep the guests happy and not have to throw away any food. While a few stragglers were doing a respectable swing dance to “In the Mood,” she and Desmond quickly distributed finger sandwiches, sliced fruit, and mini-cupcakes into boxes for those who lined up.

Desmond laughed to himself as the song faded into “Every Time I Say Goodbye.” He elbowed her lightly and whispered, “You don’t have to go home, but you can’t stay here.”

She’d been working at Fernbrook for just over two years.

In her first year, she'd done Desmond's job, assisting her predecessor. Now she was the full-time activities director at the facility, a well-regarded assisted living facility for seniors. It was *not,* as she gently corrected the family members of some of their guests, a nursing home. Their residents were mostly independent and lived in their own condos or cottages. Olivia, Desmond, and their part time assistant Julia, worked to plan social activities and outings for their guests. Hell, some of the octogenarians had more of a social life than Olivia did.

Maisie Jones, elegant and poised as always, approached the table. Her glittering red dress was flawless, as was her silver hair. If Olivia aged half as well, she'd be thankful. "Excuse me, Ms. Pierce and Mr. Lewis?" Maisie said, with a drawl that was sweet and thick as clover honey.

"Miss Maisie," Desmond said. "You know you can call me Dez."

"I can, but I won't," she said archly. She waved off his attempt to give her a to-go box. "I saw on the Facebook that some older folks have been disappearing from communities around the city. I've voiced my concerns to Mr. Talbot, but he assures me that our security is quite good."

"Yes, ma'am," Olivia said. The rumor of the Senior Snatcher had been circulating for a few weeks. The reality was that the elderly, particularly those with cognitive disorders, were prone to wander off. Several had returned, swearing they'd only just left, despite having lost days. "I don't believe any have come from communities like ours."

Maisie regarded Olivia with a stern look. "Well, I certainly don't want us to be the first. I hope you'll pass my concerns to Mr. Talbot. Perhaps he can increase security temporarily."

"Yes, of course. If you'd like, I'll walk you back to your condo tonight," Desmond said.

Her stern look faded into a smile. "I'd like that very much. Thank you." She nodded to Olivia. "Ms. Pierce, thank you for the lovely party. I speak for all of the Peach Club when I say that it was tremendous."

"Well, that is certainly high praise," Olivia said. "Please thank the ladies of the club for the wonderful desserts."

Maisie nodded, then offered her arm to Desmond. He talked animatedly to her as they left the big room, leaving Olivia to finish straightening up. She kicked off her shoes, turned the music to quiet piano music, and called on her radio for the kitchen staff.

Four workers in scrubs entered with trays. They briskly gathered the dishes and silverware from the tables. She followed close behind, folding her tablecloths, gathering candle sticks, and depositing decorations back into a plastic tote. Once the kitchen staff finished, she sent them home with their own boxes filled with generous slices of the red velvet cake the Peach Club had provided.

Thirty minutes later, she put the last of the party supplies in a storage closet and locked up. She made a quick stop by her office to grab her purse. Her phone lay on her desk, glowing insistently. From the doorway, she could see that the screen was covered with notifications. She barely had enough friends to make a social triangle, let alone a circle, so all the messages struck her as odd.

When she grabbed the phone, her blood went cold.

Danielle: *I need your help*

Danielle: *Are you there?*

Danielle: *Olivia, please answer me*

There were a dozen missed calls from Danielle over the last two hours. Olivia fumbled at the phone and texted back.

What's wrong? Call me

They hadn't spoken since the epic shouting match months ago. Within seconds of sending the text, her phone rang. "Ollie, I'm in trouble," Danielle said, breathless and quiet. "I need you to come get me."

A tsunami of terror washed over her. Olivia gripped the edge of her desk for balance as she said, "Dani, what's going on? Should I call the police?"

"No!" she blurted. "No police. I'll get in trouble."

Her stomach plunged through the floor as she felt the admonition bubbling up on her tongue. *What did you do now?* She held it back and said, "Okay, where are you? I'm leaving work right now."

"I'm at my apartment," she said. "The new one. 211 Delmore Avenue, Unit G3."

"OK, are you hurt? Did you take something?"

"Just come get me, please," she pleaded. "I have to go."

"No, stay on the—"

The call ended with four eerily final beeps. Her stomach twirled itself in a knot around her esophagus as she fumbled at her purse. She kicked off her heels and traded them for the slip-on sneakers she'd worn into the building. The world was far away as she ran down the hall. Somewhere in the distance, she heard the night receptionist speaking, but she couldn't have been speaking English.

It took her three attempts to start her car before she realized she was trying to use her house key. "Breathe," she told herself, taking a moment to ground herself like her therapist Cara had taught her. "Five things I can see," she murmured. Streetlight. Fairy lights on the gazebo. Manicured nails. A half-empty water bottle. Her phone, which had delivered the terrifying omen. "Shit."

She owned a gun, but it was stored safely at home. Did she risk going home for it? It would take another hour if she went home, and anything could happen to Danielle in that time.

Her stomach lurched as she pulled onto the road, headed for the interstate. Bracing herself for the death race of Atlanta traffic, she took a deep breath and slammed the gas to merge onto I-85.

The smart choice would be to call the cops. But if Danielle was up to something illegal, she'd get in more trouble, and she'd hate Olivia even more than she already did. As far as she knew, Dani's painkiller of choice was booze, which had gotten her into plenty of trouble while still being legal. Olivia had bailed her twin out several times, both figuratively and literally, and had made a few late-night trips to pick her up from a bad situation.

But there had been radio silence from Danielle for nearly six months, ever since the screaming match that ended with Danielle telling her to get out and never come back. Olivia had just been trying to help, but Dani hadn't seen it that way. And if Olivia was being honest with herself, she'd pushed too hard.

She'd tried to apologize, tried to reach out, but Dani had cut her off entirely.

If Dani was reaching out, it had to be bad. And maybe this was the only way to finally make things right and get her sister back.

DANIELLE'S new apartment was in a surprisingly nice community. Olivia hadn't even realized that her sister had moved until she worked up the courage a few months ago to take her a birthday gift. After pacing in the parking lot for ten minutes, she'd marched up to the door and knocked, only to find a very confused older woman who brought her a stack of mail for the previous tenant. Despite her nagging fears of prosecution for mail fraud, she still had that stack of mail addressed to Danielle at home. It was the tiniest connection, but it was all she had right now.

"Unit G3," she murmured, carefully following the signage around the neatly landscaped complex. Her heart pounded in anticipation. Whatever she found at Dani's doorstep, they'd deal with it together. Maybe she could prove that she was worth having around, and they could close this awful, aching gap between them.

All she'd ever tried to do was help Danielle. With a deadbeat mom who ran through abusive boyfriends like she'd bought them in bulk at the world's shittiest Costco, they'd had to stick together. And when Mom was with Mike Mason, dirtbag extraordinaire, they'd realized they couldn't depend on anyone else to protect them. They'd survived some bad years together, but it wasn't until they were adults that Olivia learned how much worse Danielle had it during Mike's reign of terror. Mom was still a mother in name only, listed as *Jackie* in her phone contacts. But it was some small comfort that Mike had gone to prison, pissed off the wrong guy, and got shanked with a whittled-down toothbrush. She'd never wished anyone dead, but she had celebrated the news of his death with a bottle of champagne and a slice of cheesecake.

His death hadn't fixed anything. The damage he did to both of them, particularly Danielle, was just a part of his shitty legacy. And they were still feeling the echoes of it, in bad boyfriends and quiet self-destruction.

Building F blurred past, and she honed in on Building G. It was at the back of the complex, near an access road that connected to the back of a shopping center with a huge grocery store. She parked in one of the marked visitor spots and stared up at the building.

"Whatever I find, we'll figure it out," she said. Her chest tightened, and she was bombarded with the image of her sister, pale and cold and foaming at the mouth, a needle in her arm. Her face beaten and bloody. Gunshot wounds. A dozen terrible ends that Olivia hadn't prevented. "Whatever it is, we'll figure it out," she repeated. "She's going to be okay. She's going to be okay."

Olivia gripped her keys tightly, letting the sharp blade protrude between her fingers. As she bounded up the stairs, she wished she'd gone home for the gun. The third floor was quiet and still, but she wasn't sure if that was a good sign.

She hurried around the corner to G3 and lingered at the door. Quiet voices spoke inside. She tested the handle. Locked. "Danielle?" she asked as she knocked. "Dani, it's me. Come let me in."

Adrenaline spiked through her system as the latch opened. Her sister opened the door. Though she was upright, she looked awful. Her smile was almost manic, her lips a garish red against her too-pale skin. Despite the smile, her eyes were wide with terror. "You came," she murmured.

"Dani, what's wrong? Are you on something?" she asked. At the center of a nasty purple bruise on her neck were twin trickles of blood from a pair of puncture wounds. Olivia reached for her hand and said, "Come on. Let's get out of here, okay? Let's go somewhere and talk."

A broad-shouldered man loomed behind her. He shoved Dani to the side, then held out his big hand. "You must be Olivia."

Her throat went dry. The man's eyes were blood red. Not smoked-weed-all-night bloodshot, but movie-quality contacts red. Her throat went dry as she stared up at him and said, "I just came to get Danielle."

"Ah, but now that you're here, the party can start," he said. In a blur, he grabbed her wrist and pulled her inside. She tried to pull away, but his grip was like steel. The door slammed behind her.

Her eyes flitted around the room. The apartment looked like a model, without a single touch of personality. A petite blonde woman sat on the couch with Danielle, holding her hand tightly. Her sister was staring at Olivia with terror in her eyes.

None of it added up, but one thing was clear. She needed to get Danielle the hell out of here. Shifting her hand carefully, Olivia looked up at the brawny man. He grinned, baring strangely sharp teeth. “Shit, you really are identical. Darken her hair a little, and they’ll be a matching set,” he said. As he spoke, she could see the vein in his throat shifting along his windpipe.

She had often fantasized about returning to the past, finding Mike Mason, and putting something sharp in his throat. That ship had sailed, but this would have to do. With a strength that surprised her, she stabbed the key into his throat. The man jerked in surprise and clapped a hand to his throat. Blood spurted through his fingers. “Bitch,” he gurgled.

“Dani, let’s go!” she screamed, breaking away to reach for her sister.

But Danielle just sat on the couch, staring at her. “I’m so sorry.”

Where was the blonde woman?

Hands wrapped around her shoulders and yanked her back so hard she stumbled. “You shouldn’t have done that,” a woman’s voice hissed. Inexplicably, warm lips closed on her throat. Then something sharp pierced through her skin, and a hand closed on her throat. Black closed in, and the last thing she heard was her sister crying out a fading apology.

I’m so sorry.

Consciousness was accompanied by a sharp pain in her forearm. Olivia shook awake and let out a shrill scream when she looked down to see messy dark hair swaying slightly below her. Slurping sounds accompanied the pain in her arm, sending acid through her nerve endings. Gleaming red eyes lifted to glare at her. "It's awake," the man complained. Blood dripped from his lips.

Her blood.

She tried to clamber to her feet, but something bound her limbs to a chair. Her right arm was untied, but held tightly by the man with the glowing red eyes. "Help!" she screamed.

Feet shuffled behind her, then someone shoved a cloth into her mouth. As it was tied tightly, her hair tugged painfully against her scalp. She looked around frantically. Dilapidated walls surrounded her, covered in graffiti that was dimly lit by a single electric lantern in the corner. In the far corner, a man in black folded his arms over his chest, watching her intently. The dark brown hair and well-groomed beard were the same she'd seen in Dani's apartment.

"Mmph!" she protested, lunging out of the chair. Then he was gone in a blur, and a hand closed on her throat.

Cool lips brushed her ear. "Go ahead and scream," he said, his voice curiously gentle. "It tastes better when you're afraid." Teeth sank into her arm again as he held her from behind. Panic overwhelmed her. She couldn't think straight, couldn't even grasp what had happened to her. The pain of the bite intensified, and she felt tears leaking from her eyes as she panicked, trying to catch her breath. The grip on her throat faltered, and she saw a large hand tap the other man's head. "That's enough for you. Pay up if you want more."

The man who'd bitten her raised his head. His blood-stained lips curled into a sneer. His red eyes skimmed over Olivia appreciatively. "Tasty," he said.

The dark-haired man pressed her free wrist to the chair and strapped it down. The stiff metal and tilted back reminded her of a dentist's chair designed by a sadomasochist. She tried in vain to pull at her limbs, but there was no give. Ignoring her muffled screams, the bearded man pressed his fingers to her throat. A few seconds later, he said, "That's enough for today."

He bent in front of her and pried up her eyelids. His red eyes flitted back and forth. Then he loosened the straps on her limbs and pointed a finger in her face. "Don't fight me. I'd rather not, but I've got no qualms about breaking your spine if you decide to kick me in the face or some other nonsense."

Fear prickled down her spine as he lifted her out of the seat. He moved so fast it made her head spin, and before she registered what direction she was moving, she was in a smaller room. Peeling cinderblock walls were covered in graffiti, and the warped frame of a chalkboard hung on one wall.

A classroom?

The man hauled her to the far corner of the room. The windows were all covered in black-painted wood. In the corner, a metal plate was fixed to the wall with a length of heavy chain. He secured it around her wrist, then pointed to a bucket. "Be civilized and don't do it on the floor." She stared in horror, realizing her other hand was free to untie the gag from her mouth.

She fumbled it free and said, "What are you doing with me? Who are you? Where's Dani?"

"Dani's just fine," he said. The way he said her name with such familiarity infuriated her. "And you will be, too."

"Let me go!" she screamed.

His eyebrows arched. "Or what?" He grasped her chin. "It's remarkable. You really are identical. Our patrons will love it." His eyes scraped over her, and he added, "You're a little thicker than she is. Shouldn't be a problem."

"What?" she breathed. "What are you talking about?"

"Rest up," he said, patting her cheek.

"Hey! Who are you?" she shouted.

But he walked out of the dark room without looking back. She tried in vain to pull away from the chain, but it was tight around her wrist. With about four feet of chain, she had enough slack to get to the center of the room, but no further. Everything near her had been cleared away, except a stained bucket that reeked of sewage.

She stared in horror at her surroundings. "This can't be happening," she whispered. She was still wearing the sequined dress that she'd worn to the seniors' party at Fernbrook. No personal possessions. No phone.

And no one was expecting her. No one would know where she'd gone. By the time someone called the police, she'd be dead. Her chest tightened as panic threatened to drown her.

After sucking in a ragged breath, she screamed, "Danielle! Danielle Pierce!"

Voices echoed back at her, and the broken door swung open again. This time, a petite woman with short-cropped platinum hair entered. It was the same woman who had been in Danielle's apartment. "Hey, shut up," she said sharply. "Some of us are trying to work."

"Where the hell is Danielle?" she bellowed.

In a blur, the petite woman crossed the room, pinning her to the wall. "Do you want me to rip your tongue out? You'll still taste just fine with no tongue."

Olivia's eyes widened, and she slowly shook her head.

"The next time I have to come in here, I'll make sure you don't scream again," she said. "Got it?"

She nodded. The woman's eyes were pure red. She had to be on something, just like the other guy. The smaller woman stormed out and slammed the door behind her.

Olivia sank against the wall with tears trickling down her face. She was doomed. They were going to kill her and Danielle. Probably rape them, before and after. And they were both going to be dumped somewhere, never to be found.

What did it matter anyway? No one was left to bury them, no one to cry over their graves, and—

"Get off this toxic train," she said calmly. Her therapist, Cara, had taught her a simple phrase. Olivia used to say that she was "riding the crazy train" when her anxiety took over, but Cara gently told her she wasn't allowed to call herself crazy anymore. They settled on the "toxic train," and the simple act of recognizing an unhealthy pattern of thinking was a big step, or so Cara said.

Riding the toxic train was a one-way ticket to nowhere. It usually resulted in her predicting a grim future and rendering herself blind to any other possibilities.

"Off the train. Off the train," she muttered. She closed her eyes, took a deep breath, and murmured, "Five things I can see." When she exhaled, she looked around the room to ground herself. Graffiti on the walls, spelling out *James B.* Crinkled fast food papers. A massive spider web. Yuck. Her own bloodied forearm, with the clear marks of teeth. Her scuffed gym shoes. "Four things I can feel." Mostly *ouch*. As she proceeded through the exercise, she took deep breaths to keep calm.

This situation completely sucked. But if she was going to get out of it, she had to keep her head on straight. When she finished the exercise, she was still very far from being okay, but she felt more rational.

She tugged the length of chain, then tried pulling her hand free. Her wrist was secured in both sides of a set of handcuffs hooked to the chain. Even if she could peel all the flesh off her hand, it wasn't sliding through. Then she followed the chain to where it was bolted into the wall. She pried in vain at the bolts until her fingernails were sore. If she could find a tool, she might have a chance, but her bare hands weren't budging that thing.

With her free hand, she patted herself down with her free hand. There was a zipper pull on the back of her shiny dress. If she could pull it off, maybe she could use it like a screwdriver. If she could get her bra off, there was an underwire inside. Could she bend it into a wrench?

Then she glanced down at the toes of her dirty shoes, with their long, carefully looped laces. She narrowed her eyes and hiked up her feet to pull out the laces, preparing a makeshift garrote.

Olivia pulled both laces. She tucked one into her bra for safekeeping, then prepared the other by tying small loops into the ends. She hooked one around her thumb, ready to jump whoever came in next. There was no way in hell she was going to sit here and let these jerks do whatever they wanted to her.

She spent the next solitary stretch of time listening and looking around the room. There were several plausible escape routes, but they all depended on her getting her hand unhooked. She watched intently, jolting with surprise when the door opened again. A man she hadn't yet seen, on the younger side and relatively handsome, stepped inside with a bottle of water and a paper-wrapped object in his hands. With colorful letters on white paper, it looked like a sub sandwich. If they were feeding her, maybe they didn't mean to kill her right away. She wasn't sure if that made the situation better or worse.

He looked her over as he approached and set down the items. She could see her own footprints where she'd tested the length of the chain. When his black sneakers crossed the line of her footprints, she waited. He crouched to put the items in front of her. When his head bowed for a second, she pounced on him, pulling her shoestring against his throat.

"Fuck," he croaked, pulling at the string. He whirled and backed into the wall, smashing her against the cinderblock. It knocked the wind out of her, and he pried the string away from his throat. Fury ignited in his eyes as he spun around, then smacked her hard enough to make her see stars. His canines elongated into snake-like fangs.

Horror washed over her. "What are you?"

"Hungry," he growled. He wrenched her head to the side and bit into her throat. And as the blood spilled onto her pretty sequined dress, she realized that she was in far deeper than she could swim. This was not the world she knew, but as the black pressed in, she realized it might not matter for much longer.

The Hunter's Curse will release in April of 2022!
Don't miss out!

About the Author

J.D. Monroe is a Georgia-based author with a love for all things paranormal, magical, and downright fantastical. She has not given up on the dream of riding a dragon someday. She has written a number of paranormal and fantasy novels for both young adults and adults.

When not writing, J.D. may be found playing Dungeons and Dragons, singing alto in a musical, or serving the whims of the cutest little calico kitty on the planet. She loves shiny dice, glitter eyeshadow, and gruff swordsmen with eye scars and a well-hidden soft side.

Also by J.D. Monroe

Cursed Blood

The Guardian's Curse

The Hunter's Curse - Coming Soon!

The Dragons of Ascavar

Wings of Stone (Book 1)

Wings of Exile (Book 2)

Wings of Thunder (Book 3)

Wings of Frost (Book 4)

Wings of Flame (Book 5)

Dragon's Song (Standalone)

Novellas

Midnight Flight - A Free Novella!

Dragon's Vow

Dragon's Secret

Dragon's Desire

Printed in Great Britain
by Amazon